PRAISE FOR *STILLHOUSE LAKE*

"In this rapid-fire thriller . . . Caine spins a powerful story of maternal love and individual self-realization."

—*Publishers Weekly*

"Amazing."

—*Night Owl Reviews* (Top Pick)

"A chilling thriller . . . *Stillhouse Lake* is a great summer read."

—*Criminal Element*

"*Stillhouse Lake* is a true nail-biter right up to the end."

—*Fresh Fiction*

"Highly entertaining and super intense!"

—*Novel Gossip*

"What a fantastic book!"

—*Seattle Book Review*

T0131103

BITTER FALLS

OTHER TITLES BY RACHEL CAINE

Stillhouse Lake Series

Wolfhunter River
Killman Creek
Stillhouse Lake

The Great Library

Paper and Fire
Ink and Bone
Ash and Quill
Smoke and Iron
Sword and Pen

Weather Warden

Ill Wind
Heat Stroke
Chill Factor
Windfall
Firestorm
Thin Air
Gale Force
Cape Storm
Total Eclipse

Outcast Season

Undone
Unknown

BITTER FALLS

RACHEL CAINE

THOMAS & MERCER

Text copyright © 2020 by Rachel Caine, LLC
All rights reserved.

Published by Thomas & Mercer, Seattle

www.apub.com

Amazon, the Amazon logo, and Thomas & Mercer are trademarks of Amazon.com, Inc., or its affiliates.

ISBN-13: 9781542042338
ISBN-10: 154204233X

Cover design by Shasti O'Leary Soudant

Printed in the United States of America

BITTER FALLS

PROLOGUE

It was just coming up morning when they fetched him from the cell.

He'd spent all night on his knees shivering in the cold in that thin white nightgown they'd made him wear. The few times he'd fallen asleep, a prod from the barrel of a rifle had been enough to wake him right up.

He ached all over, but then he did most days from the hard work. He'd gone from strong and athletic and cut to . . . *this*. He could see knobs of bone on his wrists, his fingers. His collarbone was showing sharp enough to slice paper. They hadn't even fed him the handful of rice they usually did this time. No water either.

It's a fast, they'd told him, but nobody fasted when they were already starving. They just starved more.

He tried not to think about food. About how he'd used to not even worry about where the next meal was coming from, about burgers and pizza and sandwiches any damn time of the day or night. French fries and beer. That whole time seemed a hazy dream. Going to classes. Girls. Parties. Flag football and Frisbee golf and the bar, the last bar that was so damn crowded with his friends. Did they ever miss him? Did they even notice he was gone?

God, he was hungry, and he just wanted to *sleep*.

Then they came for him.

Six men, shadows in the dark, but he knew they had clubs and guns. They always did. They pulled him to feet that he couldn't even feel anymore and made him stomp until the numbness went away. It hurt so bad it stole his breath. It felt unreal. *This isn't me. I have a life. I have a family. I can't be here.*

Outside the shed, dawn was a faint whisper over the trees, but it was still dark, and he could hardly see the ground as he stumbled over it. Music rose up like fog. The whole damn camp was singing. He didn't recognize the hymn; he'd been raised Catholic and right now he wanted desperately to pray. He hadn't prayed all night, even though they'd ordered him to. *God, please help me. Please.*

His feet were bare, and the rocks on the path cut deep and left blood behind, but they dragged him on anyway. Downhill. Off to his right a solid metal fence rose impossibly tall and featureless. The heavy wall that kept the whole world out. The one he'd thought he might be able to climb, once upon a time when he was a different person. He still had the scars.

Maybe they're letting me go, he thought. Deep inside he knew it wasn't true. Didn't want to know, so he stumbled along praying and hoping, all those singing voices falling behind. Now it was just him and the faithful with their guns and silence. All he could hear was his breath rattling in the bony cage of his chest.

Trees closed out the fragile light. It felt like he was going into a grave, and he wanted to run, scream, fight, do *anything* because fuck it, he'd *been somebody*, he'd been strong and sure and unafraid once, hadn't he?

He didn't run.

Better to go quietly.

The sharp chill bit like icy teeth. He just had on the thin smock, and his hands and feet were mostly numb again with the cold. The menthol scent of the trees should have been as comforting as Christmas, but all he could really smell was his own sweat and rank fear. His dry mouth felt like cotton padding. *Maybe I'm dreaming,* he thought. *Maybe it's all been a dream, maybe I got drunk at Charlie's Tavern and I'm going to wake up in the dorm next to Brie and all this will be just some stupid nightmare.*

Brie. His girlfriend. He wondered what she was doing right now. If she ever missed him at all. He thought about his parents, and the way they must be looking for him, still looking.

That hurt.

They emerged from the shadows of the trees, and he had to stop and stare. A small lake stretched out in cool ripples, painted pink with morning. And there was a waterfall . . . a waterfall that rumbled and roared over the rocks above and broke into white spray that floated weightless in the air. A faint rainbow danced on the mist.

It felt warmer here. Peaceful.

Father Tom waited at the edge of the lake. He wore a white shirt and white trousers, and his pale hair glowed the same shade. Old hair, old face, young dark eyes that seemed to know all the secrets of the universe. The eyes of a saint, the Assembly liked to say.

Father Tom was fucking batshit crazy.

"Brother," Father Tom said. "Welcome. You've labored long and fruitfully, and though you came to us a stranger, you will leave us forever part of our family. Today you'll be baptized into the Assembly, and wherever you may go, you'll always be one of us. Your old life is gone. Let your new life begin."

"New life," somebody near him said, and the others mumbled it too. He was too numb. Did this mean they were just letting him go? Could that *happen?*

Yeah, let me go, you crazy fucks. Let me go and I run straight to the cops and I put your busted asses in jail so fast even God won't know where to find you.

That was the person he used to be talking, the strong young man who'd fought and yelled and believed he could do anything. Survive anything.

But the person he was now just shivered like a lamb in the slaughterhouse. He couldn't make himself be that man again.

Maybe they'd just let him go after all if he complied. And maybe he'd never say a word about what happened here either if he got to walk away.

He walked into the water with Father Tom until it was waist deep. He could see there was a drop-off not far away, a navy-blue hole drilled down by thousands of years of relentlessly falling water. Who knew how deep it went? He was right on the edge of the abyss. God, it was cold enough to numb even the shakes out of his body. Cold enough that the water started to feel warm.

Father Tom smiled at him like he couldn't feel the chill at all, and said, "Do you believe in the power of our lord Jesus Christ, and his heavenly father?"

He just nodded. It felt like a convulsion. It hurt. He just wanted to sleep.

"Then be washed in the blood of the lamb, and begin anew. You have struggled in your faith, but no more. You are a saint of the Assembly."

He wasn't prepared for Father Tom to dunk him under the water; it was done fast, expertly, as if he'd done it a thousand times. He struggled, but Tom held him pinned for a few long seconds before he was allowed to pop up into the steaming morning air again.

He wanted to scream from the shock and the cold, but relief set in. He'd done it. He'd survived. He turned his face up to the rising sun and took in a deep, whooping breath. *I'm alive. I'm alive! I'm going to get out of this.*

"God is with you, Brother," Father Tom said. "Your service ensures our salvation."

He hadn't seen them coming, but there were two more men in the water around him now, and he realized something wasn't right. He tried to head to shore.

But one of them grabbed his shoulders, and the other ducked under the water.

He felt something tugging at him. He didn't know what it was until he put his hands into the water.

It was a big, thick chain drawn tight around his waist, and Father Tom clicked a padlock closed to secure it.

The men let go of him and stepped back.

You said you'd let me go. Begin anew, you said. That was a wail in the back of his mind, as his teeth clenched together and he felt the black, despairing rush of what was coming.

"God bless you, Saint," Father Tom said, and pushed him over the edge into the abyss.

The last thing he saw was the heavy iron weight at the end of the chain dragging him down into the dark, and the last glitters of dawn on the water above him.

So cold.

He felt himself settle on the bottom among the white bones. As his lungs ached and pulsed, he suddenly remembered being a child. Waking from a nightmare. The last thing in his mind, the very last, was his mother whispering, *Hush, baby. You're safe now.*

1

GWEN

When my personal phone rings, I check the caller ID. Force of habit. There are only six people in the world I take calls from on this number. Sure enough, it's Sam Cade. A little bubble of warmth explodes inside me as I hit the button and lift the phone to my ear.

"Hey, stranger," I say. I hear the purr in the back of my throat.

"Hey yourself," he replies. I hear the husky tone in his voice too. Oh, subtext. So sexy. "What's going on?"

"Right now? Exactly nothing," I say, and yawn. It's three thirty in the morning, and I've been sitting in this chilly rental car for three hours, not counting a quick dash into the convenience store down the road for a pee and a giant coffee I'm going to regret. "I'm waiting for my guy to make a move."

"A move to do what?"

"Good question."

"You're not going to tell me?" He sounds amused.

"Well, you know. Not until I'm sure. Anyway, you're up late. Or early. Which is it?"

"Early. Just getting some paperwork ready for the day," he says. "Kids are still fast asleep, by the way. I checked." My kids are my life, and he knows that. Sam's also well aware that he's one of a very select group of people I trust with my children. My daughter, Lanny, is at a difficult sixteen-feels-like-twenty. My son, Connor, is too adult for his age at thirteen and too young for it at the same time. Not easy people to handle, my kids.

There's no reason they should be. They've spent half their lives now with the horrifying knowledge that their father was a serial killer, and with the equally heavy burden of having people unfairly hate them by association. I want to protect them from the world. I can't, of course. But I still want to *try*.

"You going to be home before six?" he asks me, and I sigh. "Okay, fair enough. You want me to wake up Lanny when I leave?"

"Yeah, better plan on that. I can't trust her to hear the alarm and get Connor up too. I'll text and let you know when I'm on my way." I want to let my kids sleep. They have to be up at seven, but an extra hour of sleep to a teenager is like ten to me.

Neither of them will want to get up, and still less head to school, but they're used to facing unpleasant situations. I flatly refuse to home-school them. Their lives are going to be incredibly difficult given our family history. I want them to learn how to handle it now, not hit eighteen as protected little china dolls.

There lie monsters.

Counseling has done all of us some good. I started the kids in individual therapy for a few months, then together, while Sam and I met with another counselor as a couple. Now we do it as a family once every other week, and I dare to think things are . . . better.

If not for the fact that town itself has closed ranks against us.

I'm not really sure what tipped Norton residents over to utter dislike; maybe it was Sam's unintentional but ongoing feud with a bunch of drug-dealing but influential hill folk. And some of it I brought on myself by agreeing to do a TV interview. The situation had turned utterly toxic. That had triggered even more media attention to rush into the calm backwaters of Stillhouse Lake. I'd thought I was doing a good thing, but it had been like unloading a dump truck of ten-day-old garbage on my head.

The internet trolls are back, relentless and ghoulishly gleeful as ever. I'm never sure what they get out of trying to destroy my life, but I'll give them this much: they're dedicated. I recently found a post on a message board that said their goal was to drive my kids to commit suicide live on camera. The level of sociopathy that takes goes to eleven, but no mistake, it's out there. And, disturbingly, it's not that rare.

That's who we deal with on a daily basis. I don't like to call them monsters; they're just bored, angry, empathy-free humans without a cause who see me as a target for their rage. After all, I was married to Melvin Royal, the infamous serial killer. He slaughtered women for fun, so I must have been somehow responsible for that too. No, the swarm of ever-present trolls are not the monsters. I've known monsters. I've faced them down, including Melvin.

I kill monsters. You'd think they'd keep that in mind.

I talk to Sam for about half an hour, lulled into comfort and warmth and a deeply coiled need to feel him with me, but we both know that's not going to happen right now. Thanks to the closed-minded town of Norton mostly shunning us, his construction work has dried up, and he has to go farther out to find jobs. That means longer drives, shorter times at home.

I'm working for an out-of-town detective agency that tosses me a wide variety of cases within my specified driving distance; I can turn down what I can't handle or what I just don't feel like doing. But the pay's good, and I'm decent at this kind of job.

A very wealthy CEO named Greg Kingston is getting my full attention right now. The assignment came to us from his company's board of directors, who were concerned by what they considered strange behavior and some worrying financial results. I've already uncovered embezzlement out of his Florida PR firm, and his digital fingerprints are all over that. Easy enough—that goes back to his board to decide what to do about it. Kingston's days are probably numbered.

But in the process of following Mr. Kingston, I've found something that disturbs me a whole lot more. I'm not sure what it is yet, which is why I didn't say anything to Sam. Right now it's just clues, instinct, and one important question.

Why in the world would a man with Greg Kingston's hefty bank balance and social standing be staying in a no-stars motel in a shady part of Knoxville when he *also* has a room booked in the very upscale Tennessean Hotel?

There are a few reasons a man like Kingston stays in a place like this: hiring prostitutes, buying drugs, or something darker than either of those. I'm actually hoping he just has a taste for sex workers on the rougher side of town. That would be the best possible outcome here.

But it isn't what I get.

I watch as an anonymous dark car pulls up. A dumpy-looking white man gets out. He's wearing jeans and a plain jacket, and he has a ball cap pulled low over his face. No bag, so if he's a drug dealer, he's not bringing more than what's in his pockets. I don't think someone of Kingston's monstrous ego would be just in for a dime bag.

As the man opens the back door of the car, I realize that is not what he's bringing.

The girl can't be more than twelve at best, and my mouth goes dry. My heart starts hammering harder. I force myself to be calm and take as many pictures as I can. The license plate. The car's details. The best shots I can of the girl. She's in a blue dress that belongs on a younger child, and she has a vacant, defeated expression on her face that makes me want to scream.

I get an absolutely clear picture of Greg Kingston's grin as he opens up the motel room door and shakes the dumpy man's hand. He ushers the girl and the man inside the room and shuts the door.

My hands are shaking when I drop the camera and dial 911. I give the report as calmly as I can, and I tell them there's a child in serious danger, possibly being abused right now. If I'm wrong, if somehow Greg Kingston came to this shady motel to meet his cousin and his niece, then I'm screwed.

But I know I'm right. I'm watching a child being sold, and it takes every ounce of control I have to sit and wait for the police instead of beating two men senseless and taking that child someplace safe.

It doesn't take long. Less than five minutes, but it feels like an eternity. The slow, silent glide of the police cruiser into the parking lot is a relief. I get out of my car and talk to the two uniformed officers. They take me seriously, especially after they look at the photos on my camera. I'm shivering and tense as I lean against the car and they pound on the motel door.

It's over fast. Whatever they find in that room, it's enough to put Kingston and his dumpy friend in handcuffs, and when the girl comes out, she's wrapped in a blanket. Her frozen, blank look has been replaced by something that looks like real emotion.

Like the beginnings of hope.

An ambulance arrives, lights flashing, and a detective car noses in. Around the small L-shaped motel complex, the evening's occupants are making quiet getaways. Nobody wants to be caught up in this mess.

Kingston looks murderously angry. I think he ought to be looking a whole lot more scared, so I dial the city desk of the local paper and a couple of news stations. They'll love this story, especially if they can get a shot of the mighty Greg Kingston sitting in his boxer briefs with his black dress socks still on. He looks pallid and thin and exposed. Perfect front-page material.

The two detectives eventually make their way to me. I give them my business card and explain what I'm doing here. My camera's internet-enabled, so I send the photos to them directly. I add in from my phone the vague message board posts that led me to this motel. They're all in code, but it was enough to make me curious. And I can see the detectives see it too from the looks they exchange.

I give them a statement. Promise to come in for more questions if they need me. One of them clearly hasn't recognized my name; I'm always on guard for that, but he just writes it down along with my contact details and moves on.

The other detective lingers, looking at me. I can see by her expression that she's caught on. I guard myself instinctively and wait for the sneer, the distrust, the cut.

But she says, "Glad you made it through all you've had to deal with, Ms. Proctor. Can't have been easy. You taking care of yourself?"

I'm surprised. So surprised I don't really know what to say to that, so I just . . . nod. My throat feels unexpectedly tight. I don't try to thank her. Maybe she sees it anyway, because she smiles and walks away.

I feel oddly exposed now too. I'm always prepared for a fight. Not for *that*.

I get back in the car and tell Sam I'm headed home. It's a solid hour and a half drive home without traffic, but we'll have some overlap to enjoy being together. Quiet time.

I'm almost never that lucky, and today's no different. I come in the front door and reset the alarm. Connor's already up and sitting at the breakfast table nibbling on a piece of toast. At thirteen he's put on a growth spurt that caught me by surprise. He's filled out in the shoulders and chest. He's got some height going too.

But Connor doesn't look great today. Slumped shoulders. Dull, dark shadows in his eyes. Sam's cooking eggs at the stove. He flashes me a warm, quick smile and a shrug, messages received and acknowledged. Sam's in his late thirties, just a bit older than I am. Medium height, medium weight, blondish hair. A nicely symmetrical face that somehow can look older *or* younger, depending on his mood and the light.

And I love him completely. That still surprises the hell out of me; what right do I have to love a man this solid, this good? And how does he love *me*? It's a mystery I don't think I'll ever solve.

"Hey, baby," I say. I kiss my son on the top of the head. He barely reacts. "What's wrong?"

Connor doesn't answer. He looks pretty zombified, which is partly the hour and partly something else. Sam replies for him. "He says he woke up sick."

"Sick," I repeat. I sink down in the chair next to Connor. "Stomach again?"

He nods and gnaws a tiny bit of toast. There are dark circles under his eyes, and he needs a haircut. I keep intending to take him in for one, and it hits me that he looks halfway neglected right now. He's got on a favorite threadbare sweater I told him to throw away, paired with distressed blue jeans. Add the ragged hair to that, the exhausted eyes . . . If you sat him on a corner with a WILL WORK FOR FOOD sign, he'd absolutely get donations.

"You don't want to go to school?" I ask him, and get another non-verbal agreement. "How about going to the doctor?" This time it's a negative. I press the back of my hand to his forehead. He isn't running a fever. "Baby, I'm sorry, but you know you either need to go to the doctor or go to school. I can't let you just stay home. You've missed enough days already."

He gives me a miserable look, but still doesn't say a word. He just drops the toast and heads back to his room. I look at Sam, and he holds up his hand in an I-don't-know gesture. "If I had to guess, I'd say bullies," he tells me.

"Connor's been dealing with those for years."

"Connor's also been moving around town to town. He could look forward to leaving bullies in the rearview, but he's settled now. He has to face them with no end in sight. I could be wrong, but—"

"But you're probably not," I sigh. "Okay. Save me some eggs?"

"Cheese and crumbled bacon. Got it."

I knock on Connor's door and ease it open. He's sitting on the edge of his bed staring at the floor with socks he hasn't yet put on in his hands. I step in and he doesn't get mad, so I shut the door behind me. "Sam thinks it's bullies," I say. "Is he right?"

A slow nod.

"Can you talk to me about it?"

I'm not sure he will, but he finally does, in a voice so rusty it's painful. "I just . . . it's hard."

He's right. I get abuse and threats daily in my email. On social media. Even sometimes mailed right to our address. But at least those people are at a distance.

Connor's face-to-face with his bullies every day. And he can't escape.

I feel an overwhelming surge of fury, frustration, *anguish* that makes my pulse beat hard in my temples. Although I want to protect him from the pain, there's not much I can do. *Stick to your decision. He needs to learn how to cope with this as he grows up.* Wrapping him in my arms and protecting him from the world can't give him the armor he needs.

Teaching him how to guard himself . . . That will ensure he's safe when I'm not there.

"Sweetie, I know. I'm sorry. I can talk to the principal, make sure he knows that they need to back off . . ."

He's already shaking his head. "Mom. No. If you do anything it'll be worse."

I take a deep breath. "So what do you want me to do?"

"Nothing," he says. "Just like . . ." He doesn't finish that. His voice trails off, but I know what he meant to say. *Just like always.* It must seem that way. Even though he knows how much of my life I devote to protecting them. It hurts, but I endure that. "I'll be okay."

"I can make you an extra appointment at the counselor if you—"

He puts his socks on, then his shoes. Calm, methodical motions, like it's important he gets it right. "Sure." His voice is bland now. Disturbingly empty. "Whatever."

The dreaded *whatever*. It's a steel door slamming in my face. I'm used to getting it from my daughter, not Connor. But he's growing up, becoming his own person. I'm no longer his shelter.

Now I'm in his way. That hurts.

I have to take a breath against the cold that stabs through me. "Who is it?" I ask him.

He doesn't pause in tying his shoelaces. "Why? What are you going to do, beat them up?"

"Maybe," I say. "Because it kills me to see you hurting, baby. It really does." I hear the very real tremble in my voice at the end.

So does he. He looks up quickly. I can't read what's on his face and he turns his head again so fast it's a blur.

"It was easier when we moved," he says. "When we didn't have to just *take it*."

"I know. Do you want to move? I thought you liked being in one place."

"I did. I mean, I like the idea. It's just—" He sits back with a sigh but doesn't look at me. "I'm going over to Reggie's house after school, remember?" He says it as if we've already agreed on that. We haven't. But I just nod and let it go. My son needs to feel like he's got something to look forward to.

"Call me when you get there?" I make it a question, not an order. He looks relieved.

"Sure, Mom." He stands up. "I guess I should eat pancakes."

"Good call."

I want to hold him but I can see he doesn't want that. My heart aches for him. I'm so afraid that the whole world is coming to hurt him, but I can't stop the whole world. I know I can't.

Maybe that's the worst part.

By the time Connor's at the breakfast table, my daughter shuffles in, dark hair lank around her face. She's dressed in a fuzzy red bathrobe with cartoon Draculas all over it. She yawns so widely I can check her tonsils. "Crap," she says. "School *again*?"

"Again," I agree. "Eggs?"

"Sure," she says. "Coffee?"

"Elixir of life with plenty of cream and sugar, coming up."

We eat like a family. It's precious to me even if it isn't to the half-asleep kids; I have to hustle Lanny off when she wants to dawdle. If I'm not riding herd, both of them will miss the bus, and Sam's got to be on his way.

I share a sweet kiss with Sam at the door. I read the regret in his eyes. We missed our short window of privacy today.

Tonight, I hope. If nothing comes up.

"Sam?" I call after him. He turns back on the way to his truck. "Be careful."

"So many rules," he says, and flashes me a grin. Dawn's breaking behind the trees and it bathes everything in a benevolent, soft light. It glints off the glass of our car and truck windows, and for a second I think I'm imagining things, because the bright red spot on Sam's chest seems so out of place.

I feel my heart start to hammer before I work out what it is. By then the laser dot is moving.

"Sam!" The alarm in my voice is clear, but I can tell he doesn't know what I'm warning him about. I'm about to yell *get down* when the side window of his truck goes milky white as the safety glass crazes. There's a hole in the center the size of a quarter.

The boom of a shot echoes out over the hills behind the house.

Adrenaline hits me hard, and I start out the door before I check myself. Sam's not hurt, but he's an open target. He's ducked, but he's clearly looking for the origin of the shot. I yell, "Get in here!"

He dashes for the door. The shot has come from behind the house, and above. Someone's in the tree line up there. Someone wanted me to see that he had a bead on Sam, and could have put a round through Sam's chest as easily as through that window.

"Jesus *Christ*," Sam says. He sounds remarkably calm, though his face has gone pale. "I didn't see him."

I drag him back from the doorway. Slam the door shut. Throw the locks. Engage the alarm with lightning-fast stabs of my trembling fingers. The kids have bolted out of their bedrooms and stand frozen, faces stark with worry. "Back from the windows," I tell them, and point to the kitchen. "Get in the safe room and *stay down!*"

"Mom, was that a shot?" Lanny asks.

"Get Connor in the safe room *now!*" She grabs her brother and drags him that direction. I frantically look Sam up and down for any wounds. It hits people that way sometimes, that in the rush of adrenaline they don't feel the shot. But he's not bleeding.

The sniper had him marked dead to rights, then deliberately missed him. A warning.

"Are you okay?" I ask him.

He looks at me with that same odd calm. "Apart from wishing I'd taken out more car insurance? Sure. He missed."

"He didn't *miss*. He had a laser sight on your chest."

"And you know laser sights at that distance are bullshit," Sam says. "Bullets curve." He puts his hands on my shoulders, then moves them to cup my face. "Gwen. *Breathe*. It's okay, it's just a window."

"No," I say. "It was a threat."

I turn away, grab my cell phone, and speed-dial the Norton police.

2

GWEN

It's probably no surprise that the cops don't turn up anything much.

They find the bullet embedded in the truck's seat, but it's mashed all to hell. The forensic tech—who I know is competent—doesn't seem confident that they'll be able to do much.

No sign of a shooter. Or rather too many. These woods are well used by hunters.

The young cop who interviews us is a uniformed officer I don't know. Seems barely older than my daughter. He tries to be professional about it but comes off patronizing. "Ms. Proctor, I know what you think you saw, but—"

I interrupt him, because I am *pissed*. "Come on. I saw the laser sight!"

"Ma'am, just because someone's a lousy shot don't mean nothing sinister at work here. Chances are it was just an accident. Lucky nobody was hurt, is all."

I bare my teeth. Before I can put more bite with my bark Sam lays a hand on my arm. "Thanks, officer. We'll be fine. If I can have a report for my insurance company—"

"Sure thing," the young man says. He warms up to Sam. Of course. "Glad *you* understand, sir."

I get the message. Sam's the adult here. I'm the hysterical female. I want to slug the cop right in the mouth. Don't, of course. I just grit my teeth. I'm surprised I have teeth left at this point.

I can tell Sam knows that when he says, "Thank you for coming out, Officer," in as neutral a tone as anyone could have, and the cop takes it as the goodbye it is. He goes to confer with the forensic tech, who's heard the exchange and sends me a look of silent apology and an eye roll of *what can you do?*

I turn to Sam. "Really?"

"Really," he replies. "Gear down, Gwen. Picking a fight with the cops isn't going to help."

He's right, of course, but I want to fight *somebody*. And there's nobody to hit except people I love, so I push that instinct right down and take a deep breath. "Okay. Who do you think it was?"

"If I had to guess? One of the Belldenes."

It's what I expect him to say. The Belldenes are a tight-knit family of hill folk who are both paramilitary and criminal. Sam's run afoul of them a couple of times. Always in defense of someone else.

I've never met any of them face-to-face, though their reputation is large and well documented in the Norton and Tennessee state police records. They specialize in dealing all kinds of opiates. Word is that they've got some doc-in-a-box a few counties over who provides them with prescriptions, but so far nothing's been proven. A little meth cooking on the side.

I'm used to being harassed. I've endured years of being relentlessly stalked and threatened by internet vigilantes. Organized groups like the Lost Angels, who number relatives and friends of my ex-husband's victims among them. Random weirdos who idolized Melvin and want to either get close to me or kill me. Stalkers who think my kids might be budding serial killers. I have plenty of enemies to choose from, but this is different. It's someone who lives within easy driving distance. Who can show up to my kids' schools, my partner's work, our grocery store.

Or our house.

Normally I act pretty aggressively against threats, but Sam's impressed on me that the Belldenes treat feuds like sporting events. Anything I do to one of them stirs up a nest of very angry hornets. They're baiting us.

I can't afford to bite.

Still, I hate to let it go. "So we do—"

"Nothing," he finishes, and gives me a look I recognize all too well. "Right?"

"Maybe."

"Gwen."

"He could have killed you."

"If he'd wanted me dead, I'd be dead," he tells me. "If it gets worse, we'll level up. But right now he just wants an excuse, so don't give it to him. Okay?"

I reluctantly nod. Neither of us knows which *him* it is exactly. There are a confusing number of Belldenes, and likely all of them are decent shots with a rifle. One's a military-grade sniper but that doesn't mean he's the one who was out poking us today.

I think they save him for when they're serious.

I walk the kids down to the bus, hyperalert for any threats, but they board without incident. Sam gets the all clear from the police as they leave the scene. He breaks out his damaged window and promises me he'll call a repair service from his jobsite. This time our goodbye kiss is longer, more fraught.

We've struggled to get back to a sweet, warm balance of trust. It's never been easy. Sam's the brother of one of Melvin's victims. That shadow will always fall over us. So, too, will the difficult fact that he helped form the Lost Angels, one of the most vocal groups that hounds us.

They now see Sam as a traitor, and still believe I was a participant in my ex-husband's crimes. But I know Sam. I trust him completely with the most precious of all things to me, my children. And with my scarred, scared, closely guarded heart.

That frightens me sometimes. Letting anyone that close, giving anyone that power over me . . . it's both thrilling and terrifying. But at moments like these it's precious indeed.

I submit my finished reports, photos, and financial findings in the Kingston investigation to my boss. J. B. Hall owns the private detective agency I work for, and she's a hell of a smart, tough woman.

She acknowledges receipt, and she'll be the one to review the work, document the findings, and present it in a client-friendly way to the final customer. The board of directors won't find it very palatable, though they'll almost certainly hear about his arrest well before the report arrives.

I'm just as glad to not be on that end of things. I have too much drama in my life.

J. B.'s already sent me more work, I realize. I open her message. This is an odd one, she says. Cold case of a missing young man, and you'd think it would be the parents hiring us, but it's not. It's a nonprofit foundation. Maybe on behalf of the parents? It's unclear, so go carefully. It's so thin that really all we need to do is check the boxes. And it's in your neck of the woods. Take a look?

I download the file attachment. It's a not-very-thick police report about a missing person: a young man who vanished from a bar on a night out with his friends. He is—was?—a senior at University of Tennessee in Knoxville. The facts are slight and sketchy. Remy Landry, twenty-one years old, white, originally from Louisiana.

Remy had gone out with six friends on a Friday night and hit two different bars with the group. When they finally regrouped at the second bar, Remy was nowhere to be found. They'd all assumed he'd hooked up with someone and left, but texts and calls to his cell hadn't been answered. He had his own car. It was found parked and locked back at the campus. That made sense; he'd ridden to the bars with his friends.

Surveillance footage attached to the digital file shows Remy at the first bar; the compiled footage shows him ordering drinks, dancing with his friends, chatting up girls. Seeing him makes me feel cold inside: he's a handsome kid with an easy smile, strong and lean and agile. He looks like he's on top of the world. The only odd thing is that he's carrying a backpack. I wonder if that's why the police assumed he was a runaway.

The second bar doesn't have as much footage, but it catches Remy and his friends arriving at the club, and the friends leaving. There's a note on the file that says the back exit had no surveillance camera, but that they'd viewed every minute of footage from the front. Remy had come in. He'd never left, not by that door. And he'd taken that backpack.

The police had done a thorough search of the club and turned up nothing. They hadn't acted immediately, of course. The search had been done days later. Nobody takes missing college students—particularly missing young men—that seriously, especially if they don't come home from a bar. Not when there's no obvious evidence of a crime.

He'd been gone a long time before anyone believed it was a problem. And he'd vanished into thin air. No clues. No witnesses that the police had been able to locate.

And that was when I realized the date of the disappearance.

Three years ago.

I text J. B. This thing is way cold. Are there any new leads?

My business cell rings a minute after I send the text, and I pick it up to hear J. B.'s warm, confident voice. "You're asking about new leads in the Remy Landry case, and we don't have any. I'll be honest, the police did a pretty decent investigation once they got on it. Not sure who this nonprofit is that's paying for our work, but it seems like it's church-related. I'm digging into it."

"You sound like you have a bad feeling about this one," I say. I know J. B. pretty well by now, and her instincts are razor sharp.

"I do. And yet . . . something happened to this young man. Regardless of the people who are putting up money, finding out what happened has to be a good thing for his parents." She sighs. "You're a mother too. You know."

I do. The thought of one of my kids disappearing, never to be seen again . . . it keeps me awake at night. I know how much darkness there is out there.

I know the predators swimming in it like sharks.

"I can start by talking to the parents," I tell her. "They're in Louisiana?"

"The mom's in Knoxville, which is why I'm sending it to you. The dad's still living in their house in Louisiana. Running the business."

I'm already nodding. "In case the kid shows up at the family home," I say. "I'll talk to the mom first, then."

"Tread lightly, and be gentle. Their marriage isn't in good shape." That's also not surprising. A lot of couples fall apart after the disappearance or death of a child. Especially an only child like Remy Landry.

"I'll be careful. Did they ever find anything else? Something that didn't make it to the file?"

"No. No cell phone traces, no leads from friends, nothing from bar patrons. Nobody saw anything. Like I said . . . it's frustrating. Like chasing shadows. But if we can offer some closure to this family . . ."

I don't like being anyone's last resort. "And if I can't come up with anything new?"

"Then maybe that's also an answer. Maybe they'll finally let go," she says. "Sometimes we're just there to mark the boxes and cash the check. It's part of the job, Gwen. Like it or not."

"Okay," I tell her. "I'll go over everything one more time." I hesitate. "And . . . what if I find something?"

"I sincerely hope you don't, unless it's a real breakthrough that helps us find him," J. B. says. "But I'd like to give these parents whatever peace we can, one way or another. You find anything, you bring it to me and we'll do our best."

"You don't think he's alive, do you?"

"Three years on, without a single confirmed sighting, with his credit cards and phone unused? What young man does that?"

"No history of mental illness? Drugs?"

"Casual drugs, same as most college kids. But negative on mental illness. Whatever happened to him, I don't think he had a sudden psychotic break in a college bar."

She's right, of course.

"And . . . you're going to keep digging into who hired us, right?"

"Absolutely," she says. "Back to you as soon as I find out more."

I thank her for the work and get off the phone, and then I start to dig.

Remy Landry seems like a normal young man for his age. A little wild, but nothing out of the ordinary. A bit of a player with a string of ex-girlfriends, but none of them seem more than normally annoyed at him. Like J. B. said, his friends admitted to club drugs and pot use, but Remy was body-conscious; whatever he took, or drank, he did it in relative moderation. I look at his selfies and watch videos on his social media pages. He's a handsome guy with a bright, easy smile and the confidence of someone who's never doubted he's going to succeed. He was loved. His friends clearly enjoyed his company.

What makes a guy like that disappear from a crowded bar in the middle of a night out? My instinctive answer is *a girl*, but I don't see him paying special attention to anyone on the footage.

I spend a couple of hours combing through files, making notes, then review the attached video surveillance footage from the bars twice more. J. B. has noted where my guy appears on the recording, but I log into the cloud and start the full video from the time that Remy and his friends arrive at the club. I want to watch every camera and every second. Maybe someone missed something. Maybe someone around him seems suspicious. I don't know what I'm looking for, but I know that if it's there, I'll see it.

Only I don't. I don't see anything.

By the time my personal phone rings at two in the afternoon, I'm tired, achy, and yawning; I put the camera footage on pause and snatch up my phone because I'm half-desperate for a break anyway. I check the number.

It's my son. He never calls from school unless there's an emergency—usually with Lanny, who's more of a trouble magnet than Connor.

I answer and feel my heart kick-start to a faster rhythm. "Connor? What is it?"

I hear noise, but not my son's voice. Then an adult—a woman—says, "Ms. Proctor?" She sounds scared. I feel the whole world lurch around me. This isn't okay. Not at all.

"Is my son all right?" My voice comes fast and full of dread.

"Yes," she says. "Well. Relatively. This is Mrs. Prowd, I'm your son's—"

"History teacher," I say. My mouth has gone dry, my hand tense on the phone. "What's wrong?"

"There was an, ah, altercation during our drill—"

"What drill?" I say, and then I remember. It's like the floor falls from under me. *I should have known this.* Connor's reluctance to go to the school today makes total, blinding sense. I was advised but I had the date wrong. *Oh my God.*

Today was his active shooter drill at school.

"Look, I'm sorry, I should have talked to him about it," I say to the woman on the other end of the line. "If he didn't act appropriately, I'll talk to him. He's going to counseling for—"

She takes a deep, audible breath. "Connor's been taken to the hospital."

"What?" I'm on my feet, the chair zipping across the room on its wheels and banging hard into the wall. I barely notice. I'm clutching the phone so tightly now that the edges dig into my skin. "Is he okay?"

"He may have a broken nose," she says. "There were three of them involved."

"Involved in *what*?"

"There was a fight in the classroom," she says. "I'm sorry—"

"Which hospital?" I demand, but then I correct myself. There's only one ER in town. "Norton General."

"Yes, ma'am. I'm really sorry. I tried—"

I hang up while she's still talking. I'm already on the way to the door, grabbing keys and purse and punching in the alarm code to disarm the system.

I'm halfway to my car when I see the shiny sprinkle of window glass on the pavement and remember, too late, that I'm a sitting duck out here.

I stop. I turn toward the tree line and make a slow half circle. If they're out there, I want the Belldenes to see that I am not fucking afraid of them.

If they're out there, they don't let me know.

3

CONNOR

I've been having the dream again. The one where there's a man with a gun, and he's coming after me. I can hear his footsteps. I'm in the dark, trying to get away, but he keeps coming, no matter how hard I run. I don't remember how I get home, but then I'm just inside, standing there, and everybody's dead. Mom's on the floor. Sam's slumped over at the table. I can't really see Lanny, except for her feet sticking out from behind the kitchen counter, but I know she's dead too.

Then I feel the barrel of a gun against my head in this cold, perfect circle, and my dead dad's voice says, "I'll always come for you, kid," and I wake up shaking and wanting to throw up.

I always have these dreams before school shooter drills. I never tell Mom, because she hates the drills, hates the whole idea of them, but she also wants me to know what to do. And I have learned. Run, hide, fight—it's been said to us so often I wonder where "learn" fits in.

The first time I had to do it, it was in a school in Massachusetts, and I didn't really mind; I was a little kid, and it felt a little bit like a game. But here in Tennessee they really get into it. They run it like they're training us for the military.

I lied to Mom this morning when she came to talk to me; she thought it was bullies and I let her. It's easier. It's something she can understand. She grew up in a world where you were safe at school, or at least where bullies were the worst thing that could happen besides tornadoes and fires.

But that's not how it is now.

They've told us there's going to be a drill today, but we don't know *when*. So I spend the whole day waiting for it, not listening to the teachers, not paying attention to anything, because I'm waiting for the alarm tones to go off to tell us to shelter.

It finally happens in history. I hear the tones, and the PA says, "Attention. This is a drill."

I'm already falling into a nightmare. I'm sitting in a brightly lit classroom with twenty other kids, but I feel like I'm alone in the dark with a monster. I can hear it coming. *Him* coming. I see Mom and Sam and Lanny dead just like in the dream.

My teacher is trying to be calm and telling us to execute our plan. I don't remember a plan. I don't remember anything. I keep thinking about the dream. My dad's voice saying he'll always come for me. Is this how it happens? Is he sending somebody after me again?

I flinch because now it's not in my head, I'm really hearing *gunshots*. And *screams*. That's not me having a flashback—the sounds are echoing all around us.

People are moving, but I'm frozen in place. Students are shoving their desks around to block the door. One wraps a belt around the slow-close hinge at the top of the door to jam it shut, while a girl, hands shaking, pushes thick rubber stoppers under the door to keep it closed against kicks.

There's a newly installed deadbolt, and I hear somebody turn it with a click. Someone tapes a poster over the glass window so whoever's outside can't see in. They've put it up with the image facing us. George

Washington giving us the thumbs-up, with neon letters around him saying HISTORY IS AWESOME.

Most of the students have already fled to the corners, huddling together. Some are crying and screaming, too, because the gunshots and the noises are *so loud*, and all I can think about is my mom on the floor, bleeding. Sam dead at the kitchen table. Lanny's motionless feet sticking out.

My father's voice whispers in my ear. *I'll always come for you, kid. You're mine.*

I feel like I'm falling down a black, black hole, and there's no bottom. My skin's cold. I can't move. It's like I'm in a cage but I'm just sitting there at my desk. I keep screaming at myself to *move* but I can't.

Someone bangs on the door from outside and tries to shove it open. The teacher's shouting at me, but I don't know what she's saying. I hear only the gunshots. The screams. *I can't move.*

Then there's someone right next to me, grabbing me, and I think, *I'm not going to die today*, and without even thinking about it I pick up the stapler that's under my desk—we're supposed to throw staplers at anybody who gets in, I remember. But instead of throwing it I wrap my fist around it and punch him. Hard enough that I feel something twinge in my hand with a bright zip like electricity. I don't stop. I hit him again. He's screaming, but so is everybody else, and the *pop-pop-pop* of the gunshots is still echoing from overhead, and all I can think is, *I got him. I got him. I'm safe now.*

Then someone else jumps on me. I hit him too. Then a bunch of them have me out of my desk, and I'm down on the floor. Everybody's yelling. Someone's kicking my hand to make me let go of the stapler, and now I'm yelling too. I'm screaming, *Make it stop*, and finally . . . it does.

No more gunshots. No more screaming. It's quiet. I'm curled up on the floor and there's blood smeared red on the old linoleum floor. I see a yellow hair ribbon next to me, a broken phone, fallen schoolbooks, a tipped-over backpack. I look up to see the stark faces of my classmates. They're all staring at me.

The teacher's standing over me, calling my name, but I don't answer. I don't know what to do anymore. I just shut my eyes.

"It's just a drill!" one of the guys on the floor a few feet away is sobbing. I open my eyes and realize that I know him. He's not a shooter. He's in my class. It's Aaron Moore, everybody here just calls him Bubba. He's holding a hand to his cheek, where he's dripping blood. One of his hands is swelling up too. Another one of my classmates is down next to him. Hank. He's whimpering and holding his jaw with both hands. Blood's dripping from his mouth.

Blood's on the stapler lying on the floor between us.

I did this.

I'm the monster.

"Are those real gunshots?" someone is shouting at our teacher. Kids are quietly crying. Holding on to each other. "Is someone really shooting?"

"No, it's okay. It's just a drill, calm down, everybody please calm down," my teacher says. She bends down next to me, and touches me on the shoulder. "Connor? Connor, can you hear me?" Her fingers are shaking. I don't say anything. I don't want to. "Brock, get that door open. Run and get Principal Loughlin. Tell him we need an ambulance. Two ambulances. Go!"

Brock's a skinny kid with glasses. He looks scared to death, but he runs over to the door and starts pushing desks away. Someone helps. It takes a while for them to get all the barriers out of the way. By the time they get the door open again, I'm slowly realizing that I did something really, really bad.

But I heard gunshots. Real gunshots. Real screams. I don't understand *why this is happening.*

Then the PA comes on, and someone says, "Attention, everyone: there is *no active shooter,* I repeat, there is *no active shooter on the premises.*

For the purposes of today's drill, we used a recording of gunshots to simulate the environment you might encounter if an actual shooting were to occur. *There were no gunshots fired.* Teachers, please remain calm and encourage your students to follow their coping strategies. This concludes today's active shooter drill. Thank you."

He says *thank you.* I don't know why he would say that.

I'm listening to people crying, and the boy whose jaw I broke—Henry Charterhouse—is glaring at me with blood all over his face, and I can still hear those gunshots echoing in my head around and around and around.

I don't have a coping strategy for this.

Once I start crying I can't stop. They give me a shot when they put me on a rolling bed to take me to the ambulance, and it makes everything go soft at the edges and fuzzy and I quit fighting them so much, but I'm trying to tell them that *he's here* even though I know that isn't right either. There is nobody. Dad wasn't after me. Dad's dead.

I'm sorry. I hear myself saying it, over and over, but I don't know what I'm sorry for either. Shouldn't I have fought? They tell us to fight. Not to give up. Not to let people get us.

Nothing makes sense until it does and I really know exactly what I did. It tastes like swallowing ashes and it feels worse, like I'm falling off a dark cliff into icy water.

I'm screwed. I'm so screwed. If they put up with my weirdness before, that was one thing. But this?

I freaked out in front of an entire class. I busted up two of my classmates and yeah, they were jerks, they'd pushed me around before, but I didn't even know who they were when I lashed out. They were just *there.*

I can never come back to school.

Not ever.

4

GWEN

My son is injured, and I don't know how bad it is. I barely remember the drive; everything's a gray blur until I see the hospital. Norton General is a boxy three-story brick structure that dates back to the 1950s, at least. It's the only thing that's in focus for me. I pull into the parking lot for the emergency room and suddenly I'm inside without remembering the run, or even whether I closed the door and locked the SUV. I probably did. Muscle memory is smarter than I am right now. My heart is pounding like I ran all the way from Stillhouse Lake.

The nurse on duty at the desk looks up at me. I can tell from her expression that she knows just who I am: the serial killer's ex, the stain on the good name of the town. Pursed lips, raised eyebrows, cool judgmental stare.

"Connor Proctor," I manage to say. "I'm his mother."

"Room four," she says. I don't ask how he is. I shove through the double doors and look at room numbers. In the first two there are other kids, each with family present. Room three holds a sweet little old lady who's whimpering in pain as a nurse takes blood.

My son is in the room across the hall from her. Relief douses me like an ice bath, because he's okay, conscious, *alive*. He's half-reclined in a hospital bed and holding an ice pack to his swollen face. When he pulls it away to look at me, I wince. Both eyes and his nose are going to be vividly black and blue. One cheek is red and puffy. I force myself to slow down, calm down, and I walk over to his bedside and take his free hand. His knuckles are bruised and cut. He smells of Betadine and blood and sweat. He's still in the clothes he wore to school, but his sweater is now a total wreck.

"Sorry," he mumbles. He looks away but he doesn't move his hand. I place a gentle palm on his forehead. He feels warm, but it's the warmth of someone whose adrenaline is still running at peak volume. He'll cool down, probably too fast. When that happens he'll need a blanket.

"What happened?" I ask him. I feel better now. Yes, my son has been beaten up. Yes, it makes me want to rip the skin off the two boys down the hall. But he's conscious, he's alive, he's talking. "I'm not angry, Connor."

"You're going to be."

That sounds . . . ominous. "Your teacher said there was a fight?"

He turns and looks right at me this time. I see something awful in his swollen eyes. "Not really a fight," he says. "It was my fault. It was just—the noise. There were gunshots, Mom. And screaming."

I go cold. "There was a shooting at your school?"

He's already shaking his head and wincing at the pain that must cause. "No, there *wasn't*. It was . . . they played a recording of gunshots and screaming. Over the speakers. To make it more real."

"They *what*?" I'm stunned. At first I'm appalled, physically flinching with revulsion that they would do that *to kids*. Then I get angry, so angry it eats into my bones and sets my marrow on fire. I was uncomfortable enough with the active shooter events without the mental trauma he's describing. It's bad enough they have to be drilled in how to react to danger, but I understand that, given the world around them. But terrifying them deliberately? Some very misguided jackass probably thought it would *toughen them up*. It won't. They're not volunteers in an army. They're not someone like me who's chosen to run toward danger. They're just kids, traumatized kids trying not to live their lives in terror.

I hug my son. I hug him so fiercely. He's trembling.

"I'm sorry," he says again. "I just—I don't know what happened. I just couldn't let them touch me."

Of course he couldn't. My son is tough, but he's also cracked by his father's crimes and the terror constantly stalking us. Multiple times he's been in danger of being killed. All that trauma hasn't made him immune; it can't, not at his age. But it has made him violently self-protective, and that means that anyone who comes at him in those circumstances will be seen and treated as a serious threat.

Even classmates.

I can't fix this. It's going to take even more time and even more therapy and most definitely more patience, making him aware of exactly what's going on inside his very complicated head. My son is hardwired by his parentage and trauma to *survive*. Finding ways to moderate those instincts is going to be a long, difficult process.

I just hold his hand and watch him fight tears and hate myself in an ever-increasing spiral. I should have seen this coming. He's been acting more and more off around days when these active shooter drills—six a year, now—are scheduled. It was my job to understand, but I completely misread the signs.

I remember telling him, with so much confidence, that I knew how he felt. I didn't. I don't. At his age, I was a sheltered, protected little girl for whom danger was an abstract concept, and the idea of being killed nothing but fiction. I can't really understand what this is like for him; handling it as an adult is far different from handling it at thirteen. I should have known that.

My self-loathing is interrupted by a woman's harsh voice. "There's that little bastard."

I turn to look, and in the doorway there's a rail-thin woman with frizzy, dark hair and big blue eyes that look baleful with anger. She's pointing at my son. I stand up, instinctively shielding him.

There's a big man beside her. He's older, grayer, with a boxer's flattened nose. Heavy but powerful. He lowers his head and glares at me. I glare right back, switching it between the two of them. "What do you want?" I say, though I already know.

"That little shit broke my son's jaw!" the mom says. "They have to wire his mouth shut! Your damn kid went crazy, and my son was just trying to help. You're going to pay for my kid's medical, bitch!"

I want to get in her face but that isn't going to help. And she's right. "Okay," I say, and wince at what paying for medical care is going to cost. "I'll do that. But this wasn't Connor's fault—"

"No, it's *your* fault he's so crazy. You and his murderer father! That bad apple ain't gone far from the tree."

My first impulse is to attack. I'm not very much different from my son in the way I've fractured inside under the stress. But I've got more experience. I can stop myself. I keep my voice calm as I say, "It might be my fault, but it isn't my son's. Don't blame him."

"Bitch, I'll blame whoever I want, and I'll sue you for everything you got! Henry was just trying to get your kid to do what the teacher said!"

She probably will sue, I think. There's real rage in her heart. But the name of her son strikes a note with me. "Henry," I repeat. I know that name. "Henry Charterhouse? The school's worst bully. How many kids has he punched out at school?"

The accusation hits home, I can tell; the mom looks at the dad, then rallies up her bravado again for another charge. "Hank gets into scraps. Boys being boys. But your son hit him with a goddamn metal stapler!"

"My son's got bruises and black eyes," I snap. "And I'm pretty sure I can call a long string of school administrators to tell us exactly who the problem kids in Norton Junior High are in a court of law. That what you want?"

She doesn't. She hasn't thought it through. She knows her boy's a bully; she knows damn well she's skating on thin ice. I see it written all over her thin, angry face. So of course she attacks again. "You *bitch!*" she yells. "Calling my son a bully when your damn kid's the son of a goddamn *murdering rapist who killed half a dozen girls* and ripped their goddamn skins off. The nerve of you. You come on out in this hall and I'll kick your city-girl ass!" Her accent's thickened so much it's hard to make out that last part.

No way am I going to get into a fight with this woman. People think badly enough of me in Norton; infamy's a curse, particularly in rural backwaters like this one. I make most of the locals uncomfortable. I don't fit. I refuse to accept blame for what my husband did. Women are always, somehow, to blame for the acts of men; that's more true now than it ever has been.

And all that free-floating anger I won't accept rebounds on my kids. And while I want to punch her several times for that, I don't. I just turn my back on her and take my seat again beside Connor, who's staring at me in outright confusion. He's never seen me walk away from a fight.

Maybe he needs to.

"It's okay," I tell him and take his hand again. "Ignore the noise."

"It's not just noise," he says. "Mom, I'm sorry. I shouldn't have hit him like that, but I couldn't . . . It felt like I was drowning. Like I had to get *out of there* but at the same time I just . . . couldn't move." He takes a deep breath, and I can hear the sob buried somewhere deep underneath. It cuts me deep. "I'm not *you.* I'm not Lanny. I can't be that brave."

The woman at the door is still yelling abuse, but I hear the no-nonsense raised voice of a nurse telling her to settle down if she doesn't want to be ejected from the hospital. When I look, the couple is gone from view, but not from hearing. The argument drifts down the hallway, full of angry swears and quelling icy warnings on the nurse's part.

The nurse checks in a few moments later. She's a plump African American woman with triangular features and a sharp cut to her natural hair. She gives me a look, as if she's waiting to see if I'm going to be trouble too; I just thank her for looking after my son. She relaxes. No smile, though.

"The doctor's reviewed the X-rays," she says. "That nose isn't broken, just pretty badly bruised. It might not hurt yet, but it will, and those bruises will be spectacular. Over-the-counter pain relief will help. Connor, keep an ice pack on your face for the rest of the day, as much as you can stand. It'll help."

I nod. Connor's already swinging his legs off the bed. "Can I go now?" he asks. She shakes her head.

"It'll take about an hour to get paperwork finished," she says. "I'll let you know."

She's right on target. It's nearly four thirty by the time we get the discharge paperwork. I sign for it on Connor's behalf. When I'm done, she says, "Last thing is you'll need to check out at the front counter."

She means pay the bill. I nod and thank God that I have a real job now, with real health benefits for me and the kids. J. B.'s been generous on the per-hour rate on these investigations I'm doing, too, so we're a lot less pressed for cash now than we were. When we landed at Stillhouse Lake, I blew most of my remaining cash buying and fixing up the house, and my internet office work hadn't exactly been completely plugging the money drain, not with two kids. Sam helps with bills, but I don't let him give more than is strictly necessary. I remember, grimly, that I'm going to have to pick up the check for at least one other kid's treatment bill. So maybe we're not less cash-strapped, after all.

Connor looks mournfully down at the blood on his sweater. "I look like hell."

"You look like you've been hurt," I tell him. "And we're going straight home. You can take a shower and get clean clothes."

He doesn't look up. "And tomorrow? Do I have to go back to school?"

I sigh. "We'll discuss it."

I walk between him and the room with the angry parents; they glare at us from the doorway, but don't come charging out. We walk briskly to the front desk, collect the discharge instructions, pay the bill, arrange for the Charterhouse kid's bills to be sent to me, and are out and at the SUV in record time.

We both slow down as we come closer.

My tires are flat. All four of them. And when I crouch down to inspect them, there are jagged slashes in the rubber.

I swallow a burst of rage so thick it tastes like metal in my mouth, and call a cop for the second time in a day.

It's a relief when we finally get home. Sam's already there waiting, worrying because it's getting dark. He's been texting me. I had Connor type a reply, but I have no idea what he's said. Probably not much, knowing my son.

Sam meets us at the door, with Lanny close behind. Both of them look anxious. Neither of them looks surprised at the state of Connor's face. Just grim, in Sam's case, and horrified, in Lanny's. She gets over that disturbingly fast and says, "Does it hurt?" She's studying him closely. He nods. "Wow. You look like you survived a *Saw* movie. I didn't know a nose could bleed that much."

"Well, it did," he says, and shoves past her and off down the hall. "Thanks for the sympathy."

"Squirtle—"

He whirls back. He's as tall as she is now, and probably a year from topping her by several inches. "Stop calling me that!" There's real anger in it. He doesn't wait for an answer. He heads toward his room.

"Dinner's almost ready!" she calls after him. "I made pizza!" No answer. Lanny looks disappointed.

"Frozen pizza?" I ask as I put my arm around her. She shrugs. "I think the word is 'heated.'"

"Hey, I added stuff. I'm good like that." She gets serious quickly. "Is he okay?"

"I think so, but . . ." I take a breath and let it out before I say it. "Lanny, you never really talk about how it feels to do the active shooter drills. Neither does he. But he's not dealing well with it. How about you? Are you okay?"

Lanny doesn't answer, which is not usually her thing. I see it in that moment: she's not okay, either, but she hides it better than my son. I made him go to school today. I did that out of a blind desire to have my kids lead a normal life when they patently and manifestly do not, and maybe never will.

I squeeze her shoulder a little. "Honey? Was it okay today for you?"

She's quiet for a long few seconds, and she doesn't meet my eyes. "It's scary," she says, and from her that's quite an admission. "I was in the library. We got locked up in the book storage until it was over. The lights were out, and people were crying, and . . ." She audibly swallows. "It's just hard, Mom. For some of them it's just a game. But I know it's not. I know what can happen. And it's hard not to feel . . . trapped."

I turn and hug her. I do it slowly and gently, because I'm trying not to show her how appalled I feel. She's a tough kid, but I hear the vulnerability underneath. She's not okay. My son's not okay. I should have known.

Her strength wavers and cracks. "Mom." It comes in a more subdued tone than I'm used to hearing from her. "You can't send Connor back to that school. It was already bad before. They're going to come after him twice as hard now."

"Okay," I say. "I'm going to keep him out. Maybe for a while. I can homeschool him. And you, unless you want to keep going—"

"I don't," she says, and it's decisive beyond question. She gives me a half-ashamed look. "I tried, Mom. I really did. But it *sucks*. Dahlia won't even talk to me. She avoids me like I've got the plague, and her clique are all totally shitty to me." Dahlia's her ex-girlfriend; I'd been really hoping it would last, but it hadn't. Dahlia had moved on hard, and Lanny's been trying. Not entirely successfully. "It's hard enough to make friends here. And the ones I made all turned on me when—" She shuts up, but I know. *When you went on TV.* My fault. I made a bad decision to go on national television to try to vindicate myself, and instead I just fanned the fires of rage that were already burning. I've still got a few friends and allies here, but that doesn't help my kids trying to navigate the already treacherous waters of small-town school social life.

I've made this worse for them. And the trauma being inflicted on all the kids—not just mine—by the active shooter drills has special meaning for Lanny and Connor, since they've been through threats most others haven't. Lanny and Connor keep paying the price, and I *hate it*.

And now the thing I didn't want to do—insulate them—is the only choice I have. That, or move again and try to start over. I'm stubborn, but when it comes to my children, I need to use that in their defense. Not to their detriment. My instincts tell me to hold fast. But I'm no longer sure that's right.

"Okay," I tell her, and kiss her forehead. She makes a face and twists away. "I'll call the schools tomorrow and formally withdraw you both. But that doesn't mean you get to run wild either. You'll have school hours, tests, standard textbooks. And I *will* be the toughest teacher you've ever had."

Lanny rolls her eyes. "Oh yeah, I know," she says. "Believe me." But she's relieved; I can see it in the way she walks away. There's a confidence in her step that has been flagging recently.

It's the right move. It has to be. I'll make it work, and we'll figure things out as we go.

As long as we're together, things will be okay.

Sam's been watching this silently, but now he puts an arm around me, and I turn into his embrace and take in a deep, shuddering breath. "Connor's okay?" he asks. I hear the worry in his voice. I manage a nod.

"He's going to need some more sessions with our therapist," I say. "It was a classic PTSD episode, from what I could gather. He froze up, and then when somebody pushed him, he lashed out. He broke one kid's jaw." I laugh bitterly. It sounds shaky. "What's really broken is the fact all these kids have to endure imaginary trauma six times a year. It changes people. Sam, he didn't even know what he was *doing.*"

"I understand the theory. They need to be ready to react in an emergency," Sam says, but he sounds subdued. "But this can't be good for him."

Lanny's gone down the hall. So I lower my voice and say, "Sam—this town. I don't know what to do. They're shutting us out, closing ranks. You've felt it. So have I."

"I know. I also know you swore you weren't going to run anymore."

"Maybe that's just blind, stubborn pride," I tell him. "I picked this place because we were anonymous. But we're not anymore, and maybe I just need to accept that we never will be again." I take a deep breath, and I look around. This house . . . it means something to me. We bought it as a half-ruined shell, and Lanny and Connor and I made it a home. We put in the new floor. New drywall. Paint and sweat and love. We chose this place, and it's *ours.*

But the truth is, it's just a house. We can find another place to make home. And . . . and I think we should. Moving to Knoxville would be expensive, but Sam would have a chance to fly again, and I—I already have a job, and the move would put me closer to my boss, and the resources of her offices.

I take a deep breath and say, "I think we need to move."

Sam's been carefully expressionless but now he looks relieved, and it makes me feel a real wave of guilt. He's been worried more than he's told me. He puts his hands on my face and leans forward and kisses me gently on the forehead. "I think that's good," he says. "But I know you put a lot into this place. I don't want you to feel like I'm pushing you."

"You're not," I tell him, and smile. "But maybe you should. You're part of this too."

"Okay. Consider this a push." For a second, his smile is so genuine that it makes me forget everything else. "Oh, by the way . . . hope this doesn't make you uncomfortable, but since you're talking about home-schooling, I've got the details on Tennessee Virtual Academy. It could take us a while to get settled somewhere else, and I'm not sure you want to have them out of school that long." When I pull back, surprised, he shrugs. "I figured it might come to this. You can enroll them in the online academy, but you have to withdraw them formally from the Norton schools first."

"Wow," I say. "Thank you."

He shrugs. "I was worried. I thought it'd be good to know what to do if things went wrong. Backup plan."

I kiss him. It's impulsive, and it surprises him, but he doesn't pull away. We're still healing a very large rift that opened between the two of us in the rough, creepy town of Wolfhunter. Things came out about his past that I hadn't known, had never suspected, and . . . it had hurt. A lot. Now we're slowly rebuilding a bridge that will hold the enormous weight of both our pasts.

Something in this kiss ignites fires deep inside me, melts me like butter, and sends warmth coiling deeper in my body. We're both a little unsteady. A little frantic. Sam's thumb traces my lips, sealing the kiss, and the look in his eyes makes me think he's feeling the same urgency I am.

But we don't get a chance to indulge it, because Lanny comes around the corner and says, "Hey, do you want me to make a salad or—" She catches the mood right away because we react like startled teens, taking a step back from each other even though there's no reason in the world for that to happen. "Really? Wow."

"Lanny." I try to make my voice sound firm and adult. I probably fail. "Why don't you decide?"

"Sure," she says, with a load of meaning in it that I don't really feel like unpacking at the moment. "I'll, uh, take my time."

I take Sam's hand.

"Bedroom?" he asks me.

"Bedroom," I say.

I pretend I don't hear my daughter's muttered *ugh* as we pass.

5

LANNY

I suppose I should feel weird about the prospect of not going to school tomorrow morning, but I just feel *great*. Like a huge weight rolled off me, and now I can actually breathe again. School's an armed camp, and I was always an outnumbered enemy soldier. Girls don't fight the same ways—normally—so it's more snark and bitchy cuts and exclusion than straight-up fights. Though I've put a beatdown on a couple of guys—and girls—who came at me that way when I first got here. Nobody's tried it recently. But I've never really felt included; I'm still the *new girl*, at best. At worst, I'm the serial killer's daughter. The polite ones don't say it, but that doesn't mean they aren't thinking it.

It's an early night. Connor feels like shit, and not even a rewatch of his favorite superhero movie cheers him up, so afterward I run away to my room. I'm in bed listening to a playlist and luxuriating in the fact that even though Mom's probably going to roust me up at some horrible hour, I can just do online studies and take some quizzes and get on with my life.

It sounds amazing.

Rain clouds have been moving in, and by the time I finish watching a movie on my laptop and checking out a few makeup tutorials on

YouTube, I hear thunder rumbling. It's low and far away, but the rain's already here. It's a nice, steady drum on the roof and the windows.

It's nearly two in the morning, and I'm almost asleep when I hear something tapping at my window. At first I think it's a branch.

Then all my sleepiness flies away and I sit straight up in bed, because there's a shadow out there.

It's a person out in the rain, knocking on my window.

I start to scream for Mom, but then some weird instinct kicks in. I know that silhouette. I pick up my phone, activate the flashlight function, and shine it right at her.

It's Vera Crockett—Vee, to her friends. Vee from Wolfhunter. What the *hell?*

Vee's a little older than me, but only by months. She's survived as much bad shit as I have, but maybe she hasn't come through it as well. She lost her mom, for one thing, and that was after a rough childhood and even rougher teen experience. Vee's one of the few people I can trade top-this trauma stories with, and she wins. Hey, at least *I* haven't been put in jail and falsely accused of murder.

But Vee's supposed to have a new home with some aunt or something out of state. How the hell is she here, and why, especially at this time of night?

Doesn't matter. I like Vee. And she's out there soaked and shivering and far, far from home.

I grab a piece of paper and write in black marker, *Wait there.* I press it to the window glass, and she signals she's gotten the message. Then I slip out of my room and into the hall. I listen at the door to Mom and Sam's bedroom. I hear nothing. They're asleep.

I move quietly down the hall to the keypad by the front door, and I hesitate for a few seconds. Mom *probably* won't hear me bypassing my window sensor when I enter the code. But the question is, should I? Or should I tell Mom that Vee's here, outside? But I know what will happen. Mom will be worried, and she'll send Vee away. Okay, maybe she wouldn't; she saved Vee in the first place, back in Wolfhunter. But I can't take the chance.

A big part of me really wants to hear what Vee has to say.

Screw it.

I put in the code to take my window out of the alarm system, wincing at the beeps the keypad makes, but it's in the front room and Mom's bedroom is all the way at the back. If she hears something, I can say I was just checking to make sure it was on.

I hover near Mom's bedroom door, breathless, until I'm sure she and Sam have slept through it, then go back to my room and slide the glass up. The rain is cold, and it cascades in all over my bare feet; it's all I can do not to yelp. Vee's taken off the screen already. She slithers in fast and dumps a soaked duffel bag on the rug by my bed. "Quiet!" I hiss, and slide the window shut again. When I turn around, Vee's hugging me, and I freeze up for a second before I relax. She's really, really wet, and even with that she doesn't smell great, but she *feels* great. "What are you doing here?" I keep it a fierce whisper.

When I pull back, I don't like the shine in her eyes. She looks weird. And kind of high. Her wet hair's dirty and matted. "I need to use your bathroom," she whispers back. "Can I take a shower?"

Oh man. I think about it, biting my lip. "Make it fast," I tell her. I'm hoping that the sound of the rain will mask the shower noise. "Keep it quiet. And, uh, maybe wash your hair?"

She smiles at me, and boy, I like her smile. I always have since the first minute I saw her in jail. She was trying to be all cool and strong, but I'd seen something under that too. Somebody worth getting to know. Vee's got problems, I know that, but I always thought she kind of liked me too. *And here she is.*

But why?

Vee doesn't tell me. She turns and digs in her duffel bag and comes up with sweatpants, underwear, a T-shirt. I take her to the door and point out the bathroom down the hall, and she waves and heads that way. I wait until she's in there with the door locked before I go back to the alarm system and put my window sensor back online.

The rain covers the shower sound pretty well; I can barely hear it myself, and it's even farther away from Mom and Sam. Vee's quiet, at least.

I wait tensely, chewing my fingernails, until she comes back. She's showered and changed, and she sinks down on my bed with a sigh. Her dark hair is wet and dripping on the T-shirt, turning spots transparent. She looks better. And a little less high.

I lean close and say, "What the hell are you doing here?"

"Well," she says, and her rural accent drags the word out. "The courts said they'd put me with my aunt, but she couldn't take me after all, so then they put me in a foster home, and I ain't taking that shit. Would you, Lanta?"

Vee is the only one who calls me Lanta, short for Atlanta; everybody else just says Lanny. I kind of like her version. And I'm also afraid of liking it. "Probably not," I reply. "Were the foster people mean or something?"

She shrugs. "They told me when to go to bed, when to get up, what to wear, what to eat. Didn't care for that shit."

"And you came here? Have you *met* my mom?"

"Your momma's a badass bitch," Vee says. "And she saved my life when the cops would have killed me back there in Wolfhunter. So did you." She says that casually, but I feel it. I feel the look she gives me too. "I been thinking about you a lot, Lanta."

I don't say I've been thinking about her, too, but it would be true. I have. Not in a serious way; I thought she was long gone out of my life. But there's something about Vee. Maybe it's just that dangerous edge I like.

"So what are you doing?" I ask her.

"In general?" Her shoulders rise and fall. "You know. Bummin' around."

"You just took off from your foster home?"

"A while back, yeah. Then I found myself at a bus stop not too far away and I thought, hell, why not find you. And here I am."

That is not Vee's story. I know she's lying to me but I don't know why. "Look, you can stay tonight, but you've got to go before my mom gets up in the morning, okay? I'll get you some food and—"

"Lanta." She puts both hands on my shoulders and leans close. I freeze. Her eyes are so pretty, and my heart is beating so fast it hurts. "Atlanta Proctor, you don't have to do nothin' you don't want to do. You know that, don't you? I'll be gone if you want me gone. Ain't no big thing."

I feel warm. Weightless. Strange. I want to run to my mother. I want to kiss this girl. I don't know what's going on right now.

I don't answer. I just lie down and pull the covers up. Vee watches me for a few seconds, then slips in beside me under the sheet and blankets and the heavy duvet, and the sheer animal warmth of her makes me forget how to breathe.

She moves closer, and I can feel her *almost* touching me. I shiver, waiting.

I feel her warm breath on the back of my neck as Vee whispers, "Good night, Lanta."

I catch myself on a gasp, and reach over and turn the light out.

I don't think I can sleep at all, having her beside me. My mind is racing. My pulse is too. I feel hot and cold and exhilarated and terrified, and I know none of it is right but I don't care. *I don't care.* I wasn't even hardly alone with Vee back in Wolfhunter; when I was, there were lots of other problems to worry about. But I've spent time thinking about her after that. It feels unreal that she's just . . . shown up. Like this is a dream, and when I wake up, she'll be gone.

When Vee's arms go around my waist and pull me close, I moan, and it feels *so good.* It feels like the best kiss in the world, even though we haven't kissed at all.

I feel her sigh on the skin at the back of my neck, and then she just . . . falls asleep. I know she does. I feel her relax. I hear the rhythm of her breath change.

She's drunk or high or something, I tell myself. *You shouldn't have let her in here. You shouldn't be in the bed with her right now. Get up.*

I don't.

I fall asleep, too, despite all the fear and uncertainty and longing inside me.

Because as wrong as this is, Vee Crockett makes me feel . . . safe. And I know that's *very* wrong; Vee isn't a safe person. But maybe it's just feeling, well, wanted again.

Vee says she came here for *me*.

Maybe she's not lying.

When I wake up again, it's because Vee is moving. She's pulling her arms back from me, and yawning. I blink at the dull glow from the window. It's not dawn yet, but it's coming fast. Mom will be up soon, if she isn't already. *Holy shit,* I need to get Vee out of here. Now.

I slip out of bed and hold a finger to my lips as I slide on my house shoes. Vee smiles at me, a warm and lazy kind of smile, and burrows into the pillows like she intends to stay. I open the door and listen. No sounds in the house yet. I hurry down the hall and into the living room, and I'm just entering the code for my window again when I hear the bright chime of Sam's alarm going off. *Shit shit shit.* I nearly miss the buttons, I'm going so fast, but I manage to get it right, and I rush back to my room and shut and lock the door. I can hear Mom and Sam getting up.

"You have to go," I whisper to Vee. "Now. Now!" I pull her up to a sitting position, and she winks at me, yawns again, and jams her bare feet into the boots she left on the floor. Her hair has dried all crazy, but she doesn't seem to care about that. She puts her dirty clothes in the duffel bag. I open the window. She dumps the bag out and sits on the sill and looks at me, dangling her feet like a little kid.

49

"Can I come back tonight?" she asks me. I shake my head. "Oh, come on now, girl. That was fun, wasn't it? And I was nice. I didn't take no advantages."

"Vee, if my mom finds you here, she'll freak the hell out. You're supposed to be in a foster home! You can't just . . . run away."

"Yes, I can. You send me back there I'll do it again." Her smile fades. I see that cool distance in her eyes, the same as I saw back in Wolfhunter when she was in jail. Vee's complicated. And I know she's got the death of her mom to deal with, and she's probably doing that the bad way, with drinking and drugs. My mother will absolutely kill me if I don't tell her about Vee being here.

But I'm still not sure I will.

"Come back tonight," I tell Vee. "I can wash your clothes for you, maybe." I have no idea why I'm making that offer, but I've already said it and it's too late, and Vee's smile makes me go weak inside.

She kisses me. It's fast, and hot, and then she's rolling backward out the window and springing up like a gymnast. She hits the ground running. I quickly shut the window and try to catch my breath. I feel like I have a fever.

Someone taps on the door. I flinch and rush over and unlock it. I fling it open. "What?" I sound bitchy. I'm just scared. "I'm up!"

It's Mom, and she doesn't look pleased. "You left towels all over the bathroom floor," she says. "You know better, Lanny. Clean it up. Go. Now."

I was afraid that she'd seen Vee running from the house, that somehow she just *knew*, like I was wearing a neon sign or something. But it's not that at all.

I rush to the bathroom. It's a wreck. Vee left shampoo bottles in a mess, wet towels on the floor. I take the towels to the laundry machine, then come back and clean up the spills. By the time I'm done it looks okay again, and I'm calmer. A little.

"Sorry," I mumble to Mom as I head into the kitchen. "I think I was sleepwalking."

"Really."

"Maybe I was just really tired."

She doesn't buy it, not for a second.

I told Vee to come back.

Oh God.

This isn't going to work. Not at all.

6

GWEN

In the morning I make it official: I write a letter, using the format approved by the state of Tennessee, to remove my kids from the Norton Independent School District, and I enroll them in the Tennessee Virtual Academy. Both Lanny and Connor seem relieved, and so am I. I'll make arrangements to pick up the contents of their lockers later, and that'll be it. I think about calling a real estate agent, but I know I need to think about this and talk to the kids. Decide as a family. My impulse is to move on from Stillhouse Lake, but something the kids have been angry about in the past few years is that I run from things. I do it to keep them safe, but I understand their frustration. If we're moving this time we have to decide it together.

Meanwhile, I'm glad the kids are safer now, but it does make my job harder. I'd planned to take off for Knoxville today and interview the mother of the missing young man I'd been hired to locate, but even though Lanny insists (of course) that she and Connor can stay by themselves while Sam's at work, I don't buy it. So after letting them log into their new virtual schools and get their assignments, I order them into the car with me.

Road trip.

They're not thrilled, which is annoying but typical; they've both reached the age where anything I want or need them to do is a horrific burden, but I know that beneath that facade they're actually okay with it. Lanny's subdued after the weirdness this morning; she warms up once we're in the SUV and heading out on the road—with doughnuts, of course—and commandeers the sound system to play her own driving soundtrack, which I allow because it makes life easier and my daughter actually has decent taste in music.

Connor asks me about the case I'm working on.

"It's a missing college student," I tell him. "His name is Remy."

"*His* name," my son repeats. "I thought only women went missing."

That's troubling, but I can see why he'd think so. The big media blitzes almost exclusively happen for missing children, teen girls, and adult women. White and pretty, preferably. It's rare to see the major networks covering a missing young woman of color as a priority.

And almost never young men of any race, even though they can and do go missing too.

Connor's still curious. "Did something happen to him?"

"Maybe. He disappeared one night when he was out with his friends."

"Maybe he doesn't want to be found?"

"College students don't run away," Lanny says. "They *already* ran away from home. Legally."

"Sometimes they run from other things," I tell her. "Life. Responsibility. Problems with relationships. And it's also possible he could have gotten involved with bad people, or gotten into drugs, or had a mental break. Maybe even an accident, though that'd be unlikely under these circumstances. It's impossible to tell right now. That's why I'm going to talk to his mom, to get a better picture of who he was and what could have happened."

"Can we come in with you?" she asks. She hates being left out, and I have to admit she's certainly got a case for being able to handle serious issues. But her behavior this morning concerns me. I don't know what's going on in her head right now.

"Sorry, no. I can't," I say. "I'm on the clock, and it won't help my client trust me if I bring you guys along. So . . . I was thinking that I could take you both to that zip line place you like so much—"

"Navitat?" Connor beats Lanny to it by a couple of seconds. "Cool."

"Yes, Navitat, and let you guys off on your own for a couple of hours; then I pick you up. Lanny—"

"I'm in charge," she said. "Like I don't know?" But she's not displeased. Neither is Connor, come to that; my kids have pulled together recently, where they'd been pulling apart before. And they both nag me regularly for a little more autonomy. Navitat's a safe place with good security, and I can trust them that much.

I don't *want* to, though.

It's just for a couple of hours, I tell myself, and try not to think of all the people out there who'd love to terrify, hurt, or even kill my children. On top of the usual child predators, there are more personal enemies who'd jump at the chance to "avenge"—their word, not mine—Melvin Royal's victims by taking out his own family. Some of them have at least some reason to feel that way, because they lost their own loved ones. Most of them just like an excuse to indulge their constant and free-floating hatred.

But my kids are at an age where a little freedom can help them feel more confident in their own abilities. It's part of growing up.

Much as I hate it.

We arrive in Knoxville. It's an interesting place. The winters can get cold, but snow's typically rare; ice is a much bigger problem. Today's a sweetly sunny day with temperatures in the high sixties, and it gives the city a shine it doesn't altogether deserve.

For an otherwise typical small southern city, it's had a fair number of truly awful murderers. And as we drive through, I start identifying nondescript locations where bodies were found, crimes committed, murderers caught. It isn't that I want to know these things. I just don't really have much of a choice. After Melvin, after his abductions and murders of young women were carried out under the roof of the home we shared . . . I needed to understand *why* he was what he was. So I looked deep and long into a very dark abyss. I can't say I'm any wiser for it, but I am far more . . . aware.

Knoxville—and Nashville even more—will always have a darkness under the shine, at least for me.

Thankfully, Navitat—which specializes in nature trails and zip line adventures—doesn't have much in the way of horror stories, and it's well managed and guarded. I give Lanny and Connor spending money and make them promise to not lose sight of each other, *ever*, and I quiz them on emergency procedures. They know the drill. Scream and run. Emergency calls on their cells. Attract attention and get help. Never let anyone get them off alone. I keep reinforcing it, even though I know kids will always find a reason and a way to break rules and take risks. If I can make them hesitate for a second, think just a little more, that's all I can ask.

"Panic buttons?" I ask them. They both show me their key chains. The buttons activate an alert on my phone, plus an ear-piercing alarm that I hope to never have to hear again in person. "Okay. Be safe, be smart, be—"

"Careful, yeah, we know," Connor says, and slides out of the SUV. He looks back inside. "Thanks, Mom."

"I love you."

He's at that age where he just nods. Saying it back feels wrong. It doesn't matter. I know he loves me too.

Lanny gives me a quick hug and is gone in seconds.

I idle at the curb until I see them pass through the security gate, and then I look up the address of Remy's mother.

Fifteen minutes away.

I head that direction, and find myself sliding not into middle-class suburbs, but bustling streets crowded with apartments. I know Remy's mother moved to Knoxville, but this isn't a place a middle-aged woman fits in. Every person I see is well under thirty, most loaded down with backpacks and heading to or from the university.

It hits me then. *She's living in her son's old apartment.* He's been gone for three years, and she's paying the rent and . . . waiting. I take a breath. Think about what I'd do in the same situation after the police gave up and the case went cold. If Connor disappeared and I couldn't find him, would I be able to give up a place he'd once called his home?

No. That would be like giving him up too.

The address takes me to a not-very-impressive apartment block that screams that it was built in the mid-1980s, but has at least been repaired and repainted on a regular basis. The unit number in my notes is 303.

I park and climb the stairs. Someone on the second-floor landing has a nice fern soaking up sun, and it gives me a welcome scent of damp earth to replace the faint odor of dust and age and wood rot.

I knock on the faded brown door with the tarnished number 303 on it.

"Who is it?" A shadow darkens the peephole.

"Gwen Proctor. I work for J. B. Hall; I believe she's already been in contact with you to let you know I'm coming. I'm a private investigator," I say. "I'd like to talk to you about your son, Remy."

I don't make it a question. I'm not a tentative person. And she responds, after a few seconds, by inching the door open. "Do you have ID?"

I silently produce my wallet and show her my private investigator license and photo ID. She opens the door fully and steps back, and I cross the threshold.

It's like stepping into a tomb someone lives in. Everything *looks* right—the lamps are burning, the blinds are open. But this place has a young man's style imprint everywhere, from the sports posters on the wall (soccer is a favorite) to a frayed plaid couch that most women would put right out on the curb. A gaming console near the big-screen television. Two controllers perfectly positioned on the coffee table, like monuments. There's still a hoodie thrown over the back of a gaming chair, and a pair of tumbled sneakers nearby.

As if he were just here. Just stepped away, and this life here is like a game on pause.

The thing that's out of place is the woman standing in front of me. She's older than me by at least ten years, but looks older still; there's an indefinable *grayness* about her, as if she's the ghost that haunts this place, not her son. She's wearing plain black pants, a soft pullover with the University of Tennessee seal on it. It fits a little snugly, and I wonder if it belongs—belonged—to Remy. The thought makes me feel both sad and a little wary.

"I'm Ruth," she says, and holds out her hand to me. "Ruth Landry." There's a faintly Cajun spice to her words, but I don't think she was born to it. Married into it, most likely. "Thank you for taking our case, Mrs. Proctor."

I don't know why she's assumed I'm a *Mrs.*, but I correct her quickly and efficiently. "Either Ms. or Gwen is fine," I say, and leaven it with a smile. "Haven't been Mrs. for a while, and I prefer it that way."

"Oh," she says, and then doesn't quite know what to follow up with. I realize she honestly doesn't recognize my name at all. She must have lived her life in a hazy bubble of nice things happening to nice people, until her son's disappearance dropped her with brutal suddenness here in the real world.

I'm honestly grateful that I'm just a regular person to her. And more than a little sad it doesn't happen more often.

"I'm here to ask about your son," I tell her, and she nods. She seems awkward and flustered, as if she's forgotten how to talk to strangers at all. "Could I trouble you for a glass of water, ma'am?"

It gives her something to do, and while she's filling the glass, I study the apartment some more. Not that it will tell me much on the surface except what I already know.

She hands me the glass, water beading like jewels down the side, and I take it and drink. It tastes surprisingly chemical to me. I'm used to rural water, and in Norton and around Stillhouse Lake, our water tastes delicious. City water . . . isn't. I drain a couple of mouthfuls and find a coaster to set it on as she motions me to sit. I take the gaming chair as she settles on the couch. It's an odd feeling, as if Remy's still sitting in it with me. There's a comfortable, worn-in feel to the back and seat. I can picture him here—no, wait, I've actually seen him here in this chair. Pictures on his social media, with his long legs stretched out to rest on that coffee table. That game controller in his hand.

I lean forward, not eager to sink into that sadness, and take out my phone. "Mrs. Landry, do you mind if I record this? It helps me focus if I'm listening, not taking notes."

"Of course, anything," she says. I believe her. There's a feverish light of hope in her eyes. I'm the first person who's been here in a long time, who's asked her to invoke her son and bring him back to reality. "Where should I start?"

"Let's start with the last time you spoke to him," I say, and I see her flinch a little. Tender territory. She looks down. Her skin is sallow, a healthy Louisiana tan fading to pallor. Dry and uncared for, as is her hair. I'm not criticizing her, even in my mind; I'm just noting details. I've seen photos of her before his disappearance, and she took good care of her body and appearance. She's abandoned all that now as wasted effort.

"It wasn't such a good conversation," she says. "I wish—well. Wishing doesn't help, now does it?" I don't answer, and she rushes on. "My Remy was a good boy, he was just—you know, not willing to listen so much to his momma anymore. I can't blame him. He grew up, and he thought he knew best."

I wait. She's getting to something. And sure enough, she finally blurts out, "We had a little bit of a fight, I'm afraid."

"About what?" I ask.

"About this girl he liked."

"What was her name?"

"Carol," she said. "From somewhere up north." She dismisses the entire north with a wave. "City people."

I don't tell her she's living in a city. I just nod. "Okay. Did you ever meet Carol?"

"No. He just talked about her some. He said he was going to help her out. I didn't think that was a real good idea; seemed like she was a drifter of some kind. Real religious."

"Was she his girlfriend? Were they dating?"

"No. He said she was just a friend who needed help. But I don't know if that's the real truth. He'd been dating this girl named Karen Forbes, she was a nice one but I don't think she liked him as much as he liked her. She was a junior at the university. Biology, I think. Real smart."

"Do you have Carol's last name?"

"No, he never said, and since she wasn't his girlfriend I didn't really ask."

"Any pictures of her, or maybe some contact information for Karen Forbes you can give me?"

"I'll go look." She rushes off toward what I assume will be the bedroom. *She's sleeping in his bed. Wearing his clothes.* Man. This isn't good, and I wonder if her husband understands the depth of his wife's obsession. But I'm not here to play counselor. I'm here to find her son, and if I understand anything at all about Ruth Landry, it's that her cure will be the answer to what happened to her son, living or dead. This limbo is a living hell.

She comes back with a framed photo—Remy, with his easy grin, and his arm around a young woman. She's blonde, tall, curvy, and has a magazine-cover smile. Pretty and lively. The picture tells me nothing about her other than that, but I take it, position it on the coffee table, and take a photo for the records. Then I turn the frame over and pull the picture out, hoping for a note on the back, but it's just smooth photo paper. I put it back and hand it to Ruth. She repositions it on the coffee table and stares at her son.

"He was pretty serious about her," she says. "More than he ought to have been at his age. I wanted him back home. His father wanted Remy to inherit the business and run it. But he just wasn't interested in all that. I think he was going to ask Karen to marry him. But I don't know that she would have said yes, or if she did, if they'd have made it for long."

"What kind of business does your husband have?" I ask her. It's probably in the records, but it's something to keep her moving. She can't seem to look away from her son's face.

"Cars," she says. "We're the biggest distributor in our parish. And boats too. Do a good trade in those as well. A few RVs, mostly used, though."

I nod. I can't imagine she's been out of this apartment for quite a while, so when she's saying *we*, I understand that means *my husband*. Her job now is tending this graveyard. "Okay. Thank you, that's very helpful. Now, let's talk more about Remy, if that's okay . . . Your last conversation was about this Carol, is that right?"

"Fight," she corrects. "Well, more or less. I didn't like him being around someone who was in trouble, like Carol was."

"What kind of trouble?"

She shakes her head. "I don't really know. He didn't give me any details about that, and he got sharp with me when I tried to find out. Then we fought about how he wanted to spend Thanksgiving with Karen and her family, can you even imagine? In *Connecticut*. I put my foot down and said, 'No, Remy, you come on home. You let that girl go be with her family and you come be with yours.' He didn't like that, and he told me he'd think about it." Her eyes are welling up with shimmering tears, and her face is reddening under the pressure of her grief. Her voice takes on an unsteady shiver. "Thanksgiving was just a week away when we had that conversation, you know. I was already planning the meal. He told me to keep on like I was doing while he thought about it, so I did. Even after I couldn't get hold of him to be sure he was coming, I cooked dinner. I thought he'd just show up. Or at least *call*. But we sat there at the table and just . . ."

She breaks. I can see it in my mind—the family gathered at the table, the empty place, the food cooling in the bowls while they stare and wait and wait until it's obvious there will be no Thanksgiving miracle, no Remy knocking on the door, flashing them that easy, wonderful grin and telling them he was sorry to worry them.

I push a box of Kleenex on the table toward her, and she takes a handful and presses them to her face as she sobs. It takes a while, and as I wait I begin to smell something baking. I wonder if it's coming from the other apartments around us, but then a kitchen timer dings, and Ruth gasps and jumps up, loose tissues fluttering toward the coffee table as she drops them.

She heads into the kitchen. I follow and stand at the doorway as she pulls on oven mitts and takes a tray of cookies from the oven. She places it on the stove and shoots me a trembling smile. "Remy's favorites," she says. "Peanut butter chocolate chip." She moves the tray to the kitchen counter under the window, slides it open, and I feel the breeze drift in. "Want one?"

"Sure," I tell her.

She expertly slides one from the baking tray onto a little plate and hands it to me. "Coffee with that?"

I nod, and she pours me a cup from an already-brewed pot. We sit down at the small colonial kitchen table with our coffee and cookies, and Ruth says, "I make these every week now. Every day, when I first moved here. I keep thinking . . . I keep thinking that if he smells those fresh cookies, he might just come home. I open the window so he can smell them from out there. Wherever he is. I know I should stop, but I can't. Stupid, isn't it?"

I take a bite of the cookie. "It's delicious," I tell her. "And no. It's not stupid at all. Desperate, maybe, and painful, but that's normal, Ruth. You need a little hope."

"I do, yes." She takes a deep breath and drinks some coffee, visibly steeling herself. "Do you think he's dead, Ms. Proctor?"

"I don't know," I tell her, which is the truth, but not all of it by any stretch. "I'm starting from scratch right now. I'm going to go over everything. The police are good at this, but they also have lots of priorities, lots of cases on their desks. It isn't that they don't try, but that when clues dry up, they have to move on to the next critical window for another family. The reason we're able to do more is that we just have more time to devote to you. And I promise you, I'll take this as far as I can."

She's looking at me oddly now. Frowning a little, with an intentness to her stare that means she's actually taking me in as a person instead of a placeholder. "You seem really familiar. Don't I know you?" she asks.

"We've never met," I say. I know where she's going. I just don't want to help. I take another bite of the mourning cookie. "Ruth, never mind about me. Did Remy have a car?"

"A car? Yes. It's here. In the apartment garage. The police went over it, didn't find anything at all. He didn't drive that night."

"Okay. Who did he go out with?"

She lists names as easily as if they were her own lifelong friends. A kind of mantra, really. I make sure the recorder catches all of them, but the list sounds the same as what was in the files; I just like to be sure.

"Did Remy mention anything odd happening in the weeks before he disappeared?" I ask her. "Phone calls, emails, anything strange on his social media?"

"No. Nothing. He kept some old letters and cards from friends and girlfriends. Do you want those?"

"Yes," I say. "I can just take photos of them, that way you can keep them. And anything about this Carol he was helping."

She nods, but I can tell that she's still thinking about me instead of her son. Maybe that's better. I don't know. "I *know* I've seen you somewhere," she says, and shakes her head. "Well. Let me get those things for you." She stands up. I stand up too.

"Would you mind if I took a look around?" I ask her. "Just to get a sense of things."

"Oh. Of course, you go right ahead."

I take the coffee with me—it's good and fresh, and I long ago learned that life is better with it than not. I sip it and stare at what's in the living room first. He's not much of a reader, Remy, but he does love his sports. Most of the books in the one bookshelf are either textbooks, what look to be old favorites from high school, or sports-related biographies. I flip through idly, and find a couple of notes used as bookmarks, but they don't seem important. I photograph them anyway.

By that time Ruth is back with correspondence. I take photos of them and the envelopes, but don't read them; doing that in front of her will feel too intrusive. I can study them later.

I head for the bedroom. I'm unsurprised to find he has a futon for a bed.

Mom's influence is stronger here, as I suppose it would be; her book on the nightstand, her hand cream, her clothes hanging in the closet next to his. I push her hangers aside and look at what he left behind. Jeans, T-shirts, a couple of sport jackets, one good suit, probably only for formal occasions. A pair of flip-flops on the closet floor, a pair of nicer lace-up shoes he probably wears with the suit. With the sneakers abandoned by the couch, I wonder what shoes he was wearing when he disappeared.

I discover sex toys in a box up on the shelf. It's a relatively small collection, nothing too radical. Fluffy handcuffs, yawn. A couple of vibrators his ladies might like.

I put it back where I found it, and continue on.

I'm looking in his medicine cabinet when Ruth's voice from the doorway says, "I do know you."

There's a brand-new tone in her voice. I recognize it. I take a photo of the contents of the medicine cabinet before I say, "Oh?"

"You're that killer's wife."

"Not anymore," I say. "I divorced him. And then I killed him in self-defense." I close the door and turn to face her. "I'm also trying to help you."

"I don't need *your* help," she says. There are stiff lines bracketing her lips now, and a dull fury driving out her grief. I'm toxic by association. A reminder that not everything works out for the best.

I try not to sigh as I reply, "Mrs. Landry, you're more than welcome to ask J. B. for another investigator, but I'm the closest, and frankly speaking, I have a better idea of what you're going through than you realize."

"Just because your husband stole those girls away from their families, you think you understand what this is like?"

"No," I tell her quietly. "I understand because my own children are constantly under threat. Ruth . . . my children have gone missing before, and I thought I would die. I got them back, thank God, but those hours they were gone felt like eternity. I'm on your side. Please let me help."

She doesn't like it. She's afraid of the violence that surrounded me and still does. And maybe she's right to be afraid, but she should also be reassured.

Nobody else is going to take this as seriously as I do.

She takes her time before she finally, stiffly nods. "You got what you need?" The subtext is that I'd better.

"Yes," I tell her. "I'd like to also talk to your husband—"

"If you can get him to do that, I'll be amazed," she says. "Joe doesn't like talking about Remy. He can't face the fact our son's gone."

Hearing the word *gone*, I instinctively know that some part of her has accepted the likely truth: her son is dead, beyond even a mother's desperate reach. But as if she realizes what she's said, she quickly rejects it again. "I know he'll be back," she says, and lifts her chin as if daring me to correct her.

I don't. This woman is fragile, frightened, clinging to a lie she's telling herself, but I won't break her heart. Not until I know for sure I have to.

I say, "Thank you for your help, Mrs. Landry. I'll be in touch as soon as I know anything."

She's reluctant to say it. My history and infamy are weighing on us now, but she finally says, "Please find him for me. Please."

I don't promise. I can't.

But it's hard for me not to recognize the despair and horror in her eyes. She's living a nightmare but pretending everything is just . . . normal. For so many years I lived with Melvin, struggled to please him, to pretend that everything was *fine*. I pretended so hard that I thought it really was okay. All that changed the day a drunk driver opened up a wall of our house and revealed all of Melvin's evil, horrible secrets. The sight of that poor dead woman—Sam's sister—will haunt me forever.

The knowledge that if I'd only been more curious, maybe I could have *done something* . . . that's even worse. I'll do anything I can to finally end Ruth Landry's nightmare . . . one way or another. Maybe I'm doing it for her. Maybe for myself.

But either way, I'm committed.

7

GWEN

As I idle in the parking lot at Navitat and wait for the kids to finish their last zip line run, I try to focus on the case, the clues. I can't shake the unsettling truth that is Ruth Landry. Baking cookies no one eats. Begging for a ghost to come home.

I don't know what I'd be if I lost Connor and Lanny.

I'm looking things up using a bespoke app that J. B. Hall commissioned—like Google on steroids, built solely for finding traces of people by their names or other significant identifiers—when Connor and Lanny pile into the car. Instantly, they're both talking.

"Mom, that was *great*, you should have come in with us, the lines weren't bad at all—"

"Did you find out where he went? What happened to him?" Connor's voice overrides his sister's.

Lanny glares at him. "How the hell is she supposed to solve a case in, like, two hours?"

"It's *Mom*."

I laugh as they strap themselves in. "Nice vote of confidence," I tell him. "But your sister's right. This is going to take a while, I'm afraid."

"Oh. So, are we going somewhere else?" My son seems entirely too intrigued by that possibility. "We can help you."

"Nope," I tell him. "I'll make some calls once we're home. A lot of this is just making appointments and convincing people to talk to me. Honestly, it's boring."

He doesn't believe me, and neither does Lanny, but they devolve into squabbling in a few short minutes. Apparently he thinks Lanny admired another girl on a zip line, and teasing is required. I don't shut it down too hard. He isn't harassing her because she's gay; he'd have razzed her if it were a hot boy too.

Lanny insists it never happened anyway. They lapse into a mutinous silence after I finally order the two of them to drop the feud, and that rumbles between them the whole rest of the way home.

"Right," I tell them as we pull into the driveway. "I want you two to make up and get to your lessons. I'm going to check your work tonight—" My voice stops hard when I see that there's an unfamiliar vehicle parked by our house. A big, muddy truck plastered with NRA decals and a bunch of cling-film American flags. The paint job is dull jungle camouflage.

I stop the SUV halfway up the hill and wait to see what's going on. Lanny and Connor fall silent as they, too, register the presence of an intruder. I feel Lanny leaning closer, but I don't look back. "Who is that?" she asks.

"I don't know," I say. I put the SUV in park and leave the engine running. A million things flash through my mind, including the stalkers and trolls who regularly email in death threats. "I'm going to find out. Lanny, you get behind the wheel. Get ready to reverse down the driveway if anything goes wrong and drive straight for the Norton police station. Connor, you call 911 the second Lanny puts it in reverse. You *do not* wait for me, no matter what you see. All right? Everybody know their jobs?"

My kids nod, but I can see the look in Connor's eyes. He's scared again. This is yet another traumatic event . . . like yesterday's active shooter drill.

"Connor," I say, and he blinks. "Everything is okay. Breathe and count. Do what Lanny tells you. You can do this. I believe in you." It's not enough, not nearly, but I don't have time for more. I just have to hope he can keep it together.

I step out of the SUV, and Lanny moves to the front seat. She locks the doors without me telling her. And then I have to focus on what's ahead of me, not what's behind.

I walk up the driveway, gravel crunching underfoot, and two doors on the pickup truck open with rusty squeals. One disgorges an old white man in faded, distressed overalls and a flannel shirt underneath; he's not visibly armed, unless you count the giant bristling beard.

The person coming out of the truck on the other side is a woman—tall, lumpy, wearing an American flag T-shirt and jeans worn so much the color's almost gone.

She's got thin gray hair, a soft, wrinkled, pale face, and she's . . . carrying a casserole dish.

I take my hand off the gun under my jacket.

"Ma'am," the man says, and touches the brim of his trucker hat; if it has a logo, it's buried deep under decades of oily grime. "Sorry to disturb you, but we thought we needed to make some amends."

"Amends?" I echo. I'm trying to work out who they are. "I'm sorry, I don't know you. Maybe you have the wrong address . . ."

"You're Gwen Proctor," the woman says. She's smiling, and it looks disturbingly friendly. "Our boy accidentally shot out your truck window. Such a fuss, he was out potshotting squirrels and put one right through that glass, and he is just *so* sorry about that. We're so happy to pay for that repair."

"Your boy." It all seems deeply strange. Yes, it's the South; yes, people show up to be neighborly. But not to *me*. I'm the pariah of the entire county.

"Well, we're just being rude, haven't even introduced our damn selves," the man says, and steps forward with his big hand outstretched. "I'm Jasper Belldene."

Jasper Belldene. Uncrowned king of the drug business in this county. Head of a twisted family tree that includes several militant relatives who aren't above killing to make a point. I've never met the man, or even seen a picture. Sam's met one of his sons, unfortunately. That little confrontation kicked off this whole strange feud. It's odd to think that for once, it isn't *my* past that's driving all this. Just a fistfight between Sam and a drunk man acting the fool at our local gun range.

I shake Belldene's hand, because it's the only real option. He's got a firm, businesslike grip. I hope mine is the same. "Mr. Belldene."

"Oh, don't go calling me *mister*. Jasper'll do just fine. And this here's my better half, Lilah. What you got in that pan, Lilah?"

"It's a Tennessee meatloaf, just like Nanaw used to make," she says. "Made with pork we raised ourselves, and that secret ingredient is oats, not bread crumbs. Gives it some real texture. I hope your family takes this as a peace offering, Mrs. Proctor."

My knee-jerk reaction is to correct the honorific to *Ms.*, but I don't. I don't know what's going on here. They seem so incredibly down-home genuine, but that's not who the Belldenes are, and I know that. They're hardened criminals.

And they brought *meatloaf.*

"Thank you," I say, and accept the heavy Pyrex dish from her. Close up, the illusion of the kindly older lady fades; her eyes are too sharp, too emotionless.

The meatloaf smells of sage and tangy sauce. I'll bet it's delicious.

"I'll let my partner, Sam, know you stopped by," I tell them, and I don't miss the little flicker of anger that disrupts Jasper Belldene's cozy smile, like a flash of static in a signal. "He'll be sorry he missed you."

"We're real sorry we missed *him*," Lilah says, and I hear the not-so-sly double meaning. I want to be my usual bitchy, confrontational self, but this isn't the right moment. They're putting on a show. And I need to find out why.

Besides, they've very effectively tied my hands in holding the damn casserole dish.

I realize that whatever they intend, this isn't just a covered-dish exchange. They want to talk. The meatloaf is the food equivalent of a white flag, and I admit it: I'm curious what they really want. So I wave to the kids to let them know everything's okay, and then I walk to the door and open it, turn off the alarm while I balance the dish, and aim what I hope is a radiant smile on the two Belldenes. "Can I ask you in for coffee?"

"Well," Jasper says. "Can't turn down good coffee. Don't mind if we do, do we, Mother?"

Mother. I shudder a little. I *could* have accepted the gift and sent them on their way, but that isn't southern polite protocol, and from the smooth, instant way Belldene accepts, it's what he wanted.

Lanny drives our SUV up and parks it beside the big, muddy truck. She and Connor get out and head inside, and as I set the dish down on the kitchen counter, I see the look that the Belldenes exchange as my children enter the doorway. It's like two robots exchanging information, and it feels eerily dispassionate. Then the smiles are back, and Jasper gives a hearty chuckle and says, "Well, well, and who are these fine kids now?"

They don't introduce themselves. They look to me. "My daughter, Lanny, and my son, Connor," I say. "Say hi, kids."

"Hi," they say in unison. Unenthusiastically. Lanny looks at me with an obvious question in her eyes: *Are you okay?* I don't honestly know right now, but one thing I'm absolutely sure about: I don't want them in the middle. Connor's doing a good job of keeping a blank expression, but I'm very mindful of how he reacted to his last crisis.

"Kids, you'd better get to your rooms and do those lessons," I tell them. "You've got four hours of school time to log today."

"Yes, Mom," Lanny says, which is the easiest agreement I think I've ever heard from her. Connor follows her into her room, and the door closes behind them. I can't hear it, but I imagine they're furiously whispering to each other, trying to figure out what to do. I hope Lanny's conclusion is to do nothing, at least until she hears some sign of trouble. And then if something pops off, I hope her decision will be to grab her brother, get out the window, and run for the SUV. She's kept the keys, I notice. Smart girl.

Once the door's shut, I turn on the coffeepot. Hot liquid can be a weapon. I get down cups that could break into jagged pieces for cutting instruments. When you're in fear of your life, everything around you can be useful. Everything.

And it all looks so outwardly normal. I'm aware of the Belldenes sitting in my living room like land mines, and I make enough coffee to fill two mugs and bring it out on a small tray with cream and sugar.

I settle in the chair nearest the door and watch as they adjust their coffee—she takes cream and sugar, he only takes sugar—and smack their lips appreciatively. "Sorry I don't have any snacks," I tell them. "I didn't expect you. Well, not to show up so politely, I mean. I was looking for something more direct. Shooting up the house, maybe. Or a brisk round of firebombing."

The good manners stay, but the smiles disappear on both of them. "Now, now, Mrs. Proctor," the Belldene patriarch says reproachfully, and stirs his coffee some more. "If I'd wanted any of you dead, you'd damn well be dead."

I let the hateful *Mrs.* go this time. "You left a rattlesnake in my mailbox last year!" I'm angry now that the gloves are off, and I'm not shy about it. "One of my kids could have been bitten!"

"*Awww,* just a timber rattler, and it was milked first. I been bit by the damn things a dozen times, ain't no big deal. Hospital's got plenty of antivenin."

"And it wasn't our idea anyway," his wife chimes in. "That was our boy Jesse's bright notion. He ain't got no damn sense. We just told him to send y'all a warning."

"Warning for what?"

They exchange a long look. "I knew city people were dumb, but this fills up the whole bucket," Jasper says, and articulates the next two words very precisely. "*To leave.* We'd like you to get the hell out of our county, pretty please. Our state, if you can manage. We want y'all gone."

"Not personal," Lilah puts in crisply. "But you stir things up like mud in a pond, and worse, you brought all those reporter people poking around. People just love to see themselves on TV and in the papers, so they say things they shouldn't. Your family moves on somewhere else, things will settle."

"Bad press," I say, and they nod. "You think I'm bringing you *bad press?*" I have to hold in a wild laugh. "The *drug dealers* don't approve of me?"

"Now, that's never been proved in a court of law," Jasper says indignantly, "and ain't right for you to go spreading falsehoods. But even if we did have a little supply for folks as need it, we're just performing a service; we didn't get all these folks addicted to fancy painkillers and then cut them off and leave them desperate. That was your rich doctors and pill companies. Besides, none of that holds a candle to what *you* did."

"I didn't do—"

"Child." Lilah leans forward. "You were that man's wife. Now, I've been married to this old man for pretty near my whole life, and there ain't a thing he does I don't know about. Whatever you made that jury believe, I know you knew. Maybe you didn't help him kill any of those women, maybe you did, I'm not judging. But don't try to sell me that load of pinfeathers."

The absurdity grabs me by the throat, and it's all I can do to hold back a bark of a laugh. These people—leaders of a criminal gang, the worst in this county, at the very least—think *I'm* too terrible to remain their neighbor. There's absolutely no point in telling them I didn't know about Melvin's crimes. Lilah Belldene won't have any sympathy or understanding for who I was: a sheltered young woman hemmed in by my own fear. Melvin had done a great job of keeping his secrets. And whatever I might have guessed, my own fear had taught me to ignore.

"Okay," I tell them, and let a smile slide like oil over my lips. "Let's explore that idea for a minute. What if I *did* know? I'd have to be very, very cold. You think you want to start a fight with me? You're a mother, Lilah. How far would you go to protect your children?"

"All the way to hell," she replies. "But we both know the best way to win a fight is not to have one. That's why you should move on. That's how you protect them kids. By getting out of our territory."

"I'll think about it," I tell them. "Truth be told, Stillhouse Lake isn't all that great a place. But make no mistake: If I move on, it's because *we* want to move. Not because you ran us off."

"Does that matter to you?" Jasper asks. "Comes down to the same thing."

"It matters," I say, and meet his gaze calmly. "You know it does."

He nods. "So how long before you're gone, Mrs. Proctor?"

"I don't know. A few months. We have to find a place, and sell this one first—"

"That doesn't work for us," Lilah interrupts. "We need you gone by next month."

I shake my head. "That's not going to happen, Mrs. Belldene. We go on our schedule. *If* we decide to go."

Jasper looks around at this haven we've so carefully rebuilt, decorated, made into a home. He slowly nods and takes a long drink of his coffee. He sets the cup down with a sigh. "Mighty good coffee, ma'am," he says. "And I sure wish you had good sense to match. But you don't, and I can't help that. You'll learn. When you do, remember: we tried being neighborly about this."

Lilah nods. "Y'all enjoy that meatloaf, now. You want to give that dish back, you just bring it on out to our place. If not, we'll come back for it."

I understand what that means. One way or another, this is going to get ugly.

No sense in pretending to be social anymore.

I go into the kitchen, get out a garbage bag, and scrape the meatloaf into it. I run hot water and grab the soap and scrub her dish until it's sparkling clean. I dry it on a hand towel and walk out to thrust it at her.

"You're a rude bitch," she says, and takes it. "But still, I thank you kindly. It's my company dish."

"You can go now. Both of you. Out." I let them see it then: the ice and steel and fury that's carried me through these past few years. The ache and fear and relentless need to protect my kids.

They blink.

"Well," Lilah says, and raises her eyebrows. "You drop by anytime, *Ms.* Proctor. And you bring that man of yours too. One of our sons owes him a broken cheekbone and a couple of teeth from last year. He'll be wanting his payback."

"Time to go," I tell her. "Now."

She heads for the truck. Jasper follows, shooting me one last, flat look, and I shut the door and lock it behind them. I stay at the window, hand on the butt of my gun, until their truck starts and reverses back down the driveway in a flurry of gravel and dust.

"Mom?"

Lanny's back, clutching the SUV's keys and looking tense and worried.

"We're okay," I tell her, and put my arm around her. Then I wrap both arms around her. "We're going to be okay."

I don't really believe that.

Neither, from the stiffness of her shoulders, does she.

Sam comes home late and exhausted. We're having barbecued chicken and corn bread dressing, which pleases everyone; I have the Belldenes' meatloaf in a plastic sack in the kitchen. I'm considering having it tested for rat poison.

Sam's filthy and sweaty. His hands are raw from the work, and it makes me ache to see it. He does this for us. Sam likes building things, but it's a job, not a passion. He's a pilot. He ought to be flying. And he isn't because . . . because of his commitment to us, at least for now. I didn't ask him to do that. That's just who he is: a solid, real, stand-up man willing to sacrifice for the people he loves. He doesn't want to leave us here on our own; he knows things are fragile.

But that sacrifice shouldn't be forever. And that's yet another reason to give up my devotion to Stillhouse Lake.

I follow him to the bedroom and silently help him with his dirty clothes; he groans a little as he works one shoulder, and I massage it for him. "Thanks, Gwen," he says. "Sorry. I pulled something."

"I'd be surprised if you weren't sore every day," I tell him. "Shower, mister. Dinner's ready in half an hour."

"Oh, half an hour?" He raises his eyebrows. Sam Cade has a surprisingly innocent face, considering all that he has seen and knows and is capable of doing. He keeps secrets shockingly well, even from me. Like me, he diligently practices his firearms, and while he's never told me everything he's had to do to protect me and the kids, I'm sure there are deep waters there too. All that is an interesting contrast to the light that dances in his eyes right now. "Plenty of time, then."

"Hmmm." I pretend to consider it, then slip off my shoes and unbutton my jeans. "Good point."

Sex in the shower is wonderful, of course, and the running water drowns out any sounds that might disturb the kids. I love this man, and he loves me, and even though things might never be perfect between us, at moments like this they are damn close. I hang on to him, breathless and trembling, as the hot water runs over us and washes us clean. There's always a flash of memory of the pain Melvin used to inflict on me during sex. But Melvin's gone now. That's all gone.

This is real and sweetly hot, and Sam is the best lover I have ever known, and I am very, very lucky.

We cling together and kiss with the clean water cascading down our faces, sealing us together, and then, reluctantly, we part. I step out and towel dry; my hair's a damp mess, but I don't care. I let it go.

I wait until he steps out, half-dressed already, and then I say, "We had some visitors while you were gone." Better tell him before Lanny or Connor blurt it out.

"Oh?" He stops in the act of pulling a T-shirt over his head to look at my expression, to verify what he sensed in my tone. "Who?"

"Jasper and Lilah Belldene. Apologizing for their son's shooting 'accident.'" I air-quote that last part, and his expression darkens. "But in reality? Declaring war on us."

"War? Why? What the hell did we do?" He backtracks immediately. "Except for me socking her son stupid that one time at the gun range. Which he deserved."

"It's me, not you," I tell him. "I'm the bad apple. More reporters, more focus by cops, and they haven't forgotten that failed documentary that Miranda Tidewell started on me." That documentary had come for us out of the blue, a purely malicious attempt to make my life hell, and it had worked until her death put a stop to it. "I see their point, really.

It's hard to keep a low criminal profile when I put a spotlight squarely on this place every time I step out the door."

He finishes putting his shirt on and shoves his feet into flat loafers. I can tell by the fast, staccato movements he's pissed off, but not—I hope—at me. "Some nerve coming up here. Did they think they were going to intimidate you?"

"I'm not really sure. Maybe it was just their version of another warning shot." I wonder if I should talk about moving. I know I should, but this doesn't seem to be a conversation for right now. Tomorrow, maybe. I sense something more than a pulled muscle is bothering him.

"The actual warning shot cost me two hundred bucks. I'd say their point was already made."

"Sorry, Sam."

"Not your fault." He stands up and kisses me, light and gentle. "Your hair's wet."

"Keep doing that, it won't be the only thing."

"Gwen."

I kiss the corner of his mouth. "Dinner," I tell him. "Then we figure out what we're going to do."

Before I can even broach the subject at dinner, Lanny's all over it. "Mom, come *on*, who were those people? The old people?"

Sam looks at me, and I look at him. He shrugs. And he's right, of course; I can't protect my kids anymore by keeping things from them. "Remember the folks who might have put the rattlesnake in our mailbox?" I ask her.

"Oh *shit*," she says. I give her a look. "Crap. Whatever. The Hillbilly Mafia?"

"They want us gone from Stillhouse Lake."

"Why?" Connor asks.

I remember Lilah Belldene's words. *Not personal.* But it was, and is, deeply personal. It always is when my kids are involved. "Same reason people in Norton don't like us. We bring too much attention."

"Mom?" My son's put away his sunglasses, and his bruised eyes make me wince. The swelling's not so bad, at least. "Maybe it's also what I did. Hank Charterhouse is hurt pretty bad."

"Who's Hank Charterhouse?" Sam asks.

"One of the kids Connor hit. Also, first cousin to the Belldenes," Lanny says. "I mean, everybody in town knows that's why Hank gets away with stuff."

The idea that Connor's also someone they may hold a grudge against is unsettling, and it raises my hackles high. *Don't you dare come for my kids.*

Melvin Royal tried coming for our kids. Melvin Royal is rotting in a cardboard coffin in a pauper's grave, marked only with a number. I did that.

The Belldenes ought to take a lesson.

I eat a few bites of chicken before I say, "Okay, here's what we're going to do. Now that you kids are enrolled in the Virtual Academy, you can do your lessons anywhere, right?"

"Yeah?" Lanny, at least, doesn't sound sure she likes where this is going. "Uh, we did our lessons, Mom. I mean, you can check."

"I already did, and thank you. But I need to ask you all a serious question." That gets all their attention, and for a second I doubt myself. Maybe I shouldn't start this. Maybe I'm doing the entirely wrong thing, running away again. But I have to open the question. "What do you guys think about not fighting this war with the Belldenes?"

Sam slowly sits back. "You're talking about moving."

"Well, yes. I think it might be the right thing to do." I take a deep breath and plunge in. "Look, we've got no reason to fight with them; we've got nothing to win here except staying put in a place that barely tolerates us, in a house that's now listed on message boards and websites all over the internet to make it convenient for even more people to harass and threaten us. Sam, I know finding work has been tougher for you since—since all that mess with the documentary. And kids—" I look at Lanny and Connor. "You haven't had an easy time of it here. I'm sorry for that. I thought I was doing something good making you part of the community, but . . . the community's not taking us in. And I know how much that hurts."

Connor doesn't say anything. He just stares down at his plate. Lanny says, "Well, there are some nice people here. Kez and Javier, even Detective Prester. A few teachers aren't terrible." She's trying to be fair, but I know it hasn't been easy for her either. The friends she made a year ago aren't her friends now. I don't like my kids feeling so . . . alone.

Sam's not giving me anything. He's gone quiet, which means he's trying not to put too much weight into this conversation—which is less a conversation right now and more of a monologue. I need him to jump in, but when he doesn't, I feel compelled to keep going.

"I can ask in town about selling the house," I tell him. "That doesn't mean we have to make a commitment right now, just . . . look at our options. Hell, we could even rent the place out, the way some others around the lake do." Nothing except a slow nod. So I keep talking. "I need to interview the dad of my missing person in Louisiana, check with the victim's friends there, things like that. It'll take some legwork to cover all the bases." I pause and look at my children. "I can take you guys along if—and this is a big *if*—you promise me that you're going to treat this seriously. I can leave you at the hotel while I'm doing my work, and you can do your school assignments. And—"

Sam says, "I can come along."

I don't expect that, and I'm left not quite knowing what to think about it. I scramble, because I don't know what he's thinking. "Don't you have work?"

"Yeah, well, seems like my services are no longer required at the jobsite."

I'm stunned. "Why?"

"At a guess? The Belldenes have put the word out they don't want me working anywhere in this county."

I feel a pulse of real, vicious anger toward everybody who had a hand in putting that bitter misery in his eyes. It's there for only a moment, then quickly gone, and he's smiling again.

"Bright side, that's a lot less gas I burn. Downside . . . not sure what I'm going to do now." His voice is even, his eyes steady. Whatever fury he has boiling in there, he's not letting it out.

"Damn, I'm so sorry. This is all—" I gesture helplessly at the world. At myself. The whole package, bound up with a past I can't control and can never shed. Scars and wounds and armor and agony.

I'm angry for him. A little angry *at* him, truthfully, that he didn't tell me before we sat down here. But it's why he was so noncommittal earlier. He wanted me to have reasons to leave this place that weren't about him.

I make my tone lighter, my smile brighter. "In that case," I say, "I don't see any reason why you can't join us for our epic road trip out to Louisiana." And honestly, now that I've said it, I realize that I'm actually relieved. I don't even know why for a moment; it hasn't occurred to me until now that this case is leading me back to a place I desperately never wanted to go.

Back to the bayous. To a sweaty green hell like the place I faced down my ex-husband and my own personal nightmares. *No, this isn't anything like that,* I tell myself sternly. *This is me, going to help someone else. I'm in control.*

That doesn't stop my heart from racing, or my muscles from tensing. I've made strides in overcoming the trauma that I suffered after the night I was forced to kill Melvin. But that doesn't mean it's completely behind me either. *I need to call my therapist,* I think. And that's probably a good impulse; I already booked Connor in for a session next week. I should make sure I get myself right too. Between the impending threat of the Belldenes and this foreboding trip . . . I can feel myself starting to spin out.

And Sam knows it, I think, because he says, "Louisiana. Where exactly—"

"Not there," I tell him, shorthand that he understands perfectly. "But you know, same state. Similar area. So I . . . I appreciate your company."

"And after that?"

I take a deep breath. "Kids? What do you think?"

They're quiet, looking at each other, and then Connor slowly raises his hand. "I vote we move," he says.

"Where?"

"Anywhere but here?"

That's pretty definitive. I fix my gaze on Lanny, who crosses her arms. "Sure," she says. "I guess. Not like I've got any social life here anyway. But not anyplace small, okay? Someplace interesting. Maybe somewhere with more than two fast food choices."

"I'll take that under consideration," I tell her. Back to Sam. "You?"

"I know you hate giving up."

"I do. I really, really do," I reply. "But you know what I hate more? Watching the people I love get hurt. No home is worth that. Not to me." I swallow hard, because the warmth in his gaze nearly undoes me. "What's your vote, Sam?"

"I feel selfish voting given the circumstances. But . . ." He raises his hand. "Yeah. Move."

"Okay," I say. "We move. So say we all." I feel a weirdly mixed wave of emotion. Frustration, yes; I put a real emotional stake in holding on here. Stillhouse Lake, for me, has become less of a refuge and more of a fortress, with enemies at the gates. But I feel relief too. It's easy to get locked in, get tunnel vision, and feel utterly trapped by my own decisions. But I just proved to myself that we could change that future.

And it feels good. Terrifying, but good.

"You know it'll take months to sell this place, if we intend to sell it," Sam says. "The Belldenes going to be that patient, do you think?"

"I doubt it. They'll make sure we get gone, one way or another." I give him a smile, but I know it looks grim. "What do you want to bet they give us a lowball offer and strong-arm us to take it?"

"Seems likely," he says. "They've got their fingers everywhere."

"Well, we'll worry about that later," I say. "Meanwhile: road trip. Hey . . . since you're currently available—"

"That's one way of putting it," Sam deadpans. "And before you ask, no. I don't mind watching the kids while you interview the dad."

"Mind reader."

"One of my many talents." Sam winks at Lanny as they both reach for the corn bread, and he beats her. "Gotta be fast, kid."

We all have to be fast to outrun what's circling around our calm little haven of a house.

Fast, and smart.

Lanny goes to bed early. She says she's got a headache. I wonder, privately, if she's really got a new girlfriend she's sending messages to. I almost hope so; the breakup with her first love, Dahlia, nearly broke her. Rebound crushes are rarely healthy, but at least it'll help repair her self-worth, and develop more armor for next time.

I worry, just a little, that she's hiding something from me. But part of being a mom is knowing when to push and when not to. I decide not to this time. I've introduced enough chaos today.

And I pray it's not a mistake.

8

LANNY

Vee's back at midnight, of course. I'm nervous and scared and wishing I'd told Mom, but I still make sure my window's off the alarm sensor when I go outside to take out the trash. Mom doesn't notice. Nobody does. And that makes me feel pretty guilty.

When Vee shows up with her big duffel bag again, I slide that window up and get her inside, quickly. I've also greased it, so it doesn't make a sound as it glides up and down. And Vee's quiet coming in too. She's even taken her boots off, so she's in bare feet when she steps inside.

She gives me a vivid, wild smile, and I can't help but smile back. Then she hugs me. Since she showered last night she smells pretty good, still, but there's a hint of sweat and forest to her.

It kind of turns me on, to be honest.

Vee shuts the window, puts her duffel bag aside, and whispers, "So, how about that laundry?"

"Can't tonight. Mom's on high alert after what happened today."

I expect her to ask what happened, but she doesn't. She shrugs. "Okay, then. Can I borrow a cool shirt or something?"

"For what?"

"You didn't hear? There's a big-ass party tonight at Killing Rock! You're goin', right?"

"What? No!" I haven't even heard about a party. Nobody has called me. Nobody texted me. And since Mom keeps us off social media, I didn't even have that public heads-up. "Uh, I mean, I wasn't invited."

"Not an invitation kind of party," Vee says. "You just . . . go. Like a rave. You know?"

I've never been to a rave either. I've only been to a few parties, honestly, and mostly those were closely supervised things. And I took presents to them. God, I'm sixteen and a total loser. Yeah, okay, I've been out to Killing Rock before. That's a place where kids hang out and get up to all kinds of stuff, and I went there with Dahlia a few times. But never in the dark.

"You're not goin'?" Vee seems disappointed. Disappointed in *me*. "I thought you'd be happy to get out from under and have some fun."

Vee's definition of fun and mine are probably not the same things, I think. But still, I'm intrigued. "Who's supposed to be there?"

"Everybody from town who's our age. Norton's the town close to here, right?"

I nod. I wonder if she's been there yet. Then I wonder why she's here at all. I hope it's to see me, but honestly: I'm not sure. But what if it's just that simple? That Vee has a thing for me?

I don't know how I feel about it. Flattered, I guess? Definitely interested. But there's something weird and out of control about this. *Am I in trouble here?* I don't know. But now I'm kind of trapped. I let Vee in. It's my fault she's here. I could have told Mom at any time, and I didn't.

I could go tell Mom now, but then I'd have to explain how Vee got in, and Vee would probably say she was here before tonight, and . . . I don't want that discussion. And . . . and I don't want Vee to be disappointed in me.

It's easier just to say, "Uh, okay. We can go, I guess. For a little while. It's not very far, just around the lake. But I'm not going to get drunk or whatever."

She's already nodding, and her shaggy, dark hair flops down over her bright eyes. There's color in her cheeks, and I get a flash of teeth as she smiles. "Too scared of your momma?" She keeps it to a careful, low whisper.

"Damn right I am," I whisper back. "What time is the party?"

"Right about now," Vee says, and points out the window. I ease up and take a look. I can just see the end of the lake where Killing Rock juts out over the water, and sure enough, there's a flicker of a bonfire down by the shore. And I can hear music drifting over the water.

I know it's a bad idea, but even if some of the bullies are there, I can deal with that. Unlike school, I can leave whenever I want, and maybe, just maybe, I'll have a little fun for a change.

Yeah, I'm making all the excuses to myself. I know I shouldn't go. But . . . I never do what I want to do. I've been *so good*. And maybe being a little bad, especially if we're going to leave this stupid town anyway . . . maybe that's okay. Just once.

We use stuffed animals and pillows under the covers to make it look like I'm there. It's pretty convincing. Vee finds some dramatic glittery purple eye shadow and demands I let her do my makeup. I sit down, and she kneels in front of me. It feels weird and intimate, and I close my eyes and try not to jump at the featherlight touch of the brush across my lids. Then her fingers, blending it with expert little sweeps. "Hold still," she tells me, and I hear her cracking open another shadow container. "I'm good at smoky eyes. You just hang on there. Trust me."

It isn't that I do trust her, exactly, but there's something about feeling taken care of that's so . . . easy. I sit and let her do my makeup, and I'm secretly enjoying the way she's touching me, the warmth of her pressing in between my thighs. It's not sexual, but it's sexy, and I have to swallow nervously. "Almost there?" I ask.

"One sec . . ." Another long, deliberate pull of her thumbs across my eyelids. "Perfect."

I open my eyes and she's right there, bending over and staring into my eyes. For a heart-stopping few seconds I think she's going to kiss me, but then she winks and puts a hand mirror between us.

I look *good*. I mean, wow. She's amazing.

We get dressed; I keep my back to her while I change, but I wonder if she sneaks looks. My skin tingles, and I feel awkward and off balance and nearly fall over trying to pull on my distressed black jeans. When I finally turn around, Vee's leaning against the wall openly staring. Her arms are crossed. It's a little disorienting to see my clothes on her, like looking at a funhouse mirror. But great too. Like we're sharing something secret. I feel breathless at that. I've wanted to feel part of something outside my family for *so long*, and for a while I had Dahlia, but . . . that's over, and I've been so alone.

Vee makes me feel seen. Present. Wanted. Even cool for a change. And I need that so much.

She grabs my hand as she ducks through the open window and outside, and pulls me along with her. Not that I'm resisting, really.

Vee Crockett is maybe the most interesting girl I've met, *ever*. She's dangerous and wild and sleek and unpredictable, and she makes me feel like I don't know what's going to happen from one second to the next. Growing up like I did, where there were no good surprises . . . it feels like being on the best amusement park ride in the world.

But I also know our speeding roller coaster car could fly off the rails anytime, and part of my brain is nagging me as we head down to the road. We can see the bonfire clearly, and hear the shouts and laughter and pulsing music.

"Come on, let's get there before the cops bust the party!" Vee calls, and breaks into a run. I catch and pass her easily. This, I'm good at. I don't even break a sweat, and in fact I have to slow down to let her catch up. She's laughing and wheezing a little by the time we get there.

The area under the cliff—Killing Rock—is mostly imported sand, a pretend beach in the middle of Tennessee. The night air's crisp and cold, but that isn't stopping anybody from swimming in the lake or cannonballing off the top of the cliff. It's not *that* bad; it hasn't even been below freezing. Fall in Tennessee can sometimes be summer with more leaf colors, and winter can be fall with more Christmas decorations. No sign of any change tonight. The skies are a little cloudy, but the wispy kind of clouds that look decorative instead of threatening.

There are maybe a hundred teens around Norton, Tennessee, and about eighty of them are here right now on this end of the lake. The rest are probably on their way.

"Well, this looks just perfect," Vee says, and turns a wide smile on a boy who stumbles by. He's already blind drunk, but she doesn't seem to mind; she looks him over twice. I feel a little twinge of . . . something. I don't want to think it's jealousy. I tell myself that Vee's not into me anyway, that I was just imagining things back in Wolfhunter when it seemed like she really liked me. *Oh yeah, then why is she here, if she isn't here for you?*

Okay. Maybe I'm jealous, after all.

I pause just in time to see one of my kinda-girlcrushes Lottie come cannonballing off the top of the rock, knees hugged tight to her chest, and she hits the lake with a tremendous splash that's greeted with cheers from camp chairs near the dock. Dozens of teens are gathered around the bonfire, which spills red and gold light onto rippling water. I see Vee walk away out of the corner of my eye, but I wait for Lottie to surface. She does, waving, and gets another round of cheers as she strokes for the shore. Lottie's gorgeous. She's a redhead with big green eyes and an upturned nose and a Tennessee accent so slow it drips like honey. Yeah, I might have kind of a thing for her. Lottie barely knows I'm alive, though. At least she hasn't actively hated me. So I can still crush on her a little.

Killing Rock probably isn't the real name of the big cliff that juts out over the lake; it has some boring-ass official title like Lookout Point or Sunset View or something. But it's been called Killing Rock among the students in Norton for as far back as anyone can remember; even the teachers call it that. Nobody can ever say *who* exactly got killed here, though. There's some vague legend of a Native American princess committing suicide by jumping off it onto rocks, the stupid bullshit that white people say to make themselves all romantic about the original residents they killed off in the first place. I don't buy the myth. But the name has to come from somewhere.

When I look around for Vee, I don't see her. She's vanished into the crowd. I frown and search a little, but I finally figure she'll come back when she's ready. *Yeah, maybe she found that drunk guy and is making out with him right now.* I don't like to think about that. I'm not sure if Vee is gay, or bi, or poly, or what; she hasn't exactly said anything to lead me one way or another. But I do know one thing, deep down: she's bad for me. I first met her when she was in *jail*, and yeah, maybe she didn't kill her mom, but she'd done plenty of bad stuff by that point. She had a drug problem. Drinking too. And she was willing to do a lot of sketchy things to get what she wanted.

Doesn't mean I don't still want her.

"Hey, Lanny." I turn. Someone—a shadow in the trees—holds out a beer to me, but I shake my head. Last thing I need is Mom smelling it on me when I get home. He passes me a water instead. I check to make sure the seal is intact before I open it and take a sip. Growing up paranoid has its good points; nobody is going to get me with the normal predator tactics. *Oh yeah, dummy, coming out here in the dark was super cautious.* I hate the mocking voice in my head, but I can't turn it off either. At least it's making sense right now. Usually it's just a constant litany of how dumb my hair looks, how my eyes aren't the same exact size, that I'm too thin or too fat or too short or not sexy enough or whatever. The only thing that makes it better is that I know everybody else has that same voice too.

Well. Not the assholes, I guess.

There is just enough firelight bleeding out to the fringes to see that the guy handing me water is Bon Casey, kicked back in a folding lounge chair. Like me, he goes by a nickname, but at least Atlanta is a decent first name. *Bonaventure?* Ugh, not so much. He's older than me by a couple of years, a senior, and I'm struck by a little shiver of shyness.

"Bon," I say, and toast him with the water. He kicks a bedraggled old camp chair my way, and I sink into it. "How's it going?"

He shrugs. "You know." Bon's technically a senior, but he got held back a couple of grades. He's really an adult, which makes it borderline weird for him to be out here. "Heard about your brother. He okay?"

"Yeah. He's fine."

"Yeah, well, Hank Charterhouse is not okay," Bon says. "Got his jaw all wired up. You know the Charterhouses are hooked up, right?"

"Cousins to the Belldenes."

"Fair warning, Hank will be looking for some payback once he's healed. So y'all better keep an eye out. Belldene clan don't play."

"Thanks," I say. I don't tell him the old couple already came to our house and low-key tried to scare us. "My mom's not somebody they really want to mess with, I can tell you that."

Bon laughs. It sounds a little high and loony. "Yeah, she's a scary bitch."

"Runs in the fam," I tell him. He offers his beer, and I tap it with my water bottle. I ought to get up and walk, but truth is, I'm not really sure how accepting the main group will be if I go over toward the bonfire; looks like the Cool Kids Coalition to me. Some are already passed out, wrapped in flannel jackets and blankets. If the cops aren't already on their way, surely this will all be busted up within the next hour. It's kind of a scene.

I look around for Vee again but I still don't see her. I'm disappointed that she ditched me, but on some level, I guess I'm also not surprised.

I end up watching as Lottie chats with a cluster of boys and drinks too much, too fast. I feel very alone, despite Bon, Lottie, the eighty or so teens within a dozen feet of me whooping it up. Someone else—a boy this time—cannonballs off the rock, and the splash reaches all the way to the shore. I hear the fake-outraged screams of Instagram bunnies who are taking selfies around the fire. Lottie among them. Yeah, I keep noticing, even while I'm starting to get mad at Vee for putting me in this lonely, weird position.

"Boo!"

I yelp as someone grabs me from behind, and drop my water bottle. It's Vee, I realize as I spin around; she has a wide, maniacal grin that has a chemical sheen to it. She's so damn high I'm surprised she isn't floating off the ground. "Fuck! Don't do that!"

"Sorry," she says, but not like she means it. "Come on. Let's dance."

"Hey, new girl, you want to party?" Bon says. She ignores him completely, drags me over closer to the fire in an empty stretch of sand. She starts dancing. She puts her arms around me and pulls me close, and I hear boys whooping and clapping behind us. I don't like it. I'm not here to put more deposits in their spank banks.

So I push away from Vee a little and say, "Hey, this party is bound to get busted soon. We should go back."

"Back where?" She shouts it over the music. Someone's turned it up so loud I can feel it in my bones, vibrating uncomfortably through my body.

"Home!" I'm tired, and I feel weird. My instincts are telling me to get the hell out of here; there's something brewing under all the cheer and campfires and energy. Just a feeling, but Mom's always taught me to trust my instincts.

"Oh *hell* no, Lanta, we ain't goin' *home*. We're going to stay out here all night and party!" She draws the last word out and does a wild spinning dance, flinging her arms wide. I have to move back to avoid getting hit. She's way too high, and she's not making good decisions. I grab her hand and drag her away, dump her into the chair next to Bon, and get another water bottle from his cooler. He chokes on his beer. "Hey, girl, those cost, you know!"

I dig five bucks out of my pants pocket and fling it at him. He grumbles, but he takes it. I get Vee to drink, and she guzzles the entire thing, then bends over, gasping like she's going to throw up. She doesn't. She's a little more sober when she sits back. The feverish glitter is mostly gone. She's sweating. I can smell the harsh body odor coming off her. She needs another shower, bad.

"Oh man, too much. I fucked up," she says, and puts her head in her hands. "Sorry. I just—Lanta, I just want to have some *fun*. Is that wrong?"

She's shaking. The drugs are turning on her, fast, and I'm worried. "What did you take, Vee?"

She doesn't know, that's clear from the look she gives me. She downed some pills, probably. Maybe smoked something. Hard to tell.

She's not okay. And I can't leave her out here. Anything could happen to her.

"Hey," I say to Bon. "Want to give us a ride home? For cash?"

"I ain't Uber, girl. Hike it."

Another cannonball hits the lake to applause and cheers. The party noise keeps getting louder. I look over. It's just a sea of distorted faces and writhing bodies. Firelight makes people I know look like dangerous strangers.

"So. You buying something more than water? 'Cause if you're not, move on. Chairs are for closers." Bon's here selling weed and pills. Of course. I should have known. Nobody's nice to me for nothing.

"Fine." I grab Vee and haul her to her feet.

"I don't feel so good," she says.

"That's okay. We're going home. You can sleep it off there."

She breaks free of me and runs. I mean, *runs*, and I immediately start after her because this isn't good. She's not heading home. She's heading up the cliff. "Vee! *Stop!*"

She doesn't. She takes the steep path up, scrambling, laughing wildly, and I follow her. Somehow she stays ahead of me, even though I'm a runner; I guess whatever she's on has given her a real burst of energy. Switchback turns in the dark, slippery rocks, but she makes it, and I burst out onto the cliff just a step behind her.

Vee lets out a whoop and turns back toward me. Throws her arms out and collapses against me. She's sweaty and gasping, and I feel every inch of her. "Holy shit," she says. "You are *fast*."

"When I need to be," I say. My urge to yell at her melts away. "Vee, you really need to stop taking that shit. Do you even know what it was?"

"That's half the fun," Vee says, a rough purr in the back of her throat, and I feel that vibrate inside me. Heat blooms deep. "Want to know what the other half is?"

"No," I lie.

"You're no fun, Lanta Proctor," she says, and before I can think about it, before I can even start to number off why this is a terrible idea, we're kissing, and oh my God. I forget about why I shouldn't be here and that Vee is a bad idea walking, because this kiss is the best I've ever had, and I just want *more*.

Vee pulls back with a gasp and says, "What the hell was that?" And I think she's joking until I hear it too. I'd been so surprised and focused that I didn't hear the rustling under the tree, and the moan. Or maybe I thought we were making that noise. But we weren't.

My eyes have adjusted to the dark now, and I see Vee's face clearly, and beyond her, someone else lying on the ground. A pale stretch of legs.

I fumble for my phone and key on the light. It illuminates everything with brutal detail. It glistens on the pale skin of a girl's thigh, blonde hair tangled in tree roots. She's crumpled like a broken doll.

My heart races so hard it hurts. For a few seconds I freeze, and then I squeeze in behind the boulders and crouch down next to her. She isn't dead. She's moaning.

Vee says from behind me, "Jesus, what the hell is wrong with her? Don't touch her!"

"She's alive," I say. The girl's facedown, shrouded in her loose blonde hair, and I can't tell who she is, but I don't want to move her either. I'm shaking with the fear boiling inside, but at the same time, I need to see what's wrong with her. Something is. I freeze when my light catches a red streak of blood on a thick piece of rock lying next to her. There's blood in her hair. *Oh God.*

"We should go," Vee says. "Right now! Come on, Lanta!" She sounds panicked.

"I can't just leave her!" What's happened to her? Did she just fall down? Or did someone take that rock and bash her in the head? I can't think straight, and I don't want to make the wrong choice here.

I lift my phone and start pressing numbers.

"What the hell you doin'?" Vee's voice is sharp. Angry. "Lanta! Oh *hell* no, you ain't callin' the cops!" Her accent's getting stronger.

I don't answer her. I dial.

"Norton 911, what's your emergency?" asks a voice that sounds about as lazy as summer on the lake. Smooth and calm and weirdly reassuring.

"There's a girl here. I think . . . she's hurt." I turn to Vee. She gives me a cold look. Then she's gone, heading for the path down the cliff. Taking her chances, I guess. I'm shattered. I've gone from the best kiss I've ever had to being left behind so fast, and it crashes in on me that I'm all alone.

Again. I feel short of breath now, and I'm trembling. I stand up and look around, and for a second the lure of that pathway seems so strong. I turn away from it, and look out toward the lake.

I can see my house, a pretty little beacon in the darkness lit by security lamps on the corners. I think about Mom, asleep in her bed. Trusting me to do the right thing. The 911 lady is telling me I need to check the girl to see where she's hurt. I don't want to, but I know I have to. I'm all she's got. I try a couple of times before I can swallow my fear and actually do it. I carefully touch her head, and I can't find anything but blood. "I don't know where she's hurt," I tell the lady on the phone. "She's lying facedown."

"Okay, I need you to roll her on her side, gently. I'm here with you." The operator sounds warm and calm, and that gives me the strength to put the phone down and press the speaker function. *I don't want to do this,* some part of me wails. But I carefully roll the girl over. From this side I see that the whole left of her head looks . . . *wrong.* Flattened. Her sleek blonde hair is matted down in one spot, and part of her scalp is hanging loose. *Oh God.* I have to fight not to scuttle backward, and I squeeze my eyes tight shut but I can't *not* see it, it's right there like it's been branded into my eyelids. I want to throw up. Scream. But the lady on the phone is talking to me, and I cling to that hard. "Yeah," I say, though I don't really know what she's just said. "Uh, her head's injured. I think—I think she's hit it on a rock or something. It looks real bad."

It takes me a second to realize that I know the girl. She's Candy Clark, one of the popular kids. A senior, I think; she just turned eighteen. She has on glittery eye shadow. Just like I do. And that hurts. I feel tears running down my cheeks—shock, I think. I'm shivering in the chilly wind, but when I touch Candy she feels even colder. I take off the jacket I'm wearing and put it over her, in case that helps.

Vee left. She just left me here.

The voice on the phone tells me to stay calm, she's sending an ambulance and the police and that I should keep monitoring Candy's pulse. I try. But my fingers feel cold, and I'm not really sure if I'm feeling her pulse at all, or just imagining it. I'm shaking so hard my teeth are chattering.

I want my mom. Mom would know what to do.

Down on the beach, the music's still blasting, but I can hear the sirens now far in the distance. I hear people shouting, "Cops!" I can't go look, but I imagine everybody who isn't passed out is running for it. I try to stay calm and count the pulse beats I can barely feel struggling against my fingers.

"Hey," I say. "Candy? Can you hear me?" I don't think she can. I'm crying, and my voice is weird, and I have to wipe my nose and swallow hard before I try again. "Candy, it's Lanny Proctor. I'm here. I'm not going to leave you, okay? It's going to be all right. I promise."

Down around the lake, I hear engines starting up. People are getting the hell out.

That leaves me even more alone.

The operator's busy telling me help is coming. She sounds professional and calm, and that helps some, but I still feel so isolated up here, like I'm the only thing alive except for Candy. I wish someone else were here. Anyone else.

And it's like I wish it into existence when I hear footsteps coming up the path. Maybe it's Vee, coming back? But no.

It's Bon. What's Bon doing here?

In the moonlight he looks pale and sweaty.

I instinctively put the 911 call on mute.

"Hey," he says. "Saw your friend take off. You okay?"

I want to throw myself into his arms and cry, but I don't. Barely. I just point toward the girl. In the glare of my phone's light she looks pale and dead, but I can see the pulse still beating at her throat. Bon's eyes widen.

"Is she alive?" he asks. I nod. I don't think I can form whole sentences right now. *It's okay. Bon's here. He's older. He'll know what to do.*

The operator asks me if I'm by myself again, and I hold a finger up to my lips to warn Bon before I unmute it and say, "Just me. I'm alone with her." Bon's brave for coming up here after me, but he's probably got half a dozen drugs on him that could get him in big trouble. He could have run away. Everybody else did. I don't want to get him arrested.

"Have you seen anybody else up there?" the operator asks.

"No," I tell her. "Well, yeah. People have been doing cannonballs off the cliff. But I don't know who." That's a direct lie. I should mention Lottie. But I don't, because I don't want to get her in trouble either.

Bon is gesturing at me, and I realize he's asking for the phone. I instantly give him the phone, and transferring that responsibility feels so good it makes me shudder with relief. I mouth *thank you* to him.

But instead of talking to the operator, Bon just ends the call and turns it off. *What the hell?*

Then he says, "I'm sorry you had to find her, Lanny."

I don't get it for a long few seconds. I really, really don't.

Then I realize just how dangerous this is, and it feels like electricity crawling all over my skin. The jolt of fear feels like lightning striking, but I push that away. I need to be smart now if I want to get through this, but my brain is racing, babbling, wondering what Bon is doing, *why* he could have done this to Candy, *when* . . . so many questions. But I don't ask them. I just breathe, and watch. As Bon pockets my phone, I slowly get up off my knees and back away from Candy. I never take my eyes off him.

"Cops are coming," I say, which seems dumb even as I say it. We can both hear the sirens in the distance. But that doesn't mean they're really close, either, not out in the country like this.

"Just means we have to do this fast," he says, and he gets a knife out of the sheath at his belt. "Sorry, Lanny. Nothing personal."

Oh shit.

9

LANNY

"You did this?" I choke on that, because I don't want to think that, to realize that I had a nice, comfortable time sitting next to a man who'd bashed one of my classmates in the head.

He shrugs. "Look, she ripped me off. She knew better. Things got out of hand. Besides, I got a partner, and he don't play."

The cops are coming, but I have no idea when they'll get here. Minutes? I might not have minutes. He's between me and the path down to the beach. So I stall, because my only real hope is that the cops come fast, and maybe he'll decide to run instead. But I know he won't.

He can't.

"Maybe—" My voice sounds small and weak, and I'm shaking all over now. Can't get my breath. "Maybe it was an accident. She fell and hit her head. I could tell them she said that."

"What if she gets better and says different?" He shakes his head. "Look, I didn't mean to hurt her. I shook her and pushed her, and she fell on the rock." I'm not sure that's true. But I just nod. He's turning the knife over and over, and I can tell he doesn't want to do this. Not really.

I hear someone scrambling up the path. Relief hits me like a truck, slamming through my body and turning me weak at the knees. The cops are here. Thank God.

But it isn't the cops. The sirens are still screaming, getting closer, but they're not here yet. In place of that wonderful relief, I get a wave of real fear that makes my mouth dry up and my fists clench. The young man who comes out of the path is sweaty, greasy, older than Bon. He's wearing a stained old muscle tee, and he's got an honest-to-God mullet. I can smell his acrid body odor from three feet away. He *doesn't* look high like Bon, and I think that scares me more than anything.

He looks at Bon, then at me, and says, "What the hell you thinking?" Like he knows Bon. "Oh shit. Boy, I told you to get the money, not kill somebody! Well, we're in it now."

"I'll fix it," Bon says, and starts walking toward me with the knife. I don't have time to stall anymore, and panic drowns me for a second before I fight my way through to a plan. It's not much, but it's all I have.

I run straight for the darkness looming at the edge of the cliff.

I launch.

But I don't make it.

Bon's lunged in pursuit. His arms are *just* long enough that he takes a hard grip on the back of my shirt and hauls me backward off balance. My arms make windmills as I struggle to keep upright, but he yanks again and I feel myself falling. I twist and hit the stone in a fetal position, head protected, and realize he's hauling me like a sack back from the edge. "Let go!" I yell, and then I scream. I hear it echo out across the water. Maybe someone—anyone—will hear.

But kids have been out here partying and screaming all night.

Panic is burning a hole in my chest. I punch and kick at Bon as he drags me, and as he bends over to get a better grip, my phone tumbles out of his pocket. I grab it and hold down the button; that brings up an emergency menu, and I hit the button to call 911. I can't hear when they answer, I just scream, "Help me, I'm up at Killing Rock, I'm being—"

He slaps the phone out of my hand. It skitters across stone to the edge and disappears, and I feel like I've lost my only hope. I feel naked now. I can't call Mom. I can't call the cops. I don't even know if the 911 operator heard me at all.

I'm so scared now. This feels *final*. And I can't stop crying, tears cold in my eyes and down my cheeks and it all floods through my mind in a rush, all the things I'll never have again: hugs from my mom, from Sam, from Connor; kisses from pretty girls; movies and games and laughing and running and knowing for sure my mom is coming to save me. It's all a blur, suddenly, and then it goes still in my mind. Crystal clear.

I have to stay alive on my own.

Nobody's coming to help.

I stop fighting. I go limp and heavy, but it doesn't stop Bon's effortless pull. There's nothing I can grab on to . . . but then I remember all the things Mom's taught me. These moves always seemed like a game before. Not now. Now they're all I have.

I hear her say, *If you don't have anything else, you have to use your own body.*

I roll, fast, and Bon's wrist is turned and his shoulder jerked hard; I set the soles of my running shoes on the rock and lunge up at the waist, breaking his hold on my shirt. I think it rips, but I don't care. I let momentum work for me; it carries me up into a crouch, and I duck and roll as mullet guy makes a grab for me. "Get her!" Bon says. I dodge.

I spin, coil myself, and leap into a run again for the edge.

I've never done this, never jumped off this damn rock, and it's black down there, no way to tell where the water is, where dangerous rocks could be. I'm jumping blind, but I know instinctively it's my only shot at making it out of here alive. I'm scared out of my mind as I go off into the dark.

It's a long two seconds of falling. If I hit a rock, I'll shatter my legs—maybe not even know I've done it until I'm underwater. *No no no no no not like this* . . . I don't want to end up drowning. I can't. Every cell in my body screams at the thought, an incoherent blur of the dreams I've had of floating in the water, of my dad's underwater garden of dead women. *Not like this.*

I somehow avoid any deadly boulders. I tuck myself and hit the water in an enormous splash that stings like I dove into fire, and I sink, I sink as I unfold and instinctively begin to stroke for the black surface. I think it's the surface. It's so *dark*. I'm blind in the water. If I've lost my direction, I could be swimming down. My lungs are already burning, but that's panic, and I need to stop it before it makes me thrash and lose everything. *Calm down. Swim. Break the surface.*

It seems like an eternity before I feel air on my flailing fingers, and then my head is up and I take a shuddering gasp. I try to orient myself. Where am I? Close to the shore on the Killing Rock side, but I don't want to go back there; the beach is practically deserted now, everybody running for the hills, their cars, wherever they can go to get away. *The cops. Where are the cops?* I can see flashing lights somewhere up on the horizon.

I can't see Vee anywhere. She left me here. *She left me.*

I'm a good runner, but I'm not a great swimmer. I get tired fast, and I have to pause to tread water. I know this isn't safe. Stillhouse Lake is deep, and dark, and people have died in it. Nobody knows I'm out here but Bon and his drug-dealing friend. My phone is gone.

I need to save myself. But I'm *tired.*

I can't see if they're chasing me, but it doesn't matter. The lake is so cold, and I feel sluggish. I need to get out. Now.

So I swim for shore.

The first police car is pulling around, lights flashing, and there's an ambulance right behind it. I can't even feel relieved. I'm too cold.

The two cops who get out of the police car don't see me swimming toward them. Their backs are to me, and before I can get enough breath to yell, they're already heading up the path. I wonder if they're going to think *I* hurt Candy. That's a new idea. I don't like it, and I tread water again. Maybe I shouldn't go up to the shore.

I don't even realize that I'm slowing down and slipping under the water for a few seconds until the water closes over my nose and I panic. I flail up again, gasping, and I guess the splashing attracts the paramedic's attention, because he shouts at me to get out of the water.

I swim until I finally feel the bottom again. I feel a hundred pounds heavier coming out, and I'm not at the beach sand part—it's rocky here and slick—and I slip and crawl up until I'm finally on dry land. I flip over on my back and just . . . breathe. I cough out water I didn't know I breathed in. I'm shaking so hard it hurts, and the paramedic runs over with a blanket and puts it around me. He's yelling questions at me, but I don't answer. I'm not sure what to say. I just want to go *home*.

The paramedic is asking me my name, and I manage to stammer it out. I guess he recognizes it, because the next thing I know he's dialing a cell phone and hands it to me. "Lanny?" It's Mom's voice. It's like a rush of warm water through my cold veins, and I almost gasp in relief. "What's going on?"

I burst into tears. I stammer out something, I don't even know what it is, or if she can understand it through the gasps and chokes and sobs. But she tells me she's coming for me, so I tell her I'm okay and the second she's off the call I drop to the ground, shivering and soaking wet and freezing cold, and I cry my heart out.

They pile more blankets on me, but I'm still cold when Sam's truck slides to a stop on the road. More cops have arrived. They try to intercept my mom as she bails out, but she dodges them and races to me, and the desperation on her face makes me feel safe, finally safe. I struggle up from where I'm sitting, and before I can even get out of the blankets her arms are around me, holding me so tight it ought to hurt. It feels so right. I hug her back.

The relief lasts between us for maybe ten seconds, and then she pushes me back and says, "What the hell were you *thinking*? Why would you leave the house like that? Without telling me?"

I don't know what to say to her. I don't want to lie, but I also don't want to tell her about Vee. I'm ashamed of myself, and I'm angry that Vee left me, and I have no idea where she's gone. So after I fumble for a few seconds, I say, "I just—I wanted to go to the party, Mom. I knew you wouldn't—"

My voice is quavering, voice unsteady, on the verge of tears. My tough-girl persona has melted away, and I feel like I'm a little kid again. I remember being twelve and showing off for Connor; I'd gotten Mom's gun out of the lockbox and unloaded it and reloaded it, and the expression on her face when she found us was just like this. Angry, terrified, disappointed, so *worried*. It hurts. I just want to curl up in a ball and cry myself sick.

I'm the only real witness.

If the cops don't get Bon and the guy with the mullet, I'm going to be in real trouble.

10

GWEN

It's hard to even fathom the relief I'm feeling right now. Lanny's cold and soaking wet and shivering, but she's alive. Uninjured, but terrified. I need to get her home and into dry clothes, but the police officer who stopped Sam's truck and has directed him to park over by the side is coming at us, with Sam and Connor close behind.

"I'm going to need y'all to wait for the detectives," he tells us. "They're on the way right now."

Lanny says, "Is she okay? Candy, the girl up there?" She's pale, shaking, but steady enough.

Up where? What girl? I wonder, but it's not the time to ask. I turn to the paramedic and he says to my daughter, "We're headed up there right now." He directs the rest to me. "Lanny's okay. Get her warmed up and let her rest. Her lungs are going to be sore and irritated for a while, so take her in to see her doctor; he may want to give her some treatments for that." Then he and his partner are gone, carrying a lightweight stretcher and heading for the cliff the kids call Killing Rock.

I turn to Lanny and say, "Baby, what *happened?*"

She doesn't want to tell me, and I don't know if that's shock or her physical misery or something else. I want to press, but Sam puts a hand on my shoulder and says, quietly, "Gwen. She's okay. Take a breath."

"I just wanted to go to the party," she whispers. Her lips are getting a little color back, but she still looks half-drowned. "I'm sorry."

"It's dangerous for you to go out like this, you remember what happened with your dad—"

My son's been silent until now, but he shoots me a look full of resentment and impatience. "Yes, Mom. We remember. She just wants to be normal. Do normal stuff."

I stop myself from telling him that it's never going to be normal, because I don't want that to be true. We need to *find* normal. *Work* for normal. Now, more than ever, it hits me that we can't stay here. Being a teen is hard in any circumstances. The level of difficulty my kids have to navigate now is crushing.

We can't go on this way.

I just hold Lanny and rub her arms and try to warm her up. The area's littered with discarded bottles; a huge bonfire is still raging on the shore. Abandoned camp chairs and discarded bottles are a testament to how many were here. There's absolutely nobody in sight, and there's an eerie silence to the whole thing.

I can see a light up on top of the cliff: the paramedics, working on the girl Lanny mentioned. They're not up there long, and they come down carrying a still form on the stretcher. She's still alive, but her pallor is awful. From the bandages, she's got a serious head wound. Lanny found her up there, clearly. But then why was my daughter in the lake? I want to pepper her with questions, but before I can, the detectives pull up in their old black sedan. I see Detective Prester climb out first; then my friend Kezia Claremont exits from the passenger side. Prester looks like he doesn't much relish a climb; he considers the cliff trail, then dispatches Kezia up and instead comes straight for us. As he approaches, his seamed old face blurs history with present; I remember him coming like this at me before, when a body was dragged out of Stillhouse Lake and I was a suspect in her death. I don't want him interrogating my daughter the same way.

"Hey, Gwen. Sam." Prester exchanges sober handshakes with the two of us, then looks at Lanny. He's got the sort of face that can seem kind and supportive right up to the moment he slams the cell door on you. And I'm not reassured by his good manners. "Young lady, I'm going to need to talk to you. Gwen, you can come along."

"Fine," I say, as Lanny draws breath to tell me she can do it alone. I'm not about to let her get trapped. Not that I think she's done anything wrong, but . . . still. "Maybe in your car?"

"Yeah, that works, I'll get that heater going. Miss Atlanta, you get into the front seat with me. Gwen, mind sitting in the back?"

I don't until the door shuts, and I remember that I probably can't open it by myself. But I'm not the one in trouble here. My daughter looks tough, but I see the scared little girl inside, and it hurts.

Detective Prester takes out his phone and presses a recording app. "This is Detective Timothy Prester interviewing Atlanta Proctor. Lanny, state your address and birth date for the record, please."

She does, stammering a little; I'm not sure whether that's the chill she's still feeling, or nerves. Prester gives her a warm, reassuring smile. It puts me on guard. "Right, the time right now is . . . two fifteen a.m. Okay, I promise we won't be long, I know you've been through a lot tonight. You doing okay? You need anything?"

Lanny shakes her head, but she's still shivering. Prester turns on the engine, and the heater starts blasting. "You just tell me the story the way it happened, Lanny. I'm listening."

Lanny's unusually reticent, but he coaxes it out of her, step by step. Sneaking out. Arriving at the party. Hanging out with a senior named Bon. Going up to the cliff to get away from the crowd. Finding the victim.

I know she's telling the truth about the sequence of events. I also know she's leaving things out. Prester will too.

She recounts the terrifying story of being confronted on the cliff, tells him about Bon Casey and a second man. And Prester just nods. He looks, if possible, even more grim. "From your description, sounds like it's probably Olly Belldene," he says. "Bon Casey does some grunt work for him, pushing pills and weed at parties. We'll look into that."

I know this isn't good. We didn't need another reason to be at war with the Belldenes, but here it is. My daughter's the only witness to what seems to be a crime that Olly Belldene is involved in, and that makes me very, very worried.

Lanny must realize it too. Her shoulders are hunched, and though she's stopped shivering, she seems drawn into a tight ball of nerves. Prester gives her a break and thanks her for her help. I let out a breath and realize that my whole body is aching. I've been trying so hard not to interfere.

Lanny reaches for the handle, and Prester says, "One last thing, Lanny. I'd like to get a DNA swab so we can eliminate you from the scene, okay?"

I want to object. I'm frozen with doubt, but Lanny just turns her head and opens her mouth as he takes a sealed swab from his jacket. Before I can tell her it's a bad idea, it's done; Prester's as slick as a stage magician. And, truthfully, her DNA will probably be found on Candy, there's no doubt about that; she must have touched her, checked her pulse at least. So maybe this is a good step, not the start of something worse. But I can think of a thousand ways this can go sideways.

Prester tells us we can go home after that. I'm exhausted but jittering with nerves, and I just want to get my kids home. But I linger just a moment to ask him a blunt question. "Are we safe here?"

He takes his time with the answer. "Ms. Proctor, I wish I could say you were. But you've got trouble with the Belldenes already, and now this? Might want to take your family on a vacation, if you know what I mean. If I need you back here, I can call."

I heave a sigh. "Thanks, I will. Speaking of the Belldenes, though . . . I got a visit from the top today. Jasper and Lilah Belldene. Lilah made me meatloaf."

He stares at me. For the first time, I've surprised Detective Prester. "Did you eat it?"

"Nope. I was afraid it might have a nasty surprise inside."

"Well, I doubt that; Lilah's a damn good cook, and her meatloaf's pretty near legendary around these parts. She wouldn't want to cast a shadow on her reputation. What did they want?"

"They want us gone," I tell him. "And that was before this happened. Can't imagine this will make them like us any better."

"The good thing is that since we're going to be looking for Olly, we get to sweep that compound of theirs pretty thoroughly. That should set them on their heels a bit." Prester looks grim. He knows better than me how dangerous this could be. "You need to be real careful, Gwen. I don't like this. None of it."

I don't either. I take my family home, to a house I'm no longer sure is really safe. It's a very short night. I try to talk to Lanny, but she seems too exhausted and distraught, and I feel like a bad mom for keeping her awake. There'll be time.

I don't sleep at all.

11

GWEN

Our escape is the case of Remy Landry.

We leave Stillhouse Lake in the morning, all of us, and head for Louisiana. It's a good eleven-hour drive heading south by southwest. We take the SUV, which at least allows us to ride in relative comfort, and I admit I feel a sense of existential relief putting our home in the rearview right now. Too much trouble.

Leaving it behind feels like freedom, even though I know that's a temporary relief; regardless of what happens while we travel, we'll come back to the Belldenes, who must be mad as a nest of poked hornets by now that my daughter is the main witness against one of their own. They wanted us gone, and I'm willing to make them happy on that front. But I'm not going to ask my child to lie for them.

The chill of the morning morphs into rain before we hit Mississippi, but the temperature rises along with it. Sam drives, and I sleep as much as I can before I call ahead to Remy's father. No answer, I get voice mail. I explain to him that I will be coming into town and would like a meeting to talk about his son. I leave my phone number and the address of the place we'll be staying, since I booked ahead.

We're all tired and cranky by the time we arrive.

Remy's hometown isn't anything much—a wide spot in the road, basically, with a few thousand residents, the usual Dairy Queen and Sonic and truck stops. A few Cajun restaurants, all brightly lit with neon signs.

We slide into the motel pretty close to 10:00 p.m., and I have a flashback of all the cheap wayside inns I've stayed at these past few years, as the kids and I fled from one compromised home to another. I stayed at even more with Sam as we went on the hunt for Melvin. It's strange how simultaneously depressed and nostalgic I feel about motels in general.

I deliberately chose something nicer this trip. Clean, well lit, relatively modern if not fancy. J. B. probably would have paid for something really upscale, but I'm more comfortable here, and it's the best place that's close-ish to the Landry family home. I haven't gotten a call back yet, but I'm hoping Joe Landry will reach out in the morning. If not, I'm prepared to doorstep him. For tonight, we pile into our rooms—one for me and Sam, one for Lanny and Connor, though Lanny's already making mutinous noises about wanting her own room and why does she have to share a bathroom anyway. But they're okay. She's relieved, I think, to be away from Stillhouse Lake right now. So is Connor.

Sam and I settle in, but I find I'm restless in the heavy humidity. I can't get comfortable. I give up and coax a cup of coffee from the coffeemaker in the room—the results are surprisingly good—and open up my laptop to check messages.

There are quite a few, which is odd. I've put in certain keyword filters, so anything that contains *rape* or *fuck* or *kill* goes into a folder called RADIOACTIVE unless it's from someone I already know. But these have bypassed that filter setup. They're all from anonymous accounts, most just strings of numbers.

The message contents are nothing but pictures.

It takes a lot to shock me these days, to be honest. I've seen gruesome crime scenes, in real life and in vividly colored high-resolution photographs. I've seen mutilations and violations and so much more; a lot of it has been forced on me through accounts just like these, designed to horrify and incite terror.

But these are still disturbing. One's a crime scene photo—God knows from where—in saturated color so the blood is a distinctively bright hue. A woman lies on the ground. She's got no face, just a ragged mashed hole where it ought to be. One eye lies on the ground next to her. It's a cloudy brown.

The caption on the picture says *Soon, bitch.*

I brace myself for the next message. And the next. And the next. It's all bad, but some stand out. One's a direct death threat against Sam. I put that one aside. I linger, horrified, over threats to both my children. There have always been assholes who fixate on me. But threatening to rape and murder my children just to make *me* feel the pain is beyond monstrous. They don't care about Lanny and Connor; to these sick bastards my kids are just flesh dolls they can rip apart for effect. It makes me rage inside, and shake with fear, which is what they want. I know that and still can't help it.

I tell myself this is normal, that panic comes in waves and it'll subside again soon . . . but even if it does, this avenue of attack never closes. There's always someone new stumbling upon a message board, a thread, a call for action. They feel powerless. It makes them happy to lash out.

The internet enables and organizes hate very effectively; it lets people believe they're righteous warriors for justice when in reality they're just clicking keys. All the emotional hit of adrenaline, none of the risk. Most of them will never do anything else; one shot, and they're gone.

But there's always a possibility that one of these messages is from a stalker with time and inclination to travel. To shadow our family until an opportunity presents itself. And that terrifies me, because I know better than anyone that safety is an illusion.

I stop at the thirty-fourth message, because that one is a picture of the four of us together. Me, Sam, the kids. We're in front of the cabin, talking as we carry in groceries. Lanny's smiling. I'm wearing my favorite red sweater. There are targets on each of us.

This picture is *recent*, within the last month, because I just bought that damn sweater when the weather started to turn.

The caption feels like a knife at my back. *You don't get to be happy.* How many times have I heard that? From the lips of victims' families, former friends, perfect strangers.

Often enough that I have to work not to believe it.

I archive all the emails, complete with all the header information, onto a thumb drive, and then I dive into the radioactive folder for another unsettling swim in the sewer. It's even worse, but at least most of it is just words, not pictures. I put those on a separate drive. Close to two hundred of those.

Sam's hand falls on my shoulder, and I flinch. "You're quiet," he says.

"Yeah." I shut the lid on the computer and turn with a smile. But my smile dies at the serious look on his face.

"I need to talk to you," he says. "Got a minute?"

"Sure. Remy's father hasn't called back yet anyway." I let a second go by before I ask the question I'm kind of dreading. "What is it?"

He sits on the edge of the bed across from me and rubs his hands together. That's a tell of his; it means he's feeling very uncomfortable, working himself up to something personal. "I've been contacted by the Lost Angels," he says.

Contacted. Not targeted? I don't answer, because I'm not sure what to say. He doesn't, either, for a moment.

"They wanted me to know that they're about to do a podcast. You know how popular those are right now."

They are. Listeners in the millions. I even subscribe to some myself.

"About me?" I ask. He shakes his head. He's looking down now. It alarms me more than the rest of it.

"Not directly," he says. "It's about me. They believe I had something to do with Miranda's death."

Miranda Tidewell and Sam had a . . . relationship. Not the traditional, sexual kind as far as I'm aware, though she was possessive of him; she and Sam shared a deep trauma. Miranda's daughter had been murdered by my ex-husband. And so had Sam's sister. She'd been the one to help him through that grief, not me. She'd been the one who'd channeled Sam's grief into a pure, burning rage against Melvin, and against the woman she believed had enabled Melvin to commit his crimes.

Me.

Miranda had sharpened Sam and pointed him at me like a spear, and I thank God that he'd had enough of his soul left to recognize that he'd been used. And that I was innocent.

But Miranda hated me to her last breath, and she blamed Sam for turning on her and protecting me. I wasn't there when she was killed, but Sam was. The official verdict was that he didn't have a thing to do with it . . . but that wasn't about to satisfy the conspiracy-hungry anger addicts on the Lost Angels website.

They're coming for Sam. That horrifies me, because he *thinks* he's ready for it. He's seen what happened to me, to my kids . . . but observing isn't the same as experiencing, and he's about to get drowned in a storm of shit. Worse, a podcast like that could make him a pariah in his own right; it could ruin him professionally as well as personally. He wants to fly again, but the first thing potential employers do these days is conduct a Google search. Sam's name is about to become notorious.

I reach out and take his hands, and he looks up and meets my gaze. He manages a quirk of a smile. "Sorry," he says. "I didn't see this one coming. I guess it's nice they sent me a warning before they get the knives out." I don't think it is. I think they wanted him to start dreading it. It's psychological torture, and the Lost Angels have a lot of experience in that. I don't want to hate them; most of them are the family members of my ex-husband's victims who are genuinely grief-stricken—and probably normally good—people. But on that message board, on that website, they unite in one dark purpose: to make me pay. And now Sam, because Sam left them to side with me.

So I take a deep breath and plunge in. "Okay. So, here's what's going to happen," I tell him. "Once the podcast drops, they'll start getting momentum in a week or two as word spreads. You need to shut down your email account right now and make a new anonymous one; don't use it for anyone except people you trust. Make another one you'll put other places where you have to enter an email address, but keep it completely firewalled off. Don't do anything without logging into VPN first. Ditch your phone and get a new one. And call the people you trust and tell them what's going to happen, so they're on guard for any social engineering by trolls who want to get your new phone or email. Our real vulnerabilities come from people thinking they're doing something harmless."

"You've put thought into this," he says.

"I expected it," I admit. "The Lost Angels were never going to let you go without punishment. Look, the moment you decided to stay with us, you became a target too; I'm actually surprised it took this long. But they're coming at you now, and it will not be pleasant. They're going to say terrible things about you. Me. Maybe about the kids. Anything to spur a comeback from you." I hold his stare. He's starting to understand. "They'll smear your reputation and find people who'll swear to all of it; you've made enemies in your life, and they'll come crawling out of the woodwork like cockroaches when the lights go out."

I feel his hands tighten on mine.

"Sam, I'm sorry. They're going to take their shot, and it's going to hurt; you know these people. You trusted them. That'll make it personal. Likely other message boards and podcasters will jump on the bandwagon and keep driving it hard. And we can only hope it doesn't go viral, and keep our heads down until the storm moves on. Okay?"

He lets out a slow breath and blinks. "Okay," he says. It isn't. "Sorry. I know there's a lot of bullshit right now, and you didn't need this too."

"But I need you," I say, and I mean it. "Sam. You hear me? I need *you.*"

He just nods. I come and sit next to him and fold him into an embrace. I wish I could stop it. I'd hoped that once Miranda was gone, the Lost Angels would lose some steam. But someone's pushing them onward—probably out of a very sincere belief that Sam killed Miranda and got away with it. It's an ominous sign that behind the scenes, some new leader has taken charge.

They're smart to change targets. It'll throw us all off.

Especially Sam.

"I'll get on that stuff you mentioned," Sam says, and I can actually feel the effort he makes to shift to another topic. "So, no answer from Remy's dad yet?"

"No."

"Maybe he's working late. Maybe he hasn't been home to pick up the message. Hell, maybe he's on vacation in the Bahamas." Sam's really trying to put his problems behind him and focus on mine. I don't know if that's entirely healthy.

"That'd be just my luck," I agree. "But I would think—"

My phone rings. I exchange a look with Sam, eyebrows raised, and pick it up. It's a Louisiana number, all right. But not the one I called earlier. Cell phone, maybe.

I hit the button to accept the call. "Gwen Proctor," I say. There's a brief silence.

"You should go on home," a voice says on the other end. It sounds drunk.

"Mr. Landry?"

"You should go on home and tell whoever's stirring all this up to let it go." Definitely drunk, slurring words. "Got nothing to tell you, cher. Nothing you can do for my boy now. He's long gone. Sorry for your trouble." I was right about Mr. Landry's Cajun roots. The music of it weaves through his words, however intoxicated he might be.

"Mr. Landry, why don't we talk about this in the morning—"

"No," he says. His breathing's ragged. I think he's crying. "I can't. Can't do it. No."

He hangs up. I frown at the phone, not so much disturbed as thinking.

"Doesn't want to talk, I assume," Sam says. "What are you going to do?"

"I'll drop in at his office tomorrow," I say. "He runs a car place, so that's my best option. Less chance of some kind of scene. If I don't get much from him, I'll check with Remy's friends in the area. I have a list from his social media."

Sam nods. "Okay. Sounds like a plan. Do you need me along, or—"

"I always need you, didn't I just say that?" I nudge him. "Always. Let's talk about plans later. It's late."

"Yeah," he agrees, and turns his head to look at me. His smile is so warm, his eyes even better. "And you're tired."

"Not that tired," I say, and kiss him, and then we're falling back to the bed, and we both spontaneously laugh because this bed is hard as a damn *rock*, but then that doesn't matter anymore, and I'm able to forget the specter of the Lost Angels coming for us, and the dark, ugly hatred still arriving in my email, second by second, drip by drip until it floods over onto us.

Trouble's coming.

But the only cure for that is surviving it.

Morning comes early, but it comes with coffee and a decent breakfast. Lanny wants to go with me on my visit; she wants to be my assistant, but I'm not making that mistake again. Sam promises the kids that they'll do something fun while I'm interviewing Remy's dad. Neither of my children look convinced, but at least they cooperate. For now.

Remy Landry's father has a nice car dealership right on the main drag; it has an inflatable gorilla waving in the breeze and lots of colorful pennons. I park and walk in. I'm greeted by a comfortably padded woman of about forty at the reception desk, and I ask to see the boss. She looks instantly wary. I guess I don't look like someone in the market for a new ride. "What for?" she asks. "Are you one of our customers?"

"Just tell him Gwen Proctor is here," I say, and I walk over to admire a shiny, hulking SUV spinning slowly on a turntable in the middle of the dealership floor.

I hear his footsteps behind me, but I don't turn until he says, "I said I don't have anything to tell you."

I turn then, hand outstretched. He takes it, but it's just instinct; his gaze on me is bloodshot and fiercely unhappy. Like his wife in Knoxville, he looks like an old man. His hair's gone thoroughly gray, and frown lines groove the skin above his eyebrows and down the sides of his face. They look deep, almost painful. His color's a sickly yellow under a fading tan. The suit he's wearing hangs like a sack. For all that, it's a nice suit, and the tie is neatly knotted to cinch in a gaping neckline on his shirt. A good watch on his wrist, good shoes on his feet. He's got money.

Money clearly doesn't help.

"Mr. Landry, I know you don't want to do this," I tell him. "It's tough. It's painful to have this dragged up all over again. I know all that, and I promise you, if you'll sit down with me for an hour, I will not bother you again. There's every chance this investigation could bring up news about your son."

"I didn't hire you to do this," he says. "And I know my wife didn't either. Who's paying you to do this? Why?" That last part comes out as a muted cry of pain, and I feel it like a slap. I knew this might be tough, but it's worse than that. I have a strong impulse to apologize and walk away, but I steady myself.

"The firm I work for was hired by a nonprofit organization to look into Remy's disappearance," I tell him. "I'm sorry this is so painful for you, Mr. Landry. But it's possible we might be able to find him."

"My son's dead," he says. It's flat and dark the way he says it. "I let hope go a long time back." Still, there's a flicker of . . . something. And it leads me to continue.

"I'm not saying I can bring him home alive," I reply. "But maybe I can help you find some peace, and bring someone to justice."

He studies me. Sizes me up like I'm a potential car buyer. Decides I'm worth the trouble. He finally sighs and says, "Let's just get it over with. Follow me."

We go to an office and sit. I close the door. As I sit down, I realize this room is a shrine. There are photos of Remy on every wall. There, he's a small boy grinning at the camera and cuddling a puppy. There, a fresh-faced teen in a tuxedo posing for prom. In yet another he's wearing a graduation cap. A photo to my left, the largest one, is a candid shot of Remy on a soccer field, scoring a goal. He looks triumphant. He looks vividly alive.

There's a sagging sofa against one wall with a neatly folded blanket and a crumpled pillow. It dawns on me that although Mr. Landry almost certainly has a home somewhere, he sleeps here pretty often.

It feels as haunted as that sad apartment in Knoxville where Remy's mother keeps her vigil.

"Okay, I guess you talked to my wife," Mr. Landry says. "She tell you yet that I'm crazy?"

"She said you thought you needed to move on, but she wasn't quite ready to do that," I reply. But despite his declaration that his son's dead, nothing about the office says that this man has moved one inch from the moment he learned Remy was missing. Joe Landry seems to be trapped in a windowless coffin lined with the past. "I'm interested in any correspondence you had with him by email or in letters, and anything he mentioned in phone calls that might have struck you as odd. Anything at all."

Joe Landry reaches into a drawer and pulls out a shoebox. He slides it across the desk at me. "That's every letter or card I have from him since he went off to college," he says. "Emails too. I put it all together for the police, but they never were interested."

It's as complete an archive as I could have wanted. I accept it, and it's heavy. "I'll scan everything," I tell him. "I'll get it back to you."

"I don't want it," he says. His gray eyes wash with tears, and he blinks them away. "Maybe take it to Ruth when you're done."

I nod and fold my hands on top of the box. "What about phone calls?"

"He didn't call too often," Joe says. "Mostly spoke to his mother, and mostly on birthdays and holidays and the like. Last time, though—" I see his eyes go up and to the right, tracking a memory. "Last time I talked to him he sure was interested in a girl."

I feel an instinct come alive. "What girl?" I don't want to lead him. I want to follow.

"Not that girlfriend he had," Landry says, and a smile flits over his lips for an instant. "Remy liked the ladies, and they sure liked him too. No, this one's name was Carol. Definitely Carol, I remember because it seemed like such an old-fashioned name for a young woman."

"What did he say about her?" I take out a small notebook and make note to check the date of Remy's last call to his dad. It's clear that he doesn't know what his wife insisted: that her son was helping Carol out of a jam of some kind. I don't tell him.

"I know he met her at church," he said. "Good churchgoing boy, Remy. She was real different from the girls at school, he said. I think he was taken with her."

"Different from the other girls how, exactly?"

Landry sits back in his chair. The old leather creaks. "She was evangelical, for a start. Wore long skirts and wouldn't cut her hair, like that. No makeup. It surprised me he'd go for that, but I think he saw her as . . . kind of pure."

I keep my dislike for the pure/impure dynamic forced on women to myself. "Did he tell you a last name at all?"

"No. Just Carol. But you can check at that church he was going to. Gospel Witness Church up there in Knoxville, Tennessee. Somebody must recall her, even if she ain't there now."

The rest of the conversation goes without much real information; he reiterates things his wife's already told me, with minor variations. He has no theories about what happened to his son. He doesn't want to think about it, though clearly from this room he can't think about anything else.

When I'm leaving, he shakes my hand a second time. This time I think he means it. The numbed look is still in his eyes, but he seems slightly more . . . present. "You'll let me know if something turns up?" he asks. It isn't hope, exactly, but it's better than the dead apathy I saw earlier.

"I will," I tell him, and give him my card. He nods over it and puts it in his coat pocket. "Keep the faith, Mr. Landry."

"I'll pray for you," he says. Which is as much as I could reasonably ask.

When I check my watch, it's been almost exactly an hour. I don't know if Landry was watching the clock or instinctively timed things right like the businessman he is.

The receptionist gives me a frown as I leave. Protective. Good for her. Landry probably needs a gatekeeper.

I put the box of correspondence on the seat beside me and open up Remy's digital file. There's a brief note buried deep that he was a member of the Gospel Witness Church in Knoxville, where he sang in the choir. I pull up the web page, and the church seems pretty standard and bland. I call the number and ask for the pastor.

I get a man with a slow, deep voice who says, "Pastor Wallace, how may I help you today?"

"Pastor, my name is Gwen Proctor. I'm a private investigator, looking to follow up on the disappearance of a young man named Remy Landry. He was a member of your church, and—"

He hangs up on me.

For a second I think my cell phone dropped the call, but no. That was definitely, and deliberately, a hang-up. The pastor doesn't want to talk to me. Not about Remy.

Well. That's very, very interesting.

12

Sam

Gwen's onto something hot, and she needs to follow it. Driving back isn't an option; neither is abandoning our vehicle, and besides, we're supposed to be avoiding the Belldenes. So I volunteer to take her to the nearest airport in New Orleans. We see her off, and the kids and I start the long drive back.

I end the drive for the night at a nice upscale hotel and get a small suite; the kids each get their own room and bed, and I get the fold-out couch, which is actually pretty comfortable. Good food, movies on demand. As avoiding the Hillbilly Mafia goes, it's a pretty great escape.

I make sure everything's locked down after the kids go off to their own rooms. Connor's reading a book as thick as my biceps. Lanny's listening to her headphones, eyes closed. Relaxed and unguarded and happy, they look like the small kids they once were. Vulnerable. Precious. Kids I need to protect.

I'm worried for Lanny. She's still jumpy, and I don't want her on the wrong side of the Belldenes. It isn't a good place to be.

Which is partly why I've taken the sofa bed: it puts me between them and the door. Just in case.

I can't avoid it any longer. I grab my laptop and surf to the Lost Angels tribute site. I helped create this site, back in the early days. Me and Miranda, deciding on layout and colors. She'd drawn the abstract logo, and seeing it hovering there in the corner makes my mouth go dry. I didn't love her, but we had a complicated, messy history. We knew each other at our worst, our rawest. Never at our best.

I still would have saved her if I could.

My sister's picture sits last in the row of Melvin Royal's victims. She's the one who got him caught; I know she'd take some small satisfaction in that, at least. But justice still feels hollow. And always will.

I'm already dreading it before I click the link that leads to the message boards. It's secured with passwords, and I hesitate for a long few minutes before I enter my old admin codes and hit the "Enter" key. They still work. Not too surprising—volunteer groups aren't the best at the little things like that.

I'd halfway hoped they'd cut me off from access.

It's just a message board, I tell myself. Old-school tech that predates modern social media by a decade. Used by old losers like me. It ought to be harmless.

It isn't, of course. It's a boiling sewer of hatred, and I used to swim in it with real delight. I used to believe I was getting justice the only way I could after the courts failed our families. But really, I'd just been trying to fill up a void inside me.

Some people turn to drink and drugs. I got addicted to something just as poisonous. It was only getting away from that seductive hatred, and closer to Gwen, that saved me. I'd been planning to hurt her when I moved to Stillhouse Lake, but watching her with her kids broke that spell. Made her a real person to me, not a paper target. Seeing her protect other people—people she didn't even know—made me realize how bent my compass had become.

Gwen saved my soul. Not that Lost Angels will ever accept that.

I start reading posts. The new one pinned at the top is in honor of Miranda Tidewell. It starts as a eulogy, but then it turns, as I expect, to anger. Every topic on this board eventually shifts to rage. Their civility is as fragile as flash paper.

There's plenty of violence here aimed toward Gwen, of course. There's a whole thread that links together even more murdered women on the thinnest of evidence and assigns the role of serial killer to Gwen, not her ex-husband. Because just being an innocent wife of a monster, a victim in and of herself, isn't an option.

You started it, asshole. You hated her hard enough to come across the country to torment her.

I acknowledge that, though it stings, and keep moving. And sure enough, I find a whole new thread about me. It's massive, more than a hundred pages. It started after it became clear I wasn't betraying Gwen as I'd intended, and though it begins with reasonable posts about how maybe I was playing out a long game, that quickly disappears. My motives, according to the thread, range from being brainwashed to never having been *really* part of the Lost Angels at all; some even think I was a plant that Gwen, the master manipulator, had placed to watch them from the start. It's a fantastically unlikely theory, but they leap right on it and ride it for pages. They gather every bit of gossip they can find in the media and online, piling supposition upon wild leap upon outright lie.

Up until Melvin's death, there's real speculation that I'm one of his secret admirers, which makes me have to step away from the laptop so I don't punch the screen. I drink a little bottle of bourbon from the minibar, and when I feel calmer, I go back and keep reading.

Gwen's right; I need to pay attention to all this. I can't defend myself if I don't know what's coming.

After the media circus that erupted due to Gwen's appearance on the *Howie Hamlin Show*, and the subsequent trouble we found in Wolfhunter, the tone of the posts changes again.

They really, *really* hate me now. I'm a traitor to the memory of all the victims, and to the families. But most of all, I was there when Miranda was killed. And just like they assume about Gwen, my proximity to evil is enough to convict me in their message board courtroom. If I was there, I was responsible. The fact that I was shackled at the time, and had no possibility of saving her . . . that doesn't matter.

They're going to run with the idea that I shot her myself, and that the FBI—specifically, my friend Mike Lustig—covered it up. That's going to be their last podcast episode, of course, not their first. I'm sure every enemy I've ever made, from grade school on up, will be given a microphone to set the stage for my culpability before they get down to real facts. They'll build their case carefully, if completely wrong.

Gwen's right that I need to get myself locked down for this. Just reading these posts has made me feel achingly tense and devastatingly uncertain. Even when you know better, it's hard to see so many people agreeing about your guilt. It feels like a losing battle from the start.

I click away and skim through the other posts. Lost Angels doesn't spend all their time targeting Gwen and me, of course; there are remembrance posts for lost loved ones. Casual conversations. Discussions about the worrying popularity of true crime books, movies, shows, and podcasts. Sanity, in the midst of pathological hatred.

There are also, ironically, speculation threads about other serial killers and killing sprees. Some are hashing over old cases. Some are genuinely trying to connect dots. Trying to do some good.

On the fourth page of threads one catches my eye: a post about missing young men. That's unusual enough to make me look closer. The poster has the thinnest of evidence. Sketchy logic. But something makes me slow down and read more carefully. The writer is piecing together disappearances from all over the southeast, and I know one of those names.

Remy Landry.

What the hell?

I back up and read the whole thing again, and as I do I feel a cold shiver run up my spine. Yes, the evidence is thin, but he could be right. There may be something going on here. His conclusions are bullshit and have to do with Satan worshippers, but these cases do seem, on the surface of it, to have common links.

I pick up my phone and call Gwen. I get voice mail, and I read her the pertinent parts of the post. Then I say, "Could be that Remy's just one victim. If this proves out, you could be looking at half a dozen connected cases. Maybe more. So . . . watch yourself. Because if this is correct, if there is somebody out there picking young men off and making them disappear . . . they know how to get to people quietly. Call me."

I shut down the laptop and lie awake, staring at the ceiling, until I finally give up and flip on the TV and get another overpriced miniature bottle of liquor.

13

GWEN

The Gospel Witness Church isn't exactly the megachurch I'd envisioned; the South normally goes in for massive structures in their houses-of-holy, but this is a modest, cheap clapboard chapel that's clearly in need of repairs and a fresh coat of paint. The message sign board out front that faces the street is sun-faded and antique. The message spelled out in black slide-in letters says **BEHOLD! I COME QUICKLY!** and I have to snort-laugh at the double meaning that was probably unintentional. This doesn't look like a place that has a sly sense of humor, at least not at Jesus's expense.

It's late afternoon when I pull into the mostly empty parking lot; it's also a Friday, which means there's probably no evening service, since Pentecostals lean toward Sundays and Wednesdays, though there could be Bible study or other classes this evening. If there are, they're not popular.

I slide my rental car into a parking space off to the side, near a cluster of bushes losing their leaves. Opening the car door slaps me with a blast of chilly wind. I don't have a coat; I hadn't needed one for Louisiana. I duck around to the trunk and open my suitcase to find my blazer jacket. Under that lies my gun with the trigger lock in place, and the ammo stored in a separate locked box. I open both, load the gun, don the shoulder holster, and ease the Sig Sauer into a comfortable position. Jacket on after. I grab my purse and lock the car as I leave it.

The sound of the horn's beep will probably alert people inside, if they're paying attention.

I try the church's main doors. They're locked. Always-open doors in city churches went out of favor about the same time that serial killers and drug addiction became front-page news; can't really blame them for scheduling the faithful. I go around to the side. There's a worn wooden door with a push-button, cracked doorbell and a sign that says OFFICE.

I ring.

The door opens, and a very young white man with a very short haircut says, "Hello, can I help you?"

"I'd like to talk to the pastor, please," I say. "Is he here?"

"No ma'am, I'm sorry, he isn't available." He starts to close the door. I put a hand on it, but I make sure to keep myself looking meek. Well, as meek as I can.

"I just—I just really need to talk to someone," I tell him. I channel the woman I used to be, back when my name was Gina Royal: hesitant, uncertain, submissive. I change my body language. I thicken my voice and make it more timid. "*Please*. I really need his help!"

It's a scam, and I'm slightly ashamed to use it, but it works. The young man's eyes widen, he opens the door wider, and he looks over his shoulder at someone I can't see. He must get permission, because he steps back.

I give him a grateful smile and go into the office. It's suffocatingly small, crowded with a battered old desk. A clunky, ancient desktop computer takes up much of the space on top. Cheap metal utility shelves hold stacks of paper and printed materials. There's an avocado-green landline telephone perched on the desk's corner that dates from about the same period as the computer, and a collection of porcelain angels occupies the rest of the available space. The gray carpet underfoot feels threadbare, and looks worse.

The desk has no one behind it, and I realize it must belong to the young man facing me; there's another narrow doorway to my right, and beyond that a slightly larger office with a nearly identical desk, minus the angels and computer.

And an older man rises from the chair behind it as I go that way.

"Ma'am," he says, and extends his hand not to shake mine, but to indicate the visitor chair set opposite. "Sorry about that—we were just closing for the night. I'm Pastor Dean Wallace, how may I help you?"

I'm reading him the second I see him. He fits the southern-pastor profile: dark hair swept back in a stiff style that hasn't been popular anywhere else since the 1980s, milk-pale skin, a sober dark-blue suit. No tie, but then, he's not at the pulpit today, so this must be his version of Casual Friday. He seems to be genuinely welcoming, if a little frustrated at staying late. I sit down in the visitor chair; it's a stiff, wooden thing with no comfort but a lot of structure. I'm careful to keep my jacket from gaping to show the gun, and I fold my hands primly in my lap. Body language is everything when you're trying to play to preconceptions. "I'm sorry, could we . . . shut the door?" I only meet his gaze in fast glances.

"Ma'am, I'm about to head home," he tells me, and I can see he's a little doubtful. "Maybe we could take this up tomorrow . . ."

"It can't wait," I tell him. "Please? I promise, I just need to talk for a few minutes. It would mean so much to me."

I think I might lose him, but then he nods and forces out a smile. "All right," he says. He steps around me and goes to close the door, and I have a chance to study him as he passes. The light's not great in here— the window faces east, so darkness has already descended on this side of the building, and there's only a single, weak desk lamp illuminating the room. He has a jowly face that falls naturally into an expression of disapproval; he's fighting to look engaged, and I think he's telling the truth that he'd like to be out of here and on his way home.

I don't know what I think about him. Not yet.

He looks at the young man in the other office and says, "You go on home, Jeremy. I'm fine here, I'll be along shortly. Tell your ma to keep dinner waiting."

"Yes sir," the young man—his son?—says, and the pastor closes the door. He looks around and, as if realizing how dim it is, turns on an overhead fixture. That's too bright, and it reveals shabby carpet curling in the corners, dust on shelves. He goes back to his desk and regards me from the safety of the barrier between us.

"And what's your name, young lady?"

He probably means that to be complimentary, but I have to control the urge to bristle. It's a diminishment; I'm not that damn young. "Gwen," I say. I don't volunteer a last name.

"Well, Gwen, you can talk to me about what's troubling you, and we can pray about it. Would that be all right?"

I wait until I've heard the door shut to the outer office. His son's gone now. It's just the two of us. I relax my posture, open it, tilt my head up, and look him right in the eyes. The scared little wife is gone, and I see him sit back in his chair in surprise. "You might not want to pray with me after we talk, I'm afraid. I spoke with you on the phone early today. About Remy Landry. You hung up on me."

He looks like I've punched him, and his eyes go so wide I can see white all around. *He's scared.* That's a surprise. Somehow I'd expected him to be aggressive. He rallies and makes a run at that a few seconds later as he stands. "You need to go," he says. "Right now, ma'am. I don't mean to be rude, but I've got nothing to say about that."

"I'm not going anywhere," I tell him, and when he tries to head for the exit, I scoot my heavy chair back until it blocks his path and, as a bonus, holds the door firmly shut. "Not until we have a conversation about Remy. If you want to get home to your dinner, let's do this quickly."

"Who are you?" he barks, and his hands are in fists now. I watch him carefully. I stay seated. It's not likely he's going to come at me, but he's trying to loom and intimidate. He's not very good at it. "You got no business here in the house of the Lord, coming in here with lies!"

I produce my private investigator identification and show it to him. "I've been hired by Remy's family," I tell him. "And that gives me business with you, because Remy was a member of your congregation. Why wouldn't you want to help us find him, Pastor?"

He doesn't like that. It's his turn to bristle, and also to retreat. I sit calmly and let him decide what he wants to do. His glare doesn't disturb me at all.

"I'll call the police," he says, and makes for his desk. "You're trespassing."

I don't answer. I just watch. He picks up the receiver, punches in a couple of numbers, and then eases the receiver back onto the cradle without completing his call. That tells me quite a lot. "You really need to leave," he tells me. "Right now. I'm asking you." His moral authority is melting like butter in the summer.

"Remy Landry was a member of your church," I say. "And you owe it to that young man who put his trust in you. He's been missing *three years*. His parents deserve answers."

"I don't know where that boy might have gone! Why, he might have just run away. You don't know what these kids get up to these days, all the drink and drugs . . ." His voice trails off because I'm not responding. And I can hear the hollow core of what he's trying to say. He doesn't believe it himself. "You're not going to find anything here to help. I'm sorry for his folks, I truly am. But I don't know anything. I'd have told the police if I did."

"Are you sure about that?" I lean forward, hands clasped. "Because it sounds to me like you have something you need to get off your chest,

Pastor. Do the right thing. You want to, I can see that. You know how much his family is suffering. And you know God doesn't want that to continue when you have the power to help them."

He sinks down in his chair as if I've cut his legs out from under him. "I don't know," he says. It sounds weak now. "I don't know where he is."

"But you do know something," I say. "Maybe about the girl he met at this church. Carol."

It's like I've stuck a red-hot pin in him. If he was scared before, he's definitely terrified at the sound of that name on my lips. Enough that his lips part, but he doesn't have an answer for me.

"You know who I'm talking about, Pastor. She's very conservative. No makeup. Long hair that she doesn't cut. Very plain clothes." I take a leap of faith. "You're protecting her, aren't you? You think if you talk to me about Remy, you expose her to danger."

He lowers his hands and takes in a deep breath. "Who *are* you?"

"Gwen Proctor," I tell him. I can see the name means nothing to him. Good. "Like I said: I'm just someone hired by Remy's family to find out what's happened to him. You've got a son, sir. I know you understand what kind of true horror they're going through right now not knowing where he is, what he's suffering, or even if he's never coming back. You understand that they can't move on. And I know that Remy was a good kid. You talking about drinking and drugs and how maybe he went off on his own—you know that isn't true. You're smearing his good name when you say it."

He's looking down now, and his hands are clasped together so tightly it looks like it hurts. But he still doesn't answer.

"Pastor Wallace, you were that boy's shepherd," I say. "And Carol's too. So if there's anything you can tell me that can help me understand where to look for him—"

"Forget Carol," he says. "Please. I'm begging you to leave her alone. You could put her in so much danger just by mentioning her."

He seems truly anguished. It's not an act. He's pallid and sweating, and I want to ease up on him, but if I do I won't get anywhere.

"Remy mentioned to his mom that he was going to try to help her out. What happened? Did he run into people who were after Carol?" No answer. But I think I'm on the right track. Things are clicking together. "Was she on the run from an ex-boyfriend, is that it?"

Some of the tension bleeds out of him, and he sits up straighter. I'm playing a game of blindman's bluff, and I just got colder. "You're right," he says. "She was having boyfriend troubles. Remy never should have gotten involved. But that didn't have anything to do with his disappearance."

He's lying again. I switch gears. "She told *Remy* she had boyfriend troubles," I say. The key to this game is sounding like you know what you're talking about, especially when you don't. "But you knew better, didn't you? And you still do. Carol was never on the run from a relationship. It was bigger than that."

Warmer. Red hot. He looks so stunned that I know I've got my finger right on it, and he's clearly really frightened of what else I might know.

"Just let me talk to her," I tell him. "I'll keep her identity a secret, I'll leave her completely out of my reports. Nobody will ever hear her name. It won't even go in my notes." When he convulsively shakes his head, I realize I'm going to have to give a little. So I say, "Pastor Wallace . . . I understand what it's like to be running and hiding from people who want to hurt you. My husband was Melvin Royal. The serial killer. Maybe you've heard of him."

That name, he knows. His body language changes, but I'm not clear on what he's feeling at that moment. "You—you're the one who killed him."

"Yes. I didn't have a choice." When I say it, there's a split second of it flashing before my eyes: Melvin coming at me. Bracing my shaking hand on Sam's shoulder and taking aim. Seeing him end, forever. It's not as traumatic as it used to be, but it still holds power. "The point is, I've been hunted by his admirers, and by the people who hate him, and by others who just get their kicks out of hitting people when they're down. I understand vulnerability in a way very few people do. So when I tell you I will protect Carol's identity, I promise you this: I will *protect it with my life*. Just as you have."

He takes his time thinking about it. I let him. And I finally see him come to the correct—but difficult—decision. The fight goes out of him, and his shoulders sag. "I'll ask," he says. "If she won't see you, then that's the end of it. All right?"

"Ask her now," I say.

"No ma'am. I'll go to her, but you can't come with me. I'm not going to risk her life like that."

I don't move away from the door. "Then call her. Let me talk to her on the phone."

"She doesn't have a phone." He's wavering, but starting to get his backbone assembled. "If she wants to talk, I'll arrange for a meeting somewhere safe. But if she *doesn't* agree, and she probably won't, then you need to accept that and forget all about this."

"Would you?" I ask him calmly. "If Jeremy went missing, and someone could tell you where he'd gone? Could you possibly walk away and forget?"

He looks away, but I see the muscles corded along his jaw. He's not going to give me any more.

So I move my chair back to where it was; there are still divots in the thin carpeting to mark the spot. I place my business card in the exact center of his old desk. And I say, "Thanks for your help, Pastor. I'm not the enemy here. If this young woman's in trouble, I'm on her side, and I would never put her knowingly in danger. If that computer is current enough to have an internet connection, look me up. I'll put myself on the line for her. That's a promise."

I know that he marks the gun I'm wearing as I straighten up; I see the flash of awareness that I could have pulled it, threatened him into spilling her location. The fact I didn't has to be a point in my favor.

We don't shake hands. I just leave. I head straight to my car, get in, and call J. B. Hall. She picks up on the second ring. "Gwen? Everything okay?"

"Yes. I made contact with the preacher, and I may have something. You can look at landline phone records, right?"

"Not officially."

"But realistically?"

"Maybe."

"I need the destination number of the next call that comes out of Gospel Witness Church. And an address or location, if that's possible."

Because the pastor's comment that Carol didn't have a phone had come too fast and too emphatically, and the last thing he'd done before I left was dart a quick, unintentional glance at his clunky desk phone. Simple to put together. He is going to warn her.

J. B. says she'll pull some favors, and I back my rental car out of the church's parking lot. I don't go very far, just a block down, and I take a spot in a convenience store space that faces the street. The pastor's car—a big, white, boxy thing that must be twenty years old—emerges. The pastor uses turn signals; I approve, makes it easier for me. He passes me, and I maneuver out of the lot and onto the busy street in his wake. His car's going to be easy to follow. It stands out like a shaggy dog in a road full of sleek cats.

We've gone about four miles by my odometer when my phone rings. I put it on speaker. "Hey, you've got Gwen," I say. I'm not surprised it's J. B.

My boss says, "I'm texting you the number he called. It's a burner phone, though. It's going to take time to get the data on location from my source; it's an, ah, extralegal use of legal software. Technically okay, if you squint, but she doesn't want to get caught doing it either. Not without a warrant."

"I'm on the pastor," I tell her. "He knows something. It's possible he'll lead me to her." I tell her in quick sentences about what I've learned from Remy's parents and about the mysterious Carol. I'm still behind the pastor's car, shielded by two vehicles between us. He drives cautiously and obeys the speed limits. Useful, for my purposes.

"Is it remotely possible this kid ran away with Carol? That he's living with her and somehow keeping her safe?"

"I don't know," I tell her. "But it's more than we had. I'll be in touch, I think the pastor's coming to a destination."

He is, but it's his home; I recognize the car parked in the small driveway as another that had been in the church parking lot—the son's ride, most likely. That one has a bumper sticker that says UNDER GOD surrounded by the red and blue of an American flag. Makes it extra easy to spot. I park and watch a moment, in case there's something interesting to see, but there isn't. Through the handy picture window into the dining room I can see food being set out. Three place settings, so Carol isn't hiding here.

Something's making my breath come faster, sweat prickle hot on the back of my neck, and for a second or two I don't even know what it is.

Then I blink, and I see a house of similar lines superimposed over this one. A normal house on a normal street. A broken exterior wall to the garage with a wrecked vehicle jutting out of it.

My normal house. My normal street in a normal Kansas town.

And a dead girl hanging from a wire gallows in the exposed garage, the day all that ended. All those years spent in that house, living next to a monster, not knowing what was going on under the same roof. Making dinner. Setting the table, just as this woman's doing.

I flinch and gasp and close my eyes. I have coping mechanisms for these flashbacks, and I use them, slowing my racing heartbeat and gearing myself down from the blind horror and panic that never, ever quit being fresh. I press my shaking hands down on my thighs. *Past is past. Put yourself here, now. Feel the air. Take in the smells. Listen. Be* here.

The overwhelming sense of being trapped slowly fades. Panic recedes. And when I look again, it isn't my house, it isn't my dining room, and the three people sitting down at that table are not my family. There isn't horror hiding behind that wall, or if there is, it's not mine to endure.

I check my text messages. J. B. has sent me the number that Pastor Wallace called. I know I should wait for J. B. to get that tracking data; it might—*might*—send me in the right direction. Or, if he's told the young woman to run, I might lose her altogether.

On balance, I feel a real and urgent need to *act.* So I dial the number. Roll the dice.

A woman answers. "Hello?" She sounds young and tentative, and also worried.

"Don't hang up," I say. "I'm a friend, Carol. I know you're afraid. Let me help you."

I half expect her to hang up, but she seems to hesitate. Then she says, "You're the one the pastor talked about." She has an accent, but it isn't from Tennessee. Sounds more northern states to me. Maybe even as far as Maine or Vermont. "The detective?"

"Yes," I tell her. "My name is Gwen Proctor. And I can help, if you're in trouble."

"I don't think you understand," she says. "Nobody can help me."

"Maybe I can."

"He'll never let that happen."

"Who's *he*?"

"Doesn't matter," she says. She sounds quiet now. Resigned. "I'm sorry, but I can't help you. I got out. I can't ever get free. I thought I could, but . . . it's never going to work." I squeeze my eyes shut and listen desperately for any environmental clues. I hear a babble of voices in the background. An indistinct PA announcement. A metallic squeal.

I sense she's about to cut me off, and I quickly say, "Carol, can you tell me what happened to Remy? Where he is?"

Silence. Silence for so long that I think the call's dropped and she's vanished into the air. But then she says, "Remy's with the saints."

Click.

But I heard enough. I can guess where she is.

She's at the bus station.

14

GWEN

I'm taking a shot in the dark as to *which* bus station. She could have been at a regional stop, but if she wants to get out of town, Carol will be at the main Greyhound bus terminal. I've made it a point to know the city, since I do a fair amount of work for J. B. around here. I race across town, driving far more recklessly than Pastor Wallace would have approved, and I pull into the bus station in just under thirteen minutes, which isn't bad.

But if Carol was about to board a bus when I called, it's too late.

I head inside. There's a sign on the doors of the station that guns aren't allowed, and I approve of that, but I don't have time to retreat and secure my weapon, and leaving it in a rental car's glove compartment isn't a great idea anyway. I make sure my coat conceals it and stroll inside. Or try to. The station is a fairly new construction, all glass and steel and open areas that ought to seem spacious but don't, because it's crowded with people and bags. Bus travel generally doesn't draw in the first-class passengers, so most often it's duffel bags, battered old suitcases, and backpacks. Lots of people who seem exhausted and dispirited.

I spot Carol because she's sitting close to a group of Amish or Mennonite travelers; the women are in neat, long dresses with aprons and bonnets, the men in uncomfortable-looking square suits with beards bristling down over their starched shirts. Carol *almost* blends in, except that she lacks a bonnet. She's a young, pale woman wearing a long-sleeved white blouse with a bow tied in front of the high neck, no jewelry or makeup, a long, straight dark-blue skirt. Waist-length dark hair. She's got a fairly new-looking backpack with her, and for some reason it strikes me as . . . wrong. I'm not sure why. Yet.

She's scanning the room like her life depends on it, evaluating every person who comes into view. She looks me over and moves on; I'm not what she's afraid of spotting, clearly. Good. I was worried she'd run at the first hint of my presence.

I get all the way through the crowd. There's an empty seat across from her, and I take it. Her gaze still searches the entrances until I say, "Hi, Carol. I'm Gwen."

She shrinks back on her bench, crowded next to an older Amish woman, who turns, clearly concerned about her. That's better than Carol bolting, but not by much. I don't want a public incident, especially since I'm carrying a gun. That'll get me arrested.

I quickly hold up both empty hands, palms out. Surrender, and placation. "I'm sorry I startled you," I say, and smile. "Honest, I'm here to help. You're looking out for someone, but it isn't me. Right?"

Carol slowly relaxes. The Amish woman says, "Are you all right?" and gives me a doubtful look. "Should I get help for you?"

Carol has big, dark eyes. Doe eyes. I can see why a young college-age man would be so drawn to her; there's a real vulnerability there, a fragility that would appeal to someone who has an instinct for protection. *And predators,* I think. *Melvin would have loved her.* Just as I appealed to him, coming to him as an innocent girl fresh from a religious home. Looking at this young woman, I see myself, and I want to shake her and scream at her to *wake up.*

"I'm okay, thank you," Carol says, almost in a whisper, and the Amish woman settles back but keeps a stern eye on me. I make damn sure I keep my body language correct and unthreatening. "You're the one who called me."

"Yes."

Carol shakes her head. Her satiny curtain of hair shimmers as it moves. "I can't help you."

"But you can tell me what you know about Remy," I counter. "That's all I want. I swear. I just want to find him for his folks. They're suffering, Carol, and I know you don't want that for them."

She looks down. She's a willowy, tall young woman, graceful. Long-fingered hands that are reddened and roughened, as if she's recently done hard work as a cleaner. Short, plain, strong fingernails. Her head snaps up as the speakers above us announce that a bus for Pennsylvania is ready to board, and I know I'm about to lose her. The Amish are getting up, gathering their things. She's going with them, or at least getting on the same bus.

The backpack she's holding still bothers me. It's got faded stickers on it for University of Tennessee football. She doesn't strike me as an alumna.

I nod toward it. "That's Remy's backpack," I say. "Isn't it?"

She looks shocked. "I—he gave it to me!"

"When?"

"When I told him I had to leave," she said. "I should have gone. I would have, but then . . ."

"Then Remy vanished?"

She doesn't blink, doesn't nod, doesn't answer at all. Then she just stands up.

"Who's after you, Carol?" I stand up, too, and her paranoia is catching; I scan the crowd, looking for trouble. Lots of motion, and no obvious threats. "The same people who took him? What happened to him? Did they question him to find out where you were?"

140

"He'd never tell," she says.

She turns and walks away. I move up to go with her. I don't have a whole lot of time. This boarding line is long, but the second I get to the agent collecting tickets I'll be done. She'll be beyond my reach. "Carol, please. Please, I'm asking you to give me *something* I can use. You know what happened to him, I can see that. Remy tried to help you. And something happened to him. Just give me a place where I can start looking for him, that's all I need!"

We've moved up two feet in the line by the time I finish saying that. Carol's clutching Remy's backpack like it's a life preserver in a thrashing ocean. She's crying, I realize. Silent tears, racing down her cheeks and dripping on her blouse. She hastily wipes them away and shakes her head again.

Then she suddenly dashes for the bathroom. I hesitate, not sure if she's trying to actually escape or wanting me to follow her. She doesn't look back. I take the chance anyway. Worst case, I can claim to be needing the toilet.

Carol's waiting by the sinks, jittering from one foot to another.

"Sorry," she says. "Look, maybe . . . maybe I can tell you a few things. Thing is, I don't have any money for another ticket." She wipes tears from her face and takes a deep breath. "And I don't want you knowing where I'm headed either."

"So you just want me to hand over cash? No, Carol. That won't happen. Not here."

She blinks. "Then where?"

"I'll take you to a restaurant," I tell her. "Buy you dinner. Get you a room for the night. And I'll buy you a plane ticket to anywhere you want to go in the morning, plus enough money that you can disappear for good. All you need to do is tell me about Remy and what happened to him. Deal?"

She's silent for a moment before she says, "You're going to be sorry you ever got into this. Because it's bad."

I don't doubt that for a second.

We head outside, and I'm alert for any sign she's about to bolt, but the lure of what I've offered seems to have a magnetic attraction for her. I don't try to make small talk; she doesn't seem the type.

My rental car is behind the bus station, in a parking lot that's an adjunct to the full, busy one; we walk toward it, and I notice that there's a dilapidated RV circling the lot, restlessly looking for a place to park.

Carol suddenly grabs my arm and pulls me to a stop. Her grip is so tight it hurts. "Have you got a gun?" she asks.

"Even if I do, I'm not going to start anything in a Greyhound parking lot," I tell her. "What's the matter?"

She nods toward the RV. It's sun-faded, the kind of antique that nobody wants. It probably dates from the mid-1980s, at best. I'm surprised it's still running. She pulls me off to the side, beside an overflowing dumpster, and I try not to breathe in the reek of garbage and urine. Carol doesn't seem to notice. Her attention is all focused on that RV. "They found me," she says. "Oh, Lord help me." Then she turns an angry, narrow stare on me. "They found me because of *you*. Stirring things up."

"Who are *they*, Carol?"

She doesn't answer. The RV cruises the lot, doesn't park, rambles on over to the next lot. When it finally pulls out onto the main road again, she says, "We have to hurry. They'll come back."

I don't know what she's thinking, or who she's afraid of, but one thing's for sure: she's not bluffing. We race to the car, start it up, and I tell her to get down out of sight.

I pass the RV going the opposite direction, and when I try to read the back license plate in the rearview, it's useless. They're Tennessee plates, but dirty and mud-splattered, and I can't make out anything but an *M*.

The interior's completely hidden by tinted glass.

We keep moving. I hold my speed down to just below the speed limit, and look for the RV to follow us.

It doesn't. I watch for several blocks before I tell Carol we're in the clear.

"We aren't," she says, but she climbs back up into the passenger seat. Her shoulders are hunched, her hair a curtain that hides her face. "I need to go. Now."

"We have a deal."

"We *had* a deal," she says. "But they're *here*. Looking."

"And if they're chasing us in an RV, they're going to be damn easy to spot," I tell her. "There's no sign of them now. We're okay. How about that food? You still hungry?"

She stares straight ahead for a long time before she finally nods.

Then she folds her hands and starts to pray.

At dinner, she wolfs down buttermilk fried chicken like it's her last meal. She's chosen a seat near the back, by the kitchen, where she can watch the entry doors. It's not by a window.

High vigilance. I understand that impulse. I've had it for years.

I wonder how often she gets real food. There's a certain way she hovers over the plate, like she's guarding it. People who've been starved do that. Maybe it's a consequence of how she's been living. Or maybe it's worse than that. She's not giving me much, and she doesn't talk other than to say *yes* or *no* or *can I have that butter.*

When she is finally filled up and sits back with a sigh, I pay the bill and hustle her back to the rental car. Still no sign of the RV. There's a good selection of hotels around the airport. I choose the Best Western, which seems like a low-profile destination, and check us in. One room. One key, and I keep it. I make sure to park the anonymous rental car in the covered garage, backed in so the license plate is invisible. I've always hated the Tennessee rule that says front license plates aren't required . . . until now. It makes this a whole lot easier. If whoever's in that RV wants to check every white rental car in Knoxville, they're going to have a long job of it.

I have that weird déjà vu again as I lock the door behind us; the room's nice enough, but it's another anonymous, temporary shelter. So many in my history that it's disorienting. I got two beds. Carol sits down on one of them, testing the mattress and running her fingers wistfully over the clean covers. She bounces tentatively on it, as if she's forgotten what a bed feels like.

"What's your real name?" I ask her. She doesn't look at me. She keeps smoothing her hand over the sheets.

"Hickenlooper," she says. "Carol Hickenlooper."

I don't believe her, but I let it go. Something's nagging at me, but I can't put my finger on it. "If you want a shower, go ahead," I tell her. "I'm fine." I've brought in my small suitcase, and I unzip it to take out my laptop from the front pocket. I set it out on the small work table. The young woman practically jumps at the chance for the shower; she takes underwear and clean clothes—another plain shirt and long skirt, from what I can see—out of the backpack and goes into the small, clean bath area. I hear the click as the lock engages.

I lose no time before examining the backpack she's left behind, and just as I expected, I see Remy's initials in black permanent marker on the inside of the front pocket. That makes it real. And grim. And I don't believe that he gave it to her before his disappearance; he had it with him the night he disappeared from the bar. I saw it on the video.

She knows something. Saw something.

There's nothing else of his left inside it. The large back part holds women's underwear, a sports bra, a worn white nightgown made of cheap, light fabric with no adornments. Dirty clothing toward the bottom, neatly rolled and ready to be washed. In the smaller front area I find a battered paperback copy of the Bible—King James Version—with plenty of inked annotations. Some basic toiletries. A pair of cheap folding flat shoes, though it seems like those are for emergencies, since the soles are still clean. A washcloth almost certainly stolen from a hotel, a few miniature bars of soap, some nearly empty hotel complimentary shampoo bottles and lotions.

Carol may be homeless, at least for now, but she cares about being clean.

The shower's still running by the time I've examined everything. I end up looking at the Bible more closely, because the annotations seem . . . odd. Often they have dates attached to them.

I try something. I close the book, set it spine down on the work table, and let it fall open. It flops to a page that Carol must have frequently read. One verse—Colossians 1:26—stands out. It's been decorated with childish-looking stars.

Even the mystery which hath been hid from ages and from generations, but now is made manifest to his saints.

Saints. It rings a bell from something she said earlier. *Remy's with the saints.* I check a few more annotations. Chillingly, she's heavily marked the passages that have to do with the subjugation of women, with the note *memorize.* There's a quote written out on the inside cover of the Bible that I don't recognize: *So shall you bring Me saints, that I may take them unto Me for the war to come.*

The attribution at the bottom of that is F.T. No chapter or verse number.

I try scanning First Thessalonians. It's only four chapters, and short verses. I find only one reference to saints at the end, but it doesn't match this quote at all. I'm no Bible scholar, but something seems off, and I don't know what it is exactly. I try riffling through the copy again, looking for notations, and finally in Lamentations I find something circled with a star beside it, and a handwritten note in the margins: *Father Tom's message 4/2012.*

F.T. Father Tom.

I abandon the Bible and move to the computer, but a Google search for Father Tom just turns up dozens of entries for parish priests. That bothers me, and then it comes into sharp focus. *This is a King James Version Bible.* She's not Catholic. She's some flavor of Protestant, apparently. And Protestant churches have pastors, not priests or fathers. Unless there's a sect I don't know about.

I glance up at the old-fashioned nightstand clock on the bedside table. It's coming close on midnight now. No wonder I'm exhausted.

I keep staring at the digital display, not blinking. I don't even know why until I see the white scripted name of the maker on the corner of the device. It's small, but I can still read it from where I sit.

Hickenlooper.

No wonder that name seemed off.

I've missed a call; I had my ringer off. My phone buzzes to alert me to a voice mail, and I check the sender. It's from Sam. But it'll have to wait, because I hear the shower cut off, so I put the Bible back where I found it. I zip the backpack shut, and am at my laptop checking emails when she opens the bathroom door a few minutes later.

Her hair is up in a towel, but she's completely dressed. Pink-cheeked and relaxed from the shower. She sinks down on the bed with a sigh and moves the backpack farther away. "That felt really good," she says. "Thank you."

"Sure."

"And for the meal too. I haven't eaten like that in a while."

I sit back from the laptop and close the lid. I swivel the chair to face her. "How long have you been running from the cult?" It's a blind guess, but the verses she's marked, the name *Father Tom*, the dichotomy between that and the Protestant Bible, the RV following her . . . I think it's a good one.

Her lips open in surprise, and I see panic flash through her. She glances toward the door. I raise my eyebrows, but I don't say anything.

Her escape impulse is strong, but momentary. "A while," she says, then looks down. Her comfort is gone again. "Years now."

"Three years?"

She nods.

"Remy helped you escape?"

Another nod.

"Carol, you need to tell me what happened."

She's going to lie to me; I can feel it. But she looks like she's being completely frank.

"I'd already run away when I met Remy," she says. "I was hanging around Knoxville, and I started going to Gospel Witness. The pastor, he was really nice to me, and he let me stay at his house. He found me a safe place to live after that, and for a while it was fine. I met Remy at Bible study." She's very still. Unnaturally so, I think. Trying not to betray anything with her body language. It works, because it's hard to read a blank page. "He wasn't—I mean, we weren't together. We were just friendly. He had a girlfriend, I think, and I wasn't looking for anything from him. It was just nice to talk to him. He was concerned."

"He found out you'd been in a cult."

That got a slow nod. "He caught me crying one day. I shouldn't have told him, but . . . Remy was so easy to talk to. He wanted to help me," she says. "He was a nice young man. Godly."

Remy wasn't *that* godly, from what I've gathered; he liked a good time just fine. But I let that slide by. "What happened the night he disappeared, Carol?"

She's quiet for a few long seconds. She takes the towel off her head, and her damp hair cascades down, curling at the ends a little. She lets it shroud her face. "He was going to help me get out of town," she says. "He was supposed to meet me and give me some money. But he never showed up. I waited, but . . . he just never came, and nobody ever saw him again. I thought maybe he got grabbed."

"By the cult?"

She shrugs.

"Why would they take him? To get to you?"

Another shrug. She's not meeting my gaze anymore. She's lying to me. But at least she's talking.

"Carol. Look at me." She does, finally. There's a bleak light in her eyes. Resignation. "Where would they have taken him?"

"I don't know. They move around. They drive these RVs."

A mobile cult? That sounds terrifying. "How does the cult work, exactly?"

"The usual way." A bitter twist to her lips. "They drive us around and we preach to people, get gifts. Sometimes we recruit them, and they give up their family and money to get into heaven."

"Do they? Get into heaven?"

"I thought so, once. But . . ." She hesitates, then looks away again. "But maybe it was really just a lie. We never had any money, and it wasn't—it wasn't like I think heaven would be. And the way they treated us . . . like chattel. You know what chattel are?"

"Yes."

"Women especially. We had no say in anything. Not even in ourselves." She's talking around something dreadful, I can tell that from the tension in her body, as if she's tiptoeing along a cliff's edge. She pulls back, and laughs. It's a strangely empty sound. "Anyway."

"So how did you escape?"

"I didn't. Not on purpose, at first. I was late coming back after I went into this little store, and this man, he—he tried to pull me into his car. The convenience store clerk, he saw what was happening and called the police, and they arrested the man who tried to get me. But I couldn't leave, the police wouldn't let me until I gave a statement. The RV left, and I saw it parked down the block; they don't like to talk to the police. That's when I realized . . . I realized I had a chance. I just decided to get away. I don't really know why, exactly. I didn't know what I'd do, where I'd go."

"Couldn't you have gone home?" Three years ago she must have been a minor. She looks like she's barely twenty, if that.

"I didn't really have a home before Father Tom took me in. I was in foster care."

Vulnerable, no self-worth . . . ideal for a cult. Though she probably hadn't brought them much material wealth, being accepted and feeling loved would have made her loyal. It was a minor miracle she'd broken free, actually. Most people don't leave until things get so bad they just can't excuse it anymore, they're rescued . . . or they die.

I know part of the story she's told me is true. But I strongly suspect that she's still lying too. Maybe about small things; most people do. But she's unnervingly good, and it's impossible for me to judge whether she's really being straight with me about the most important parts of her story.

"When did you get the backpack?" I ask that because I have nothing to lose, and it might rattle her.

It doesn't. She blinks once, then says, "The day before he was supposed to meet me. Remy said it was an old one, he didn't need it." There's a slight edge to it, though. Something that tells me I brushed a nerve. "I didn't steal from him."

"I didn't mean to imply you did, Carol. What's your real name?"

"Hicken—"

"I saw the name on the clock."

She shuts up fast. Looks at me with a great deal more intensity than before. And I revise my assessment of her. She plays vulnerable with great skill. But she's not vulnerable. Not where it counts. There's an iron to her that shows only in flashes, and quickly vanishes beneath the camouflage.

She finally says, "I don't know what my birth last name was; they never told me. My last foster family was called Sadler. So I guess Carol Sadler, not that it matters so much. I don't even have anything to prove that. The church took it all when I joined."

She says *church* unconsciously. Not *cult*. And I know she's not talking about the little clapboard place where she was finding refuge with Pastor Wallace.

"What was it called? This church?" *Cult.*

She stares down for a long, long moment, then says, "It's called the Assembly of Saints. Anyway. I'm really tired now. I need to sleep."

Before I can even comment, she's pulling back the covers and climbing in, still fully dressed. She pulls the covers and a pillow over her head and burrows in like she intends to vanish into the soft cotton.

I'm not going to get anything else from her tonight. I'll try in the morning, but for now I leave it alone and go back to my computer. I send a summary of what I've learned to J. B., and document it in my online case notes. I make a note to investigate the name Carol Sadler, not that I think it's going to lead me anywhere useful. By the time I'm done, I'm pretty exhausted, but I still need to check Sam's voice mail.

I listen to what he reads me, and I open a document and run the message again as I type in names from the post he's narrating. There are six. One of them is Remy Landry. If the post's author is correct, five other young men have gone missing in the past few years. Just . . . vanished. Two left their dorm rooms at college and were never seen again. One was in high school and vanished after track practice. One on his way home from work. And the last one from a bar. Just like Remy.

I quickly run their names on J. B.'s proprietary company search, and there are open investigations into all of them. There's no commonality of place; they're all over the southeast. But they're all white, fit young men of a certain age: the youngest is seventeen, the oldest is twenty-two.

I step out of the room, lean against the hallway wall, and call Sam. He answers on the second ring. When I check the time, it's after one in the morning. "Hey," I say. "You still awake?"

"Yeah, I was hoping you'd call. Can't seem to sleep, even though I'm tired enough to crash like the Hindenburg."

"Ouch."

"Too soon?"

"Too accurate. Are you home?"

"No, we stopped at another hotel. I figure we'll hang here until Kezia gives us the all clear. Which shouldn't be too long, right? Bon Casey and Olly Belldene don't sound like masterminds."

I'm relieved he hasn't driven straight back to Stillhouse Lake. Far too many unknown threats there. "Enjoy the room service," I tell him. "I'm at a hotel too."

"How's the case going?"

"Interestingly," I say. I press my back against the wall. There's a head-ache forming behind my eyes, and I shut them for a moment. "She says she was supposed to meet Remy, and he was going to give her money to get out of Knoxville. But he never showed up, and nobody saw him again. And she's got his backpack. Now that I know there's a pattern of disappearances—thank you for that, by the way—I'll hit her up with the other names in the morning and see what happens." I debate for a second whether to tell him this, but plunge in. "She says she belonged to a cult. Well, she says 'church,' but everything about it screams 'cult' to me."

"Oh." I hear the shift in his voice. "Like Wolfhunter?" Wolfhunter had been a toxic tangle, but at the rotten heart of it had been a nasty cult, with a cruel philosophy of oppressing women. *Chattel.* Carol had said that. Most of the cult was dead; the leader, I'd heard, had gotten away. But surely that wasn't the same cult that Carol meant. As far as I knew, it hadn't been recruiting openly like this one.

"I don't know," I admit. "I can't get her to tell me much yet."

"She's still with you?"

"Yeah. My plan was to get her information and then let her leave in the morning. Buy her a plane ticket and get her somewhere safe."

"Maybe it's the connection, but I'm hearing a silent 'but,'" Sam says. I love talking to him. He's always either just a step behind or a step ahead. I never have to wait for him to catch up. "You don't believe her."

"Not entirely, no. I'm afraid that she's too good at playing the victim."

"Do you think she had something to do directly with Remy's abduction?"

"Maybe? I think there's a whole lot she hasn't said. Which means I can't really afford to put her on a plane and have her drop completely out of sight. I don't know what I'm going to do, exactly. I'm going to sleep on it tonight and decide in the morning."

"I wish we were home together," he says. "And I wish you weren't on your own with this."

"You've got my back."

"Always."

I let a beat go by. "How are they?"

"Sleeping," he says. "And in the morning they'll be missing you as much as I do."

"Tell them I love them," I say, and I hear the warmth flooding my voice. "And I love you too. Be safe."

"Love you, Gwen. Be safe."

I'm about to card back into the hotel room when I hear footsteps. I look up and toward the end of the hall where the elevators are; I've asked for a room close to the stairs, even though that's also the one with the most risk of break-ins, because it presents a fast escape if necessary. I'm being paranoid, of course. There's no way her cult could have traced us here.

Unless they have a car in addition to the RV. No. I'd have noticed. One thing I never am: complacent.

I relax when I see two uniformed police officers. Both African American women. They are walking briskly in my direction. I nod toward them, but I don't get a nod back. They head for me with laser purpose.

One of them says, "Back away from the door, ma'am."

They both put their hands on their guns.

I'm still wearing mine, and all of a sudden it feels more like a hot red bullet magnet than a means of defense. I don't know what's happening, but I do as they say. I back up against the far wall. I put my hands up above my shoulders, key card still in my right hand.

They turn me to face the wall. I don't resist, because I've looked over their gear and they look utterly authentic. And very, very tense. "I'm armed," I tell them. "Shoulder holster, left side. I have a carry permit in my wallet, but it's in the room."

"Keep your hands flat on the wall," one of them tells me, and I feel my gun being tugged free. "Okay. Hands down and behind your back."

"You're handcuffing me? What did I do?"

"It's for your safety, ma'am." The handcuffs click on, and I instinctively pull against them. It hurts.

"What the hell is happening?" I ask.

"Sit down," the officer facing me orders. She's got thick eyebrows and a harsh set to her jaw, and I silently slide down. "Cross your legs and *do not move* until I tell you."

"Officer, my name is Gwen Proctor—"

"I know what your name is," she snaps. "You have the right to stay silent, and you'd best use it."

The other officer is knocking on the door, and it's only a heartbeat later that Carol flings it open.

She's got a large red mark forming on her face that's going to be a bruise soon. One eye is already swelling.

And her hands are tied in front of her with one of the zip-tie flex cuffs I keep in my suitcase.

Fuck. I almost have to admire her.

"Help me," she says. She's sobbing. "Please help me!" She's utterly believable as a terror-stricken victim.

I feel the ground dropping out from under me, and at the same time a grim sense of my own stupidity. I went through her bag. I should have known she'd do the same the second I left her alone.

Should have seen this coming.

15

SAM

I get the call at 6:00 a.m. from Kezia that both of their suspects from Killing Rock are in custody, and we're clear to head home. That's good. I've tossed and turned all night, feeling like something wasn't right. Like I needed to be on the move.

"Thanks for the heads-up," I tell her. "Great work."

"Wasn't all that great, or much work," she says, and I hear the amusement in her voice. "Bon turned himself in; he's no fool. Olly Belldene was a surprise; I figured his old pappy would hide him out in the hills, but instead they called us to come get him. I can only guess they don't want us back on their property." She quickly gets serious again. "Sam, I'm going to need Lanny to come in and make formal IDs, and give another statement on the record. When do you think you can get here?"

"I'm a few hours out of town, just heading back," I tell her. "I'll give you a call." I don't commit to bringing Lanny in, or even what time we'll be home. For one thing, I might be taking care of her now, but I'm not her parent or legal guardian; they won't let me sit with her for the statement or lineup, and I want Gwen present. Not that I don't trust

Kez or Detective Prester; they're both straight arrows. But things have been known to go sideways, and sometimes it's nobody's fault.

I get the kids up. They're not happy at the early wake-up call, but after the initial grumpiness they're glad that the bad guys are safely behind bars, and we can get on our way. I don't tell Lanny the police want to talk to her again; there's no point in making her nervous. I get everybody in the car and on the road in an hour, which I figure is a world record, and we start the drive home.

I receive a phone call when I'm about an hour out from Stillhouse Lake, and check my phone. The phone, as Gwen advised, is new; I put all my usual close contacts in last night. I wouldn't normally accept a call from anyone off that list, but the caller ID says it's Gwen's boss, J. B. Hall. I feel ice form along my bones. I pull the car over to the side of the road and put the flashers on as I answer. "Hello?"

"Mr. Cade?" The voice on the other end is warm but serious. "Gwen gave me your new number. I promise you I won't give it out, first of all, I understand it needs to be kept confidential—"

I interrupt, because I can't wait. "Has something happened to Gwen?" I can't think of any other reason this woman would be calling me. None. And I feel my heart racing, and taste the acrid, bitter surge of adrenaline.

"She's safe," J. B. says, and I let my breath out in a rush. *Oh, thank God.* Connor was sleeping in the passenger seat, but the tension in my voice has woken him up, and he's staring at me with worry. His sister's still crashed out behind us with her headphones on. "She's perfectly fine, Sam. I've just seen her."

"Okay. So why are you calling me?"

"Because she's been arrested on charges of assault."

I open my mouth and close it without saying anything. I can legitimately think of a dozen situations where Gwen might go mixed martial arts, but when I spoke to her last night, she wasn't in any of those. J. B. doesn't wait for me to ask, and continues, "The young woman she was

155

interviewing? Carol? She set Gwen up the second Gwen left the room to talk to you. Self-inflicted injuries and a call to 911, and Gwen found herself off to a cell for the rest of the night. Carol refused hospital treatment and vanished as soon as she gave her statement, and the police are already figuring out the whole thing is bogus. I'm at the courthouse now, and she'll be out on bail soon. Don't worry, the case will be dropped. The detective in charge understands what's going on here."

I remember the call with Gwen, the easy way we'd talked. Everything had been fine when we'd ended it, but things must have gone wrong immediately after. Gwen's not easily fooled, or easily manipulated. This Carol must have been really, really good to pull it off.

"Sam—" J. B. seems like she's hating what she's about to say next. "You realize that the story's about to break that she's been arrested for assault, right? The circumstances will be gas on a bonfire. The fact that a young woman accused Gwen of holding her prisoner—"

I squeeze my eyes shut and take a deep breath before I say, "Media feeding frenzy. I understand."

"It won't take them long to get to Stillhouse Lake and lay siege to your house. You can bring the kids to Knoxville—"

"Yeah, bit of a problem with that. We need to talk to the cops in Norton. Lanny's a witness to something that happened the other night, and she needs to make an identification. Can't avoid that." I think about it for a few seconds. J. B. waits. "Okay, we'll go home, get what we need, go to the police station, and leave from there for your offices." More hotels in our future . . . or maybe not. Maybe we just find a place in Knoxville and send movers back to pack us up at the house. Maybe this is just the clean break we really need. It won't be easy for Gwen to make that move, but this does make it a more clear-cut decision. Solves our Belldene problems at the same time.

But damn, I hate to think about the reporters who are going to come hunting us. J. B. will protect our privacy as much as she can, but inevitably we'll be found. I can already imagine the clever questions: *So, as the brother of one of Melvin Royal's victims, how does it feel to hear Gina Royal is being charged in connection with assault and abduction?* Or, *Do you believe, given this new accusation, that Gina Royal is still innocent of involvement in her husband's crimes?* I've got zero interest in answering any of those things, unless my response starts and ends with *fuck off.*

I finish with J. B. and click the flashers off. I pull back into the sparse traffic before I ask Connor, "Did you get all that?"

"Some of it," he says. "Mom's in trouble?"

"Maybe not for long," I tell him. I don't want the kid worrying. "We'll see her this afternoon at the latest, okay?"

"Okay." He's quiet for a moment before he says, "Sam? I—I wish things could just go back to the way they used to be."

"Oh yeah? When?" That's bitter, and I wish I hadn't said it. "I'm sorry, Connor. Didn't mean that. You mean a couple of summers back, when we were building the deck?" That was when we'd gotten to really know each other, and I'd realized what amazing kids Gwen had raised. And what a good woman she was. And yes, it had been a sweetly glorious time.

"Yeah," he says softly. "I just want things to be okay again. Not all the reporters and the people hating us and coming after us all the time."

"Normal life," I say, and he nods. "Okay. I promise you that we'll try to get there. It's never going to be boring, though. You know that, right?"

He smiles and looks out the window. "Yeah," he says. "I mean, Mom. Not boring."

"Nope. Me, I'm pretty boring, though. Maybe it'll even out."

"I don't think you're boring."

"Good to hear." I ruffle his hair, and he punches my arm, and we're okay again. For now. But the kid's right. We need normal. Badly. Between Connor's horrible experience at school, Lanny's close call at the lake, Gwen's arrest . . . not our best of times. I'm looking forward to the relative peace of Knoxville, and I'm hoping that J. B. will take Gwen off this case and let us just deal with things.

We're a few miles from Norton when I get another call. This one's in my phone book, and even though it's not legal to talk and drive, I grab the phone and lift it to my ear instead of putting it on speaker. Connor's already on edge. I don't want to make things worse.

"Hey," I say. "Javi?"

Javier Esparza says, "Man, when you guys fall in the shit, you really get in there, don't you?"

"You calling just to cheer me up or what?" Javier is a good friend, a good dude and retired marine; he calls me Chair Force, and I call him Jarhead, and we're still brothers in arms in every sense. He runs the local gun range, which is one of my favorite places around Stillhouse Lake. We have a friendly game of center bull's-eyes at the target range. So far, he's up by one point out of thirtysomething matches. He's way better than me at longer-range matches, but short range, I can give him a run. Javier is a genuinely stand-up guy who's had our backs in several nasty situations.

Speaking of which, I owe him either a round of cleaning toilets at the range for losing that last shooting match, or letting him teach me how to scuba dive. I have no intention of scuba diving. I hate swimming. I'd rather scrub the men's room.

"Wish I was," he says. "Kez is worried." Kezia is Javier's mostly live-in girlfriend.

"What's she worried about, exactly?"

"She'd kill me if she knew I said anything to you, so I didn't say anything, right?"

"Absolutely."

"She's worried that this is going to fall wrong for Lanny. Look, Bon and Olly aren't good people; everybody knows that. Problem is they're telling consistent stories. And she hasn't disclosed everything."

"Meaning?"

"She was with somebody else at that party, man. She didn't come alone. Some girlfriend or something. You need to get her to come clean before this goes bad. She can't hold back if she wants them to believe her story over theirs. Hell, they turned themselves in. That earns them a listen, at least."

I want to argue Lanny's innocence, but fact is, I wasn't there. Gwen and I entered this particular story after most of it happened, and though I believe the kid, I can't *know* what happened. He's right. Having one of the Belldenes, of all people, turn themselves in? That's a pretty strong statement.

"Okay," I say. "I'll talk to her." I make sure not to glance back at Lanny, though I'm tempted. This can all wait until we're home. In the rearview mirror I can see she's still lying down, eyes shut. I can hear the tinny rattle of headphones from here. "Any other good news?"

"Well, I booked the pool for tomorrow like we agreed," he says.

"Javi—okay, first of all, I never said I'd *do* it . . ."

"You lost the bet, man. You owe me. You put on the gear and get in the water. Hey, if you'd won, you'd have definitely taken me up in one of those prop planes and barrel-rolled me until I puked."

"I would," I admit. "But given the circumstances with Lanny . . . maybe I'd better just go for cleaning the toilets. Option B."

"You ever seen what these toilets look like? I get hill people and truckers in here. None of them have good aim off the range. But sure. Your choice."

He's trying hard to lighten the mood, even though the Lanny thing is serious. I appreciate that. "I will personally scrub that porcelain until it shines. You can't make me a marine no matter how hard you try."

Javier sounds like he's suppressing a laugh when he replies. "Okay, okay, I know. Hey, I'll be kind. I won't even make you use a toothbrush to clean the place."

"Better than boot camp."

He lets a beat go by, and when he comes back, he's serious. "You take care out there, my friend. And remember: you got people who care."

"I know," I tell him. "So do you. In case you were wondering."

"I'm not the one in trouble. When I am, you're my first call. Well, second. After Kez."

"Fair enough."

We sign off, and despite the worries, I do feel better. We aren't hunted and alone.

Well, not alone anyway.

The road turns familiar. Norton's the same sleepy place it always is, and then we're past it on the road out to the lake. I glance over at the beach at Killing Rock as we pass it; someone's made an effort to clean it up while we were gone. No debris that I can spot, though there's a torn flutter of police tape still tied to a tree. It just reminds me that our troubles aren't over.

And I'm going to have to have a serious conversation with Lanny, as soon as we're inside.

As we pull to a stop in the driveway, my instincts wake up. I don't even know why until I fix my gaze on Lanny's bedroom window.

It's open about three inches, and a little flutter of sheer curtain is ruffling.

Lanny's yawning, and she and Connor are already bickering about who's going to get the shower first when I say, "Quiet."

I get their instant and baffled attention. "Uh, sorry?" Lanny says. "Did you just tell us to shut up—"

"Why is your window open?"

I'm looking at her in the rearview mirror, and I see the exact second guilt hits her. She knows what I'm talking about, but she says, "I don't know! Maybe somebody broke in?"

"Without setting the alarm off."

She doesn't answer that. I've already figured it out: she cut her window out of the alarm system. That's how she got out the other night, and I should have realized that and fixed it before we left. *Dammit.* We were too distracted. And too worried about her.

But I can see by her expression that sneaking out isn't the whole story. I think about Javier's call, the fact that she was *with* someone at the party. And I say, "Who's inside our house, Lanny?"

"I don't know!"

"Yes, you do," Connor says. "It's probably Vee."

"Shut up, you traitor!" Lanny snaps.

He shrugs. "Your fault," he replies, and turns to me. "Vee's been coming to the house."

"Vee Crockett," I say. Jesus, Vee is one messed-up kid. I care about her, but . . . there's no denying how much baggage she carries. She had problems even before her mom's death, and I can't imagine that made things better. I don't want Lanny caught up in her drama. "You didn't tell your mom about this either?"

She just shakes her head.

Dammit. I'm realizing this explains a lot. "Vee's the reason you went to the party at Killing Rock." It was well out of character for Lanny to do that; Vee instigating the whole thing makes perfect sense.

No answer that time, but I'm sure I'm right. I'm not *that* old. I remember why I sneaked out to parties at that age, and it wasn't just to hang out with my buddies. It was usually to impress girls.

I keep going. "Lanny, you outright lied to the cops about being alone at the party. And to us. Was she up on that rock with you too?"

"Vee didn't do anything!"

"Oh? And were you with her the whole time at the party?"

She doesn't say anything to that, which is an answer in itself. Vee tearing through a party, with Lanny chasing after. It's incredibly worrying that Lanny's covering up for her, when it's Lanny's ass on the line now.

Connor's still watching the open window. He says, "You shouldn't go in there. What if it's one of those Belldenes, not Vee?"

He's got a point, but I'm pretty certain that the Belldenes would have set off the alarm. They're not subtle; they'd just put a boot through our front door, trash the place, and be gone before anyone arrived. And how would they even know the window was off the system?

Still, he's got a point. It isn't as if we don't have multiple threats coming our way. So I tell them to stay in the car. Lanny grips her cell phone in white-knuckled hands; she'll call for help if it comes to that. I can count on her for that much, at least.

I walk up to Lanny's window and part the curtains to look inside.

Vee Crockett is sitting on the edge of the bed staring at me, gripping a bat she's grabbed up off the floor. She's panicked and ready to swing. In Wolfhunter, she alternated between feral and traumatized. I can't say this is miles better. "Easy, Vee. It's just me. Sam Cade. Remember? I live here."

It takes her a second, but the bat gets lowered. She still hangs on to it. "Oh. You're back," she says. "I was asleep." She looks it. Her heavy makeup is smeared, her hair's a mess, and she seems completely hungover.

"I'm coming in the front door," I tell her. "Stay there. Don't run; you're not in trouble."

She doesn't believe that; I can see it. I shut the window in case that will delay her a couple of seconds, go to the front door, unlock it, and type in the code as I step in. Then I move back to the window, where Vee has thrown out a dirty blue duffel bag and has one leg out to follow it. "Please don't," I tell her again. "We're not your problem. Come in, take a shower, rest. It's okay."

She's wary, but she's also bone tired, I can see it. And scared. "Is Lanny here?"

"Yeah." I turn and gesture for the kids to come out of the SUV. They do, and both join me at the window.

"Hey, Vee," Connor says. "You look like hell."

"Nobody asked you," she snaps back, but she's looking at Lanny. And Lanny's looking at her. And I know that expression. I get it myself from time to time when I see Gwen.

Man, I really don't need these two to be in love.

"Inside," I tell everybody. "We'll get the bags later." I head to Lanny's window and pick up Vee's duffel bag from the ground. "Except this one. This one goes into the living room with me." Because I know she's not going to abandon it. If she would have, she'd have run and left it behind when I gave her the shot.

"Hey!" Vee protests, and makes a grab for the bag. I step back out of reach. She's still half out the window, glaring.

"Come on. I'll make coffee."

I don't know if it's the promise of coffee or me hijacking her bag, but when I look back, she's ducked back inside Lanny's room and slammed the window. I've earned a few minutes of her time, at least. I'm sure that isn't how Gwen would have done it, but I feel pretty sad for the kid. She's had a shit life, and it looks like it hasn't gotten much better since we left her in Wolfhunter.

We get in. Coffee gets made. Lanny and Vee perch together on the sofa; I say *perch* because Vee looks like she's ready to launch herself up to fight or run at any second. I recognize that bone-deep wariness. I see it in Gwen from time to time, and I know where it comes from.

I keep it light and calm and easy. I make the coffee the way they ask for it—not for Connor; he gets hot cocoa—and make an offer of lunch once the coffee's down. Vee looks less likely to bite and flee, and at the prospect of a home-cooked meal she has a moment of real longing. "Spaghetti's easy," I tell them. "Fifteen minutes." That's cutting corners, but I don't feel like this is a situation where attention to the culinary details is going to be useful. Lanny's gaze begs her to say yes, and Vee finally nods. Stiffly, like her neck's a steel rod.

I still don't talk about anything but the drive back until we're around the table, and Vee's fully invested in her spaghetti and meatballs. Then I say, "Okay. So. Vee, you bolted from the foster home. Right? Easy, I'm not judging you. I just need to know facts."

She's not running from her food. She's got her hand curled protectively around the bowl. But her eyes warn me not to push.

Too bad.

"Yeah," she finally says. "I ran. So?"

"You got a good reason?"

"They were assholes."

"What made them assholes?"

"Nothing," she says. "I was better off on my own."

I don't debate that. I don't know the full story, and I don't want to quiz her about potential abuse. That's for the cops to sort out. It's important I don't doubt her, or alienate her; she'll be off like a shot if I do. Probably taking the bowl with her.

"You got a place to stay?" I ask her. I know she doesn't; if she did, she wouldn't have been sneaking into our house.

"Little place in the woods," she says. "More of a lean-to. It ain't a palace."

"Doesn't sound very safe," I say. "You want to stay here? With us?"

Her eyes widen. She looks around, as if she can't believe anybody shares in such luxury. I just see a regular middle-class house with a fairly comfortable couch and a good on-sale TV. But mileage varies. "Here?" she says. "Where?"

"My room," Lanny says, at the same time that I say, "The couch folds out," and that's awkward. But I'm damn sure not putting a lovestruck kid in bed with Vee Crockett and trusting nothing's going to happen. I'm pretty sure Gwen would say the same. Which reminds me, again, how much I miss Gwen's presence in this conversation. I'd expected J. B. to call by now, but when I glance at my phone, there's nothing yet.

"She's staying with me. In my room," Lanny declares, as if she's the decision-maker here.

"Nope," I say, and eat some more spaghetti. I'm not going to argue about it, and she knows that. She glares. "The couch bed is comfortable. I should know, I slept there for a couple of months." Gwen and I had things to work out after she discovered how involved I was with the Lost Angels. That wasn't fun, but I'm not lying about the comfortable bed.

"It's fine," Vee says to Lanny. "Not that I don't like *your* bed." She winks, and I open my mouth to ask how many times *that's* happened, but then I think better of it. Lanny's face has blotched scarlet, and she looks deeply shocked that Vee's said that in front of me.

"Vee," I say instead of running after that bait, "are we going to be getting a knock on the door from the police, looking for you? Would anything you're running from cause that? I don't mean just bouncing from the foster home—I grew up in the system, and I bounced from a few too. I mean actual crimes they can tie back to you."

She stops eating. She looks at me, and I remember that flat, simmering resentment in her eyes. It hasn't changed since Wolfhunter. "I ain't killed nobody recently," she says. "If that's what you're asking." It's sarcastic. Vee Crockett was accused of her mother's murder. As far as I know, she's never actually killed anyone.

Doesn't make me trust her.

"I was clear," I say. "Straight answer, Vee. If you want to stay."

She's aware that I'm serious. I see her calculating. She's a smart kid—not book-smart, but she reads people well. It's something kids who live on the edges develop early. Some turn it into pure con artistry. Some use it defensively, like she does. She'll try to game me if she thinks that will work.

She must see it won't, because she says, "I done what I had to do. Some of it might not be strictly legal, I guess."

"Bad enough to have warrants out?"

She just shakes her head on that one. I don't think she's lying. "Okay. You can stay until Gwen gets back. Then we have a deeper conversation. Finish lunch. You three get to Roshambo for who does dishes." I eat the rest of my spaghetti and check my phone. No calls from Gwen. I text her one-handed. Funny story, we have a new house-guest. If anything will make her get back to me, I figure that will do it.

I watch the screen.

No answer.

I start feeling that tension creep up my spine, knotting muscles as it goes. The kids are talking. I'm not listening. My focus is all on that screen.

Nothing.

"Cleanup duty, all of you," I tell them as I stand up. "I need to make a call. Lanny, put the window back on the alarm circuit and lock it up. Vee, that alarm stays on all the time. You're free to leave if you want to, but you ask before you open that door. Understand?"

She gives me a tired salute. "Yes, boss."

"Don't be a smart-ass, we're full up." I'm already walking for the office. Gwen's added soundproofing, since so many of her phone calls are confidential. I don't want the kids to hear me right now.

I call J. B.'s number, and she picks up on the first ring. "Sorry, I was about to call you. The court isn't quite running on time. Gwen's being arraigned in about an hour, and then I can post her bail."

"I was hoping the whole thing would be dismissed."

"I know. I was hoping for that, too, but the local DA is getting his fifteen minutes of press attention before he lets it fall apart; Carol's already disappeared, and the phone number Gwen used to track her is already dead, so they've got nothing. I doubt the cops are going to find her again; this girl seems to have a real talent for vanishing. Did Gwen tell you about—" She leaves it for me to fill in. So I do.

"About the cult the girl's running from? Yeah. It sounds familiar."

"There are definitely similarities to the Wolfhunter cult, but that got cut off at the knees. It's very possible that the Wolfhunter location was just one of several, though. You should check with your friend Mike Lustig. FBI, right?"

"Right," I say. Mike was intensely involved in our Wolfhunter problems; he saw how it all worked firsthand, and knowing Mike, he'd still be digging into that cult if there were anything left to find. "I'll ask him about it if it would help."

"It might," she admits. "Okay. I'll get back in touch once Gwen's free. Just take care out there. Fallout from this is inevitable, I'm afraid."

"Copy that. Tell Gwen—ah, hell. She knows."

I hang up after polite goodbyes and pull up the Knoxville criminal courts docket. If the reporters haven't already recognized her name, the firestorm will start burning our direction soon. I have until then to make sure the kids—including Vee Crockett, now, because I just made her our responsibility—are safe and our defenses are solid.

The first call I make is to Kezia to alert her; she'll notify the rest of the Norton PD that we're going to need eyes on our house to control any journalists who stampede this way. We've got protocols, so I'm not really worried until Kez says, "I was hoping not to talk to you, Sam."

I don't like that. At all. "Why?"

"Because the statements that our suspects are giving contradict what Lanny told us. They say that they knew nothing about Candy, but that they only chased Lanny because they thought she was the one who did it and they were—I'm quoting a Belldene here, remember—trying to bring her to justice."

"Bullshit," I bark.

"And they're shoveling it high and deep. Anyway, we're going to need that girl in sooner rather than later."

"I'm not doing that."

"Sam."

"Come on. I know you're fair. But will the county DA, or the judges, or a jury around here be that fair? Kez. It's not like this tie will go to the killer's daughter." I can hear the arguments now. We're the newcomers. The strangers. Lanny's got *bad influences*. The Belldenes have been part of this town since before the Civil War. Tie goes to the locals.

"Sam, I'm going to do what I can, you know that. But you've got to bring her in and get this cleared up."

"Can't," I say. "I'm not her legal guardian. Gwen's not here right now." I've never been so glad of that. They can't interview someone Lanny's age without a parent or legal guardian's permission. And Gwen's very unavailable right now. "I'll let you know when she's back."

Kez sighs. "Dammit, don't try to pull something clever. I don't want to be looking for you too."

She's a good friend, Kezia. But that doesn't mean she won't come after me and throw my ass in jail. I know that.

"I'll call when I get Gwen back," I tell her. "Until then, you're not talking to Atlanta Proctor. No offense meant."

"None taken. I'm glad she's got advocates. Talk to you soon, Sam. A patrol unit's going to be hanging around the lake, like you asked." That's both to help out with the reporters who will descend, and also to alert Kez when Gwen gets back. Dual duty.

I think about what else I can do. Not much, as it turns out, which is frustrating. By the time I could get to Knoxville, Gwen will be bailed out and headed home. But hunkering down here, however logical it is right now, that feels wrong too.

I look up at a knock on the office door, and get up to open it. It's Vee Crockett. "Hey," she says. "Can I come in a minute?"

I gesture her into the room and, on a hunch, shut the door behind her. She settles into Gwen's office chair and spins it around, leaning back at such an angle I'm afraid she's going to tip and break her neck. I reach over and close down the laptop screen.

"I wasn't looking," she says, and suddenly stops spinning to stare at me. "You wonder why I come all the way here, right?"

"You're not here for Lanny?"

She smiles. It's not quite right, that smile. Makes me tense up. "Nope," she says. "Well, I like Lanta all right. She's a cutie pie. But there's something I wanted to tell Ms. Proctor."

"Okay. What is it?"

"You ain't Ms. Proctor," she says.

"Vee, I have had a shitty day, I'm really tired, and I've got no patience for bullshit right now. Just spit it out."

She sizes me up, then nods. "It's about Vernon Carr. The man what owned that compound outside Wolfhunter? Owned the garage too?"

Cult leader. All-around asshole too. "What about him?"

"I know where he's at."

I don't honestly know whether to believe her. She looks smug enough. But I shake my head. "Tell the FBI; they're the ones looking for him."

"I figure there could be a reward. But they won't give it to me. I ain't old enough. But you could get it and give it to me."

I'm way too tired for this. Too worried about Gwen and Lanny and Connor. "We're not cops, we're not agents, and I'm not lying to the FBI for you. Okay, Vee? You can stay here until Gwen gets back, and then we'll have a conversation about what comes next. That's the best offer you're getting. How's that?"

"Sucks," she says crisply. "And you're kind of an asshole, Sam."

"When I need to be. But mostly I'm just too tired to sugarcoat things right now." I expect her to leave. She doesn't. She spins the chair again, but more slowly. "Vee. Go. I need to make some calls."

"In a minute." She faces me again. "What if I told you ol' Vern ran off to join up with Father Tom?"

"I don't know who that is, either, so—"

"You don't know a hell of a lot, do you? *Everybody* up in Wolfhunter knew about Father Tom."

"Because . . ."

"Because he started there. He's the one started the Assembly."

"A church?"

"Some might say." She nods. "It's what Carr was heading up when everybody out there got shot. Assembly's short for Assembly of Saints, which is Father Tom's place. Stands to reason that's where you ought to be looking for Carr. Where Father Tom is."

Not a church. A cult. I'd never found out the name of the group living out on Carr's land, or even if it had one. And . . . Gwen's looking for a cult now too. I lean forward, suddenly very interested. "Wait," I say. "Carr didn't start that cult living in his compound?"

"Nope, just ran it. Father Tom started it, but then he left. Got a bigger place, more followers. He didn't want to stay in Wolfhunter. Who would?"

Legitimate question. "Do you know where Father Tom moved his cult, then?"

She shrugs, and for the first time she looks away. Picks at the material of her pants. She's nervous, and Vee Crockett doesn't *get* nervous.

"Vee? You can tell me."

She whips her head back toward me, and I see her consciously armor herself up again. "I don't know nothing about *that*."

"You told me you knew where Carr was."

"Yeah, I just *told* you, he's up with Father Tom! I don't know where it is on a map!"

"Are you sure you're telling me the truth?"

"Because I'm a liar, right?" she says, and is instantly on her feet. She's got unnerving eyes, but never more so than when she's angry, and right now, she's burning with it. "Fine, I'm a liar. Fuck you, I'm out."

As quickly as she came, she's gone out the office door and slamming it behind her. I put my head in my hands and squeeze in frustration.

My headache's getting worse. I need to figure out what the hell game Vera is really playing here. She's a clever kid, but she's also dangerous.

Some painkillers and a cold shower slap some energy back into my bloodstream. It does wake me up, though it doesn't do much for the aches. I make more coffee, and I'm drinking it when I realize that I don't know where Vee has gone. Or Lanny, for that matter. I knock on Lanny's closed door.

"Yeah?" she calls. "I'm not dressed!"

"Is Vee in there with you?" I ask.

"No. She's in the living room!"

Vee isn't in the living room. She also isn't in the rest of the house. I search it methodically, room by room, closets included. Anything large enough for her to hide inside.

When I check the security system, it's disabled. I quickly reset it. *Fuck.* I know I covered the panel when I keyed in the code, how the hell did she . . .

And then I realize. I'd automatically put the SUV's keys on the hanging rack by the door . . . and there's a remote control for the system on the key chain. All she had to do was press the button. And in the shower, I missed the telltale beep.

When Lanny opens her door I check her room, but there's no sign of Vee there either. She's gone.

And she took her duffel bag with her. She's not coming back.

"What did you say to her, Sam?" That's Lanny, glaring at me. "Did you make her leave?"

"I said she could stay. I didn't make her go anywhere."

"But you must have said something!"

Maybe it was my fault. I pushed her, and she went off like a Roman candle. Which, I realize now, would be consistent for someone with her particular combination of aggressiveness and trauma. I got close to something that scared her or was painful to her. Either way, her instinct was to run.

"We have to go find her," Lanny says. I stop her as she heads for the door, and set the alarm back when she keys it in. I change the code while I'm at it. "Sam!"

"No," I say. "Not until your mom is back. You're not going anywhere."

"*We have to—*"

"Lanny! We're not going anywhere. That's enough." We don't have *time* for Vera Crockett and her maybe-made-up stories.

I don't expect Lanny to defy me. That's a failure of imagination on my part, because she glares at me and throws the front door wide open. The alarm starts blaring. I quickly key it off, but by then Lanny's running down the hill. And she's fast.

Dammit, kid . . .

I shut and lock the door and run after her, but she darts into the tree line, and I lose her within the next couple of minutes. If she doesn't want to be found, I'm not going to find her like this. So I stop, pull out my phone, and call up the tracking app.

She's disabled it on her new phone already. *Dammit.*

Not enough coffee in the world for this day.

"Lanny!" I shout. "Come *on*. Don't do this. Not today."

I know she's heard me. But there's no answer. I turn and head back toward the house. As I do, I see something in the trees on the other side. A glint from glass. Could be a camera lens, and my first thought is that the reporters are back, and *dammit*, not now.

But then I realize there's a man sitting almost motionless in the shadows. He's a young man with a ragged beard in high-quality, dirty camouflage. Probably one of the Belldene clan.

The fact that he's looking through a rifle scope at me is what I realize next, and I don't think. I just spin and flatten myself behind the thickest available tree.

And I see Lanny coming out of the underbrush toward me. She's got a red scratch on her cheek, and a dry leaf caught in her hair, and I let out a wordless yell and tackle her to the leaf litter because if *she gets shot because of me . . .*

But there's no shot.

Lanny yelps and beats at me with her fists until I roll away; I fishtail around and crawl to where I can get a look at the nest where the man aiming at me is.

But he's gone. Just . . . gone. Like he never existed.

Lanny's furious, but I rush her into the house, grab my handgun, and go out to check the spot, and what I find there proves to me I wasn't imagining things. It's a printed picture of me standing on the porch, talking to Gwen. Couldn't have been taken too long ago, maybe a couple of weeks at most; I can see that dead leaves are piled up near the steps, and I raked those away ten days ago.

The writing on it says SOON.

And there's a sharp-pointed rifle round sitting on top of the picture, right over my face.

16

GWEN

Jail brings flashbacks of being arrested on the day Melvin was caught. I was held for days before they finally charged me too. Not pleasant memories, and I try to remember that time is over, and this is a different situation. I still have to spend my time behind bars going through all my coping exercises, one after another, to keep myself from feeling the panic that knocks on the door of my head. It almost works.

When they call me out for my hearing, I fight to keep my head above the tide of utter despair that threatens to engulf me, the impulse to panic and fight and run. I think I'm succeeding at that too.

Until I'm not. Because the small courtroom is packed to the gills with reporters. I should have realized that would happen; no doubt they were given the heads-up, and ever since Melvin's trial my name is instant news catnip. I'm dealing with that, or at least I think I am, until the sight of J. B. Hall's friendly middle-aged face takes my knees out from under me. Relief hits so hard it feels abusive. I sway, and the deputy puts a hand on my shoulder to steady me. She's a big woman, and she gives me a concerned look. "You okay?"

"I'm fine," I tell her, though it's true only in the broadest sense. She takes me through the wooden gate to the defendant's table, where my lawyer is standing up studying a file folder. He's a round African American man with triple chins and an old suit, and he greets me professionally and seems damn competent. I'll get through this. I've been through this before, charged as Melvin's accomplice. Charged, and acquitted. I survived that, with a packed courtroom full of shouting, angry people beaming real hate at me. I can certainly do this.

The fact that I want to curl up in a ball and scream uncontrollably that I have to go through this again is beside the point. I put on my game face and nod to my lawyer like I'm a pro, and he shakes my hand. I sit. He does, too, a little abruptly. "This should go fast," he says. "They're arraigning you for felony assault. I assume you're pleading . . ."

"Not guilty."

"Okay, that keeps it simple. Anything you need to tell me?"

"It's total bullshit."

"Good enough."

I turn to look at J. B. Hall, who's claimed the seat right behind me. She looks as sharp as I remember: an older pale woman, dressed in an effortlessly intimidating pantsuit. No makeup, a blunt haircut, and everything about her radiates competence and power.

She leans forward. There are journalists on either side of her, but she cheerfully ignores them.

"Hey," she says. "So. I was hoping this would get dismissed before we got to this point, but the DA is a prick and he wants to coast on your notoriety while he can. You all right?"

I'm not, but I nod. "Thanks for coming," I say.

"No problem. Soon as this is done, I'll get you out of here." We're talking in low tones; even though the two reporters are leaning in and trying to get a listen—discreetly, of course—the hubbub of the room works in our favor.

"What about Carol? Do they have her in custody?"

"I'm afraid not. They got her statement, and as soon as their backs were turned, she ghosted. The address she gave them is a liquor store, by the way. They know they've been had on this one. And forensics is casting serious shade on her entire story."

"And they're still doing it?"

She shrugs. "Our fearless DA here is eager to get some press attention before the upcoming election cycle. He'd like to be known as tough on crime, and it helps that your connection with a serial killer always gets attention. It's just politics. My information is that they'll drop the charges in twenty-four hours. Quietly. It'll be buried on the back pages."

I'd like to reply with what I think of that, but it's too late. The judge enters, we all rise, and the dry proceedings . . . proceed. My lawyer at least tries to argue the merits for dismissal, but it's over fast. He knows it's a political stunt, and in ten minutes we're done. Bail is set at $50,000; J. B. is already headed for the clerk to pay it when I'm led away again.

It takes another hour to bust me loose into her custody, and once we're outside and I'm breathing free air again, the shakes set in hard. I have to sit down on the closest bench. J. B. waits calmly next to me. "Hey," she finally says. "You did good work, Gwen. It's not your fault that you got taken by an expert. All indications are this Carol is one hell of a con artist."

I swallow back my tide of anxiety. "Do you think there was any truth to the cult thing? That she's on the run from them?"

"Do you?"

I don't know why she'd fake that Bible, or wear the clothes she does, if it wasn't on some level authentic. And how Carol, the brash con woman, seemed completely helpless at the sight of that circling RV. That's conditioning. And terror. "Yeah, I do. It feels like she might have some thread of truth in all this. The story she told me was of a cult that operated some mobile preaching/recruitment mission out of RVs. You ever heard of anything like that? Maybe something run by a guy named Father Tom?"

"Doesn't ring a bell, but I'll ask around. Unfortunately, religious cults are always in style." She slides me a sideways look. "You got anything else for me to go on?"

"Yeah." I take a deep breath. "Got a pen?" She does. I reel off the five extra names Sam gave me last night.

"Okay, what am I looking for?"

"It might all be connected," I tell her. J. B. looks up, frowning. "These young men also disappeared. I don't think Remy's the only one."

"Lord Almighty, are you telling me that they've all joined this cult?"

"If they have, it might not have been under their own power," I say. "And from what Carol said—if we can believe anything she said—they might not have survived."

J. B. looks shaken. I feel it too. It's like cracking open an egg and getting a flood of spiders. "I'll look into it," she says. "If it's true, this may be bigger than we can handle."

"Did you check into the nonprofit who hired us?"

"Yeah. It's a religious group called All Saints International. It traces back to what is essentially a business park that runs an administrative service for small organizations, some of which look pretty shady to me. I don't know they would have . . ."

Her voice fades away in my ears, because I feel a sudden snap of realization and a hot burn of anxiety. *All Saints International.* All those marked passages about saints. The quote in the front of the Bible. Carol saying that Remy's with the saints.

That cannot be a coincidence. But why the hell would they hire us to investigate Remy if they'd actually taken him?

Because they know we're not going to find him. They want to find Carol. Holy shit. We've been played. Carol knew someone would come looking. It wasn't a coincidence that they'd found her at the bus station; *I'd* found her for them. She ran because she knew that.

Carol knows things they can't afford to have revealed.

"Gwen?" J. B. asks, and I snap back to focus on her again. I explain my theory, and I see the grimness set into her expression when she thinks it through. "Those bastards. They used us."

"I can't look for Carol anymore," I tell her. "But maybe someone else can. I can keep them focused on me. You can locate Carol and get her to safety."

"How? She's not about to trust me any more than you. Or anyone, as far as I can tell."

J. B. has a point. And I don't have an answer. It's frustrating, and I desperately want to find out what happened to Remy, but I need to back away from Carol. At least for now.

I sigh. "Just try, okay? By the way, sorry about the bail. I appreciate it."

"This? This is nothing. I've had to rescue my people from way worse situations than this. But stay out of trouble for a while, okay? This case will go away; a news cycle of coverage is all the DA's going to need, and then he'll quietly dismiss. I'll dig into All Saints International a little deeper, particularly the corporate officers. Might be something there. I'll follow up on these other cases too. But you need to get home."

"My rental car's still at the hotel."

"I'll drive you back to Stillhouse Lake, and have one of my local guys take the rental back. Deal?"

The idea of going home to my family sounds like heaven. "Deal," I agree. "Thank you."

Once we're at J. B.'s spacious sedan, she stops and opens the trunk. There's a solid lockbox inside, and she takes it out and hands it to me, along with a set of small keys. "It's a loaner," she says. "Since they're not releasing your gun back to you until the case is dismissed, and I don't want you running around without anything. Lose it and you're dead to me."

She's not kidding, and I nod. I get into the passenger seat and open the lockbox. Inside is a pretty fine Browning 9 mm, and ammunition to go with it. There's even a belt clip holster. I prefer a shoulder holster, but I'm grateful for anything. I put it on my right side, and the weight makes tension unspool inside me.

Really need to work on that, I think. I want guns to be tools of my job, not security blankets. But with my history that's a long, tough therapeutic road.

It's an hour and a half to Stillhouse Lake, and we arrive after dark. I can feel weariness pulling me apart, fraying my edges, and I yawn as J. B. pulls up in the drive of the house. The lights are on, and the warmth of it makes me feel a wave of relief. Everybody's okay. The SUV's parked in front, so they made it back safely.

All will be well.

I thank J. B. again, and she heads back for her home in Knoxville—or the office, maybe; J. B. has a boundless amount of energy. I don't right now. The emotional demand of enduring jail and court again sapped me dry.

When Sam opens the door, I sink into his arms and drag in a deep, shuddering breath. "Hey," he whispers against my hair. "Hey, it's okay. Come inside."

I need to get it together, and I do because Lanny and Connor are there, anxiously waiting too. I hug them both. I have to swallow tears, and it tastes like blood; my throat is so raw and tight it hurts. But I smile through that and kiss them on their foreheads and tell them I love them, and I mean it with every cell in my body.

That's when the stories start to tumble out.

"Mom, Vee ran off, and there was a man out there with a gun in the trees," Lanny says, "and Sam went after him, and—"

It's the casual drop of *Vee* that makes me hold up a hand. "Hang on," I say. "Vee? Vera Crockett?"

"Uh . . . yeah." Lanny's taken aback, and I realize that Sam already knows this part. Lanny just forgot that I didn't. I look to him, and he takes up the story.

"Turns out Vera's been coming around and talking to Lanny," he says. "She skated on her foster family."

I don't know whether to be more alarmed by Vee's appearance here or Lanny not telling me about it. Neither one is a good sign. "Vee's supposed to be with her aunt."

"Well, she's not," Lanny says. She folds her arms and sits back, chin thrust forward. Aggressive and defensive at the same time. "Her aunt didn't take her. And she got put in foster care, and *that* was awful. So she came here because—because she just wanted to be close to people she knows." Not the real story, I know that. But I don't have time to mine for information. I look at Sam.

"She wanted someone she trusted to front some information to the FBI," he says. "For the reward money. I said no."

Lanny's mouth drops open, and her head swivels around toward him. She looks like someone just sucker-punched her—shock, pain, and betrayal. Her crossed arms drop. She didn't know this. Vee never told her.

Vee probably told her that she'd just come for her. And that makes me want to shake that girl hard for hurting my daughter like that.

"What information?" I ask him.

"She claims that she knows where Vernon Carr is hiding." He shrugs. "I don't know. Maybe she's being honest."

Vernon Carr. I remember him vividly: a bitter, lean old man who wasn't above kidnapping, abusing, and murdering women. He'd had his own little cult out there. Creepy.

Then Sam says, "She thinks he's gotten shelter with a bigger off-shoot of the same cult he was running out of Wolfhunter. She says it's called the Assembly of Saints."

He says more, but I don't hear it; there's a high-pitched buzzing in my ears, and I feel my heartbeat accelerate hard. *Saints.* We were hired to find Remy Landry by *All Saints International.* And Carol, with her marked-up Bible, all those passages marked with stars that referred to saints. I hear her voice whisper, *Remy's with the saints.*

I lick my lips and focus back on Sam. "How does she know?"

He frowns at me and cocks his head. "You mean how does Vee know where Carr is?"

"Yes."

"I don't think she does; she talked around it, but didn't tell me a place. She said Father Tom started the cult in Wolfhunter, then took most of his followers and formed his own, bigger compound. So maybe she just assumed that's where Carr would go. If I had to bet, I'd say she doesn't know exactly where it is. But she's not lying about this Father Tom."

Father Tom. F.T.

"I think someone in Wolfhunter told her where Carr is," I say, and stand up. "Sam. *Somebody told her.* And they knew she'd come to us. Maybe they even suggested it."

"Whoa, whoa, Gwen, calm down. What are you talking about?"

"Something is very wrong about all this. We have to go," I say. "Right now. *Now.* Lanny, Connor: get your bugout bags." I fall back on old terminology; from the time I got reunited with my children to when we landed at Stillhouse Lake, I'd insisted they pack emergency bags with everything they'd need to take in the event we had to evacuate quickly. Bugout bags. We'd even decorated Lanny's with painted ladybugs. Connor had decorated his with rhinoceros beetles, which he thought were really cool.

My kids just sit there. They exchange looks, and Connor says, "Uh . . . we don't have any? I mean, we've been here awhile, and we didn't . . . we didn't think we needed those anymore?"

Oh God *dammit.* I jam the heels of my hands against my burning eyes and take a deep breath. I can't freak out right now. I need to stay calm. But we are *exposed.* "Okay," I say, and I can hear the false normality in my voice. "We're going to get packed and leave. Now. Tonight."

"Mom—" Lanny says. "What's wrong? Why? We just got home!"

I shout, "What did I just say?" I never yell at my kids, never, and I see both of them flinch and it makes me heartsick, but they *move*.

Sam's standing up now, too, and he says, "Gwen, what the hell?"

"They're going to come for us," I tell him. "They used me to get to Carol. Maybe they already have her. But they aimed Vee right at us. They want us to chase a lead right back to the Assembly of Saints, and *we're not doing that*. We need to get out of here."

"Hey. You're not making a lot of sense here. Maybe we just need to sit down and think this—"

Now I'm shouting at *him*. "We are not safe!" I'm acting irrationally, in his eyes. And maybe he's even right. Maybe I've gone a little crazy. But I remember how Remy slipped off into the night without a ripple to mark his disappearance. And those other young men. I remember the oppressive horrors I saw in Wolfhunter, and *I don't want to be here*.

Sam steps into it. Into my chaos and rage and fear. He puts his hands on my face, and the touch stills me a little. Centers me. I catch a breath, and he stares into my eyes. "Gwen," he says. "If you want to go, we'll go. No more questions."

I am so grateful for that I nearly choke on the swell of relief. I sag into his embrace for a warm, precious second, and I feel safe there. I know it's an illusion, but it helps.

When I push back, I say, "Thank you for trusting me."

"Always," he replies, low in his throat. And I realize that it's true. He *does* trust me. And I haven't given him that same respect, not consistently. He's not demanding for me to explain. He's just trusting my instincts. "Come on. Let's get packed and go."

I stop to open up the gun safe under the couch, and take out the weapon I keep there. I grab extra ammo from the supply I keep behind books on the bookcase. All of it goes into a backpack. When it comes to clothes, I just grab a couple of changes and shove them in on top. Doesn't matter if it looks good. Shirts, pants, underwear. Good enough.

Sam's shoving toiletries into a bag and tossing it to me to throw in as he heads for his side of the closet.

Five minutes.

Lanny and Connor are done ahead of us, which is flat-out amazing; I'm zipping the backpack when Sam freezes for a second and says, "Shit. I forgot to tell you. There's a police cruiser out on the road, they want to take us to the station. Lanny needs to give a statement about what happened at Killing Rock."

"We're not going," I tell him. "They're not going to arrest her, Sam. Not tonight anyway. And we can make amends on that tomorrow." I'm afraid right now. Deeply, viscerally afraid that everything, *everything* is going to go completely wrong. If the Assembly of Saints thinks I know where Carol is, they'll come for us. Or they'll just come for revenge. Or to find out what we know. Or . . . any of a thousand reasons, and I know, because ice-cold Carol is afraid of these people, that I cannot risk my family here. I want to hunt *them*. I don't want them to hunt *me*. Stillhouse Lake no longer feels safe to me. It feels like a trap.

"Okay," he says. Another gift of trust. He takes the backpack.

I hear the doorbell ring, and absolute terror bolts through me. I move the borrowed Browning in the holster until it's snug against the small of my back. I draw the gun and ease ahead of Sam. "Lanny," I say, as she turns toward me, eyes wide. "Open the safe room."

She drops the backpack she's holding and runs to push the chairs and dining room table another foot back. Our safe room—original to this house when we bought it—isn't fancy, but it's secure, and she clicks open the hidden door in the wall and starts keying in the code. I leave her to that and look out the peephole.

There's a Norton police cruiser parked in our driveway with its red and blue lights flashing, and two uniformed officers standing there on the porch. I can't see their faces; the brims of their caps throw dark shadows. But the uniforms look authentic.

"False alarm," I say to Sam, and put my gun away. I hear Lanny still pressing buttons. She's trying too hard; she's erroring out the code. "Lanny, it's okay. Never mind. Kezia sent a cruiser. I'm going to send them away, and then we're out of here."

"Kezia was pretty firm that she wanted her statement immediately," Sam warns.

"And I'm going to tell them, very politely, to fuck off."

I disarm the system and open the door.

That's my mistake, but I don't know it for a few long seconds. All I see is uniforms . . . and then I see the faces. One of them has a beard.

There are no Norton cops with beards. It's a rule. And their uniforms don't fit.

They've taken out the cops.

I go for my gun, but I'm already too late; the first man started moving the second the door opened, and now he stiff-arms it and forces me back, and his gun is in *his* hand while mine is still holstered. He puts the barrel to my forehead and drives me backward. Shock blows through me like an explosion, but it leaves something else: rage and fear, tearing along my nerves and pooling cold in my stomach.

I back away. He follows and keeps the gun to my head. One slight pressure on that trigger and I'm gone. I want to look for my kids, but I don't dare. I can only pray they're getting into that safe room.

Oh God, Sam . . . "Sam!" I say sharply. I raise my hands. It's a gesture of surrender.

It also shows him the gun clipped on the back of my belt. I'm between the incoming intruders and him. If he's fast . . .

He's fast.

I feel the tug on the back of my jeans, and then Sam is stepping sideways and aiming my gun. "Drop it," he tells the fake cop. I can feel the menace in his voice like a heat wave shivering the air.

But then the man's partner *also* steps in, and he's holding a shotgun. He racks and raises it, and I can almost sense the moment that Sam does the bloody calculus. If he fires, the shotgun blast takes us both out. He's outgunned, and I'm the hostage.

I hear beeps. Lanny's at the safe room door, and she's going to get it open. My kids are going to be okay.

"Hey," the second fake cop says. "You. Girl. Stop. Get over here now, or I blow both their heads off. You. Asshole. Put the gun on the floor and kick it to me."

"Lanny, get in the goddamn safe room!" Sam snaps. I can hear my daughter crying. She's trying. I hear the rapid beeping of the locking mechanism refusing the code she's entered. I used to drill them on this stuff, made sure they could enter the code at a moment's notice. We'd made it a game.

But this is *my fault*. I stopped drilling them. I stopped insisting that we be that ready, that careful, that paranoid.

I hear the beeps stop.

I see Lanny shuffle slowly forward out of my peripheral vision, and I risk a quick glance toward her. She's crying. Trembling as she holds up her hands. Sam makes a growling sound in the back of his throat, pure frustration, and when the second fake cop points the shotgun at Lanny, Sam crouches down and puts his gun on the floor. He kicks it across, too hard, and it smacks the far wall behind the man with the shotgun. But if Sam meant it for a distraction, it doesn't quite work. The man doesn't go for it. He just leaves it where it stops.

I can't see Connor. I'm praying that he had time to get down the hall, that maybe, *maybe*, he's getting out of the house. *Go, baby. Run.*

I'm flooded with panic-flavored adrenaline and shaking, and every cell of my body is screaming with rage. "What do you want?" *Oh God.* I turned the alarm off. I let them in. All this is my fault.

"I want the girl," the man facing me says. At first I think he's talking about Lanny, or even Vee, but then I know what he means.

"Carol isn't here," I say. I'm lowering my hands, but he doesn't like that. He presses the barrel of the gun so hard against my forehead it

185

feels like being branded, and I lean back and put my hands up again. "I don't know where she is!"

"You have ten seconds to tell me the truth, or I blow the back of your head off. Understand me?" he snaps. "I want her, and I want the child. You tell me where they are, and you all live. Fuck with me, and you all die."

The front door is still open, and stripes of red and blue light cascade through the doorway behind him; the glow makes him look like angel and devil in fast strobes. But then that color washes out, and I realize headlights are coming up the driveway. Bright, high headlights.

I draw my breath to scream for help, but I stop, panic trickling down my backbone in ice-cold drops. There's no point in screaming for help.

It's a big, old recreational vehicle. Boxy and faded from age.

It's brought reinforcements.

A third man, the driver, steps out of the RV and heads inside. He shuts the front door and stands against it.

"Hey," says the man holding me at gunpoint. As if I could have possibly forgotten him. "Focus. I'm still counting down from ten. Where's Carol? Where's the kid?"

"I don't know anything about a kid!" I say. And that's true. I don't. "Carol vanished after I was arrested. I don't have any idea where she'd go."

"Four seconds," he says.

"I don't know!" I shout it at him, hopeless now, furious that after all that I've survived it comes to this, *this*. "Don't hurt my family!" It's all I can do in those last few seconds, beg for their lives. I feel like my skin's too tight, too cold, like it might split open like a drum and let all the darkness inside spill out.

Time's up. I get ready to die.

He doesn't shoot.

He stares at me with dead, dark eyes and then turns to look at the man with the shotgun. "There's supposed to be a boy here too," he says. "Go find him. You, bitch. Down. On your knees." He holsters my sidearm and takes the shotgun from the man who passes. He aims it right at me. "Down."

If he was intending to kill me, he'd have done it by now. I risk a question. "Are you from the Assembly?"

It's like I hit each of them with an electric cattle prod. They stiffen their posture and exchange looks. "Carol tell you that?" the man holding the shotgun asks. He sounds angry. "Get on your knees, woman. Pray. All of you! Down! Now!"

I lower myself down to my knees, hands still raised. Sam manages to move up so he's next to me; I can feel the vibrating tension in him, the need to *do something*. But we are doing something. We're buying time for Connor to get away and get help.

"Just let my daughter go," I say. "Please. She's a child. She doesn't have anything to do with this."

"She's old enough," he says, and I don't like the way he looks at her, like she's a piece of meat in a market. If I have to go out fighting, I will, and *one move* toward my daughter . . . My whole body is trembling in time with the heavy, racing thud of my heartbeat. I'm coiled like a watch spring and ready to explode.

"Carol took a bus to Pennsylvania." The lie comes out of me in a rush, and the words feel like they cut my tongue, they're so sharp.

"A false witness shall not be unpunished, and he that speaketh lies shall perish," the man with the shotgun says. "Proverbs." He aims at me, and I draw in a sharp breath. Fear is like a knife down my spine. "You're lying."

There are only two men now. The one with the shotgun, and the one who came from the RV and is blocking the front door. The third is looking through the house for Connor. I hear him opening doors down the hall.

I need to play for time.

"Check my phone," I say. "I have a text."

"God is watching you, woman," the man with the shotgun says. I can tell he's chewing it over, and I see a flash of frustration in his eyes. "Phone. Now."

"It's in the other room," I lie. "The office. On my desk." If I can split them up even more, maybe we'll have a chance. If nothing else, it delays them.

The man who went in search of Connor comes back. "Not here," he says. "Maybe went out a window."

"Go find him," the man with the shotgun says. He's in charge, no doubt about it. I watch as the man opens the door and rushes outside. *Run, baby. Just run.* "You. You're stalling." He's talking to me again. There's real confidence in him, and that scares me. "I studied up on you, Gwen Proctor. Gina Royal. And your phone ain't in your office."

"It is."

"You sure about that? Because liars get punished." He takes a phone out of the pocket of his police uniform and dials.

I clearly hear the low buzz from the purse that sits on the coffee table. I don't say anything. I can't.

He hangs up the call, and my phone stops buzzing. He raises the shotgun to his shoulder, and I feel him aiming. It's like a spotlight on my face.

The front door opens, and his friend is back. Strong and lean and merciless.

He's got my son.

He's holding a knife to Connor's throat. And I feel all my fragile plans come apart, and now there's nothing but fear, waves of it.

"Put him in the RV," the man in charge says without looking away from me. I let out a little cry and lean forward, reaching out. "We want Carol. If you want your boy back, you find him. You, her, and the child. You've got two days." He tosses a small disposable phone on the carpet next to me, but I can't look away from Connor as he's yanked away. The stark look on his face, the pleading in his eyes . . . I let out a sound that's half-scream, but before I can launch myself up and *fight*, the man in charge shuts the door, and Connor's just . . . gone. "There's a number programmed in. Call when you have her. Better be fast."

"She's *gone!*" I yell it at him, hopeless and furious and hating myself. "Carol's gone, and I don't know how to find her!"

"If you don't, then your son joins the saints," he tells me. "You should be honored. As Exodus says, *the males belong to the Lord.*"

"Amen," the other man says solemnly.

I'm going to fucking kill them all.

I hear a sound erupt outside, a shrieking howl that splits the night, and in an instant I know what it is. My son's hit the panic button on his key chain.

"Mel!" the man in charge snaps. "Go shut that racket up!" The man who's been on the door opens it and moves out. There's a split second where the noise ramps up as the door swings, and the man with the shotgun glances that direction.

Lanny's slipping her own key chain out of her pocket, and I see it. Sam sees it too. We have one shot. Just one. And we have to do this together.

Lanny hits the panic button on her own key chain, and the noise is explosive, like a sonic grenade; it feels like being hit in the head with a hammer, but I'm braced for that.

The man in charge is not.

Sam and I launch as one, while Lanny rolls away to take shelter at the end of the couch. I'm screaming, but I can't hear it, the noise is a red blur pulsing through my brain. I'm moving fast, but I don't know if I'm fast enough. Sam and I hit him with all our weight and momentum. The shotgun goes off with a boom, but it's only blown a ragged hole in the ceiling.

The leader slams the butt of the shotgun into Sam's head, and Sam staggers back. He's wide open, off balance; I kick out wildly at our enemy, and connect. It spoils his shot at Sam, and the buckshot rips a hole in the wall instead.

Sam hits the coffee table and topples drunkenly sideways. He's half-out, struggling to stay in the fight.

I see my gun still lying by the wall, and I scramble for it. I get it and roll over and take aim at the leader just as he swings the shotgun toward me, and we both freeze. The shriek of Lanny's panic alarm is so loud it drowns out anything I could say.

But we both know that even if I get him, he's going to get me, too, and that shotgun will rip me to ribbons.

I'm sitting up on the carpet. My back's to the door. I don't feel movement behind me until the last second, and then it's too late.

Something hits me in the back of the head with such force everything explodes into a flash of white, and I feel myself falling, losing the gun. The world is a long, loud smear.

When I blink again, I'm down. My whole head is pulsing with red-hot pain, and I'm struggling to make sense of things. My gun's beside me, and I grope for it. A boot kicks it away.

He's getting away. The man with the shotgun. He's leaving. I crawl toward the gun but things go gray. I'm lying on the carpet. My gun isn't where it was.

I see Sam, bloody and stark with fury, lunging out the door. He's got my gun. He's going after Connor.

Lanny's next to me. I can see her terrified face, but I can't hear her over the scream of the panic siren. I can't turn my head; my body feels heavy and cold. The sound of the siren gets dimmer, slower, and then . . .

. . . then, despite the racing of my heart, the desperate need to *get up* and go after my son, everything fades to black.

17

GWEN

I wake up in a red mist of pain, and the first thing I try to do is touch the throbbing spot on my head.

Someone pushes my hand down. I open my eyes, but all I can see is a blur of shapes and shadows, and then slowly I focus on a face looming over me. It isn't Lanny.

It's Vee Crockett. She's holding a cold cloth to my head, and when I try to get up, she shakes her head and presses me back. "Nope," she says. "You need to rest, Ms. Proctor."

"Connor," I whisper, and this time I don't let her stop me from sitting up. The whole world does a greasy slide around me, and I gag from the pain of the headache. I sit, shaking, until it subsides a little. "Where's Connor?"

"I got help," Vee tells me. "I heard the sirens, but I thought it was the cops at first. There was a cop car here. But then I saw them assholes dragging Connor to their RV, and I knew it was trouble."

"Where's my son?"

Vee sits back and looks up, and I realize that Lanny's put her hand on Vee's shoulder. My daughter looks pale but steady, and she crouches down and takes my hand. "Mom, I need you to be calm," she says. "Okay?"

"Are you all right?" It bursts out of me in a blind panic, because if she's been hurt . . . but she looks okay. I think she's okay.

"I'm not hurt," she says. "Mom . . . I'm sorry." Her reluctance to tell me what she has to say makes me shake, and tears burn like acid, boiling up in a hot, melting rush.

"They took Connor," she says. And I immediately, irrationally react, trying to move, to stand, to *find him*. "Mom. *Mom!* He's going to be okay. They won't hurt him, they're just—they're holding on to him until you get this Carol person, right? And we'll do that. We'll get her."

She's trying so hard to be the adult right now. She's scared to death, and she's holding on to Vee for support. "You said you found help?" I say to Vee, and I realize I'm still not myself; I didn't mean to say that out loud. "Who—"

She points, and I turn my head. I'm expecting Kezia, a full contingent of Norton police, but instead I see an old man with a thick white beard and cold blue eyes.

It's *Jasper Belldene*. The pill-pushing Santa of Norton. I'm hallucinating. I have to be. But the blinding headache I'm fighting off, the taste of metallic blood—that's all too real.

"Easy," Jasper is saying, and holds up steady when I try to scramble up to my feet. "Hold on, there, woman, take it easy!"

The effort makes my head go gray and throb even harder, and I need all their help to get me upright and standing. "Sam," I say. "Where's Sam?"

I'm still in my own living room. The silence is as deafening as the panic alarms I remember before I passed out. The damage to the ceiling and the wall looks raw. Spots of blood on the rug, but I think it's mine, or maybe Sam's. *Where is he?*

Jasper Belldene looks at me with a mix of dispassion and keen focus. "Best I can tell, your man tried to take on two out there," he

192

says. "Signs read that there was a hell of a fight. Looks like he made it into the RV, but the RV done took off. So I guess they've got him and your son too."

It's like an icy stab to my chest. I have trouble getting my breath. *Focus!* I scream at myself inside. *Think!* I can't. I pull free of Lanny's hands and stagger to the front window. It's still dark outside. The police car is there, but someone's turned the flashing lights off. My SUV and Sam's truck are still parked. "Where are the police?" I ask. "You called them?"

"No," Jasper says. "And neither will you, if you want those boys back."

It isn't that I forget the headache, or the pain; it's that they cease to matter. I shove it aside, along with the fear. Fear will only slow me down. I turn my face toward Jasper and say, "You're part of this. You said you'd come after us." He's an old man, and I'm barely standing, but I'm about to lunge for him anyway.

He must see it, because he holds up both hands. "Ain't saying we don't have issues," he says. "But you agreed you'd move, and I think you mean to keep that promise. I wouldn't have nothing to do with kidnapping your boy. Whoever these people are, they ain't mine."

"Then why are you *here?*"

He points at Vee. "Girl there called," he says. "She's a friend of my boy Olly. She said there was trouble here. Ms. Proctor, we ain't got time for this. Your neighbors might be hunkering down, but I guarantee they're on 911 right now—"

"Why would *you* help me?"

"Fact is, you live 'round here, Ms. Proctor. You're our neighbor. They're strangers come in to do you harm." He smiles. It's cold, and I see the predator under the friendly disguise. "Besides, this is a chance for us to horse-trade a little. I help you find these bastards, you get your girl to say my son didn't have nothing to do with that girl getting hurt up at Killing Rock."

"Police are going to get involved," I tell him. "These kidnappers took their car and uniforms. Did you find the officers?"

"Trunk of their own cruiser," he says. "Trussed up like Thanksgiving turkeys in their undies. My son Jesse took some photos for posterity. They're all right. But the clock's running fast, Ms. Proctor. Better decide quick if you want my help." He's staring at me, but I can't read anything in his face.

I grab for the SUV's keys. I miss.

He's shaking his head. "No good tearing off after them, even if you could drive without passing out. And you got no idea which way they went." I don't like the smile he gives me. Or the look in his eyes. "I do."

I feel every muscle in my body tighten. Painfully. "Where?"

"Favors for favors is how we do business. Now, my girl Florida, she's one hell of a smart kid. You know anything about drones?"

"Drones," I repeat.

"I had my boy Jesse follow that RV when it left; it went up onto an old logging road, don't even have a name. Florida got a drone up and landed it on top of the RV before it got off that road. So we can track it . . . or I can just have Florida fly that drone on back home." He pauses. We both register the sound of sirens coming. "Time's up. I'm good either way."

I swallow hard. I feel fragile now, all my bones turned to milky glass. I hurt. My head's throbbing so hard I see pulses of red in front of my eyes. What he's asking is a terrible thing. And I can't decide for my daughter. She's the one who'll have to lie.

I look at Lanny, and she says, without a second's pause, "I'll do it. Anything, Mom. If it gets Connor and Sam back, I'll say whatever he wants."

"And your whole clan leaves," Jasper says. "You pack up and you leave Stillhouse Lake when this is done. Agreed?"

Like my daughter, I don't hesitate. "Agreed," I say. I offer my hand. He takes it.

"If it helps salve your conscience, Olly ain't no killer. He's foolish, and he's a good man in a fight. He may sell some recreational drugs now and again. But he never wanted Candy hurt. That was all on Bon, the idjit."

Lanny bites her lip and nods. "That's true," she says. "I mean, I'm pretty sure. Bon admitted it."

I walk to her and take her in my arms. I press my forehead to hers and whisper, "I'm sorry, baby."

"It's okay," she says. "We're going to find them."

Jasper grunts, but makes no promises. His phone makes a chiming sound, and he looks down at it. "Spotters say Johnny Law's coming 'round the lake. You tell them what happened here, but leave us and that stuff about the drone out. You have your girl change her statement. Then come out to the lodge, and we'll get to finding your boys."

"Lodge?"

"I suppose you'd call it our *compound*," he says, and huffs, as if he takes that personally. "Anyway, I'll have Jesse waiting to lead you up when you're done. You bring Vee and Lanny; my wife will look after them. Best you bring what you need for some days."

"You'd better not screw me over, Jasper. I'll kill you."

"Ma'am," he says, "I'm going to consider that you've been bashed silly and not hold that against you. Hospitality's a sacred thing, and when I offer it, I mean it. No harm will come to either of you under my roof, and I'll swear to that." It's weird, but I believe him. He's actually offended that I'd think otherwise. Southern customs. In some ways they're utterly incomprehensible to me still. But right now I'm just abjectly grateful.

"Mom? I want to come with you," Lanny says. "I want to find Connor!"

I just shake my head. It's impossible for me to take my daughter into this fight, and she knows that.

Doesn't mean she likes it. At all. Doesn't mean I do either.

I give Jasper a few minutes to clear out; then I call the police and report the home invasion and the abductions—it would be strange if I didn't. I excuse the delay by telling them I was unconscious. Kezia and Prester burn rubber and arrive together just behind the patrol cars, and their professionalism and kindness shake my hard-won composure. It feels like I'm standing on a thin pane of glass over a hole as deep as the Grand Canyon, and every move I make cracks it a little more. *Please, Sam,* I pray, in the quiet moments between questions. *Please stay alive. Please watch over our son.* I know he will, if it's humanly possible. But the thought of losing one of them, or both of them . . . it destroys me.

Lanny doesn't say much to any of the officers, and I think she's going into a deeper state of shock now that there's nothing for her to do. Vee stays with us—or, more accurately, with Lanny. And I'm glad of that; Lanny needs the support.

Every second this takes feels like sandpaper grinding on my heart.

I've taken the phone that the cult's team leader left for me; it's burning a hole in the pocket of my jeans. I don't mention it to the police, not even to Kezia. She insists on having my head wound checked by a paramedic, and I don't object too fiercely, but I refuse a trip to the hospital. No time.

Within an hour, the state police are involved too. They're going to issue an Amber Alert for my son. I don't really want that; I'm desperately afraid that these cultists have nothing to lose in a fight, but the last thing I want to do is rely completely on the word of Jasper Belldene. I'm just worried that like most fanatics, these Assembly kidnappers will believe they're bound for heaven anyway and run toward the chance to die in glory if they've got no other options.

It's a relief when someone calls on my regular phone. I grab for it, hoping against hope it's Connor or Sam, but a different name comes up.

It's Mike Lustig. Sam's FBI friend. I answer and he says, "Sam's missing?"

"How did you hear?" I ask him.

"Friend in the Tennessee Bureau of Investigation gave me a heads-up. They got an abduction alert from the Staties; there's an agent on his way to you now. What do you know?"

I tell him, while the state police officers look at me impatiently; Lustig's an old friend of Sam's, fiercely loyal, and with his position in the FBI he might be of immense help right now. Or not. It depends on where he is and what he's doing. But he takes it all in, and then says, "You think Remy Landry's disappearance is connected to other similar cases. And a cult."

"Yeah, I do," I say.

"Well, we looked into those cases, but we were never able to pull any commonalities together. And we never heard of any cult in connection with it."

"I'd say it's a pretty damn solid lead, considering they *took my son*," I snap, and immediately regret it; none of this is his fault. I brought this to my own doorstep. "Any way you can help?"

"You got tracking chips in your kids?"

"On their phones." Lanny's old one is at the bottom of the lake, but she's got a brand-new disposable; I make sure my kids are never out of contact. "Can you track Connor's?"

"Staties will try, they've got the ball, but I'll help any way I can. Even if the phone's off, we can still expedite the tracking." He pauses, and his deep voice gets a little deeper. "Gwen. You know the chances they've still got that phone with them aren't very good."

"I know," I say. If the cultists have a pattern of abductions, like I believe they do, then they've learned to be methodical about covering their tracks. Leaving no trace.

Which is why keeping my agreement with Jasper Belldene is so vitally important right now.

◆ ◆ ◆

I appreciate what the authorities are trying to do, but I'm desperately impatient to be *done* with them. I talk to Kezia; I still can't tell her the whole truth, but she agrees to take Lanny's amended statement about the incident up on Killing Rock. She's really not happy about that, and she pushes Lanny hard, but my kid doesn't waver. That allows Olly Belldene his freedom, or at least a far less dire charge to plead away. I don't care what happens to Bon; he can rot in jail. He isn't part of the deal.

As soon as the police—local, state, and Tennessee Bureau of Investigation—finish with us, I tell them I need to get Vee and Lanny somewhere safe and away from here. I admit, I play the posttraumatic shock heavily; it's not entirely an act either. They agree, on the condition I tell them where I'm going. I lie glibly about a motel in Knoxville, and give them the address when I look it up on the internet. I turn over the house keys. We're already packed to go, but I make sure I collect every gun in the house, especially the Browning, which was left behind. After I identify it and get J. B. on the phone to verify that it's a work-issued weapon, they let me keep it.

J. B. asks me what she can do, and I tell her to throw every single resource at finding Carol. I don't intend to turn her over to the cult, but I want to *know* where she is. If the Belldenes' drone stops working, I may need a plan B.

Interestingly, the police don't seem to trust me as much as they should, considering we're the victims. The TBI agent tails me to Knoxville and the motel; I register for a night, and we go to the room. I watch from the window until he leaves, then order the girls back into the car.

Jesse Belldene's been following us too. He's better at it than the TBI agent; I spotted his muddy, nondescript Jeep tagging along on the road out of Norton, but he was skillful at staying just at the edge of sight, and the TBI agent was so intent on us that he probably never looked behind him. When we get down to our SUV, Jesse's Jeep is idling next to it. He just nods to us and exchanges a guarded glance with Lanny. I don't like the look of the man, but he seems polite enough when he says, "Thanks for helping my brother out with the cops. He never wanted y'all hurt, swear to that. Bon got carried away. Olly's a dumbass, but he ain't evil."

Lanny gives him a wary nod. Truce. He winks at Vee. "Want to ride with me, pretty gal?" he asks her. I fully expect Vee to say yes; everything I know about her—including the fact that she's familiar enough with the Belldenes to go to them for help—tells me she will. But she doesn't. She just shakes her head and gets in the back seat of the SUV with my daughter. Lanny takes her hand and clings to it desperately. My head still hurts, but the painkillers I've taken are doing their job of keeping it to a dull roar.

"You okay?" I ask my daughter softly as I drive, tailing Jesse's muddy bumper. "Lanny?"

She sniffs and wipes her eyes and says, "Sure. I'm fine, Mom."

"No, you ain't," Vee says. "And it's okay, Lanta. You don't have to be okay. You know that, right? You've got people."

Lanny takes a deep, uneven breath and drops her head onto Vee's shoulder. I blink as I start to put the relationship into a new light. I'm pretty sure I don't approve. "Do you think Connor and Sam are okay?" Lanny asks me. The vulnerability in her voice makes me forget my objections. For now.

"I think Sam will do everything in his power to be sure they are." That's not an answer, but I don't want to lie to her. Not about this. "Baby, I think I should take you to Javier and see if he can let you stay with him while I do this—"

"You're thinkin' the Belldenes might hurt her," Vee says. "They won't." She sounds utterly sure, and I give her a long look. "They do what they need to do, but there's a code. They're not about to break their word and hurt Lanta. Besides, I'll look after her."

It's strange, but . . . I believe her. "Why did you come, Vee?" I ask it gently. Without accusation. "Really. What happened to you?"

199

Vee looks away, and for someone like Vee, who's always on guard and armored, that's as good as a wince. Her expression is still and quiet, and when she answers, her voice is neutral. "There was a girl in that foster home. Younger than me. Real young. She . . . she ran away and got herself hurt." She swallows. "Was my fault. She kept followin' me around, treatin' me like her *sister*. I wasn't, we just had rooms in the same house is all. I told her we wasn't never goin' to be sisters." Her rural Tennessee accent is so thick it's hard to understand her on the last of that. She pauses, and I realize that she's crying—fat, silent tears sliding down her cheeks. "I just—I couldn't stay there after. I wanted to be—" She doesn't continue. Lanny puts her arm around her. Vee takes a deep breath and wipes her face with an impatient swipe. "I had to be on my own is all." I hear the armor going back on, almost an audible clank of metal plates.

"Vee," I say. "You aren't on your own. You don't have to be." Vee— fierce, independent, wildly unstable Vee—needs someone to care, and I do. I have since I met her, even though she unsettles me, even though I worry about her influence on my daughter. "You came to us for a reason, and it wasn't to get reward money like you told Sam. Right?"

She shakes her head, and I see the effort it takes for her to force the grin. "Good idea, though, ain't it?"

"I have to ask this, honey, and I need you to be completely honest with me. Do you know where Vernon Carr really is? *Exactly* where?" Because if she does, it's possible that's also where they're taking Sam and Connor. We could get there first.

But I can see it in her face before she says it. "No, ma'am. I know he's got to be at that Assembly compound. But as to where it is . . ." She shakes her head. "We never were part of those people. Momma always stayed away. She was real glad when Father Tom pulled out of Wolfhunter."

"Okay," I tell her. I'm disappointed, but I let it go. "I mean what I said, Vee. You're safe. You're not on your own."

She gives me a hard look this time, and it reminds me that she takes no bullshit. "For now. But what happens after? You sendin' me back to that foster family? They don't give a shit about me. Probably don't even know I'm gone except it's one less mouth to feed."

I don't know if she's right. Maybe they do care. Maybe they're worried out of their minds about her. But I just say, "Until I say different, you're staying with us."

The hard look fades, and I see the vulnerable child underneath. The one who crossed a hundred miles of hard country to get to us. To safety. To some hope of acceptance.

"You're with us," I tell her. "I promise."

Jesse's Jeep takes a cutoff—unmarked, and almost certainly not on any map—that leads through wild, hilly country and up into the woods; I can only vaguely guess the location, but it can't be very far from Stillhouse Lake, or from Norton either. It just looks like a rough trail, littered with rocks that challenge the suspension of my SUV. We go through three locked gates—the last warns me that trespassers will be shot—until suddenly the trail opens into a wide clearing.

Jasper Belldene might like to call it a lodge, but it sure meets my definition of a compound. There's a ramshackle collection of houses clustered around a small pond fed by a stream coming down the hill. The biggest house is fairly handsome, built of heavy timbers; the others are far less fancy. I count three homes and two very large outbuildings, but there might be more up behind the big house. There's a formidable fence all the way around—heavy-gauge chain link, with razor wire on top, and a corrugated steel fence a few feet behind it that blocks sight lines. The gate's been rolled open for us, and that makes me think they've got surveillance cameras up in the trees along the road. They'll see people coming a long way off.

Jesse parks, and I pull up next to him. The gate's already rolling closed behind us. I get out and say, "Just in case your daddy is thinking of pulling any bullshit, I sent texts to Kezia Claremont, my boss in Knoxville, and the FBI telling them where I'll be." That isn't a bluff. I really did it before we ever left the motel room. As contingency plans go, it's the best I can manage at the moment.

Jesse just grins. He's got the slick charm of a good-looking young man who skids out of every tight spot . . . until he doesn't. "No problem, ma'am," he says. "Jasper Belldene keeps his word once he gives it. Until you break yours. You planning on that?"

"No."

"Then we ain't got a worry." He turns and heads up the wooden steps to the big house, and as he does, the front door opens and Lilah Belldene steps out. She clasps her hands in front of her and gives us a warm, welcoming smile. "Come on in," she says. "I've fixed up a couple of rooms for you two girls. Gwen, I don't expect you'll be staying that long. Jasper'll be out directly, you just wait right inside."

The house is surprisingly . . . normal. Comfortable couches, a worn old recliner that's no doubt Jasper's exclusive domain. A rocking chair with a basket of colorful yarn beside it, and knitting needles stuck in. The place smells clean and feels warm. Welcoming. There's a big high-definition TV set to a news channel that plays without sound.

It's not exactly what I expected from the Hillbilly Mafia.

"Girls, you follow me," Lilah says. "I'll get you settled, and then we'll have some hot cocoa. All right?"

Lanny's still holding Vee's hand, but she drops it and turns to me to give me a hug that takes my breath. I hold her like I never intend to let her go, but I know I have to, and finally I open my arms and watch her step away. "Lilah. A moment," I say, and Mrs. Belldene stops.

She looks at me for a second, then turns to the girls and says, "Down the hall and to the right. Your rooms are across from each other.

You're going to have to share that bathroom, now, and I want it kept clean. Go on. I'll be right along."

She turns toward me and waits. I walk closer. Close enough that we could hug, if we're so inclined. We are not. "People know where they are," I tell her. "You understand me?"

She raises her thin, graying eyebrows. She looks so devastatingly grandmotherly in her red gingham shirt. She's even wearing a necklace I recognize: one that dangles a cluster of birthstones of her children and grandchildren. It's an impressive collection. A deliberate reminder that she has a family she loves. Everything this woman does, I think, is calculated to disarm.

"Trust but verify," she says, and winks. "I'd do the same. We may be friendly right now, but we sure ain't friends. Even so: if your daughter sticks to her story and my Olly comes home, we're square for now. Then you leave this county, and we're square for good." She loses the smile like it was a paper mask she'd put up. "I would not hurt your child. You can be sure of that."

I nod stiffly. It isn't that I don't believe her. It's that I don't want to *have* to believe her.

I have to wait only a couple of minutes before Jasper Belldene comes out of the kitchen. He's holding two coffee mugs, and I admit, the smell of good beans makes me lose some of my edge. I gratefully accept and drink, even without milk or sugar. I need it. "How's that head?" he asks me.

"Hurting," I reply. "But it won't hold me back."

"They're still driving," he tells me. "On the interstate. Florida's watching the GPS." He clears his throat. "You can't go at this alone, you know that."

He's right, of course. My instinct is to rush out there, but I don't know what I'll be running into even if I get a final location. I couldn't win against the men from the RV. And if this leads back to Father Tom, to the cult that Carol was so terrified would find her again . . . then it'll be infinitely darker than that. One gun won't do it.

I feel very alone.

"You're not offering, are you?" I ask.

"No. I got no dog in this fight."

"Even if I pay you."

"Ma'am, you can't pay me enough to put the lives of my own children at risk to go get yours. That's a fact. I'd advise you to look elsewhere, you want to drum up a posse. We ain't in that business. I'll point you where to go, and that's the end of our dealings."

My coffee tastes bitter for a moment. I drink it anyway. I don't know when I'll have another chance.

He drains his cup and says, "You may not have my help, but you've got my sympathy. I hope you get that boy back. No child deserves that."

I nod and I hand him my cup when I finish it. He juggles both when his phone dings for attention, and looks at the message. He stares at it for a long second, then says, "I'm real sorry."

He turns the phone toward me, and I read the text. It says Lost the signal. Batteries probably died on the drone. Last ping was up in Cumberland County, up near Catoosa.

I want to scream, and it takes every ounce of self-control I have to hold back that wild despair. Because like Remy Landry, Connor and Sam have just vanished into the dark.

Gone.

I sit with my head in my hands for a while and just let the magnitude of this roll through me. There's absolutely no guarantee that this RV is stopping anywhere in Tennessee. It could be heading farther north, into another state. It could already have disappeared completely.

I call Mike Lustig, and I sound calm when I tell him what I've learned. He promises that he'll feed the info back through the Tennessee law enforcement channels, and then he pauses. "How you doing, Gwen?"

"Not great," I tell him. "At all. I don't know what—what to *do*. I can't just—"

"Yes, you can. Until we know where to find them, there's not a hell of a lot that can happen. You know this."

"Yeah," I say. I don't believe it. "Do you have anything at all on this Assembly of Saints? Or All Saints International?"

Lustig asks the logical question about why I'd ask, and I tell him my suspicions. He considers that in silence a moment. "Got to ask the question: Why would they hire you to find a guy they kidnapped themselves?"

"Because they knew my poking around would flush Carol out of hiding, if she was still around. I made it possible for them to get a shot at her." I swallow hard. "But it won't work again. She'll cut off contact with the pastor and drop completely out of sight, if she's smart. She'll get the hell out of this state—"

"Why didn't she?" Lustig asks. It stops me cold. "You found her in Knoxville. Doesn't that strike you as odd, if she really wanted to get free? She could have been in Hawaii by now. Or Estonia."

He's right. I just assumed she didn't have the resources, but now that I've met her, that seems even less likely. Carol—or whatever her real name is—could manipulate her way in life, cash or not. There has to be a reason why she stayed.

It comes to me in a wave of anger that I've been stupid. I've got no excuse except that I'm tired and distracted and terrified for those I love. I should have nailed this the second the man who kidnapped my son told me he was looking for Carol *and the child.*

Two possibilities: either Carol escaped with a young child from the cult, or Carol ran from the cult because she was pregnant. Either way, she stays in Knoxville because she wants to see that child, even if she can't keep it with her. It makes sense now why the pastor was so committed to protecting her; he was also protecting someone more vulnerable.

I need to apologize to that man someday. "I have to go," I tell Lustig. "Any possibility you can use some kind of surveillance system to locate that RV? Satellites? Anything?"

"I'll see what I can do," he says. "Gwen? You stay put. Don't do anything stupid. Promise me."

"I promise," I say. I'm lying, of course. But Agent Lustig and I have a guarded relationship, at best; we're friends because of Sam, and it ends there. If Lustig could find evidence against me, even the thinnest, to tie me to Melvin's crimes, he'd show up with a warrant as fast as if he'd teleported. He doesn't think I'm good for Sam.

Fair enough.

I end the call and think about leaving. Lilah, who's sitting in her rocker across the room, looks up. She has been knitting steadily, and doesn't stop now. The rhythmic clicking of her needles sounds like claws on a window. I suppose it should be comforting.

"Wait until morning," she says. "You're bone tired, and those girls are too. One more night won't hurt. You're safe here. Can't guarantee what will be outside our fence."

I immediately wonder what ulterior motive *she* has, and maybe that's unfair; the Belldenes have been straightforward enough about their motives so far. Maybe in this, Lilah's being a mother and a grandmother.

I don't imagine it'll last past sunrise.

"Thank you," I tell her. I feel dispirited and horribly lost. I can't sleep, I can't rest, I can't *think*. My son is *gone*. I've tasted this bitterness before, but never quite this deeply. It's the uncertainty that kills hope. "I need to use my computer. That all right?"

"Surely," she says. "As long as you don't need our Wi-Fi password. I ain't sharing that."

I don't need that. I use my cell phone to provide the signal and yoke my computer to it, and I'm online in under a minute.

I start with the Catoosa Wildlife Management Area. It's wild and more than a little desolate. I zoom out. There are far too many possibilities, too many directions, too many backwoods small communities, towns, farms. From satellite, a cult compound looks a lot like any other place. And lots of rural people have trailers and RVs.

I search the internet for most of the rest of the two hours that remain until sunrise, but I don't come up with much. There is almost nothing on the Assembly of Saints except for a passing reference to a long-expired church in the northwest, an entirely different group. The only mobile groups I can find seem to be Romany travelers or groups of elderly retirees with a yen to see the country on the open road.

"Ms. Proctor?"

I blink and look up. Vee Crockett is standing in front of me. She's wearing a frilly white cotton nightgown that's too small for her, and the long sleeves barely cover her to the elbows. She sinks down on the sofa beside me.

"Couldn't you sleep?" I ask her, and she shakes her head. I don't think. I just put my arm around her, the way I would Lanny. She stiffens at the touch, but then she relaxes and leans against me.

"Did you find anything?" she asks me.

I wish I could say yes. But I need to be honest with her. "No."

"Can I show you something?"

I nod. Vee pulls my laptop over and surfs to a video site—not one of the major ones—and pulls something up. "Look."

It's murky and dark, and I don't know what I'm looking at, but the color finally stabilizes. "What is it?"

"These people, they explore weird abandoned places," she says.

"Why?"

"For fun. Just *look*."

The summary underneath says that it's an exploration of an old, abandoned Civil Defense facility. I don't know why she's so intent on it until they push open one of the rusting metal doors on a concrete building, and the flashlights illuminate neat rows of beds against the walls. Surplus military bunks, by the look of it; they still have mattresses on some of them. Apart from that, the place seems empty and unremarkable . . . until the lights catch on something painted on the wall, and the camera turns to bring it into focus.

It's a carefully painted quotation.

WATCH YE, STAND FAST IN THE FAITH, QUIT YOU LIKE MEN, BE STRONG.—
I CORINTHIANS 16:13

The other wall holds a more ominous verse.

GATHER MY SAINTS TOGETHER UNTO ME; THOSE THAT HAVE MADE A COV-
ENANT WITH ME BY SACRIFICE.—PSALMS 50:5

Vee freezes the video, and we stare at it together. The word *saints* seems to glow—a trick of the flashlight, but somehow it seems like a message. "Where is this?"

"Thirty miles from Wolfhunter, out in the woods," she says. "Been closed up for years, I guess." She clicks the play button. "Keep lookin'."

I'm afraid what we're going to see.

The rest of the bunkhouse seems normal enough—bathrooms, bare showers, toilets. In another few minutes they leave the concrete structure. The people shooting the video start out making jokes, but that stops soon. It's eerily quiet where they are, and as they pan around the scene, I see a long, narrow white house like a church, adorned with an outsize cross on the side. They choose to explore that next. The doors are closed but open easily, and the video shows that the large space is completely bare except for a raised platform that holds a single comfortable chair. There's something eerie about that too. I can almost picture a room full of people standing, or kneeling, on that floor while the person that chair belongs to . . . sits. And talks.

There's another building, a mirror to the one that held bunks. The sign outside isn't quite as faded. It reads **THE GARDEN**. I'm expecting some kind of plant nursery. But it's still bunk beds . . . just fewer of them. Farther along, there's a small area with playpens and old, abandoned cribs.

There's just one separate closed door, and when the exploration team opens it, they find a room with a king-size bed. Other than the single chair in the church, that bed is the only luxury in the place so far. That's all that's in the room, and yet I feel sick. Maybe it's the discolored stains on the bare mattress.

Or the quotation on the wall over the bed.

AND ADAM KNEW EVE HIS WIFE; AND SHE CONCEIVED, AND BARE CAIN, AND SAID, I HAVE GOTTEN A MAN FROM THE LORD.—GENESIS 4:1

As the explorers leave, they spotlight more quotations, carefully painted huge on the walls.

FOR THE MAN IS NOT OF THE WOMAN: BUT THE WOMAN OF THE MAN. NEITHER WAS THE MAN CREATED FOR THE WOMAN; BUT THE WOMAN FOR THE MAN.—I CORINTHIANS 11:8–9

That gem makes me flinch. It has to be proof, to these poor souls, that they were born inferior and always will be. That they have no life of their own. The other wall is arguably worse.

LET THE WOMAN LEARN IN SILENCE WITH ALL SUBJECTION.—I TIMOTHY 2:11

I feel cold staring at it. Oppressed and suffocating, trapped like the women who would have been kept here. These women likely believed in this twisted version of Christianity; they had to, to keep their sanity. But it also doesn't escape me that there are twice as many beds in the other bunkhouse—which I think must be for the men—as there are here in the Garden for women.

Women held here were outnumbered as well as indoctrinated. Relentless subjugation. I think about Carol, about her facile manipulation. Did she grow up here? Is this the place she ran away from? No, it couldn't have been. From all appearances, this place has been vacant a long time.

"It's the Assembly," Vee says. "I knew it as soon as I seen this video. Always was talk they had their own place around Wolfhunter, but I didn't know where; I was only a kid when Father Tom moved them on to a better spot." She swallows, looking at the frozen image of the last quotation. "I met him once. Father Tom. He came to our house to recruit my momma. She told him to shoo, and he left. But he was . . ." She pauses, thinking about it. "I thought I liked him back then. He was real nice to me."

Maybe he hadn't been trying to recruit Vee's mother at all. Maybe he'd been after Vee. I shudder to think that, but I remember those cribs, those playpens.

That king-size bed with the stains and the quote looming above.

I don't doubt that Vee is right. This was once the Assembly of Saints compound, before it left Wolfhunter behind completely and moved somewhere bigger. Somewhere better.

I hug Vee and say, "Thanks. This is a big help." I try to smile. She tries too. We're both a little shaken. "However did you find it? It wasn't marked as Assembly of Saints, was it?"

"No. I just looked for creepy cult videos," she says. "In Tennessee, 'cause that's where he started out. That's all I found, though. Wish I'd found the new place."

"You did great," I tell her. She needs that, as much as or more than my own kids. And she nearly glows under the light of that small encouragement. I see it, but I can hardly feel it. My heart is nearly dead, and it will be until we find Connor.

The dawn's a layer of promise on the horizon, but I go and rouse Lanny, and get Vee to change back into her clothes.

"Where are we going?" Lanny asks me as she drags a loose black shirt over her head. "Do we know where they are?"

"Not quite," I tell her. "We're going to find someone who can tell us where to look."

Because I'm going to find Carol.

And this time she's going to tell me everything.

18

Sam

I don't remember much of anything after seeing Gwen hit from behind, seeing her go down, and charging after the man who was taking Connor.

Just flashes.

The deafening shrieks of the kids' panic alarms going off.

Connor being dragged to the dirty RV parked outside.

Bracing myself and getting good aim on the craggy face of the man who had my son.

It's fuzzy after that. A sudden, spasmodic, overwhelming pain. Being down, losing the gun when it's kicked from my hand. Being kicked again until I'm out.

I try to remember more but all I can see is Connor's face, stark and terrified.

I wake up slowly, and the memory fades into an unsettling reality. I'm shackled by my feet to a U-bolt in the floor of the RV, and my hands are manacled together with a long chain through the same bolt. Just enough slack for me to sit tied in this dirty, frayed bucket chair that's also bolted down.

They didn't get me from behind, I know that; I had all three of them right in front of me. One slightly off to the left. When I concentrate, I think I remember seeing flashes of light as the pain hit and I collapsed.

One of them must have had a Taser, and he juiced me down until they could kick me unconscious. I'm bruised and sore, and I may have a cracked rib, but I'm better than I expected. One hell of a headache throbbing like a fist behind my eyeballs. None of that matters, because Connor is sitting in the chair across from me.

He's tied down, too, same manacle setup. He's bruised and scraped, but his eyes are clear and sharp, and I see the relief when he realizes I'm waking up. "Dad?" he blurts out, and I feel a complicated rush of emotion. Fear. Intense love. Rage that I can't get to him. He doesn't call me Dad often, and when he does, it means his defenses are low. It means everything to me that he trusts me that much. I can't let him down. "Are you okay?"

"I'm fine," I tell him. *We're not fine. This is bad.* We're in the dirty RV, rocking and rolling along bumpy roads; we're not traveling a main highway, at least not yet. They're taking some back way, avoiding any cops, I assume. It's still dark outside, and I don't think I've been out all that long. Minutes, I hope. Longer than that, this throbbing behind my eyes means I'm heavily concussed, and I don't need brain damage on top of everything else we're facing right now.

"Shut up," says one of the men. There's one driving, of course, and one sitting shotgun; the third one is in another bucket chair that's swiveled around to watch us. He's got a Taser sitting on the table next to him. No gun that I can see.

They don't want to kill us. That's good. That's an advantage I can use.

"You're not going to make it," I tell him. "Cops will already be looking for you. And the FBI. You abducted a kid this time, not an adult. You know what that gets you? Amber Alerts. Federal and state investigation all over your asses. They'll have you ID'd from the surveil-lance video at our house in a matter of hours, and how long do you think this piece-of-shit RV is going to stay anonymous? Just let us go. Let us go and call it good."

"Next time you talk, you get this," the man says, and touches the Taser. He isn't listening. Or believes God is going to protect him, though they have to have some awareness of just how risky this is. They've been careful before. Something about this has made them reckless enough to break their patterns.

Nothing scarier than fanatics who don't feel like they have anything to lose.

I shut up, because I need to be ready and able to protect Connor, if it comes to that. I memorize the layout of the RV. Lights are dim, yellowed with age, but they reveal matted, old carpet; a tiny, cramped kitchen with a cracked counter and locked-up shelves; four bucket-style chairs; a couple of small tables; and two bunk beds all the way at the back, just visible behind a sagging folding door. I guess the other fold-ing door hides the toilet. The inside of this thing smells like a locker room baked under a heat lamp. I assume there's usually a woman with them—the bait for their preaching—but if so, there's no sense of a woman's touch in here.

The curtains—plaid, in rust and avocado-green patterns—are clamped shut on all the windows. Nobody can see in. I'm looking for escapes. Besides the entry door across from me—bolted shut from the inside, and fastened with a padlock—there's a hatch in the floor that's probably for maintenance, and one up above with a skylight over it. No exit in the back that I can see. But options, at least.

If I get loose, I intend to kill as many of them as I need to, hijack this piece of shit, and drive to the nearest place we can get real help. If I can't manage that, I'll get Connor out through one of the escape hatches before I go down fighting. It isn't much, but at least he'll have a chance to run. Hide. Find help.

It's not the best plan. My headache is so strong it's making my stomach boil, but I doubt they're going to give me a bathroom break.

"Why do you want us?" Connor asks. He directs it straight at the man with the Taser. "What did we ever do to you?"

"Don't worry. You'll be home soon," the man says. "My name is Caleb, by the way. The woman we're after stole a baby. All we want is to find him and bring him home." He treats Connor like an equal, not a captive. I get his contempt. For Connor, he busts out the warmth.

And Connor is listening. "Are you trying to find your baby?"

"No. He's Father Tom's son. That makes him my brother. So I want him back too."

Jesus. He thinks Connor can be manipulated, I realize. I'd like to say the kid's immune to that, but at this age? No. Connor's dad played on his fears and his need to belong. Same thing cults do.

He's vulnerable.

I can't let this new asshole get a grip on Connor's soul. So even though I know I'll get punished for it, I say, "And when the babies are girls, how old are they when you marry them off to your prophet? How old do they have to be before he starts molesting them?"

That pisses Caleb right off, which is what I intend; he grabs the Taser. I see him fire it this time, and the bright pop as the electrodes hit me and start pulsing.

That's pretty much all I see before the amps fire, and then I don't see or feel anything but waves of mind-numbing agony as my muscles convulse. It stops for a second and I catch my breath, but then he presses the trigger again. More agony. I hear Connor yelling for him to stop. My lungs are pulsing, burning for air, but my muscles won't unlock enough for me to fill them. I don't think you can tase someone to death, but it feels like it.

Seems like a year until he finally runs out of juice, and the pulsing, paralyzing shocks stop coming. I gasp in a huge, whooping breath. My chains rattle from the force of the convulsions, and the metal around my wrists and ankles feels hot. Just being alive feels like a victory.

I can hear him pressing the trigger again. Nothing. He's killed the battery. *You son of a bitch.* There's a real sadistic streak in Caleb. And better I am its target than Connor.

"Leave him alone!" Connor shouts, and from the driver's seat comes a sharp command for all of us to shut up or get gagged. I manage to nod to Connor. Give him a thumbs-up signal, even though I'm limp as a landed fish and twitching with reaction. I acknowledge the pain and focus on the man who was so quick on the trigger. He gets up, unlocks one of the cabinets with a key from his pocket, and takes out another Taser, which he shows me very pointedly before he walks back to his table.

We all go quiet. I close my eyes, because the aftereffect of being hit with a shock like that brings exhaustion; I slip almost imperceptibly into a doze for a while. No point in being hyperalert when I'm chained down and there's nothing productive I can do. Air force pilots don't just train on flying and fighting; we also get a serious dose of SERE education. I've already failed the Search and Evasion parts of that course, since I'm sitting here tied up, but the Resistance and Escape parts are definitely applicable. The cult isn't likely to pull anything I haven't seen and felt and experienced before, and been trained how to counter. Wasn't fun to go through, but it's paying off in an unexpected way now.

All I have to do is get us to the last *E* of that training: Escape. Future-state visualization is important in all this, and I need to start making that real not just for me, but for Connor too. I need to coach him through this and get us home safe.

Or, if that isn't possible, at least get *him* home safe. Because that's my job.

He calls me Dad, and I need to live up to that.

I snap back out of my doze. The rocking and bumping of the RV has changed to a smoother, accelerating pace. We're on a real road, finally. It's nearly dawn outside, from the light leaking around the curtains. Caleb's stretched out in one of the bunks at the back. Complacent asshole.

I start methodically testing my restraints. Wherever we're heading, we're moving fast toward it. The U-bolt in the floor that I'm chained to is completely solid. So are the chains, of course. There's enough slack that I can twist my wrists, winding the chain in on itself tighter and tighter. I'm hoping to find a weak spot in the links, or the manacles. I don't. Connor's watching me, and trying his own bonds. The captors are just a few feet away, and periodically the man sitting shotgun swivels around to look at me. He doesn't seem worried that I'm testing the restraints, and he doesn't bother to tell me to stop.

So I keep it up. The chair is firmly bolted down. The ropes they've secured me with around the waist and chest hold firm. He's right: they know their kidnapping jobs well.

Right, I've done due diligence. Now all we can do is wait.

I doze while the drive continues, but I wake up at every sound, alert for anything they might try to do to Connor. But they leave us alone. When I wake up again, the sun's up. The old clock on the RV's wall says it's almost exactly nine thirty in the morning, and we slow down and come to a stop with a squeal of ancient brakes. I hear voices up front—someone talking to the driver. Then the sound of metal gates rolling back with a distinctive rattle.

The RV rolls forward, but not very far—the length of a football field, at most. Then it stops, and the engine dies.

"Get your lazy ass up," the driver yells back at Caleb, and he rolls out, yawning and rubbing his face. "We're home."

"Praise the Lord," Caleb says. "Been aching for a decent meal."

My stomach rumbles, right on cue. I could use some scrambled eggs and bacon. No point in denying that craving exists, so I satisfy it as best I can by imagining how that would taste. I let it go and focus on Caleb, who is releasing Connor. He unlocks a padlock at the bottom of the U-bolt, sliding the chains free; Connor starts to struggle, but he's not going anywhere. Still tied to the chair. Caleb knows his job. He gets right in the kid's face and says, "Look, I don't like to do this, but you're not giving me a choice. Stay still, or I'll shock you unconscious. Understand?" He knows Connor saw what that did to me. And I hate the fear that I see on the boy's face before he locks it down behind a calm, stiff expression. I've seen that look before. He gets it when he hides everything and tries to cope, but it's less a shield than a thin Halloween mask. It won't protect him long.

Connor locks eyes with me. I mouth, *Do what he says.* Connor nods slightly. I'd worry more if it were Lanny, who'd take the wrong opportunity to rebel, but Connor's cautious. He'll be okay.

I'll make sure of that.

My heart's beating too fast. I use breathing techniques to slow it down as I watch Connor get untied and brought to his feet. Caleb keeps the manacles on his wrists and ankles and leads him shuffling to the door and out. All my training can't lock down the worry I feel, having him out of my sight. *This was inevitable,* I try to tell myself. *They're going to separate you. Wait for your chance.*

That doesn't help the fear I feel—not for myself. For him.

I count seconds. It's a way to stay calm when I can't see what's happening. Not knowing can drive you nuts, especially when emotions run so high. When counting doesn't stop my brain, I make it do square roots. Anything to keep it occupied.

It takes ten minutes for Caleb to come for me. By this time the other two men have exited, and I'm left alone in the RV. Caleb uses the same routine with me as Connor. First, he opens my padlock and unthreads the chains. There's an opportunity, but it's not a good one—I can mule-kick him in the chest, if I'm fast enough, but that still leaves me tied up in the chair, inside a compound with a locked metal gate. Not to mention I don't know how many of them are waiting out there armed. I'd still take the chance if I knew the keys had been left in the ignition, and if I were just getting myself out.

But Connor's not here. And that means I need to be out there. The problem is that if this cult is as experienced and smart as they seem to be, they'll never keep me close to him. Isolation will be part of the disorientation tactic. Isolation and fear, coupled with acceptance and support by cult members. But for Connor, I think, not for me. I'm not their primary target; I'm the control.

Being the control has certain advantages. I'm more disposable, but at the same time, killing or even seriously injuring me will impair their ability to handle Connor, so that means they probably have a hard red line of how far they'll go. As long as I'm alive, he'll work to please them and keep me safe. Kill me, and he'll close up. From Caleb's attitude toward the boy, they'd like to recruit him. He's at a prime age. And maybe having Melvin Royal's son in the congregation would be a perverse feather in the cult leader's cap.

Caleb leaves me tied up in the chair and steps back, and that's when I realize someone new is coming on board the RV; the floor dips with his weight, and when Caleb's out of the way I see an older man with pale, almost white hair. Pale skin to match. Nothing impressive about him. He's medium height, maybe a little thin, wearing a plain white pull-on shirt and loose white trousers. Not nearly as tanned and sunbaked as his followers, which means he spends his time indoors, not working fields. Long hair that flows all the way down to brush his shoulders. He's going for the Christlike image, according to the popular paintings, and it works for him.

"Hey, it's Jesus," I say. "Is this heaven?"

Caleb's not amused. He picks up the Taser, but Fake Jesus puts his hand on Caleb's arm and shakes his head. He's smiling. "Let him joke," he says. "Brother Sam, yes, Jesus is here. Not in me, I'm not so arrogant as to think that. But in all of us. Even you." He keeps smiling.

It's unsettling. "I'm Father Tom. I know you think ill of us right now, but you'll come to see the truth. Everyone does eventually."

He sounds certain of himself—not a trace of doubt in those calm, mad eyes. I don't answer, because I get nothing if I let myself give in to my smart-ass nature. The best strategy for the rest of this, no matter what happens, is to play quiet, exaggerate weakness and injury, give nothing. I don't know if I'm valuable to them beyond being a club to beat Connor with. But even that's enough. I can use that to stay alive, and relatively unharmed.

Never agree. Never admit. Never ask. Never sign. Even a simple *yes* to something is a hook they sink into you, a crack in your armor, and it can be used in all kinds of dangerous ways. Enough hooks sunk in, and they can drag you where they want you to go.

Alert and neutral, always accept food and drink but never ask for it. The training comes back fast, as it was meant to.

I lower my gaze and say nothing.

They untie me, watching for any hint of resistance, but I don't offer any. I go along quietly, shuffling in my leg irons like a criminal on my way to a cell. I sweep in as much as I can in a long glance—multiple buildings, fields in the distance, vehicles, barns. An open central area. Lots of people moving around.

A church situated prominently near the center of the compound.

I look for Connor, and I see him; they're taking his ankle manacles off, which is good. It means he can run if he needs to. But it also means they want to instill a sense of gratitude in him. They'll wait awhile for an opportune moment, then do him the additional favor of taking off the handcuffs. Little kindnesses. Maybe paired with pain, maybe not. At his age, love will work better than torture.

And that's Connor's weakness. He needs love the way a sponge needs water. And from a father figure, doubly true. If they spot his weak points—and they will, they're experts at this game, predators always are—then they'll know how to get to him. Good cult indoctrinators can pull it off in just a couple of weeks at the most. And that's on adults.

I need to stay ready. For both our sakes.

It starts as I expected. While Connor's getting well treated, they sink a punch into my midsection. That's Caleb's job, of course, as soon as Jesus / Father Tom has turned his back and walked away; it *looks* like Father Tom isn't aware of it, but of course he is. Connor sees it, which is what they intend. Double incentives for him: cooperate with us, you get treated well. They're setting him up to have him ask for better treatment for me, which puts him in their debt psychologically. And he won't understand that. I hate that I'm the lever they're going to pull on him, but that's how it works.

I meet his frantic gaze for a second and smile. I give him a silent thumbs-up to let him know I'm okay, that it's fine, that he doesn't need to be worried. It's all I can do to insulate him before they hustle me away in a different direction, dragging me when my shackled legs don't move fast enough. I still manage to look back, and find him anxiously staring my direction. I try to put everything I can into that look—love, especially. Some steel too. I hope he gets it. I can't be sure.

Then we're around the corner of a low concrete building, and at the end of it there's a steel shed.

They throw me in the cold, cramped, pitch-black shed and leave me there.

Step one: deprivation and stress.

I can't stretch out; I have to try to get comfortable against cold, hard sides and a dirt floor. No blankets, of course. No water either. *Not even a pot to piss in.* The old lament sounds funny at the moment, but it isn't. They're not going to provide me with a toilet. I have to make one, and I do, digging in the hard dirt until I've scraped out a hole in the corner. Good enough for now. The laborious exercise also tells me that the walls have a foundation that goes down at least three inches, and probably several feet more than that. Digging out might be possible, but it'll take time, and there's no way to conceal the extra dirt from anyone who looks. So: probably useless effort.

I use the hole as intended, and try to stretch out and rest. I'm cold, and I'm thirsty, but I know they'll withhold water until they get something they want. Whatever that will be.

They've taken my cell phone; they're not that stupid. They probably left that on the side of the road long ago, or—if really clever—sent it on a wild-goose chase in exactly the wrong direction. I have no weapons. They stripped off my shoes and shirt too. The pants will be next. Eventually, every prisoner in a situation like this ends up naked.

I curl up in a ball, preserve what core warmth I can, and shiver until I can fall asleep.

I wake up to singing, and for a disoriented moment it sounds like a chorus of angels. It's *beautiful*. I sit up, listening, eyes shut against the darkness; it feels better if I control how dark it is rather than having it forced on me. They're singing a hymn, and the female voices lift it up to a clear, warm height. Feels like sunlight. Like joy.

When the song ends it's just silence, and darkness, and the cold, and it feels like forever. I need to get to Connor. But I know that need is a weakness they're going to use against me.

I'm trying not to think about Gwen, about what might have happened to her and to Lanny after I was tased out. *She's okay. These assholes cannot stop her. She'll figure it out. She'll point the goddamn army our direction if she has to.*

That comforts me just enough to let me sleep. I dream that I'm falling into a hole so dark it swallows me up completely, but then I feel Gwen's arms around me, and her strength at my back, and I hear her whisper, *I'm here.*

It's a good start to survival.

19

LANNY

I don't know why it doesn't hit me until I'm alone in my room at the Belldene house, but it all just . . . crashes on me. I'm wearing a stranger's nightgown because I forgot to pack one in my backpack. I'm lying on a bed that feels like it's molded for someone else's body. Clean sheets, clean pillows, but the room smells all wrong, and those aren't *my* posters on the walls, or *my* books on the shelves.

And as I'm lying there, I realize that my brother's really, really missing. He's *gone*. They took him away, and I was scared out of my mind and hid behind the couch and I *didn't stop them*. I'm so ashamed. I always, *always* thought I would fight, no matter what. I always told Connor that I'd protect him if something happened, and I meant it.

But I didn't. I let it happen. And Mom was hurt, and Sam—

I press my face to the pillow. My skin feels hot and tight, and tears just explode out of me like my eyes hold geysers of misery. I curl up and cry into the soft cotton pillowcase that smells like someone else's detergent, and I think about my brother's face, about how *scared* he looked. Before, I was there for him. I defended him.

But he's all alone now and *I hate this*. I hate feeling like a failure, and the worst of it is, *I blame Mom*. This is all because of her, because of her job. I thought it was cool and awesome, but it brought those men to our house, and there's nothing good about any of this.

I hear my door open, and I gasp and throw myself upright. In my room I'd know what to reach for, but here I just look around like a dumbass. All I have to defend myself is a pillow.

But then I realize that it's Vee. Vee, in a stupidly short nightgown that looks like it was made for a twelve-year-old. She puts her finger to her lips and closes the door behind her, then comes to sit on the bed next to me. I'm hugging the pillow tight, and she puts her arm around me and pulls me closer. It gets smashed between us until I toss it aside.

Vee's fingers trace the tracks the tears left. Gentle sweeps down my face. "Hey," she says. "Don't be sad. You're gonna be okay."

"No, I'm not," I say. I sound ridiculous and teary and stubborn. "Look at us, we're in some drug dealer's house, my brother's missing, and some *cult* is trying to get us, and *I'm not going to be okay, Vee!*"

Vee doesn't answer. She just holds me, and when I finally pull away, I throw myself back down on the bed and curl up into a tight ball of misery. I stare at the clock—an old-fashioned one with hands, probably doesn't even have an alarm or anything—and wonder where Connor is right now. How scared he is. What we're going to do about it.

Vee spoons up against me, and she whispers something I don't really hear, but the soothing warmth of her against my skin makes me stop crying and slowly, slowly drift away.

I wake up slow, smelling food, but when I turn over I'm all alone. Vee isn't there. For a sweet few seconds I think I'm at home, but then I focus on that stupid clock, and it's almost seven, and as I sit up I remember everything.

It hurts so bad I can hardly catch my breath.

I slide out of bed and lock the door before I strip off the nightgown and grab fresh clothes out of my backpack. I'm packed again and ready to slip into the hall bathroom in under two minutes, and all my stuff gets done fast there too.

When I open the door, there's a girl standing there. She's lean, tall, with a smart sunburned face and freckles, and long, curling dark hair. She doesn't smile. "Breakfast," she says, and turns to go. She's wearing jeans and a T-shirt so faded I can't figure out what it says. She walks fast. I skip to catch up as I settle my backpack on my shoulder.

"Who are you?" I ask.

"Florida," she says. "You're Lanny." Her accent isn't what I expect. Not Tennessee, for sure.

It hits me a second later. "Are you *English*?"

We're already at the end of the hall, and we meet the tall young man who led us here in his car coming around the corner. He pushes Florida out of his way with the ease of an older brother. "She ain't English," he tells me. "She just watches a lot of PBS."

"You shut up, Jesse!" she yells after him, and now her accent has shifted back to rural drawl. "You never let me have any fun!"

Lilah Belldene's standing in the kitchen when we walk in, and she's putting out a huge platter of bacon on the long counter. There are staggering amounts of scrambled eggs, toast, bacon, and several pots of coffee.

Vee and Mom are already here. Dressed and waiting.

Florida says, "Should I get them out plates, Ma?"

Lilah slaps her hand as she reaches for them. "They ain't staying for breakfast."

That's too bad. My stomach rumbles, but Mom turns and heads for the front door. Vee and I follow, and step into the cold morning air. It's misty and gray, with the sun a pale shadow to the east just sitting on the edge of the hill. A whole football team of Belldenes is heading toward the main house, coming from different buildings situated around the compound. No wonder she didn't ask us to breakfast.

We get into the SUV and drive to the gate, where one Belldene opens it up for us. I recognize him. Mullet man, from Killing Rock.

Seeing him, I shrink back in the seat. It brings back finding Candy up there, and I don't want that.

Vee rolls down her window and says, "Hey, Olly. You're out."

"Yeah," he says, and looks past her at me. "Thanks for that, girl." He gives me a grin he probably thinks is pretty charming. I nearly give him the finger.

"Sure," I say. "Whatever."

"See you later!" Vee shouts to him as Mom hits the gas and speeds us away. Vee flops back into her seat after waving, and looks at my mom. "Where are we going now?"

"Knoxville," she says.

I tense up. "But—what about Connor? And Sam? Aren't we going to get them?"

"Of course we are. But I need leverage, and that means I need Carol. She's the only one who knows where this compound is really located, and what we'll be up against when we find it."

"But how are you going to—"

"Lanny." She reaches over and takes my hand. Her fingers feel strong, but cold. "Just trust me. I will."

I hang on to her.

And I try to believe her.

20

CONNOR

When they take Sam away they hit him, and I know Caleb's doing it to scare me. It would have worked except for how Sam looks at me, like he's telling me to be strong. I'm not strong. I feel cracked all along the edges. As I watch him being taken off to a low concrete building that looks like a prison, a guy dressed in white starts walking over to me.

It's weird. I can *feel* him as he comes closer, like heat. Sun. Something like that. He makes me feel . . . safe. And I know I shouldn't, *obviously* I shouldn't. I remember this feeling because it's how my dad's—Melvin Royal's—voice made me feel when I was little, and when he talked to me on the phone.

All the while Dad was lying to me, planning to kidnap me and use me to hurt Mom, he made me feel just like this.

Safe.

Some people have that talent, I guess. And I already know how dangerous it is to believe it, even for a second.

"Connor," the man says, like he's known me all my life. "I'm Father Tom. I know you're worried and scared, but there's no reason to be. We're so happy to have you here. I'm going to introduce you to our church members and get you settled. You're not a prisoner here. You're a guest, and, I hope, a friend."

It sounds stupid, but it's almost like the whole abduction never happened. Like he's *invited* me here. He pats me on the shoulder. He acts like I'm here on a school retreat or something instead of dragged away with a knife to my throat while my mom was fighting to get to me. Like Sam wasn't just put in some kind of prison.

I need to remember what's true. Being around him, reality bends. *I wish I could do that.* Because if I could, I'd make myself bigger, stronger, nobody to screw with. Sam would be free. We'd be home.

Father Tom is still talking, and he's steering me at a slow walk toward a big main building. It sort of looks like a church, but there's no steeple or cross or bell, and the windows are just plain clear glass. I'm not sure I ought to go with him.

Maybe I should run? Fight? But there's nowhere to go. The gate is closed, and there are big guys with guns standing next to it. The wall is pretty high, and there's wire along the top. Mom taught me to look for these things, to think before I do anything. *Run if you can. Wait if you have to. Do what you have to do to survive.* She'd meant it for people coming to get us because of what Dad did. But it works for this too.

Right now, making Father Tom think I'm listening to him is the best thing I can do. It's easy. He thinks he's smarter than everybody else anyway. If I just agree with him, he'll start trusting me.

It's weird how calm I am. I remember how helpless and trapped I felt in class, with the gunshots blaring over the loudspeaker and everybody screaming and knowing all I could do was *hide*. Here, I *am* trapped, I *am* helpless . . . but I can also think for myself. Somehow that's different.

I haven't said much to Father Tom, but he doesn't seem to care; maybe he sees it as normal. He leads me up the steps into the building— church, I guess—and inside there are people standing on either side of a path that's marked by a narrow carpet running down the middle. They're in neat rows, and I realize after a couple of seconds that all the men are on the left side, all the women on the right. The women are standing with their hands clasped and their heads bowed. There are a few kids, too, but they seem just as quiet and serious as the adults. Even the littlest, who can't be more than three years old. They all turn to look at us, and as we pass, the men say, all together, "Hello, Brother."

I think they're talking to Father Tom, but no: they're looking at me. Smiling. Nodding. The women and kids don't say anything, they just keep looking down, and all of a sudden I remember how the ladies looked down in that basement in Wolfhunter. They stood just that way, very straight, very still, heads down, hands clasped. Like little dolls waiting for orders.

It makes me sick.

Father Tom takes me all the way down the length of the church—and I guess it has to be one—and at the end there's a wooden platform about a foot high and a big leather armchair sitting in the middle. It looks strange. I was expecting to see a podium, maybe. Or an altar, like in a real church. But it looks more like a . . . stage.

Father Tom points to an empty spot in the front row, next to the carpet, and says, "The brothers saved you a place." He expects me to go where he points, I see that. I'm not sure what's going to happen if I don't, so I try it. I just stand on the carpet like I'm too dumb to understand. He still looks friendly when he says, "Connor, would you mind taking your place? I promise, this will be quick."

I don't say anything, but I move off to the side where he points. I see the extra little curl in his smile. He thinks he's got me, because I did something he asked. But I did it to see what *he* would do. And because I can't do Sam any good if I'm locked up somewhere.

Father Tom steps up on the platform and seats himself in the big chair. When he does, the men all say, "God bless you, Father."

"And you, my brothers," Tom says. "Thank you for welcoming young Brother Connor into our number. He's only here as our guest, but I know he will appreciate your charity to a stranger. Now, I know you're all wondering what happened last night; you know we went out to retrieve our sister Carol, but as you also know, the demons in the world are clever. It's been three long years, and she's still hidden from us, along with our precious child. But with God's help, and the continuous prayers of our saints, we are going to find them. Very soon." He beams a smile right at me, and it's like getting hit with a spotlight. "With God's help, and Brother Connor's."

I want to yell back that I'm not here to help him, I've been *kidnapped*, but something tells me to keep quiet. Lanny wouldn't, she'd be kicking and screaming and maybe she'd be right to do that. But I want to see what he's planning.

This has to be about the case that Mom was working, the one with the missing young man. She'd talked about a woman named Carol.

Don't tell him anything, Mom. I know they're using me to get to her. And it's going to work, too, because if my mom has a weak spot, it's me and Lanny. And Sam, but he'd probably agree that it's more about us. I'm here to make Mom give up that lady who escaped.

"Brothers and sisters, we will pray about this tonight after work's done. But for now I want you to take young Brother Connor under your care, make him feel at home, and show him our true fellowship. We'll have a dinner this evening, Sister Harmony. A real feast to welcome him to Bitter Falls."

A tall, blonde woman on the other side of the aisle in the front row raises her head and nods, but she doesn't say anything. She's probably Mom's age, maybe a little younger. I guess she's in charge of food or something. And right on cue my stomach rumbles. I don't know how I can be hungry at a time like this, but I am, and I can't help that. Maybe I shouldn't eat anything here. Isn't there some Greek story about how if you eat and drink in the underworld, you can't leave?

Father Tom talks a little bit more, but it's all Bible verses and explaining what they mean, and I don't really listen; what he's saying about them isn't what I learned in Sunday school. He has a calm, deep voice, though, and it rises and falls almost like he's singing. It's kind of relaxing, and I fall into sort of a trance listening to it.

Then it's over.

I'm a little surprised when I realize people are moving. The women and kids are heading straight for the door, walking single file, while the men stand and wait; Father Tom is sitting in his chair talking to one of the guys who was in the RV with us, the one who drove, not the one who shocked Sam. I'm concentrating hard on them, so it comes as a surprise when I realize someone's holding a hand out to me. I blink and look up. It's one of the men who's been standing next to me. "Good to have you here, Brother Connor," he says, and shakes my hand. He claps a hand on my shoulder like we're friends, and then before I tell him I'm not his friend, that I shouldn't even be here, he's replaced by another, shorter man, who says, "Welcome, you're safe here." They're all coming at me, beaming big smiles and offering handshakes. "God bless you for visiting us," one of them says, like I had any choice. I know this has been set up, that they're under orders to make me feel like a guest. It's like they just accept Father Tom's fake reality without question. I usually know when somebody's saying things to me just to say it, but every one of these men who talks to me seems *actually* happy to see me.

I try saying, "I want to leave," to one of them. He just smiles and nods and does that shoulder-clap thing, then moves aside for the next one.

After ten of them, I start losing track. They all say slightly different things, but one thing's constant: they smile at me. They seem happy. They do that shoulder-touch thing.

It's really hard, after a while, not to smile back. I don't *want* to smile, but when people do that, when they're beaming all that happy at you . . . it's weird. It tells some part of you that you ought to seem happy too.

I don't like that I want to smile.

I catch one of the young women—my age, I think, or pretty close—giving me a quick look as she files out of the church. She's a pretty dark-haired girl, shorter than me. I watch her while some new guy tells me how glad they are to have me here. She's at the end of the line of women leaving the church.

She turns and looks at me again, and I wonder—I wonder if she's trying to tell me something. Maybe she can help me. Maybe I can find a *real* friend here who can help me get Sam free.

I can almost hear my sister mocking me. *You just want to think that because she's pretty.*

Once the girl's out the door, the men start to leave, too, and by the time the last one shakes my hand I feel exhausted with all the welcomes. I didn't see Father Tom leave, but his chair's empty now. I don't know where to go, so I follow the men as they leave the building.

The girl I noticed is standing near the steps, talking to an older woman. She shoots me another glance and smiles. It's fast, but it feels like all the air just got sucked out of the world. I feel my ears pop, or I think I do. My skin goes hot and cold at the same time, and I nearly miss a step.

It's that kind of smile.

"Hi?" I make it a question. Smooth.

She says, "Hello, Brother Connor," and I think I've never heard anybody say my name that way before. "We're all so pleased to have you with us." She bobs a little bit, like an old-fashioned curtsy. She doesn't shake hands, and I don't know what to do with mine, so I put them in my pockets and sort of nod.

The older woman walks away from us.

"Thanks," I say to the girl. "What's your name?"

"Aria," she says, and I don't think I've ever met anybody with that name before. It's pretty.

"Aria what?"

She smiles. "I'll be happy to show you around the place. Can I call you Connor?"

"Uh, sure," I say. "I'd like to talk to my dad. To Sam."

She doesn't stop smiling. "Sure, I'll ask if we can do that. But he's not your *real* father, is he?" I don't like that, and she has to see it, because immediately she draws back, like I'm about to hit her. "I'm sorry. That was mean. I shouldn't have said it."

Now I feel bad for scaring her. "No," I say, "it's okay. You're right. It's just . . . I don't like to talk about my birth dad."

"Oh. Of course. I'm so sorry, Connor. Well, I guess the first place you should see is the falls, it's the best part of this place, and then—"

"Aria!" a voice says sharply, and I look up to see the oldest of the women—Sister Harmony, Father Tom called her earlier—moving toward us. She looks mad. "Get to your work. Now!"

"But I was only doing what Father Tom—"

"Go!" Sister Harmony snaps. Aria gasps and moves away very quickly with her head down and her long hair blowing across her face. She's wearing a blue skirt long enough that only her shoes are visible, and a paler blue shirt, and she looks like a painting in a museum—beautiful, and also like someone who lived a hundred years ago. Her hands are in fists at her sides as she walks toward the fields.

Sister Harmony looks at me, and unlike everybody else who's been smiling at me, she doesn't. Her mouth is set in a flat line. "I'll show you to your quarters, Brother Connor," she says, and for the first time I hear something that isn't welcoming. She doesn't want me here. There isn't any of that feverish warmth coming off her either. She puts a firm hand around my arm. "Forgive Sister Aria, she's young and doesn't understand how inappropriate her behavior is. This way."

After all that fake brotherhood, this feels . . . real. Like fresh air in my face. And I needed that, I realize. It wasn't that I forgot being kidnapped and brought here, or Mom fighting for me, or Sam. It was just . . . a lot. And now that I've had that moment of feeling clear, I realize everything about that church was meant to make me feel *important*. Even Aria.

She was ordered to be nice to me.

If Sister Harmony was, she's ignoring that, and I'm weirdly grateful. Between the droning rhythm of Father Tom's sermon, all the smothering, Aria's flirting . . . I was way off balance.

Sister Harmony takes me to a building that's nothing but a kitchen, and inside are only women. Women slicing vegetables. Women working at large industrial stoves, stirring pots or mixing ingredients. Two of them are making bread. It smells amazing, and my mouth waters so much I have to swallow.

There's a small table in the corner, and she sits me down there. "I'll get you some food," she says, and turns away. But then she turns back. "I know you probably are thinking of ways to get out of here. But Connor: don't try. They're watching you. Break the rules, and the man they brought in with you will pay the price. Do you understand?"

I nod. She's said it very quietly, and it's hard to hear over the noise of the kitchen. Her lips are tight, her eyes darkened, and I wonder how exactly Sister Harmony got here. But that second of connection ends, and she stiffens her back and moves off. The other women all glance up and nod as she passes, but nobody smiles. She's got power here. Not a lot of friends.

I wonder if this is some other kind of game Father Tom is playing. Does she *want* me to worry about Sam? Is this supposed to make me play by the rules? I'm not sure. Maybe she means it. Or maybe she's just like Aria, sent to make me do exactly what Father Tom wants.

I need to get to Sam. Once I know where he is, maybe I can steal some keys and let him out. I close my eyes and think about that, about making some escape over the fence, and how good it will feel to get out of here and back to Mom and Lanny. That helps me remember that this place isn't *real*. Out there, that's real. This is all . . . fake.

A shy, round-faced woman of about twenty brings me a bowl of soup and some bread, and I wonder for a moment if I should eat it or not. I'm so hungry, but . . . I don't trust it either.

The woman understands immediately. She goes and gets a spoon and takes a big mouthful of soup from my bowl, and a chunk off my bread. She eats it, still smiling that weird smile. "See?" she says. "All safe. We wouldn't do anything to hurt you, Brother."

I push the bowl away anyway. "I'm really not that hungry," I tell her. I take a little bit of the bread. It's *good*.

"Well," she says, "if you're not hungry, of course, I understand. You can come here anytime you need food. Just ask for me. Sister Lyrica."

I'm regretting my choices when she picks up the bowl and takes it away, but I eat the rest of the bread. Bread that probably isn't drugged, if she ate it first, or at least that's what I tell myself because I can't stop eating it. Sister Lyrica brings me a plastic bottle of water that's still sealed, and I drink that.

"The bread's really good," I say, and finish the last bite. "Uh, is Sister Harmony your boss?"

"She is the elder wife," Lyrica says, and blinks. "She is responsible for all the sisters." She clearly thinks it's weird I don't know this. I wonder if she's ever been outside these walls, seen even a little bit of the real world.

"Elder wife?" I ask. "How many wives does he have?"

She seems confused by that question too. As if it's obvious. "We are all the brides of Father Tom," she says. "As God intended."

Harmony has noticed us talking. She comes striding over, long skirt flowing behind her, and snaps, "Sister Lyrica, back to your work, please. The young brother has no need of your conversation."

Lyrica hurries off, taking my empty bread plate and bottle of water. I got to drink only a little bit of it. Harmony stares at me for a long moment, then starts to leave. It's weird. She doesn't look like my mom, but there's something about her. Maybe it's the angry look. I don't feel like she's angry at *me*. Just . . . angry.

I ask, "Do you think all this is right?"

She turns to face me. I've kept my voice low, the way she did hers when she warned me.

"Do I think what is right?"

"How he treats you." I look around the room. "All of you."

"The Lord says, *Ye wives, be in subjection to your own husbands,*" she says. "I obey the commands of the Lord."

Yeah, but she doesn't like it. I can see that. I wonder if Father Tom sees it, too . . . but if he does, why would he put her in charge?

Then I remember what Lyrica said. *She is responsible for all the sisters.*

Just like Sam's responsible for anything I do wrong here. Putting her in charge means she has to cooperate, or other women get hurt.

The bread was delicious, but now it feels heavy in my stomach. Like I've eaten in the underworld, and now can never leave.

She leans over to sweep crumbs from the table into her palm, and while she does, she whispers, "Don't go to the falls, whatever you do." Then she straightens up. "Now come with me. I'll show you where you are to sleep."

"I want to see Sam," I tell her.

"That area is off limits."

She's not going to argue about it. She just moves off to dust the crumbs into the trash, and looks at me, waiting for me to move. I have to decide whether to follow her. I remember what Lyrica said again. If Harmony is responsible for the women, she's probably responsible for me, their *guest*, while I'm in her company. Which means if I take off on my own, she'll be punished along with Sam.

I can't take that chance.

I follow.

21

GWEN

There's a pressure inside me like a scream. It squeezes my heart and lungs, and no matter how deeply I breathe the pressure doesn't ease. Driving away from this strange, temporary alliance feels like being stripped bare. We need real help. Real options.

J. B. may be able to give us that.

We drive away from the Belldene compound, bouncing over the rutted, narrow track that leads back down to a logging road; Belldene boys are stationed at the gates to open them and lock them up after us. We eventually come to a two-lane country road, which is practically civilization compared to where they live. It's so remote that they have plenty of warning for anyone coming up there; if law enforcement shows up, they have plenty of time to hide evidence.

I hate that I owe these people.

Lanny's been quiet, too, but she suddenly says, "Mom, what if Sam and Connor get away? What if they come home and we're not there?" My whole body aches from a sudden rush of emotion, because the idea of them coming home is so powerful. So impossible right now.

"If they do, they'll let us know," I tell her. "Either one of them would call us, or call the police, and we'd hear immediately." I pull my phone out. "It's always on, honey." I realize that's a risk. The kidnappers could have Sam's phone, unless they trashed it as Mike Lustig thinks they probably did; if they didn't, they now have a powerful tool to trace me. He's got an app on it that allows tracking of my phone. I have to breathe through another surge of anxiety. Normally I'd ditch our phones and get new ones.

I have to remind myself that if they have the phone, if they turn it on, I can track *him*.

I check. It's off.

I have a flash of Remy Landry's mother baking cookies for a son who doesn't come home to eat them, and my mouth goes dry, my skin cold enough to show gooseflesh. *No. That's not going to happen. Not to us.*

"We should go home," Lanny says, but she doesn't mean it, not really. Our home's been made toxic by the men who broke into it. By the shotgun blasts in the drywall. By memories. She's imagining walking into a place without that lingering damage, and the reality would be very different. Neither of us could feel safe there now.

"J. B. will help us," I tell her. And I pray that I'm right, because if she can't, my next call has to be to the FBI. That's a trigger I'm deeply afraid to pull. If the FBI gets officially involved, good things can happen . . . but so can bad. Ruby Ridge. Waco.

Connor and Sam could get caught in a very deadly crossfire.

"But what if they—"

"If they can get free, they will. And God help anybody who gets in Sam's way of protecting Connor." I'm trying to believe that. Trying to make her believe it. And it works, a little; the insistent, choking pressure inside recedes enough that I feel like I can breathe again. I look down and check the gas gauge; it's an automatic thing born of living out in the country. We've got plenty.

But it comes to me in a sudden wave that although my SUV burns a fair amount of gas, that RV must burn a hell of a lot more.

And all of a sudden, I know how we're going to narrow down our search area. There can't be that many gas stations near a cult compound.

"It's going to be okay. I promise," I say, and for the first time I actually think it might be true. She doesn't answer, but she nods and closes her eyes. She looks exhausted, too, poor kid. I'm not tired at all. I don't think I'll ever sleep again, at least not until I have my son and Sam back safely.

I call Kezia and tell her about my gas station idea; she likes it, and says she'll start working on it by phone, and send the information on to the TBI and state police. And, God willing, that won't turn out a total disaster. I can't stop it. But I can try to make contingency plans.

The drive to Knoxville takes a torturously long time, and inside my brain a horrible litany of the abuse that my boys could be suffering loops over and over and over, and I have to keep my hands firm on the steering wheel so they don't shake. It feels like a relief when I spot the office building in the distance, and I park and hustle the girls upstairs. My key card gets us inside the plain, solid door, and we step inside the large open-plan office. Lots of desks, and some of them are occupied with people doing computer work; for some of J. B.'s investigators, that's the only kind they do. For others, their desk is just a place to type up reports and take calls.

I don't even have one, officially. I just claim one of the desks without a nameplate whenever I'm here, which isn't that often. That's the agreement I have with J. B.

Her office is a glass box near the back in the corner; she has all the blinds raised, and she sees me coming. She meets us halfway and gives me a hug. "Hey," she says. "How are you?" She shoves me back to take a good look, and shakes her head before I can try to lie. "Never mind. I know how you are. Lanny, hi. And I recognize Vee Crockett, of course." She would, from Wolfhunter. Her glance toward me clearly says she has no idea why Vee's with us now, and I don't try to explain. "Hey, girls.

Why don't you go back there to the break room and grab some snacks while I talk with Gwen?"

Lanny hangs back for a second until I nod, then takes Vee back in the direction that J. B. points. I follow J. B. to her office, and wait until she's closed the door and lowered the blinds before I sink into a chair. She leans against her desk and crosses her arms.

"I'd ask how in the world Vee Crockett figures into this, but that's probably not important right now," she says. "You need help, and not just moral support. Right?"

I nod. The suffocating pressure is closing in again. I want to be Badass Gwen, the woman she hired, the one who fights everything, all the time . . . but I've got no one to fight. I suck in a deep breath and say, "I need Carol."

J. B. doesn't move. "I put Fareed and Cicely on that after your bail hearing."

"And the case?"

"Dropped as of twenty-seven minutes ago. I checked. You're no longer out on bail. You're a free woman."

"That's a relief," I say. "Fareed and Cicely?" They're top operatives for J. B. Fareed is an absolute master of all levels of the internet; he can trace anyone, anywhere, anytime if they've ever so much as glanced at a computer. And Cicely is a little pocket dragon of a woman J. B. hired away from a top bail bondsman. Cicely is *dangerous*. And expensive. "Thanks."

She waves that aside. "Fareed got nothing, which wasn't too much of a surprise, as careful as this woman is. But Cicely hit the ground running. She had a theory that Carol might not chance public transportation again, not even a bus, so she went to domestic abuse shelters first. Carol has visible bruising and they don't ask questions."

"And?"

J. B. gives me a smile that makes me remember what hope feels like. "She found her. Cicely's sitting on the place; so far, Carol hasn't tried to leave it. She probably feels secure for now, but that shelter has a network that could get her out of Knoxville quickly and quietly, anytime she wants it."

"You're sure about this?"

"It's Cicely. She's never wrong." J. B. raises eyebrows at me. "What do you want to do? Please don't say abduct Carol; I'm not risking it. And I don't think you'll get her to come with you willingly this time."

"I'm not trying to," I tell her. "I just need a conversation. She can point to the exact location and what we'll be up against when we get there. Carol's the key to getting Connor and Sam back safe." I have a brief, dizzying moment imagining what might happen if Carol won't talk to me. What would I do then?

It occurs to me that I could put a tracker on her. Maybe in a zipper pocket of her backpack. That way, if everything fails, if I have to trade her for my son's life . . .

I flinch. I can't. *I can't.* I won't betray Carol to the people she fears, even after what she pulled on me. She was just trying to survive then. To protect her *own* child.

The thought I've been trying to avoid brings me up short, and I ask J. B., "Does she have a child with her at the shelter?"

J. B. cocks her head to one side, still unreadable. "Why would you ask?"

"Because I think when she ran from the cult she was pregnant," I say. "The men who came to my house were looking for her *and a child.* I'm sure they want to shut her up, if she's got information that could link them back to Remy's kidnapping. But they want that child just as much."

J. B. sighs and looks down. Her shoulders angle forward. "Cicely says there's a child with her, three or four years old. A boy."

Carol must have retrieved her child from whoever was keeping him for her. She's planning to get out of town as soon as the heat dies down. A domestic abuse shelter is an absolutely perfect place to hide.

"If it comes to that . . ." J. B. shakes her head. "Maybe you have to tell them where she is."

"I can't." I say it softly, but it feels heavy in the air anyway. "I won't turn her or her son over to them. I could never live with that. Everything I know about this cult tells me they see Carol as nothing but a walking incubator, and her son . . . They'd raise him to believe as they do. If Vee's right, I've seen video of one of their old compounds. J. B., it's . . ." I can't put into words the wave of slow horror I feel. I remember that nightmarish house in Wolfhunter, and what Sam told me of the women out at Carr's compound. I can't condemn Carol back to living hell, or her son.

"I know," she says. "You were never going to make that bargain, Gwen. That's why I like you." She pushes away from the desk. "Come on. I'll drive."

We leave Vee and Lanny at the office, over their protests; I don't want the girls anywhere near this. I don't know what's going to happen. Carol's desperate. She might be armed . . . I certainly am, and I'd do desperate things to protect my children. I don't want Lanny and Vee in the line of fire. They're parked on a sofa in the break room with a pizza and a stack of movies, and a stern warning to *stay put*. And J. B. assigns someone to watch them too. *Trust but verify.* I remember Lilah Belldene saying that, and I shake my head.

Dammit. She was right.

The domestic abuse shelter sits in a neighborhood that was once residential, now rezoned for commercial purposes; most of the original houses have been demolished or significantly renovated, but the one J. B. points to as we drive by it looks like the outlier. It's a large place, at least four or five bedrooms; at one time it was probably a showplace. Now it's showing its age and is in need of a good coat of paint and roof repairs. There's no sign on it except a small one that says **No Solicitors**. The front door looks normal enough, but it's painted metal. I'm sure it's solid. Bars on all the windows too.

"The main entrance is in the rear," J. B. says. "Cicely's in a neighbor's yard watching it. How do you want to do this?"

I don't want to lie to the people running this place. That would be the easiest way in; I could walk right up and tell them a horror story. It would even be true, just not current; being married to Melvin has given me that, at least. But I'd feel foul doing it. As J. B. smoothly turns the corner, I say, "Did you get back the bail money you put up for me yet?"

"I did," she says.

"Will you loan it to me? At bank rates?"

Her eyebrows raise, but I can't say she's really surprised. "Automatic deduction from your paychecks," she says. "Are you sure? Absolutely sure?"

"I am," I say. "But I'll need it in cash. She won't take a promise."

J. B. heads for the nearest bank branch. In twenty minutes we're carrying out a small bank bag with $50,000 inside, and I put it in my shoulder bag. J. B. doesn't ask again if I'm sure. She just drives me to a house that sits across the fence and at an angle to the shelter house; this one is vacant, with a **For Rent** sign in the window. We park and walk around to the backyard, which is as devastated as the front—dry grass and dead bushes, and junk left piled in the corners by a leaning shed. I don't see Cicely West until J. B. heads straight for her, because she's chosen a spot near the junk pile and is wearing clothes that nearly match the weathered gray paint on the shed. She's sitting in a folding chair and draped with a camouflage blanket. All the comforts, and I still can't spot her until we get within fifteen feet and she raises a hand. She rises, folds her chair, and leans it against the shed. She folds the thin camo blanket into a tight square and tucks it into the messenger bag hanging by her hip.

She barely reaches my chin—five feet tall, if that. Perfectly proportioned, with smooth skin as dark as walnut bark, and eyes the color of late-fall leaves. Cicely wears her hair close-cropped in tight spirals, and though she doesn't have bulk, she has serious skills. I've seen her take out a biker twice her size in three swift moves. "Your girl's still inside," she tells J. B., then looks at me with a serious expression. "Hey, Gwen. I'm so sorry. You doing okay?"

"Headache won't go away," I say, and attempt the smile she didn't. "I need to talk to Carol. What's our best play?"

"Straight up? They've got a van parked at the dentist's place right next door—which they also own and rent to him—to evacuate people if someone shows up to find them. So J. B. goes in the back and asks for Carol, they'll tell her no such person, and after they see J. B. drive off, they'll get Carol to the van and relocate her to another safe house. Van's our best chance."

It's solid, and it doesn't require me to go in and lie, so I nod agreement. J. B. goes to her car, and Cicely and I walk around the block to the dentist's office. It's a modernized, small clapboard house with a ramp access; there's a totally anonymous van with darkened windows sitting in one of the spots in the small parking lot that's replaced the yard. I leave Cicely on the porch and go inside the dental office and sit down in the slightly shabby waiting area; no one's at the front desk, and I hear the high whine of a dental drill in the back.

I need to stay out of sight until Cicely signals me, because if Carol spots me, she'll know exactly what's up.

The receptionist comes back to her desk and seems surprised to find me there; I just tell her I'm waiting for my friend, and she accepts that without question and goes back to reading a magazine. Minutes pass. I resist the urge to look out the window and see what's happening.

Cicely finally cracks the door open and nods, and I join her.

We move down the ramp. The driver is sliding the van's side door shut. He's a solid-looking man of about forty, balding, with skin a few shades lighter than Cicely's and a comfortable beer gut. He opens the driver's door, and Cicely moves faster than I would believe possible to get to the passenger side. As he's climbing in, she's slamming her door.

I step up to block his exit. She's drawn a gun. It's highly illegal, but she makes her point as he flinches and freezes. "Easy," she says. "We just want to talk to your passenger. Then we'll go, and she can do what she wants. Okay? Nod your head."

He hesitates, and I can see the fury and tension in him. But he nods. I slam his door and slide open the back.

Carol's in the rear corner of the van, and she has a wide-eyed little boy in her arms. There's a flash of relief when she recognizes me, but she doesn't let down her guard. I climb in and close the door after me, and hold up the bank bag that I've taken out of my purse. "This is for you," I tell her, and toss it. She catches it and unzips it. Stares at the $50,000 inside, then looks at me with confusion.

"Why?" she asks me. "After—" She doesn't finish, but then, she doesn't need to. I understand. She looks past me, at the van's driver, who's got his hands up. "It's okay. I'll talk to her."

That's a real relief. I see Cicely put the gun down to rest on her thigh. She doesn't put it away. The driver slowly lowers his hands and puts them on the steering wheel. "Don't you honk that horn," Cicely says. "We're all friends here. Right?"

He nods. But she's watching him like a hawk about to drive in claws, and he stays still.

"I just have a couple of questions, and you can go anywhere you want," I say to Carol. I pause and look at the little boy. He's adorable. I remember Connor at that age, his smiles and his rages and his little-boy charm. It hurts as much as it warms. "He's Father Tom's son, isn't he?" She clutches the cash, and finally, stiffly, nods. "And Father Tom wants him back."

"Of course he does," Carol says. "He never lets any of his property go. But I'm not letting him have Nick. I'll die first." I think, for the first time, she's being honest with me. Her bolting for the bus had probably been a temporary measure. She wouldn't have left him behind. Not permanently. "Father Tom corrupts everything he touches. I came as a runaway when I was thirteen. And he made me think I was *nothing* in so little time you wouldn't even believe it. But I'm not worthless. I'm not." She lifts her chin as she says it, and I can see she's still struggling to *know* that. Not just say it.

"Can I ask you a question?" I say. "When you lived with the cult, what did they call the place that women slept?"

She doesn't have to think. "The Garden," she says. "Like Eden. We're all his Eves." The bitterness in her voice makes me flinch, and remember that king-size bed in the deserted compound. She's not lying. She knows this cult.

I can still see her self-inflicted bruises, ripe blue-black splotches. But her damage goes far, far deeper than any of that.

I can't imagine what it took for her to run—not just for herself, but for the baby she carried. Dear God.

I take a deep breath and say, "They took my son, Connor, last night. They wanted me to tell them where you are. They came in an RV, just like you said. They got Sam too. My partner. My son's about the same age you were when they started on you."

She goes ghostly pale. She shoves the money bag into her backpack—the same one from before. Remy's. "I'm sorry," she says. "What did you tell them about me?"

"Nothing. But you need to leave, Carol. Right now. We found you. That means they can too. Take that money and start a new life with your son somewhere very far away." My eyes fill with tears, and I have to struggle to continue. "But before you go, please, *please* tell me where to find my son. I'm begging you. *Please.* It's in your power to help me save him."

"But . . . you already know about the Garden. You have to know . . ." Her voice fades out. "Oh. You found the old place. The one up near Wolfhunter. They moved out of there before I joined up."

"I know the new compound is somewhere up near the Catoosa Wildlife Area. Just—just tell me how to find them." I'm shaking so hard now I have to brace myself with both hands on the back of one of the seats. Tears break free, and I feel them cold as melting ice on my cheeks. I don't know what I'll do if she doesn't tell me. I don't want to think about that. "Carol. Please."

She's shaking her head, *God no*, she's shaking her head and I feel the desperation inside coil and twist like a snake through my guts. But she says, "He bought that old work camp up near Bitter Falls. But that won't help you. There's no way out. There's no way *in*. It's his fortress." I see the glitter of tears in her eyes, sharp as tinsel, but she blinks the shine away. "I know people who tried leaving. They all died there. He made them his *saints*. I'm sorry about your boy, but I can't help you anymore. I'm not going to let him drown my child like he did all those others—"

I go cold, and whatever else she says dissolves into noise. *Drown my child.* I try to swallow, but it feels like the saliva in my mouth has turned thick and hard as gravel. My voice is rusty when I say, "What do you mean, drown?"

Carol takes a horribly deep breath, like she's going under herself. "He told me Nick was going to be his new messiah. But he said that before, and then he said that baby didn't have the right marks, and he took him to the falls and came back alone." She shudders, and I feel it, too, a cell-deep revulsion. No wonder she ran. "Any man who steps out of line he calls *saints*, chosen by God. And he drowns them while he baptizes them. He says he's making an army up in heaven to defend us."

I feel colder than I've ever been, listening to this. "Is that what happened to Remy?"

"Remy thought he could buy my way out by promising to work for them for three months. That's what I told him. But he's not coming back; they never let anybody go. They've got him, and either he's one of them, or he's a saint now. I don't know which one." She wipes away tears. "That's the night I managed to slip away. The night Remy went with them. I took my chance, and I escaped. I traded him for my child's life. And I think about that every day."

She named her boy Nick. *Nicolas.* Remy's middle name. I think she's being as honest as she knows how right now. But the desperation gnawing at me won't let go. "I need to get in, Carol. Find my son. Where would they keep him at the compound?"

"He'd sleep with the men in their house if he was a convert," she says. "But it depends what they do with him during the day. Converts usually work the fields. But he's not a convert, he's a hostage, so I don't know. Maybe they'll keep him in the shed; that's where Father Tom locks up those he calls saints before he takes them away. But none of that matters. You can't get *in!*"

"I can ram the gates if I have to."

"They're too strong, and anyway, you'll be shot to pieces. He's got an army in there. Patrols all along the fences too. He preaches that the government's coming to kill them all the time. They'll fight. All of them." She swallows hard. "They kill for him already. And they'd die to the last man defending him."

"What about these falls you mentioned?"

"Doesn't matter. There're twelve-foot fences around the whole camp," she says. "Wire on top, and patrols all the time. They can shoot you dead before you make it over. Even if you do, they'll catch you. And God help you then."

I have to believe that there's a chance. I have to.

Carol says, "I used to have nightmares about those saints coming up out of that water. But it was never real to me. Not until I got pregnant." She swallows hard, as if she's fighting nausea. "Then I couldn't sleep for imagining my baby being drowned out there. I didn't know if it would be a boy or girl, but either way, I knew I couldn't let it be born with *him*. I volunteered for the missionary circuit—they send us out in the RVs, three men and one woman. Us converts were better at flirting than the ones born inside the compound anyway; those poor girls, they never knew any other life. We could charm those boys, tell them our sad stories, make them believe they were saving us." She looks down at the backpack she's holding. "Like Remy. It was so easy to do it. Spin a sad story, tell him only he could be my hero. And he thought he was doing right."

I want to go. I *need* to go. She's confirmed the place—Bitter Falls— where we might find Connor and Sam. But there's a magnetic, awful pull to her self-loathing and her guilt.

"None of this is on you," I tell her. "You were a victim. You were a child. Brainwashed. Abused. The fact you found the strength to run says everything about you. Just—live for your son. Find a place you can be safe. I promise you, if you ever need me, all you have to do is call. I'll help."

"Why?" It sounds like a cry of pain. "I screwed you over first chance I got!"

"You did what you had to do, Carol. I understand."

She's silent for another couple of seconds before she says, "He gives us all names he likes. Music names. Flower names. Mine was *Carol.*" She suddenly holds out her hand, balancing her son in one arm. "But I'm Daria. Daria Iverson. And this is Nick Iverson."

I take her hand and shake it. "Gwen Proctor," I say. "But . . . I used to be Gina Royal. I feel about that name the way you feel about Carol. It belongs to the dead."

I don't ask where she's going when she leaves. I hope she disappears. I hope she and her son find some anonymous corner of the world to make their own, far away from compounds and saints and the dead.

But me?

I'm going to war.

22

SAM

I expect beatings on the regular, so I'm not surprised when the door clanks open and three men rush in to put the boots to me. I roll into a ball and take it, to the extent one can take these things; the pain hits sharp as glass, but I don't think anything breaks, and when they leave me bleeding and breathless on the dirt floor, they toss down a half-empty bottle of water and a piece of bread.

Literal bread and water. Good they know the classics.

I sip a little, despite the urge to drink it all at once, and put the bottle aside. I save half the bread for later, and eat it in small bites. I taste blood from my split lip when I chew. I've already lost track of time, even though I tried to count out hours by scratching marks on the dirt where the sun fell, until the sun was gone.

I don't know where Connor is, and I have to stop thinking about him, because there's no way out of here—yet. I let them have their fun this time without a fight, mainly because I want them to get complacent. Next time they'll come in without so much aggression and with a lot more confidence. I'll let them have that one too. The third time, if the circumstances are right and their defenses are low, I'll get the fuck out of this hole, locate Connor, and find us both a way out.

I have to hold back from eating all the homemade bread, because it's as good as I've ever had. But best to save it for later.

I hear a quick, nervous knock on the door. For a darkly hilarious second I almost say, "Who is it?" like this is my home, like I could allow them entry if I wanted. But I keep quiet.

"Are you there?" a voice asks. I've been hoping it will be Connor, but at the same time, I don't want it to be. I want him to stay safe, obey the rules, not risk himself.

It's not Connor. It's a woman's voice, or maybe a girl's. Very tentative. I try to get up, groan, and stay down. I used to manage pain better. Maybe I'm getting old. "Where else would I be?" I ask. I scoot over and lean my head against the metal door. I'd better be grateful it's early winter, I realize. This thing would be a merciless oven in summer. The cold's got me shivering, but it's not down low enough—yet—that I need to worry about hypothermia. Going to be hell sleeping, but I've survived worse.

"What's your name?" she whispers. "I can't stay long, I'm sorry. Just tell me who you are."

"Sam Cade," I say. I don't intend to give them much beyond that, because this is probably a tactic. "Who are you?"

She doesn't answer that. She just says, "Are you his father? The boy's?"

There are alternate answers to that; I choose the simplest. "Yes."

"He's in trouble," she says. "You need to get him out of here. Soon."

That makes me forget the aches and the cold and everything else. I straighten up and look at the door like I can see past it. "What's happening?" I ask.

"It happens to all of them," she says. My mysterious stranger. "It only ends two ways. He ends up a brother, or he ends up a saint. Neither is good."

I realize that this, too, may be a tactic—a disinformation tactic designed to weaken my focus, damage my ability to resist. Naturally, they're going to play me and Connor off each other. It's textbook. And for all I know, this voice on the other side of the door is one of the true believers.

"Nothing I can do about it. He's on his own," I say, and despite how much it stings to do it, I go back to the far wall. She says my name, twice. I don't respond.

She leaves, and in her wake the night seems very dark, very cold, and very long. Because I can't be sure that she wasn't telling the truth. I can't be sure that Connor isn't being brainwashed right now. He's been susceptible before. He fell for his bio-dad's bullshit, which either immunized him—hopefully—or made him even more vulnerable. I'm praying it made him better able to see the manipulation coming, but clearly these people have a solid system that works well-nigh flawlessly. They're careful, strict—and yet coming for Gwen that way, and taking me and Connor . . . that was reckless.

Recklessness is very, very dangerous in this kind of cult. It makes them brazen and suicidal. Father Tom, like all these self-appointed ass-holes, will hang on to power until the bitter end, and making sure all his cultists precede him to the grave ensures that. Plenty of precedents for it, from David Koresh to Jim Jones.

Whether I want to believe that woman or not, Connor's danger is real. The fact that I'm sitting here shivering is humiliating and enraging, but I can't allow it to tear me up. I need to use this. Somehow.

So I do what my SERE training in the air force taught me. I eject all of it from my mind, I curl up to preserve warmth, and I sleep as best I can, for as long as I can.

◆ ◆ ◆

The next morning, I wake up when the door bangs open. I barely get myself upright before they're on me. No kicks this time. They drag me out into the soft morning sunlight. It's still cold, and my feet have gone numb, so I barely feel the cuts as I stumble over sharp rocks that form a low wall around the prison building. It's a symbolic sort of barrier, designed to warn people away. There are three men again this time, and one of them is Caleb, who's carrying an assault rifle strapped around his chest. An MP5. I wonder how good he is with it. Probably good enough to shred me like pulled pork. The other two are armed as well with more consumer-level ordnance, which decreases my chances of getting that MP5 away from him and surviving to use it. I opt to wait and see where they're taking me.

They don't say a word. They shuffle-march me down a path over more sharp, cutting rocks and then cold, packed dirt through a cathedral of silent trees. When I stumble—feeling's coming back into my feet now, and it isn't pleasant—I get a strong shove from behind that nearly sends me sprawling. The manacles on my wrists and ankles have worn my skin raw already, and I'm gnawingly hungry again. I notice that odd silence. There are no birds singing in this place.

I hear the hiss, then the full-throated roar, before I see the waterfall. It's small, but breathtaking, and in the morning light a rainbow dances around the white mist that overlays the foaming water. The pond—lake?—it plunges into looks inky and deep.

Father Tom is standing by the rocky shore staring at the waterfall. Caleb and his silent companions shove me into place beside him, and withdraw a few steps. They stand at parade rest. Sloppy jumped-up militia assholes, two of them, though I think from his superior posture that Caleb's worn a real uniform sometime in the past.

"Sam," the prophet says, and turns his head to smile at me. He looks like everybody's older best friend, dad, grandpa . . . and I have to admit, he's got a weird, compelling charm. "I wanted to have a private talk. Just us, man to man." Jailer to prisoner, he means.

I realize this could be my chance. I'm not in the middle of an exposed camp, surrounded by guards and guns. I'm in a secluded area with just three guards and the most valuable member of the cult. I click through the plan rapidly in my head. *Step one, get my manacled hands over his head, pull him back by the neck, use him for cover. Get them to throw down weapons. Grab whatever's closest and shoot every one of them if I have to. March Father Tom over to get Connor, and use him to get a vehicle and get the fuck out.*

As a plan, it's thinner than the edge on a piece of paper, but it's a chance and the best I'm going to see, I think.

I'm a hair trigger from throwing it into motion when Father Tom turns toward me and presses a huge hunting knife to my side. He's still smiling. "I know what you're thinking," he says softly, as if we're exchanging secrets. "You're making a plan on how to get out of here and get the boy out too. I respect that. But that boy is *mine*. I'll see you both dead before I let you leave."

I don't say anything. Defeat is sour in my mouth. I swallow it and don't move.

"Even if you do manage to somehow get past this knife, past me, past my men . . . my people have their orders, and they'll tear you apart before you can escape. Accept it. You're not that brave. No one is." He pauses for a moment. The knife stays right where it is, a hot point of pressure against my skin. An inch or two from kidneys, large arteries. He wouldn't have to make much of a move to watch me bleed out, right here. I feel sick and enraged and I want to *kill him*, but I force myself back into my training.

I wait. I look defeated. I waver, and I look as tired and dispirited as I can.

"That boy of yours is smart. Quiet, too, like you. Though I know who his real father is. Maybe he takes more after Melvin Royal. Do you think that's true? Would he grow up to be a ruthless killer?"

I don't say anything. Let him talk. He'll get to the point eventually. I bite down on my anger and chew it and swallow as much of it as I can. I'm sweating, even in the cold. Feverish with the need to *hurt him*.

I need to wait.

"I looked you up, Sam. Such a shame your sister had to cross paths with a monster like Royal. God really does work in mysterious ways, doesn't he? Setting you and Royal's wife together. But there's a certain triumph in that too. You don't need to destroy him if you've taken what he once had. His wife. His children." He's trying to get a reaction. I don't give it. He's jabbed me in the wrong spot if he wants to see me flinch.

His smile doesn't waver. Neither does the feeling coming off him—relaxed, friendly, calm. I'll bet he looks and feels like this right up until the moment he watches you die, and then, maybe only at the very last second, the mask will slip and the monster will show through. But only for his victims. Never for his flock of sheep and wolves.

"You seem to really care for that boy, despite all that blood and pain. So tell me, Sam: What will you do to save him?"

Now we're getting down to it. I'm almost relieved, but I still don't answer. First step in resisting interrogations: never say yes. Never give any answer that can either emotionally compromise you or be twisted into hurting others.

"Not a word?" He sounds disappointed. "I need to know this, Sam: Would you die for him? He's not your real son, not your flesh and blood. Do you love him enough to save him?"

Never say yes. Captive training is imprinted deep into me, but I've never felt such a prisoner as I feel right now, trapped in the drowning well of this man's threat and charisma. I can see some glint in this man's eyes now, some hint of what his victims see at that last, desperate moment. I need to make him angry. "I'm going to jump to the chase, since your mind games are getting boring for me. So let me make this clear: Fuck you, Tom. Fuck your twisted cult and your threats and your bullshit amateur brainwashing. Take all of it and stick it up your ass. I'll die for Connor, absolutely. You might manage to kill me before I kill you. But I've got to tell you, the person who comes for you when I'm gone will be so much worse."

If he's taken aback, thrown in any way, I can't see it. But I do hear a strangely curious note when he says, "And who do you think comes after once you're gone?"

"Gwen Proctor," I tell him.

He laughs. Genuine laughter, though I don't think someone with this much malignance and pathology is capable of understanding humor the way the rest of us do. He finally composes himself to say, "The Bible says, *Man was not made of woman, but woman made of man.* Women are made to serve, to please, and to procreate. Nothing else is important. She needs to be taught that. I'll make sure she is."

"She's going to enjoy teaching you too," I say. "If I don't get to do it first."

"Let me predict the future this time. When I'm done with him, Connor's going to be a true believer. Maybe even my long-promised messiah. He'll carry on my work, and he'll feel better and more content in that than he ever has with you or his unnatural mother." He presses the knife in closer, and I feel a bright spark of pain. I don't react. He cuts deeper. Sparks turn to fire. I don't blink. "That's the best case, of course. One of you is going to join my army of saints. It can be you, or it can be your son. I'm going to let you make that choice."

Classic.

"You're going to do exactly what you want, no matter what I say. You think you're different and special, but you're not even original. You're ISIS with a Bible. You're Jim Jones minus the poisoned drinks. You're a copy of a copy, asshole. But it doesn't matter. People like you always end badly. But the important thing is . . . *you end.*"

I've succeeded in cracking open his shell, and for a second there he is: the real Tom. Angry, feral, clever, *hungry* Tom.

This time the knife goes deeper, and it feels like he's stuck a blow-torch in me. Shock descends in a warm curtain, and that's good, because part of what shock does is pull blood into the core of your body, save it up to preserve your heart and lungs and brain, fuck everything else.

The bleeding isn't so bad from my side, though there's a steady enough flow. He didn't hit an artery. That helps me get my breath.

He stands there looking at me with the knife in his hand. Watching me bleed. He looks . . . happy as a kid at Christmas. He'd love to carve me to pieces. I think he's going to for a long few seconds, and while that happens I just . . . vanish. I think about Gwen. The kids. Good days, warm sun on my skin. If I'm going to die here, I don't want to be thinking about Father Tom.

But he doesn't kill me. He composes himself back to his normal face. He takes a handkerchief from his pocket and wipes the knife clean before he puts it in a leather sheath at his back.

"Take him," Father Tom says. "Let him bleed and fast and pray. Tomorrow we're going to make him a saint."

"You need me," I tell him. "Kill me, you've got nothing to keep him here. That kid is smart. He'll find a way out."

"Connor's already mine," he says. "And I'll do with you as the Lord moves me."

They have to drag me back to the prison. I pass out halfway there, and when I come to again, I'm locked in the little cell. Someone's dressed my wound. I have no idea if I'm bleeding internally, but it hurts like a son of a bitch, every pulsebeat a red stab of agony. I just stay as still as I can and wait for my body to start adjusting. Or my mind. Whichever can do it first.

When the pain's manageable, I drink the rest of the water and eat the rest of the bread, a miniature communion, and tell myself that whatever happens, I've done the best I can. If I'm bleeding internally, this is going to be a very bad few hours. And I have to admit to myself that I'm scared. Scared for myself and for Connor. Terrified for Gwen, who might not know what she's walking into when she comes for us.

I believe Father Tom when he says his people are lethal. I go cold and sick when I think of Gwen being caught by them. I don't want to imagine what could happen.

Don't come alone, Gwen. For the love of God, don't come here alone.

23

GWEN

I call every person I know who can be of help.

The war council convenes at Stillhouse Lake, at our old house with the shotgun holes in the drywall and signs of struggle everywhere. Before everyone arrives, I go to Connor's room and open the door. It's neat, as it usually is, like he's just stepped out. Books racked on every available shelf. He always makes his bed, even when I'm telling him that we're leaving this place, maybe for good. I know that some of that is his need to exert control over a life that's often seemed wildly chaotic. But I also think he's just careful, even at thirteen.

I sit down and pick up his pillow, then silently hug it and breathe in the scent of my son. I want to cry. I can't. The pain is fierce, but it also burns away all the worry. We can get him back. *We will.*

I put the pillow back and smooth it down, and I go to the living room as the doorbell rings. Lanny and Vee are sitting uneasily on the couch, holding hands. I don't like it, but I don't discourage it either. Lanny needs this now. And so does Vee, most probably. "Mom? Do you want me to make tea or something?" Lanny asks.

"Sure, honey," I tell her. "See what we've got. Maybe make some coffee too." I have the feeling it's going to be a long night.

Kezia and Javier Esparza are the first to get here. I haven't seen Javi much recently; he's been off doing his own thing running the gun range and visiting family, but he and Sam always keep in touch. Javier is a badass. He's an incredible shot, and one of the best, most polite shooting instructors I've ever seen, while also not putting up with anyone's bullshit—which can be considerable out here in not-exactly-liberal rural Tennessee. He doesn't talk much about his days in the Marine Corps, but I know he was highly trained and almost certainly highly decorated. Javier is someone I need at my back right now . . . and I'm grateful, so grateful, that he's willing to be here.

Javier doesn't say a word when he walks in; he just gives me a hug and sits down. From him, that's a lot. Banter is his usual way of expressing emotions, but when he's silent like this, he's very, very focused. I wouldn't want to be his enemy, ever, but especially when he's in this mood.

Kezia's right behind him, and her hug lingers a little longer. "You all right?" she asks me. I try to smile. "Yeah, okay, I see." She glances at Vee and Lanny, both in the kitchen taking down mugs from shelves. The last time she saw my daughter was when she took her statement taking the blame off Olly Belldene. "Girls okay?"

"They're all right," I say. "Worried, of course. I'm trying to keep them occupied."

"Anybody else coming?"

"A few more," I tell her. It's a bit of an understatement.

When I try to step away, she holds me in place. "You made a deal with the Belldenes, didn't you?" I don't answer that. I don't want to lie, not to her, but I can't tell her the truth either. She finally just shakes her head, lips pressed into a hard line of disapproval. "You're on the wrong side of this, Gwen."

"I'm on the side of my kids," I tell her. "And I know you are too. Thank you for being here."

"Well, Prester would have come, too, but one of us needs to be here in Norton. He also said thank God whatever mess you're in is not in our town for a change."

I have to laugh, because I can almost hear Detective Prester saying it. I didn't ask him to come tonight, but I'm not surprised, either, by the fact he knows. Norton doesn't deserve the two detectives it's got, and I'm sure the locals don't know how lucky they are.

J. B. arrives next, but when I open the door she doesn't come in. She gestures me outside and points out at the far end of the road, where it disappears down a dip in the hill. "I really hope that isn't a problem." I see the line of cars as it comes around the curve. Six of them—big, black SUVs. Two of them park down on the road. The other four turn in, and maneuver into our already-packed space in front of the house. It's a *lot*. I imagine our neighbors around the lake are paying close attention and wondering what kind of trouble I'm in this time.

We stand quietly together on the porch and watch. J. B. says, "FBI?"

I nod. "Go on inside," I tell her. "I'll be there in a minute." She goes, and I wait, breath misting in the cold air. This is the kind of night Sam and I like—crisp, bracing, the sky full of stars and the lake shattering that light into glitter. We'd sit out here on this porch with a bottle of wine, sharing a blanket, fingers twined together. Blind, contented peace.

I want that back so badly.

FBI Special Agent Mike Lustig unfolds himself from the passenger side of the first SUV. A big, powerful African American man with a handsome face that eases into a restrained smile when he sees me. More people start getting out of the SUVs—like Lustig, they're serious people in suits. Lustig's wearing his FBI badge on his hip, which he normally doesn't; he's in full Bureau mode right now.

"Agent," I say, and offer my hand. He shakes it. We're a little more formal than the rest of my friends, at least right now, after Wolfhunter. He made choices I didn't like. One of them was working with Miranda Tidewell to try to get Sam away from me. He's never fully trusted me, and I doubt that's going to change. "Thanks for coming. And"—I gesture to the rest of it—"bringing the cavalry."

"Pretty much emptied out the Knoxville and Memphis field offices," he tells me. "Specialized teams are coming down out of headquarters and heading straight for the location you provided."

I'm not stupid enough to think he took my word for it. "You have confirmation that's where their compound is?"

He nods and pulls out his phone, and in a few swipes brings up an image. It's taken from a satellite, and it's difficult to make out exactly; the area is thick with trees. But I can see an open area, and what looks like at least two buildings visible through the tree cover. One looks like a church. What seals it is the wide stream that wanders along the border, and the rocky falloff into a small lake. *Bitter Falls*. It matches what Carol—Daria—described.

"We're tasking a drone to get a better look at the compound, so we should have images real soon."

He's holding something back. That isn't surprising, but it is aggravating. "You couldn't have gotten all this done without more than what I told you," I say. "What did you find?"

He doesn't want to tell me. At all. But he can see I'm not moving until he does. "We took a look at that abandoned camp you talked about. Fact is, we were behind the curve on this; they never had anybody coming forward, escaping, selling stories. Nothing. People who were in the cult kept their mouths shut, or didn't know enough to matter. We went all the way back in the records and came up with a man called Tom Sarnovich. He started out a regular-type preacher back in the seventies, took over a church in Wolfhunter around then. One day, the church just closed down, and they moved out to Carr's property, where they built their first compound."

"The one you and Sam found."

Lustig nods. "Turns out they were there for about ten years, then Preacher Tom wanted a bigger slice. They moved to that camp you sent the video of; it was an old mining camp sold at auction." He doesn't want to tell me the next part. I can see him hesitating.

"Agent," I say. Then, in a lower tone: *"Mike."*

"Okay. We sent a team out there to look around. It was pretty much like the video showed—weird and disconcerting, but no real signs of anything criminal. But there was a small lake on the property, too, an old quarry. Smelled rotten around there. On a hunch, the agent in charge sent down a diver to take a look."

My mouth goes dry. I don't blink. I just . . . wait.

"They found bones," he says. "No way to tell how many bodies there are down there, a lot of the bones are scattered. They're all skeletonized. Divers found one still weighted down with junk iron and chains."

My lips part, but I don't say anything. All this fits. It fits with everything that Carol told me. It fits with the baptism, Father Tom's army of *saints*.

"My guess is, they moved because when you put that many bodies in a body of water that shallow, the stench can't be covered up. The whole place must have reeked. So he found some new spot to relocate and start over."

"Bitter Falls," I say, and swallow. It feels tight and painful, and my nerves are crawling with horror. "How deep is this lake?"

"Deeper than the first one," he says. "And my guess is, they're using it the same way."

I have to brace myself against the porch railing because my knees are shaking. I can't stop imagining my son out in that water, a weight around his ankle, being dragged down in the cold, black water. Then, in a blink, it's Sam. Nausea rushes up. It's too much. Too close.

Melvin anchored his victims' bodies in water. He liked to take us out on the lake where he knew they were, gliding his boat over his garden of dead women. I never knew until the trial, and I still dream about it, about plunging off the side of the boat and being down there with them. Sightless eyes and reaching arms, welcoming me.

I don't throw up. But I realize that I'm gasping for breath, and Lustig is watching me, and I manage to get myself together. Somehow.

"Normally I wouldn't let you within a country mile of one of my ops," Lustig says. "Especially not one like this. You know that, right?"

I just nod. The acid at the back of my throat burns.

"So here's the deal we're going to make. You, your friends—however badass you think they are—you can come with us, but you're staying at the perimeter. I can't have you in the line of fire, and I can't have you trying anything clever. These are not rational people we're dealing with now. You got me?"

"Yes," I tell him. "When are you going in?"

Lustig sighs and looks up at the sky. Day's turned to night. We've wasted so much time already. I expect him to say soon, or now, or at least *tonight*.

But he says, "We're not."

I just stand there for a second, looking at him blankly, because I know I *cannot* have heard him properly. "They've got *Connor*. And *Sam*. You know what they do to people!"

"They've also maybe got fifty or more other people in there, and we don't know which of them are fanatics and which are victims. Little kids in there, by your informant's account and the evidence we saw at that old compound. That's a hell of a lot of potential human shields and noncombatants. We can't do a full-on assault. They'll be looking for it."

"But . . . you said you were going to *get them out, you bastard*—"

"Hey," he interrupts me, and I realize my voice has risen, that there's a sharp, cutting edge to it. That I've lost my battle to stay calm. It feels *good*. I need to yell. I need to hit and shove and *make people listen*. "Easy. We do this right, and we make it way too expensive for them to do any harm to anybody in there. We get his followers to lay down their weapons and come out; I guarantee you there are people in there who aren't completely brainwashed and want out, and maybe more than you'd think. Trust me, this isn't a Seal Team Six situation. This works best if we convince them to walk out on their own."

Everything he says makes sense, but I don't care. The idea of waiting while my son is . . . while God knows what is actually happening to him . . . I know I can't do it. I know in my gut, just from meeting Carol and seeing the desperate lengths she took to avoid going back, that what waits behind those walls is far, far worse than Lustig is considering. I'm incandescent with rage, and worse, I know he isn't going to *listen*. He trusts Sam. Not me.

He's going to get my boys killed, and I don't know whether to blame him or myself. I should have known that getting Lustig involved was a risk; he's not a free agent, and he has protocols to follow.

But I'm not letting those rules get my son killed.

Lustig calls my name as I walk away, but I don't stop. He doesn't try twice.

I go back inside and close the door. J. B., Kezia, Javier, and the girls look at me as I close the door and lean against it. I don't know what I'm going to say to them. Then I find the words. "We're on our own," I tell them. "The FBI is going to do it their way, but their way isn't going to get Sam and Connor back alive. Not according to what Carol told me."

"They're not going in, are they?" Javier says.

"In Mike's words, this isn't a Seal Team Six situation." I put all the bitterness I feel into the words.

Javi takes that personally. "The hell does he know? Does he think we go in and just shoot up the place? That's not how it works." He pauses and shakes his head. "They're going to negotiate, aren't they?"

"Try to," I say. "And from everything Carol told me, I think Father Tom has been planning for this day for a long time. He'll see it as their final battle. Their glorious ending. Ragnarök, Armageddon, whatever religion he's cobbled together in his head. While they're sitting outside waiting, this will go very, very badly."

"Then what we need is a plan B," Kezia says. "One that gets us into the compound. We find Sam and Connor and get them out. But what about the others? Surely not everybody in there is down with the idea of dying for Father Tom. What you told us means the women are little better than slaves in there. And the kids—"

J. B. is shaking her head. "You can't count on the women," she says. "In a cult like this, the women are often the strongest believers, despite how badly they're treated. Maybe because of it; if they stop believing it *means* something, they're just victims, and they can't handle it. If you go to them for help, they're liable to raise the alarm instantly."

That's a grim prospect, and I care about them. I care about the kids. I care about the men who've been roped or kidnapped or brainwashed into this toxic sinkhole of a cult. I want to save them.

But sometimes, I know, the hard fact is you have to save yourself first. They always tell you on planes to put your mask on before helping others. My oxygen is Connor and Sam. And once they're safe, then we can work out how to get others free.

J. B. says, "I'd suggest infiltration, but there's no chance of pulling that off. Mr. Esparza, Detective Claremont . . . sorry to point it out, but so far everything we know about these people is that they go after exclusively white recruits. So that leaves you two out. Gwen, some of them already know you by sight. I'm sure this Father Tom has your dossier. He'd see you coming a mile away."

"You, then?" I ask her. "J. B., no. I can't ask you—"

"That wouldn't work anyway," she says briskly. "Cults like this don't have any use for older people. Father Tom has no use for women if they're not of childbearing age."

"Then who . . ."

I realize what she's saying, and it grabs me by the throat. I choke on it. I shake my head. Violently. "No. *No.* Absolutely not. I won't let Lanny go anywhere near this—"

"You don't have to. I'll do it," Vera Crockett says.

She sounds calm as chamomile tea. She's even smiling a little bit. We all stop and look at her. Vee, with her attitude and her fragile strength and her slightly mad eyes.

"Vera, you can't," I say. "I know I'm not your mom, but—"

"You ain't my momma," she agrees. "I can take care of myself. I took care of my own mother more often than not. I'm the right age, ain't I? They like young girls."

"No," I say flatly. "Out of the question. These people are *killers*."

Vee stares at me without a quiver. "You think I don't know that? The Assembly folk in Wolfhunter killed my momma. I know 'em better than you do. And I can act the part. I can!"

"That's a lovely offer," J. B. says, "but it won't work. If it was any other time, I'd say Vera would be an ideal candidate to let them recruit. But it would have to be done gradually, over time. Not the same night the FBI shows up. They'd kill you, Vee."

"I can sell this," Vee insists. "I *can*. And you need to let me!"

There's absolutely no way in hell I'm going to let this girl do something like this. She may not be my child, but she's my responsibility. "No!" I shout it this time, and it surprises Lanny to the point that she flinches and grabs for Vee's hand. Vee doesn't even blink. "You are *not doing anything like this, Vera!* I will not allow it!" I take a beat to get my pulse under control, my tone less sharp, and turn to the others. "I need options. Does anybody have some?"

Vee turns and walks away. She goes down the hall, and I hear a door slam. Fine. I want her out of this anyway. Her and Lanny both. My daughter looks torn; she gives me a pleading look, and I nod toward the hallway. She goes after Vee.

The four of us are silent for a few painful seconds, and then Javier says, "Tell me what the girl said again. About how they make their saints."

I repeat Carol's story, best I can. About how Father Tom drowns his captives and sinks them in the pond. It's borne out by the evidence the FBI found in the lake at the abandoned compound, so it's almost certainly still going on at Bitter Falls.

Javier listens without any expression and then nods. "I'm opening up the gun range. We'll arm up out of the stock. If the FBI isn't going in, then we're going to have to. It's risky. You and me, Gwen."

"And me," Kez says. Javier turns expressionless eyes toward her, and she stares right back. Nobody bends. "You don't decide for me, Javi."

"Fair enough," he says, and cracks a crooked smile. "I know I can't stop you when you get going anyway." He looks at J. B. "Ma'am, I don't know you, and I can't trust you can handle this. Sorry."

"It's okay," she says. "I'm past my fence-climbing days. But I've got two operatives who aren't, and they're waiting on my call. Solid people. You can count on them."

"In a firefight?" I ask her. "Because that's where this is heading, J. B."

She lifts a single shoulder. Half a shrug. "Cicely West and Joe Froud. You know them. You tell me. They volunteered, by the way, when they heard about Connor and Sam."

Joe Froud is a tall, lanky, funny man; I've met him a few times, worked with him once. But never in a dangerous situation. Cicely—well. I've already seen her in action. If J. B. thinks Joe's in her class, I'm fine with that. "Please tell them this is incredibly dangerous," I say. "And I understand if they take a look and decide it's not for them. No judgment."

"Let me make the call," J. B. says. She goes into the kitchen and turns away from us. I look at Kez and Javier.

"You two, same thing," I say. "I can't ask you for this. I don't want you risking your lives for me—"

"Hey," Kez says. "We're not doing it for you, Gwen. We're doing it for Connor. We both love that boy. If there's anybody innocent in this situation, it's him."

Javier just nods in agreement, and I have to stop for a moment. The weight of this is both welcome and crushing. I need them. But I also need them to be safe. But I need my son. There are no right answers here, and I'm flailing in the dark.

J. B. ends her call and comes back. "They're going to meet us there," she says. "Question is, how do we get out of here with the FBI parade blocking our way?"

"We don't ask," I say. I stand up and go knock on Lanny's door. There's no answer, so I swing it open.

My daughter's standing at the open window, staring out. As I watch, she slides it down and locks it before turning back to me with her arms crossed. "Vee's right," she says. "You don't get to decide for her, Mom."

"She's gone?"

Lanny just nods. *Fuck.* I can't worry about what Vee's planning. There's no way she can get there before we do. I'll have to alert the FBI that she might try to approach the place, though. I don't want anyone thinking she's a combatant.

I want to yell at Lanny, but it won't do any good. I should have known Vee Crockett would do whatever she thought was best, like it or not. And that Lanny would agree with her. I just take my daughter in my arms and hug her instead. I feel all the stiff confrontation melt out of her. "It's okay," I tell her. "It's all going to be okay."

I'm lying to my child when I say it. I feel utterly out of control, out of time, out of hope. For the first time in my life I have to depend not on myself alone, but on the goodwill of friends I've made along the way. People I respect and love. And giving up control is the hardest thing I've done in a long time.

I lead Lanny back into the living room. J. B., Javier, and Kez all look up.

"Let's do this," I tell them. I look at my daughter. "Lanny, you're going to stay with J. B. Whatever happens, I don't want you to be alone."

She nods. She was so afraid I'd leave her behind, and that hurts and heals at the same time. I know I'm taking her somewhere dangerous, but Lanny, of all people, understands how necessary this is.

Javier says, "Gwen? Once we're doing this, you follow my orders. That's how it's got to be."

I nod, though it goes against everything in my nature.

Sometimes I have to let those I love lead the way too.

24

CONNOR

It starts with the girl who tried to get me to go off with her before. Aria.

It's getting dark after dinner is served by the army of silent women. Aria's one of them. She keeps her gaze down most of the time, but she glances at me plenty. I . . . don't mind. She keeps coming by to refill our glasses. The men at the table ignore her completely, like she doesn't even exist. But I see her. And she sees me.

She needs to leave with us, I think. *She doesn't belong here.* There are younger girls here than Aria, too; there's a wispy blonde girl with really blue eyes who looks scared to death, who cowers when anyone comes near her. Another dark-haired kid, maybe nine at most, who just looks sad and lost. They're not like Aria. Aria seems to know what she's doing.

The last time she leans over my shoulder to pour more water into my glass, she whispers, "Meet me at midnight at the falls." She's gone before I'm even sure I heard right. Or heard it at all. She walks away with her heavy pitcher and doesn't look back, and the meal finishes and I have to listen to Father Tom praying for nearly an hour before we're released. When all the heads are bowed, I do it, too, but I don't close my eyes. I'm sure they're all into whatever he's droning on about, so I slowly move my hand and put it over the fork I left next to my empty plate. I'd like to have a knife, but they didn't give me one. I slowly slide the fork up my sleeve and work it around so the tines are stuck in the cotton right at the band of the long sleeves. It's the only thing I like about these clothes Father Tom's made me put on: I can hide stuff under the shirt, and the plain black jacket.

When the prayer's over, everyone stands. I start to, but the men on either side of me put their hands on my shoulders and keep me seated. My heart starts racing. I look at one of them and say, "What?" He doesn't answer. He just smiles.

Then Father Tom walks over and says, "Put it back, Connor." He sounds calm and patient, but firm. I think about bluffing, but I know that voice. It's what my mom sounds like when she knows exactly what I'm up to.

They knew I'd try it. They were ready.

I silently reach into my sleeve and take the fork out. I put it back where it was. The men let me go.

"I like your spirit," Father Tom says. "But you need to understand that when you do these things, there's a price. Not for you. For the man who calls himself your father."

I lunge to my feet. I don't even think before I do it. My fists are clenched. "Don't hurt him!" It just kind of bursts out of me.

The men on either side of me laugh, like they think I'm funny. Stupid. Weak. I shove the chair back so hard it tips over, and the laughter stops. "Pick that up and put it back," Father Tom says. "You're not a child. Don't throw tantrums."

The sick thing is that there's something about the way he says it that makes me want to obey. *Want* to please him.

I kick the chair and send it spinning down the wood floor instead. Another man down the row who's standing there stops it with a booted foot and looks at Father Tom. Then he sets it upright.

"That's disrespectful," Father Tom says. "Go get it, Connor. Put it back where it belongs. Now. Or you'll make me do something very unpleasant."

He's using Sam, and I hate it, *I hate it*. He hasn't said what he'd do, but it doesn't matter, it would be bad. And I can't get Sam hurt because I'm pissed off and scared.

I go get the chair. I bring it back to the table. I slide it in place, and then I look at Father Tom.

He smiles and pats me on the shoulder. "Good boy," he says, like I'm a pet. "You look fine in those clothes. Much better than those modern rags." He means my old blue jeans, the ones that had holes in them. The ones they've made me put on are stiff and new and cheap, and I hate them. The black jacket itches. The shirt feels thin and homemade. The only thing they let me keep were my Nike shoes.

I want to tell him his clothes suck. I stay quiet.

Father Tom follows as the men walk me back to the Quarters, a long bunkhouse where the men sleep. Long rows of identical cots, with old surplus army trunks at the foot of each bed for clothes and whatever personal items they're allowed to have. They've assigned me a bunk, and these stupid clothes to put on; my regular ones got taken away when they made me change. They said it was to wash them.

I don't think that was true.

"Our routine doesn't vary," Father Tom tells me as he walks me to my bunk. "You have thirty minutes for private prayer and contemplation; you may read your Bible if you wish. Then bed."

"I want to see Sam," I tell him.

"Sam's fine," he says. "He won't get any food tomorrow because of your disobedience. Disobey again, and he won't get water. Three times, and I'll have to assign a much worse punishment. Are we understood? I like that you are strong, Connor. But you need to know how best to use it."

With that, he's gone. He greets other men, shakes hands, claps shoulders in that way they all touched me in the church. Like a ritual.

Once he's gone, they all stop talking and go to their bunks—all except for a group who stands near the door. They're not wearing the same clothes the rest of us are; they have regular ones, checked shirts and T-shirts and jeans that don't look so stiff and awkward. They look almost normal, compared to what I have on.

They're the men from the RV, plus a few more. In a strange sort of way, they're familiar at least. So I go to them, and they stop talking and look at me with either annoyance or amusement. I focus on Caleb. "When do I get my clothes back?"

Caleb puts his hand on my shoulder. "These are your clothes, Brother. Wear them with pride."

Oh hell no, I won't. I want my clothes. I remember going with Mom to the mall in Knoxville to buy those jeans, and the Avengers T-shirt I love. I need to have them back. They're not the past. They're my future. In the real world.

That's why they took them.

I look down at myself. I look like them now. That's what they want. They're trying to change me bit by bit. Make me someone else. Just like Father Tom made me do what he said.

I need to get the hell out of here.

"Go pray," Caleb says, and pushes me away. "Thirty minutes to lights out."

I don't pray. I just sit there, pretending, watching the others. They seem to actually be doing it. The RV crew makes sure they do, I realize; they walk up and down the aisle, and they're checking. I stop pretending and actually pray when Caleb pays attention to me. *Dear God, please help Sam. Please make sure he's okay. Please help us get out of here and keep Mom and Lanny safe. Please get rid of these people.*

The time passes pretty fast. The last five minutes men start undressing, stripping down to their underwear. It's all the same, white boxers. I take off my coat and fold it up on the trunk, and pretend to be untying my shoes. I take long enough that the lights go off, and I've still got my pants and shirt on. I get in bed and pull up the covers to my neck. I have to stay still and wait until I think most everybody is asleep. When a chorus of snoring starts, it's time to go.

But I don't go.

I lie there, afraid that I'm going to get caught. This seems way too easy; Father Tom had people watching me at dinner. And he'd probably have someone watching me here too. I'm afraid that if I try to sneak out, Sam might be punished even more. But I have to *do something*. Lying here won't help.

Aria wants to meet me by the falls. Sister Harmony told me not to go there. I don't know which of them I should believe. One of them has to be lying. I *want* to believe Aria; she's pretty and my age, and she seems to like me. Sister Harmony just seems angry.

I finally make a decision. I slip out of my bed and move quietly to the door. No guards posted, everybody's in bunks now, even Caleb; I can hear him snoring when I tiptoe past him. He's closest to the exit. I'm afraid the hinges will creak, but they don't. The door opens silently, and I slip out.

Outside. I feel my heart pounding, and I stop once I get the door shut and lean against the wall to breathe for a minute. I stay in the shadows. I pause to look around. The camp is loud with croaking frogs, and I can hear the snoring from the building out here too. There's not very much moonlight. Clouds have moved in, thick masses of darkness showing thin silver at the edges. Something smells a little bad, like garbage, maybe the septic tanks.

I freeze and back up against the wall of the Quarters as I hear footsteps. There are Assembly men patrolling the camp at night, and one's walking past me. I hold my breath and flatten myself back in the shadows. *He's going to see me.* But he doesn't even look toward the building. He seems tired. He yawns, scratches his head, cracks his neck, and moves on toward the other house, the one where the women sleep. The Garden.

I can also see, across the open space in the middle, the concrete building where they took Sam. I walked by it a few times earlier, trying to figure out where he was, and finally saw a metal shed, kind of like a box, at the end of the building. It's shut with a padlock, the combination kind, not the key kind. I don't know how to pick locks, and at least before there was a guard sitting right beside that door. Maybe not at night? I don't know. But I'm pretty sure Father Tom would expect me to go there.

Sister Harmony's probably telling me the truth. Aria's probably lying. I shouldn't have been able to get out of the Quarters that easily. The guard should have seen me.

They *want* me to go to Aria. So should I go? Maybe if I do, I can convince her to help me instead of Father Tom. Maybe I can find out things from her while she's trying to make me do what she wants. Maybe I can even make her do what *I* want.

I don't like how that makes me feel, but I need to get Sam and get out. That's all that matters right now.

A path on the other side of the concrete building curves around by the big, wire-topped steel fence. It's dark over on that side. I can distantly hear the waterfall; it's the only sound out here, except the snoring and frogs. It's weird how quiet it is.

I don't have any way of telling how late it is; maybe these people can tell time from where the moon is in the sky, but I can't. But since the roaming guard has walked on, now's a good chance to leave the shadows and get moving. Maybe it wouldn't matter. Probably not. If what I think is true, I can stroll right across the middle of the compound and nobody will stop me. For a second I think about testing that.

But if I'm wrong, if I really *am* sneaking around and get caught . . . Sam gets hurt. So I stick to being sneaky.

It takes a while; I end up hiding in the small stand of trees next to a big cabin that must belong to Father Tom; it's way nicer than any of the other places here, and it still has lights on inside. Curfew's for everybody else. Not for him.

My mom would go in there and make him let her and Sam go. For a second I imagine how that would feel, seeing *him* afraid. Making *him* do what I tell him. Feels really good in fantasy, but I feel kind of dirty when I stop thinking about it. I know I can't make him do anything. Not when he's got all the guns and power and people.

I work my way around to the back of the cabin and to the shadows of the trees.

Then I'm curving on the path. It's not as easy as I thought; the gravel's sharp and tricky, and in places it slopes down at a steep angle. I don't fall, but it'd be real easy. The trees feel like they're closing in. Wind hisses through branches, and it's so cold that I wish I'd worn that stupid jacket.

The falls sound like radio static. It starts low, then builds into a heavy hiss, then a roar when I come out of the trees and see the place for the first time. It's pretty. It's not a big waterfall, maybe twenty feet up or so, but I've never seen one in person before. I like it.

The lake, though. I don't like that. It's too dark. Too still. And it smells like rotten fish.

Aria's waiting for me. She's standing by the shore with her hands clasped in front of her, but her head isn't down like it usually is. It's up, and she's smiling, and when I come toward her that smile just gets wider. "You came," she says. "Thank you, Brother Connor."

"Just Connor," I say. The moonlight is stronger here, and I'm glad. I want to be able to see what she's doing. "Why did you want to see me?"

She steps up to me and puts her hand on my chest, and it's like putting my tongue on a battery, the energy that zips through me and leaves my ears ringing. Aria's shorter than I am. Small and pretty and kind of fragile. It isn't that I wasn't aware of that before, but all of a sudden it's *real*.

She stretches up on her toes, graceful as a ballerina, and kisses me.

I'm so surprised I don't know how to react. I just . . . freeze, everything crashing and burning in my head because it feels so *good*. Kissing feels *really good*, and I never knew that. Guess I should have—everybody talks about it like it's amazing, but there's something more real about that feeling than I've ever known before. I don't know how to kiss her back, but I try, pressing my lips back on hers, moving into it . . .

. . . and then I wonder *why* she's kissing me. It feels great. But it doesn't feel *right*.

I step back, and when I turn my head, I see Father Tom standing there. Watching us. I feel angry and sick at the same time. I feel . . . *naked*. And he's *smiling* at us.

"I chose her for you," he tells me. "A flower from my garden. I see you like her."

I look at Aria. I expect her to look angry too. Or shocked. Or *something*. But she's still smiling, like she's happy. I grab her and shake her. "You're not a flower," I tell her. "And he can't tell you what to do!"

She blinks at me, and I feel bad for shaking her, because she just seems . . . confused. "Father Tom's always right," she says. "Why shouldn't I do what he says? And I do like you, Connor. You're nice."

"You don't even know me!" I yell it at her, and she flinches backward and clasps her hands and looks down, and I feel like shit. "Stop it! He can't just give you away! You don't belong to him!"

"No," she says, and looks up at me then. "I belong to you now."

"That's sick. And I'm *thirteen*."

"I'm twelve," she says. "But I'm a full woman now. It's okay."

"It's *not*!" I have no idea what to say to make her understand that. I turn back to Father Tom. *He* knows this isn't right. It's why he locks people in here in the first place. "I'm not doing this."

"Of course not," he says. Smooth as oil. "Not yet, of course. But she'll be held chaste for you, Connor. She'll be yours when you're ready."

"No." I say it flatly, and I mean it. I'll put a chair back. I'll wear the stupid clothes, if that helps. But I'm not doing this.

My old dad would tell me to do it. That's why I won't.

Father Tom just shakes his head. Sadly, as if he already knew this would happen. "All right," he says. "On your head be it." He raises his hand above his head, and people come out of the trees, up the path. There's Caleb, with a nasty-looking assault rifle slung over his chest. And the other two from the RV. They weren't asleep. Of course they weren't.

My stomach drops when I see who they're holding. *Dad.*

He's still got chains on his ankles and wrists, and he's got another one wrapped around his throat like a thick metal leash. I feel like I'm sinking into quicksand. It's awful and horrible and Caleb's leading him by that chain and *I need to do something.* Sam looks awful; he's barely standing up, and he's dirty and bloody and has no shirt on. The only clean thing about him is the white bandage that wraps around his waist.

More of the Assembly men are coming down the path behind them. Nobody was asleep. Everybody was in on this.

"Go back to the Garden, Sister Aria," Father Tom tells her. "Your job is done here."

She nods, still smiling, as she walks past me and toward the path. She passes Sam, and that's when I realize he's watching me. I take a step toward them. He shakes his head, emphatically.

"Easy, Connor," he says, and the calm sound of his voice makes me ache inside because I want him to be okay so bad. "I'm fine. I'm all right."

Caleb yanks on that chain, and Sam gags and staggers, and fury rips through me.

I lose it, just like in the classroom. But this time I know who I'm going to hit. I go straight for Caleb, and I see him drop the chain and step back and aim that gun he has and *I don't care*—I'm too angry and too scared and I just want it to *stop*.

Sam moves between us, and I skid to a stop because I don't care if I get shot, *I don't*, but not him. "Easy," he says again. "Breathe, Connor. Breathe—"

Caleb puts the muzzle of his rifle to the side of Sam's head. "Back up, Brother Connor. Right now. Or this is your fault."

"It's not," Sam says. "Remember that."

One of the other men punches Sam in the side, and he cries out and nearly goes down. Somehow he doesn't, and it's all I can stand not to go charging at them again. I know it's stupid. But I have to do *something*.

"He's right, Connor. It's not really your fault," Father Tom says, like none of this is happening. "You've been poisoned by women your whole life. Especially your mother."

Sam looks like he'd say something to that. I say it for him. "My mother's the strongest person in the world."

"It's not your fault you think so. You've been brainwashed. Female strength is inferior. They're incomplete, made from the rib of a man. They were made by God to serve."

Sam gets his breath then, and he says, "Save it. It's not going to work. Connor knows better. Weak men believe shit like this. Weak men like these assholes." He jerks his head toward Caleb, and I know Caleb's about to punch him again and I need to *make it stop*.

"Brother Caleb," Father Tom says, and stops it for me. "There's no need for that. We're not here to torture the man."

From the expression on Caleb's face, he'd like to do it anyway. But now I'm scared what's coming. Sam looks so tired; he's fighting to stay on his feet. He's doing that for me. The sound of the waterfall is like a drill whining through my skull, tunneling right through bone.

"I want to believe in your ability to change, Brother Connor," Father Tom says. "But you've shown poor judgment too many times in a short period of time. I think it's time you were baptized. I think you'd be of more use to us if you join our army of saints." I don't know what that last part means. I don't think it's good; it feels like something awful is in the air now.

The men standing around us say, "Amen."

"Come with me, boy," he says to me, and puts his hand on my shoulder, just the way all those men did in the church when they welcomed me in. "Let me anoint you with holy waters."

"No!" Sam shouts. He lunges forward, and Caleb grabs the chain again and yanks him back. He fights, and I'm afraid he's going to choke. I can't stand this, can't stand seeing them hurt him.

"Okay!" I shout. "Okay! I'll go! Dad, it's okay!"

He keeps on struggling. They push him down on his knees. I can't look. I need to do this so they'll stop. It's just water. It's nothing.

Father Tom leads me into the lake. Two steps and the bottom drops off, and I'm up to my knees. It's freezing, so cold I'm already shaking. The water, close up, has a weird oily shine on top. It stinks.

He keeps pulling me deeper. I don't want to go, but I need to do this. I can't let them kill Sam, and I know they will. I can feel it.

"One more step," Father Tom whispers in my ear. "I'll anoint you with the holy waters and you will be one of us, Connor. A full brother of the Assembly in the sight of God. Then you'll be worthy."

I take another step. It's a drop-off, and I sink fast. The water comes up to my chest. I gasp and flail. I can barely feel my feet now.

Father Tom scoops up water in both hands. I don't want this. I don't. I turn and look back at the shore and I see that Dad is still fighting his chains to get to me. He's hurting himself more.

I need to just do this and get it over with. Now.

So I take a deep, unsteady breath and nod. "Okay."

Father Tom lifts the water in his joined palms.

"Father! Someone's at the gate!" Someone shouts it from up close to the path. "You need to come! Right now!"

Everything freezes.

Father Tom pauses, and ripples go out from him across the pond to disappear into the darkness. The only sound that continues for a moment is the dull roar of the waterfall cascading down.

Father Tom lets the water fall back into the lake, grabs my shoulder, and pushes me back toward shore. "The day of reckoning," he shouts. "Hallelujah! Brothers, the day of reckoning is at hand!"

"Praise the lord," the men all say. "Let his might prevail!"

"Amen, brothers. You know what to do. God be with you."

The men all rush away, up the path, as fast as they can go. They're gone before Father Tom and I stumble back onto the rocky shore. Caleb's still there with his other two men and Dad. Dad's collapsed onto the ground, breathing hard. I'm not even sure he's fully conscious. I struggle out of the water and try to get to him, but my legs feel numb and heavy, and I don't see it coming when Father Tom grabs me from behind by the hair. I stop because the pain is intense, like he's set my scalp on fire. "Caleb. The prisoner goes back to his cell. Take the boy to the women. Tell Sister Harmony he is her prisoner now. She knows the penalty for failure."

"Yes, Father," Caleb says. He seems slightly doubtful. "So he isn't our new messiah?"

"No," Father Tom says, and shoves me at the man who comes to get me. "The devil has offspring too. Get him out of my sight."

The man who takes hold of me marches me back toward the center of the camp. When I look back, they're dragging Dad toward the shed. Father Tom is gone. I have no idea where he went.

◆　◆　◆

I'm shivering and wet, and I stink of that awful water. I want to get free and get to Dad and get the hell out. I'm terrified that they're going to hurt him more, or that he's already so bad off that he can't defend himself. I don't know what to do.

I don't know that there's anything I *can* do.

Caleb shoves me into the women's house—the Garden—and I find all the lanterns have been lit. The women's bunkhouse isn't very different; they've got the same beds, the same old military trunks, but they've tried to provide a little beauty here for themselves. There are flowers blooming in little planters in the windows.

The Garden.

They've got different Bible verses on their walls than the men do.

I count the people I see, because Mom's always told me that information is the first step to defense. There are twelve adult women, and four who are younger teens—Aria's in the back, and I hate the sight of her right now—and there are six younger kids, from two babies on up to about seven years old, boys and girls.

The women are all fully dressed in their long skirts and plain shirts, but some of them still have their hair in braids that I guess they do for sleeping. Sister Harmony's blonde braid is as thick as my arm; it looks like she could whip it like a club. She meets us a few steps into the house, and Caleb thrusts me at her. She grabs me in surprise. She glares at Caleb before she remembers to look down.

"He's your prisoner now," Caleb says. "Lose him and we'll cull the herd by half."

I feel her shudder, but she says, "It will be done as Father Tom wishes."

"Everyone stays in until you get different orders," he says. "Get them ready. Reckoning is coming."

She opens her mouth to say something, then just looks down and nods instead. Caleb turns and leaves, and Harmony closes the door. I hear locks turn, and I realize Caleb's turned a key. Locked us in.

Harmony turns to me, and for a second there's something so angry in her eyes that I hold up my hands and say, "I'm sorry. I didn't—" My teeth are chattering, I'm so cold. She sees that, and some of her anger slides away.

"It isn't your fault," she says. Her face is tense and pale, and she grabs a blanket and puts it around me. "You've done nothing wrong. You'll find no punishment here."

A few of the other women look up, and murmur to each other. Aria frowns. She steps forward and says, "If Father Tom made him a prisoner, we shouldn't be so nice to him."

"Quiet!" Harmony snaps, so sharp that I see Aria recoil. "I need to think."

"There's no need to think, Sister," one of the other women says. She sounds tentative, though. "Father Tom's told us what to do. Aren't we to prepare for the reckoning?"

Harmony ignores that. She moves past me to the window and looks out toward the gate. I join her, trying to see what's happening. She doesn't snap at me or order me away. That causes more whispers behind us, but I don't care. I'm hoping I can see Dad out there . . . but I don't. He must be back in his cell by now. There are a bunch of men gathering in the compound with guns. Some are handguns, some are rifles, but there are some that look like Caleb's rifle—real military-style weapons. I recognize them from playing *Call of Duty*. Scary, especially now. I'm still shivering and freaked out from what happened at the waterfall, and now it looks like they're prepping for a real war.

"What's the reckoning?" I ask Harmony. She doesn't answer. She looks tired and very grim. "We're in trouble."

"Tell me something I don't know," she snaps, which shocks me. It doesn't seem like something someone who buys into Father Tom's women-aren't-human shit would say. More like something my sister would, though. "Connor, it's clear Father Tom doesn't want you. You need to stick close to me, and whatever you do, *don't trust anyone else* unless I tell you it's okay. Do you understand?" It's a harsh, serious whisper.

She's got that Mom presence and energy, and I just nod.

Then she says, "They're opening the side gate. Someone's coming in."

I twist to be able to see what she sees. The men crowded up at the little door in the fence pull somebody inside, and I can't see who it is. *Please, don't be my mom.* I'd feel so relieved if she was here, but I don't want her here either. Not now. Not like this. I'm barely keeping it together, and if they hurt Mom . . . I just can't. I can't.

"Who is it?" I ask Harmony. Maybe she can see better. She's taller. But she shakes her head.

"It's just a young woman," she says. "Strange. She shouldn't be here." She turns away from the window and looks at me. "Do I need to lock you in a closet like Aria suggests? Or will you give me your word to do as I say?"

"How do you know I wouldn't lie?"

She smiles just a little. It makes her look even less happy. "I'd know," she says. "Connor, did you hear what he said? About culling the herd?"

"I don't know what it means."

"It means we'll have to draw lots," she says. "Women and children alike."

I stare. "Like . . . like in that story? 'The Lottery'?" It was a creepy story, all about a normal place and normal people but one person gets chosen and the whole town kills them.

"Just like that," she says, and my whole body wants to cringe, bones and all. "That's the culling. Only it won't be death by stoning."

She sounds scared and sick and angry. Just like me. But she's keeping her voice low, so quiet that I don't think the rest of them can hear. "I promise," I tell her. "I'll be good."

She just nods. "They're going to bring that girl in here," she says. "Whatever happens, stay quiet. Promise." She stiffens as Aria drifts closer to us. "Hush now, boy." She's louder, so Aria can hear. "You'll do as you're told without question. Do you understand?"

"I understand," I say. I can see Aria reflected in the glass, staring at us.

We turn away from the window, and Sister Harmony leads me over to the others, then turns toward the door. I do too. I can feel Aria's stare digging into me from behind, and I don't know how I ever found her pretty. I hate that I kissed her. I'm thinking about that because my brain won't shut up; it's pinging around from one thing to another—Mom, Sam, Lanny, hating myself, being scared, being angry, wanting to smash Caleb's face—and I can't slow it down. I'm still cold. I still stink, and the smell keeps making me remember how helpless I felt out there in that water, with Father Tom ready to pour it over my head. I don't know why that scares me so much.

There's a rattle of keys outside. Harmony composes herself, gaze down, hands folded, and all around me, the other women and girls do the same. The kids do it too—even the toddlers. It's weird and scary.

The door opens, and Vee Crockett walks in. I almost blurt out her name, and the relief at seeing a familiar face is *intense*. My brain even goes quiet for a few seconds, stunned by the weirdness of seeing her here.

But this isn't the Vee I know. This one is wearing one of Lanny's old plaid button-up shirts and warmup pants and she's got all her makeup washed off. She looks way younger this way, and kind of sweet.

And scared.

"Prisoner," Caleb snaps. "She says she's from Wolfhunter. She *says* her mother told her about us. Keep her here until Father Tom confirms she was a recruit. Father Tom says the reckoning will be coming. Until we say different, she's your responsibility."

"Stray lambs are always welcomed," Sister Harmony says without looking up. "God be praised."

"God be praised," everyone echoes, but from Caleb it sounds sour. He's looking at Vee in a way I don't like. "Get her cleaned up and into modest clothes. Father Tom will want to talk to her. We'll see what her real story is."

Harmony nods, and Caleb shuts and locks the door again. I stare at Vee and open my mouth, but she quickly looks away, and I realize she doesn't want me to talk to her. So I don't. But I'm burning to know *why she's here* and where Mom is and what the hell is happening.

I spot one of Caleb's RV guys looking in a window. He's watching what we do. Sister Harmony must see him, too, because she turns to the other women and kids and says, "Let's be to our beds. Lights out, please. I'll keep one on here until our new brother and sister are settled."

"He's not our brother," a voice says from near the corner. Aria, all bright, bitter eyes and smiles. "He's going to be a saint. Father Tom said so."

"Silence," Harmony snaps, and Aria's smile goes away. "Do you want me to report you as prideful and rebellious?"

"No, Sister."

"Then do as you're told, Aria."

One by one, the women and kids go to their beds, climb in, and turn out their small lamps. It's like watching stars go out, and once it's down to just the single, dim light that Sister Harmony takes from her bedside table, I feel the darkness pressing in on all sides like we're in the middle of a black glass globe. I feel like the air's gotten thicker. My breath keeps moving faster, but I feel like I'm not getting any oxygen.

I don't like the dark. I never did.

I want to talk to Vee, but I can't, not yet. She was clear about that. "This way," Harmony says, and leads us to the farthest set of beds—not near the door, but near the cribs at the other end. They're made up, but unoccupied. "You, girl, what's your name?"

"Vera. Vee."

"Your name is now Sister Melody." Harmony opens the trunk and takes out the standard uniform—long skirt, plain shirt—of the sisters. "Put those on. You may change there, in the robing room."

Vee suddenly turns to me and says, "You look super familiar to me, but you ain't from Wolfhunter." That lets me know I'm not supposed to recognize her. And I quickly wonder *why*. But then I realize Vee can't trust Harmony. She can't trust anybody but me.

"I was on TV," I tell her. "That's probably why."

"Oh yeah," she says. "Sure. Are you here by yourself?"

She's asking about Sam without mentioning him. I say, "More or less. I'm with my dad. But he's in another building." She nods, and I know she's got it. "Where did you come from?"

She shrugs and looks a little ashamed of herself. I know Vee, but it still looks like real stuff to me, even though I don't think Vee's been ashamed of herself in years. "Father Tom came to see me when I was just a little girl, and I always wanted to join up; my momma just wouldn't let me, but she's dead now. I was going to join the Assembly there, but—but the enemies destroyed it." She turns toward Harmony, who's watching us with very sharp eyes. "I guess you heard about that?"

"The Assembly group in Wolfhunter sinned," Harmony says. "They were greedy."

Vee looks down, and she seems really, really meek. She's picked up on how to act awfully fast, but then again, she *did* live in Wolfhunter. "Yes, Sister," she says. "Did Brother Carr make it here? I was told he was trying."

"Were you." Harmony's tone gets cold. "Brother Carr has joined the saints."

Vee's startled by that, and she glances up at me, then quickly away. "Oh," she just says. "Okay."

"How did you get here?" Harmony asks.

"Walked."

"Walked," Harmony repeats. "It's a very long way from Wolfhunter."

"Well, I hitched for part of it." Vee says. "Thank you for the bed. I'm so tired."

Harmony's studying her carefully. As good as Vee's act is—and it's pretty good, she's sticking close to truth—Sister Harmony is smart and careful. Vee starts to reach for the clothes that Harmony's set out on the bed.

Harmony grabs her wrist and holds her still. She lowers her voice to a low whisper I can hardly catch and says, "Who sent you?"

"Nobody," Vee says. She keeps it just as quiet. "Nobody sent me." It's weird, but I think she's telling the truth.

"You came alone?"

Vee nods. Harmony's face twists up, like she's angry; I see her grip on Vee's wrist go hard enough that the girl winces. And that's not good. Vee hits out when she's hurt, I know that, and I feel the rush of fear inside me. She doesn't know there are rules here. That people might get killed for her breaking them.

I say, "Hey, you're hurting her," to Harmony just as I see the dark flash in Vee's eyes and her other fist tighten up. Harmony lets go, and Vee sinks down on the bed. There's a red handprint where Harmony was grabbing her, and Vee rubs at it, glaring back.

That's when I realize that there are tears in Harmony's eyes. She isn't angry. She's desperate. She wants so badly to believe that someone, *anyone*, is coming to stop this.

That's when I know for sure I can trust her. But I know I can't trust any of the others in here, so I say, "I have to go to the toilet."

"Yes, go," Harmony says. She doesn't even look at me. I don't move from where I'm standing until she finally does. "What?"

"Uh, it's dark," I say. "And I don't know where it is."

She makes an impatient noise and grabs the lamp. "Come with me, then."

Vee gets it. Instantly. "Can I come too?" she asks. "I—I need to pee."

"Bring your clothes. You'll change there. I have to search you." Harmony's voice is shaking. I don't know what she's thinking, but I know she feels trapped. I do too. I feel like Vee showing up is the best thing and the worst thing all at once. If she's here, I have to think that Mom's not far behind. And probably other people too.

Day of reckoning. Maybe Father Tom was right.

The long bathroom at the back of the room doesn't have a door, but it does have stalls with curtains that pull closed. I'm warmer now, and I put the damp blanket in a woven laundry basket and go to wash my hands. I leave the water running and turn to Vee and quickly whisper, "Vee, you can trust her. It's okay."

Harmony's head whips toward me, then back to Vee. "You do know him," she says to Vee. She keeps her voice low, barely above a whisper. We all need to. "I thought so. Tell me, quickly: Are the police on the way? Did you send them?"

Vee doesn't answer her directly. She looks at me instead. "You're sure about this?" She means about Sister Harmony.

"Yes."

"Your momma didn't want me to do this. I had to get here myself. But I knew I needed to get inside and make sure you were okay. And I knew I could, 'cause . . ." She swallows. "Father Tom will remember me."

"How'd you even get here? You didn't really walk?"

She rolls her eyes, and looks exactly like the old, familiar Vee. "I stole some old guy's truck couple of houses down from your place. It ran out of gas a couple of miles back and I had to walk the rest of the way. But your mom and those others, they won't be far behind." She takes a deep breath. "And the FBI, too, I guess."

Vee suddenly hugs me, and it feels good, really good, to know there's someone here who knows me. Really knows me. While we're in that hug, she whispers, "I got this for you." It's like a magician's move the way the switchblade appears in her hand, and she presses it into my palm. I quickly slide it into my shirtsleeve, then step back and put my hands in the pockets of my stiff, weird pants. The knife slides down. I'm armed now. I don't know how I feel about that.

Harmony doesn't miss the exchange, fast as it is. "Didn't they search you at the gate?"

"Ain't no Bible-thumper going to search a lady's butt crack," Vee whispers, and grins.

Gross. I wipe my hands on my pants.

"We can't stay here," Harmony whispers. "Someone will come soon. I can't trust some of the women, or any of the girls."

Vee says, "Is there anybody here who would fight to get out? Whatever it takes?"

"Yes," Harmony says. "I can count on five of the women. We have some weapons. We knew it might come down to something like this in the end, and we aren't going to go quietly. Not this time." She blinks, and I see tears forming in her eyes. They shine in the lamplight. "How did you find us? Really?"

"There was a girl named Carol," Vee says.

Harmony puts her hand to her mouth. "Carol's still alive?"

Vee nods.

Harmony whispers something I don't catch. It might be a prayer.

I say, "Your five, plus you, plus the two of us . . . that's just eight against a whole bunch of armed men. I know you want to fight, but do you maybe have a plan?"

She opens her mouth to tell us, but two things happen in quick succession.

Aria walks into the bathroom and says, "What are you doing in here?"

And just a second later, I hear the sound of men shouting outside.

And a rattle of gunfire.

Something's just gone very, very wrong.

25
SAM

It's time for the final *E* in *SERE*. I know I came damn close to dying at the pond this time; I nearly choked myself on that chain trying to stop Connor from going into the water. He didn't know what was going to happen, and I would have done anything, *anything*, to stop it. Killing myself seemed a small price to pay, if they wanted a dead saint.

This last-second reprieve doesn't feel like victory. Our time's run out. He's going to kill my son. He *wants* to.

I'm not going to be in better shape for escape than I am now. I have to gamble everything on one throw of the dice.

Being half-dead has its privileges, and one of them is that the man assigned to take me back to my box has to help me up the hill. It's not easy moving someone who's stumbling and uncoordinated, and I accentuate it to the point that he gives up and lets me fall. I grab on to him on the way down. He's got keys clipped to his belt, and since I'm falling anyway, and distracting him with trying to take him down, too, he doesn't feel them slip away.

He's one of the guys from the RV, and I hope that means the ring has an ignition key for the vehicle, plus the keys to my handcuffs. He won't be looking for his keys to open my cell; it's a combination padlock. So I'll get a little time before he realizes they're missing.

He tosses me into the dirt inside the shed and slams the door. I hear the lock being slotted back in and clamped shut.

I hear him leave.

I try the keys on my cuffs with unsteady fingers. Hypothermia's really setting in now; I'm shaking like a tree in a hurricane as my body tries to spin up enough heat to protect my core. I'm not worried about that; it's when I stop shuddering that I'm in real trouble. But it makes trying the keys extra difficult, along with numbed fingers and exhaustion and doing it in the dark.

One of the keys finally slides into the cuffs on my ankle, and at a twist the left one is free. My side is burning where I was bandaged. I have to rest for a few seconds before attempting the right. My hands are going to be tricky, but I try to keep calm and keep at it, and after way too long I finally manage to unlock one wrist. The other's a piece of cake.

The chain's a damn good weapon, provided I can use it properly. It's heavy. I double it up and test using the closed loops of the cuffs as a handhold. Makes a hell of a flail.

Now I need to get the damn door open. I already inspected the hinges; they're outside, so no help there. But I've been methodically digging up the dirt under the doorway and putting it back in the same hole, whenever there wasn't a guard on duty. Digging a little deeper each time. I have loose-packed dirt in a hole about six inches deep, and now that I need it, I can scrape it out deep enough that I *may* be able to slide under.

It's not quite enough. I use the handcuffs as entrenchment tools and deepen the trough another three inches, all the way across. It's hard work, and painful. I try to ignore the ticking clock getting louder with every second that passes, and the liquid sound of the breaths I'm taking, and the pain in my shoulder and side and my throat. Sooner or later, the guy I took the keys from will notice their absence, and he'll know exactly where to look. I need to be gone.

The inky darkness is my friend as I slither under the heavy door. For a horrible few seconds, I can't summon the strength to push myself out when I'm halfway through; I have to lie still and gasp for breath and fight against the pulsing red pain. I'm bleeding again. *It's a slow leak. Shut up, you can make it.* I push and swallow the groan as my wound presses and scrapes against the edge. Sweat burns my eyes. *One more.*

I push, and my hips slide under and I roll over and crawl to my hands and knees, then to my feet. I'd been so focused I forgot there was normally a guard patrolling around, but he's gone, drawn off by the orders that Father Tom gave out at the lake. *Day of reckoning.* It's coming for all of us, I think. Me especially if I screw this up.

I limp to the darker end of the building and use the cover to get my breath back and try to form a plan. I need to get to the RV, get on board, drive toward the gates, and honk the horn like mad; Connor will know what it means. He'll come running, or try. Once I've got him, I'm going to ram the gates, and if these assholes get in my way, so be it. That's their choice. Mine is to save my son.

And they're going to light up that tin can with MP4 rounds, genius. What's your work-around? I don't have one. Plan A had better work, because plan B doesn't exist. *Shit.* Well, sometimes you just have to work with what you've got.

I make it to a stand of trees that marks the edge of one of the fields and stop for breath, and to check the bandage. In the thin moonlight I can see that there's a big, dark, wet spot on the white cotton. I'm bleeding, all right. That's another timer clicking down. *Move it, Cade. Now.*

But I have to wait until I get my air back and the world stops spinning, so I stare at the fields. They're mostly fallow for winter, except for a small and carefully tended garden. No winter wheat, which would have been helpful because I could have used the cover or . . .

I lean against a tree, and for the first time in what seems like a long time, I smile. Because there *is* a plan B.

I head for the barn instead of the RV. They keep cows in a small pasture; I smell the cow shit as I pass, though the cows themselves are invisible. I love that smell. Cows mean that the barn has hay.

Hay is an *excellent* distraction.

I don't have matches, but I do find a plastic gas can sitting by a tractor; it's half-full. Good enough. I douse the hay bales. Still no matches, but I grab jumper cables hanging on the barn's wall and hook them up to the battery on the parked tractor. I touch the clamps and get a nice, fat spark.

Before I ignite the hay, I make damn sure I have my next move in my head. I know where the RV is parked; I saw it on the way here. Simple enough. I hope.

I spark the hay. The gas ignites with a dry, vigorous *whoosh*. I avoid the ignition wave with a healthy retreat, and as I head out the barn door into the darkness toward the RV, I see the blurry orange glow already starting to rise behind me. The chickens in the coop outside start to squawk. There aren't any animals in the barn, thank God. Just storage. I don't want to think about what I would've done otherwise, because right now I have a ruthless streak a mile wide.

Survival's a hardwired instinct.

I'm halfway to the RV, comfortably in the cover of the darkness, when I hear shouting. I can't hear what they're saying, but my plan was to draw a good number of them to fight the fire.

That isn't what happens.

Floodlights blaze on all over the compound. A siren wails—the kind that rises and falls in pitch, like it's announcing the arrival of a tornado.

Then the noise cuts off, and something else comes over the loudspeaker. Father Tom's voice.

"Brothers, the day of reckoning is here! Today is the day that the hand of Satan is raised against us, but fear not—our army of saints is called from heaven to fight. God be praised!"

I can hear the distant shouts. Call and response. *God be praised.*

Christ. The FBI are coming, and they know. *What the shit were you thinking, Mike?* I want to scream it at him, but I'm exhausted and dirty and bleeding into the dirt, and that RV is way too far away, and I'm way too fucking slow right now to make it. The keys are in my hand. Doesn't matter.

The compound—at least here, toward the gate and near the main buildings—is lit up like Broadway. I can see Father Tom's lackeys running to assigned tactical positions. *How can Mike not know that anything but a stealth approach is a terrible idea?* Maybe it isn't Mike. Maybe it's some gloryhound local agent who doesn't realize he's about to kick off a brand-new Waco.

It takes me a few seconds to realize that I've missed something vital. The lights. The positions of the lights are mostly concentrated near the part where the cultists live and work. But the fence goes pretty far out there. Mike's not stupid. He'll know they have to try negotiating; hell, he's probably been ordered to do it. But he'll also know there aren't enough cultists to guard every foot of fence line. The feds are going to make it in, whatever happens up at the gate. All I have to do is stay down and wait. It's almost comfortable. Or it would be, except that with the barn on fire, I've put myself right in the path of anybody dispatched to put it out. I need to move.

Best I can manage is a sniper-crawl, forearms and toes. It takes me closer to the fence, which isn't ideal, but I'm harder to spot lying down.

Or so I think, right up until I hear a shotgun being racked behind me, and what feels like double barrels press into the small of my back. "Get up," a male voice says. "Now."

It's the guy I took the keys from.

So screwed.

26

GWEN

I hate waiting. Mike Lustig made me swear that Kez, J. B., Javier, Lanny, and I would stay where we were positioned on the south side of the compound, far away from the gate. He assigned two TBI agents to stay with us to make sure we'd keep the promise.

Obviously, I don't keep the promise. We wait until we hear things kicking off in the compound, and lights blaze on inside; J. B. checks her phone and sends a text. Nobody says a word. The TBI agents look like they would rather be in the thick of things than stuck out here with us.

So they're not looking when Cicely West and Joe Froud show up, materializing out of the dark like ghosts. The TBI agents instantly get out of the front of the SUV and pull their weapons. Cicely and Joe raise their hands. "We're unarmed!" Joe shouts. The TBI agents rush forward.

They don't see me, Javier, and J. B. coming up armed from behind. They'll be regretting that for a while.

Kez hangs back with Lanny. We zip-tie the agents up in the back seat of their own SUV, ankles and wrists, and for good measure we loop zip-ties onto their belts and the door handles to hold them in place. "You're all going to jail," one of them snaps. The younger one. The older one seems resigned. "Hope you know that."

"We know," Kezia says. She grins like she's looking forward to it.

J. B. pulls the SUV up close to the metal fence, and Javier and Kez grab a heavy rubber mat from the back of the vehicle and toss it over the razor wire strung along the top. Javier is the first over, jumping and landing with an athletic ease that I know I won't duplicate; Kez is almost as good.

"Mom?" I've got one foot on the bumper, ready to climb up. But my daughter is asking for me, and I step down and turn to her. She looks pale and strained, and there are tears standing in her eyes. I hug her, and I cherish that moment. "Bring Connor back." It's an unsteady whisper.

I kiss my daughter's cheek and say, "Of course I will, baby."

Then I turn away, step up on the bumper, the roof, and climb on over the fence.

I feel the landing impact all the way up through my bones, but I don't break anything; I know how to fall and roll to shed the force. Joe and Cicely are the last over. J. B. doesn't even try it. Her job is to stay on the other side of the fence with the TBI's rifle, ready to discourage anybody who comes for us.

And to guard my daughter while I can't.

Before she jumps down, Cicely hands over our gear. Javier and I are both wearing wetsuits under our light clothes; I opted for thin leggings and a T-shirt on top, nothing that will hold me down underwater, despite the chill, and quick-dry water shoes that go land-to-dive easily.

Javier's brought dive tanks, masks, and regulators. His plan is to get across fast, dark, and silent. He'd have done it alone except I've had a little scuba experience; I was certified, once upon a time, but it was years ago, before I was married. I'm just praying I remember the basics of breathing. He's right: the most direct way to the camp is straight across the lake; following the fence line would bring us into an exposed section with lighting, and almost certainly armed resistance.

The dry bags on our backs hold our weapons and ammo.

"Y'all sure about this?" Cicely asks us. "You want us to leave you here?"

"Yes," I tell her. "Watch yourself. These people are dangerous."

She nods, and she and Joe slip away through the heavy brush, making their way next to the fence around the lake. It'll take them longer, but eventually they'll make their way around to where we're going. And we'll need backup by then.

Kezia says, "I wish I was going with you."

"We need cover," Javier tells her, and kisses her lightly. He brushes his thumb across her lips to seal it. "And you're a hell of a shot, Kez."

"Oh, I know," she says coolly, and raises one eyebrow. "You hear me shooting, you stay down."

He nods. So do I. She's almost invisible in her hunter camo gear. Like J. B., she's going to cover us if things go wrong.

So much can go wrong.

The Assembly has built their wall all the way around to enclose the lake and the falls and the creek that feeds it, but they don't seem to have much interest in this side. It's thickly overgrown, and I'm glad we don't have to hack our way too far.

The FBI's negotiators will be at the front gate. Mike didn't tell me his plans, but he did let slip that he'd called for Special Teams, which means he was lying to me about not going in. This *is* going to be a firefight; he planned for that from the beginning. Yes, he'll lead with negotiators, but that doesn't mean he won't have the others going in hard at the same time. This compound may be full of fanatics, but it's too big to be impenetrable. The fence is just to keep people in. Not out.

Mike didn't tell me the plan, because he wanted us to stay out of it. But I can't do that, not when people I love are in danger. Which is why we've just committed assault on two state investigators and why we're heading for the trees by the edge of the lake. In case all this gets very, very complicated, we need to get Sam and Connor out of the middle of it.

When we get to the edge, Javier suddenly crouches down, and Kez and I follow suit. I slowly edge forward to get a look.

Something's happening by the lake on the other side. Two men drag a third, who's barely on his feet. They drop him to the muddy bank, and one kicks him viciously.

Javier's taken out a small set of field glasses from his gear, and I see the change in his body before he thrusts the glasses toward me. I dread looking. But I know I have to.

It's Sam. He's dirty, bloody, naked to the waist.

"No," I whisper. The image jitters, and I realize my hands are shaking. "Sam—"

Javier pulls the glasses away, and I gasp and try to rise. Kez holds me down. "Stop," she whispers. "Hold on. Javi? What are they doing?"

"Can't tell," he says. "They're—" He leans forward a little. "Fuck. They're wrapping a chain around him. Kez!"

She takes a knee and looks through the scope of her rifle. It's a pretty long shot, and Sam's in the middle of it. I hold my breath.

The snap of the rifle shot hangs in the air, and I don't need to have the field glasses to see that one of the men crouching over Sam goes down. She racks and takes aim, but the second man grabs Sam, pulls him up, and hides behind him.

"Gwen!" Javier snaps. "In the water. Now. *Now.*" He's putting on his tank. Kez puts down her rifle and helps me snap mine on too. I test my regulator, drawing in a shaking breath. It's working.

We stand up and run for the shoreline.

"Sam!" I shout, and I hear my voice echoing across the water. I think I see him react.

But then he's pushed forward into the water, a human shield for the man holding on to him.

"The saints will rise!" I hear the shout echoing across the lake toward us this time. That's the cultist holding Sam. "This is the day of reckoning! God be praised!"

Sam's shoved forward again. He's struggling to stand up now.

Javier and I are wading in, up to our thighs. Our waists.

Across from us, Sam vanishes with barely a ripple. The chains around him are dragging him down. The other man begins to wade back to shore.

I want to scream, but I save my breath as I pull down the mask and jam the regulator in my mouth, and then I'm under the water.

I can feel the bone-freezing chill of it through the suit, but I quickly adjust. Panic is beating inside me like a thousand moths. I just want to get to Sam; every second it takes to reach him is another second he's dying down there, alone in the dark.

One step, two, and suddenly it drops off into an abyss; the waterfall has worn this hole deep over thousands of years. My exposed skin burns with the sudden cold, and I'm sinking faster than I intend to, but I don't care. Sam's down there. *He's down there.*

He doesn't have long.

It's hard to be calm right now, and using scuba gear requires focus and a clear head; I have to fight through my instincts to slow down my actions. The lake is like an ink bottle, but when Javier turns on his dive light it cuts through like a sword, turning black water to murky green. I turn mine on too. He swims forward, and I follow close enough to touch his dive shoe. I can't afford to lose sight of him. Not here. Five feet away might as well be five hundred.

We keep going down, but I can't see Sam, *I can't see him.* How long has it been? Thirty seconds. At least.

We swim, and swim, and I want to scream out my agony at how long it takes. Not seconds. A minute. More. I don't know. We go deeper. My ears ache with the pressure, and I work to regulate. Javier starts changing his angle slightly. Our lights illuminate a sheer granite wall up ahead.

That's the drop-off on the other side of the lake. But I can't see Sam. *No, please . . .*

I look down, and a pallid face looms out of the murk, hair drifting like a dark cloud. It doesn't have eyes. The skin is wrinkled and bloated and swollen, but it's held down by a heavy chain around it, and round weights.

I want to scream, but I can't. I feel pressure in my head. We're pretty deep now, but not to the bottom yet.

And I don't see Sam. My heart is racing so fast it hurts with every pulse, like my whole body is cramping with it. My head is splitting from the pressure. I breathe faster, trying to get air, and realize I'm making myself worse. I try to slow down. No, I can't. I can't. Sam's here.

Our lights sweep over more decaying bodies. Some are just bones scattered white across the heavy black silt. Some are held together with sinew and awful twists of muscle.

Some are intact, and the suffocating horror makes me feel the need to get out of here, just *go*. But not without Sam. I'm not going.

I mistake him for one of the dead at first because he isn't moving.

But he *is* bleeding. There's a misty cloud of red around him, coming from the soaked bandage around his waist. He's just floating there, held down by another padlocked chain and what looks like a small boat anchor.

His eyes are shut.

My whole body explodes with the impact of that last burn of adrenaline, of despair, of desperation. I have to save him. I have to.

I lunge forward and touch him, and his eyes open. He starts violently struggling. He's about to breathe in water; I see it from the blind panic in his face. I grab his nose and squeeze it closed. I take in a deep breath and thrust my regulator in his mouth. *Breathe,* I beg him. *My God, please breathe, baby, please.* For a torturous second it doesn't seem he can, he's trying to bat my grip away on his nose, and then I see the relief spread over his body. He's breathing in. I let go of his nose. He cups both hands over the regulator and sucks in air, breathes out bubbles.

He's alive. *He's okay.* No, he's not, he's bleeding and it's cold and he's shirtless, pallid, terribly equipped for this. Hypothermia will kill him fast. Blood loss too. We need to get him *out.*

I fumble at the chain, and realize that it's locked tightly into place. We don't have anything with us that can remove it.

My lungs are aching and trembling with the need to breathe. Javier signals me, but I don't know what he means until he takes another regulator from his belt—something designed to share with another diver in trouble, I guess. At his signal, I take my regulator back, and Javier expertly swaps with me. I can't tell if it's working, or if Sam's breathing.

We have to get the chains off, and there's no way around it; that's going to hurt him. They're tight. Dragging them down is the only real option, and working them past the pants he's still wearing is impossible. I yank the pants free and let them float away. He's just down to underwear now. My hands are shaking, my fingers numb. I get a grip on my side of the chains and slide them down half an inch. My fingers slip off, and I yell into my regulator with frustration. Javier gets his side. We're tearing open Sam's wound, but that doesn't matter now; I can see that he's moving sluggishly but not helping. Not tracking. His body's shutting down.

I yank hard, feel sharp, needlelike pains as my fingernails crack and snap. I don't care. I get the chain lower. Sam thrashes against the pain. I keep pulling, knowing I'm hurting him, knowing I can't stop even if everything in me cries out against it. I ignore it, I *will* do this, *I will . . .*

Then the chains slip over the point of his hipbone, and go slack. They slide down his pale legs and hit the bottom with a thump of viscous silt. I drag in a sweet, canned breath, drop weights, and then we rise, me and Javier, with Sam held between us. He's barely moving. *Stay with me, baby. Almost there. Almost there.*

He's too limp as we tow him toward the bank. I'm exhausted, shaking all over, breathing way too hard and too fast. The pressure's left me with a vicious, throbbing headache, but I don't care about that. I care that *Sam isn't moving*.

I'm first out of the water, and I grab Sam's limp arms and pull him up onto dry land toward Kezia, who's waiting with a metallic survival blanket. "Sam?" I yank off my mask. "Sam!" Javier pulls Sam's mouthpiece away. Oh God, he's not responding, his eyes are open but he's not looking at me, and this *can't happen, it can't*.

Not after all we've endured. Please, no.

I see some life creep back into his eyes, and the hard, black pressure on my chest melts, and I cry out in relief. My eyes blur, and I let the tears fall.

Sam shudders and takes two huge, whooping gasps of air before he chokes out, "Connor. Get Connor!"

Everything goes still inside me. I look at the lake, and I fall back into nightmare. I lock eyes with Javier, and see he's shaken too. I can't ask. I can't. I'm so afraid of the answer.

Javier says, "Sam, is Connor in the water?" Eerily calm, his voice. I'm screaming inside. Falling apart. If my son is in that water, I will die looking for him.

Sam whispers, "No," and I squeeze my eyes shut and cry harder. It's relief, but it *hurts* in its intensity. I bend over and rest my hand on Sam's shoulder to keep myself from falling. When I can open my eyes again, Sam's looking at me. He looks ghastly—pallid, lips the color of lilac, shivering. But he's alive. "They took him to the women's quarters. He'll be there. Go get him. I'm sorry I couldn't—"

I kiss him. My lips are cold and wet and trembling, but his are like kissing a glacier. But he's there, and he's alive, and I send him all the fierce, warming devotion I can through that press of our skin. I can taste the foul water on both of us. I don't care. I'd drink the lake dry to save him.

"I'm going to get him," I tell Sam. "Javi, there should be a rope to get you back up the fence. J. B. was going to drop one. But he'll need both of you to help him up."

"You're not going by yourself," Javi says. "Gwen—"

I shake my head. Kez can't manage Sam on her own; it's a long way to the fence, and getting him up, safe, and warm will take two people. I can't go.

I need to find our son.

I put the mask back on, and the regulator, and I plunge back into the lake before anyone can stop me.

The fastest way to my son is on the other side.

27

CONNOR

Aria's a *problem*. And as she draws in breath to scream, I grab her and put my hand over her mouth. She's small enough I can pick her up off the ground and hold her there while she struggles and squeals. The water's still running, and Vee turns on even more taps, so I don't think anybody else can hear the struggle over that. But someone's going to come looking, fast.

Vee rips down one of the stall curtains. It's thin stuff, and she pulls out her own switchblade to cut long strips. One is a gag. The other two she uses to tie up Aria's hands and ankles. We dump her in the corner of the bathroom stall as she wiggles and tries to scream.

Sister Harmony pauses as a siren starts to wail somewhere outside. It sounds like a tornado alert. Then I hear Father Tom talking, but I don't know what he's saying over the running water. Sister Harmony must be able to understand it, because she grabs the lamp and charges out of the bathroom. Vee and I chase after the light.

Sister Harmony's not stopping for the screams and shouts of the other girls and women, or the crying children. She races down the aisle, and from behind she looks like a comet flying through the dark, with ghosts shouting and flailing all around her in their white nightgowns.

I don't know what Sister Harmony is going to do until she bangs on the locked door and shouts through it, "Help! Help, they're in here! Save us! They'll kill us all!" She shoves me back against the wall, and Vee realizes what she's doing before I do, because I see the gleam of that knife in her hand. I don't want to use mine. I pick up a table instead and hold it.

There are other women coming toward us. I count five, plus a wispy blonde girl of about ten, and the babies and little kids. The other women are milling around, shouting. Some are kneeling and praying. Those are the ones Harmony can't trust, I realize. The ones who won't fight. Or who believe too much to try.

Harmony smashes a plank on the floor with the heel of her shoe, and beneath it is a white sack. She pulls it out and dumps the contents on the floor. Kitchen knives. She must have taken them gradually, I guess. There aren't enough for everyone.

Vee's turning her switchblade restlessly over and over in her hand. There's a tense brilliance in her eyes that makes me worry she's going to do something stupid. But I'm holding a table. Maybe I should use the knife instead.

The door slams open before I decide, missing Sister Harmony, and as a man charges in with a gun she buries a kitchen knife in his forearm. The gun goes off, but it fires into the floorboards. I back up. I know I should be doing something, but I don't know what; I just know that everything seems to slow down, that I feel hot and clumsy, and people are in my way.

And then everything focuses and there's an opening. I swing my table and connect with the side of his head; he staggers. I drop the table and shove him, and he stumbles, off balance. Vee trips him, and I watch him crash to the floor. He looked angry when he came in the door, but now it's turned to shock. And as he realizes what's really happening, he's scared. He's down on his stomach, squirming to get up.

I should get something to tie him up, I think, and I look around, but before I can find anything Sister Harmony's dropped down on his back as he tries to rise, and with one quick thrust, she puts her kitchen knife in the back of his neck. I see it happen, and I don't really understand it for a second, not until he goes still. It's fast and clean, and I only realize that he's dead a few slow seconds later. I don't know how I feel. I only know that she's crying, and she says—not to us, to him—"This time you're the one who's culled."

Sister Harmony scoops up the gun before Vee can make a try for it, and the older woman raises it, covering the open doorway. "Vera, Connor, take the sisters and children to the RV, and find a way out of here."

"Aren't you coming?" I ask her. I know I should be afraid of her. Horrified, too; she just killed someone. But she's like Mom, a warrior, protecting those she loves. I grab a little kid who's crying by the hand, then pick him up. He's heavier than I expected. Warmer.

Sister Harmony shakes her head. That heavy golden braid hisses like a snake against the fabric of her shirt. "I'll bring the rest. As many as I can," she says. "Just go. Don't wait. Once they realize we're loose, they'll come for us."

I stop and look at her. She's never held a gun before, I can tell; her hands are shaking worse than mine. "You were supposed to kill all of them, weren't you?"

She drags in a heavy breath and nods. "Day of reckoning," she says. "I was supposed to burn the Garden and let no one live. *Go*, boy. And don't stop!"

Vee yells at the other women and children to link hands, and she goes to the back of the line. I'm up in the front, with a dark-haired woman almost Harmony's age. I remember someone saying her name: Sister Rose. She says, "We'll need to run. I know where to go. I'll lead." She's holding a knife, and she looks scared to the bone, but determined too. She holds out her hand, and I take it. Most of the kids are being carried. The little boy I'm holding has his arms around my neck, and all of a sudden I realize how dangerous this is, how he could be hurt if I fall or if somebody comes at us, and I'm not scared for myself anymore. I have to make sure he's okay.

We run.

Toward the gate there are men clustered and guns booming, but they're focused on whoever's outside the gates. FBI. *Mom.* Mom could be out there.

I need to get Sam, but first I need to get this little boy who's got his arms around me to safety. That's most important. So we run, pulling each other along, and when Sister Rose stumbles I help her up, and we keep running. A man runs toward us to try to stop us, but when Sister Rose screams and raises the knife she's holding, he stumbles back in surprise. He's got a gun, though. One of those assault rifles. And as he backs up, he raises it, and I feel a pulse of ice cold go through me. I can't do anything. Not with the kid in my arms.

Sister Rose lets go of my hand and launches herself at him, screaming. He stumbles again, and then she's on him. When she gets up, she's got the gun and there's blood on her shirt. She takes off running again, and I follow, yanking the line along with me. I can't look back. I'm scared that Vee's in trouble at the rear, or that more men are coming after us. All I can do is keep chasing Sister Rose.

There's Father Tom's cabin on the far side of the church, all lit up. The barn beyond it is on fire.

And the RV is sitting right next to Tom's cabin.

When we get there, I turn and look back, and they're all still there. Vee's at the end of the line, and she's carrying a baby in one arm. She pushes up next to me. Sister Rose is pulling on the RV's door, but it isn't opening.

Locked.

There's so much gunfire now. It sounds like the men are fighting a war. I don't know where Caleb is, or Father Tom, but as long as they aren't here, it doesn't matter.

Dad. I need to find Dad. But first I have to get everybody in this RV.

"There's a skylight up top!" I yell, and hand the little boy I'm holding to Rose. I scramble up the ladder at the back, kick at the skylight until the lock gives, and drop down inside to open the door for the rest of them. "I don't have the keys!" I yell to Vee as she gets aboard at the end of the line and slams the door shut. The kids are screaming and crying, and the women crowd in around the bucket chairs.

"I don't need 'em!" she shouts back, and shoves her way through the crowd of ladies to get to the driver's seat. She drops into it, leans over, and starts yanking wires out. I guess she knows what she's doing, because about thirty seconds later she's got the engine going, and she flashes me a brilliant grin as she slips into the driver's seat. "How you like me now?"

"I like you a lot," I say. "I need to get Dad!"

"Boy, you ain't going anywhere," she yells, but I'm already moving back to the locked cabinet where Caleb kept the Tasers. I pry it open and take one of the Tasers that's sitting in a charging cradle. I put it in my jacket pocket, and then I find what I need in the corner of the cabinet: bolt cutters.

When I turn around, Sister Rose is in my way. "Move!" I tell her. "I need to get Sam!"

She shakes her head and blocks my path to the door. I want to scream at her. Hit her. "You can't go," she says.

"Let me out! Vee!" I take the Taser out of my pocket. "I need to let him out of that cell!"

Vee's got the RV in gear now. "Don't be stupid, Connor. You get yourself killed for him, how do you think he'd feel? Besides, your momma's comin' for him." She grins. "Wouldn't want to get in the way of *that*. You! Can you drive?" She points at Sister Rose. "I need to make sure he doesn't jump out and do something stupid."

Sister Rose changes places with Vee in the driver's seat. Vee grabs my arm as I lunge for the door.

Rose hits the gas. "Everybody hold on!"

I still want to get Sam, and it burns in the pit of my stomach that Vee's right, that Sam would tell me to stay here. And the RV's moving now. I grab the Taser from the floor and hold on to it, and brace a girl standing next to me as the RV lurches into a long turn.

Rose accelerates the camper as it straightens up again. I see the church over to our right. The men's quarters. The Garden's on the other side, but she doesn't slow down for it; nobody's waiting to be picked up outside. Harmony isn't there.

Rose lays on the horn, and it echoes like a high-pitched scream as she jams the pedal to the floor and heads for the gate.

"Everybody hold on!" I yell, and brace myself.

But we don't get to ram our way out.

The men shoot our tires out, and Rose loses control and instead of hitting the gates head-on, we slide sideways and slam into them at an angle; the gates sway, but it isn't a hard-enough impact to force them open.

The jolt knocks me into window glass, and I'm dazed for a second. That's long enough for someone to yank open Rose's driver's-side door and drag her out, screaming. They've got the other door open, too, and men are coming on board and pulling the women off, and they're fighting back with knives and fists and screaming defiance. It's chaos.

My head aches, and I feel clumsy, but I get over it fast, because we're going to have to fight now. And I expected to be afraid, to want to run, but I feel a weird peace come sliding down through my body like cool water. There's nowhere to run. I'm not scared. I'm not mad. I just take the Taser and fire it at the first man I see; I remember I have to keep the trigger down, and I watch him scream and collapse, twitching. I don't know if I can use it again, and I don't care. I swing the bolt cutters at the next man who comes on board, and hit him in the guts. He topples backward.

The next one has a gun, and he lunges in and aims it at someone fighting near me. One of the older women. I grab his wrist and shove it up, and his shot goes into the ceiling instead of her face. I can't use the bolt cutters; there's no room to swing them. I punch him instead, and it hurts all the way up my arm, like I'm breaking every bone, but I don't care, I can't. I just need to stop him, and I don't care how.

But he's bigger and stronger than me, and when he punches back, I go down. It doesn't hurt so much as just make everything white out for a second, and when I blink that away he's standing over me, pointing the gun at me, and I realize I'm going to die. *Now* I'm scared, my whole body catching cold with it, and at the same time I bare my teeth and yell and I wish I'd gone for Sam, I wish he were here, *I want Mom,* but it's all too late.

Sister Harmony stabs him. She's bloody, wounded, limping, but he doesn't see her coming. She screams as she puts her blade in the back of his neck. She twists it, and I see the whole light go out in his eyes. He falls forward on top of me, and I shove him off like he's on fire. I'm shuddering and clumsy again and gasping, and everything in my chest feels too tight, but I'm already looking past the dead man, looking at the door where the next one's going to come for us.

Harmony yanks the blade free and snaps, "Get the gun, boy," and I think about the verses she's had to stare at every day, for years, written on the walls of her prison.

Let the woman learn in silence with all subjection.

She learned better than Father Tom ever expected.

There's another man coming on board now. Thin and young, maybe twenty or so. I grab the gun. It's heavy and too big for me, but I point it at him, and he freezes. Sister Harmony shakes her head and pushes my arm down. She takes the gun and hands it to the new guy. "No, he's with us," she says. "Remy! Watch the door!"

Remy. "My mom's been looking for you," I tell him. He glances at me. He's more scared than I am, but the gun's steady in his hand. "You're Remy Landry."

"I used to be," he says. "We live through this, maybe I still am. Harmony! We have to go!"

"Not without my sisters!" She plunges off the RV again, bloody knife in her hand. Remy follows, and so does Vee.

So do I. I grab up the bolt cutters as I go. They're bulky and heavy, but I tell myself that I can get to Sam, *I can*, and Sam can help us get out of here. We can all get out. Everyone.

But when we come out of the RV's door, it's worse than I thought.

Rose, two other women, and several of the little kids are backed up against the fence. All three of the women have knives, but they're all hurt too. Rose's left arm hangs limp and bloody. She's pale as chalk, but still standing. The kids are crowded in behind the three of them, and they're facing two men with assault rifles. "Give us the children," one says. "We won't hurt them."

"Liar!" Rose screams and rushes him. He's going to kill her, I realize, and I can't stop it. All I have is a switchblade and these bolt cutters, and that's not enough. I'm not fast enough. I'm not close enough.

Harmony *is* fast. She kills him the same way she did the one in the RV, quick and lethal, and ducks as the other man swings his gun toward her. Rose tackles him and sends him sprawling. She grabs his gun and points it at him, panting, wild. When he laughs, she shoots him. She misses, and shoots again, and he stops laughing. I know I ought to be curled up in a ball now, like I was back in school. Gunfire. Screams. The smell of blood in the air.

But that was fake. This is real. And I'm afraid, but I'm focused on two things: staying alive and getting to my dad. *I can get him out. I will.*

But we're pinned between the RV and the fence. There are at least twenty men with guns around us, but most aren't paying attention to us; they're firing through holes in the fence at the FBI outside the gates. And the FBI are now firing *back*. I see what look like grenades come launching over the wall and hit the ground on our side, and for a second I think we're about to blow up like in the movies, but then they let out a pulsing white fog and I can't breathe. My eyes are burning, I'm choking and coughing and gagging, and it tastes like burning paper at the back of my throat. I can see Vee, who's bent over gasping, and I grab her and hold on.

"Side gate!" she croaks. Her eyes are streaming tears, and they're red as fire. Mine probably are, too—they're blurry and aching, and I'm disoriented. I don't know where I am. Guns are still firing. "That way!" She shoves me, and we slide along the fence. I shove the switchblade in my pocket and grab blindly for a coughing little kid. Vee grabs someone else. Harmony, who's holding on to Remy. Rose, staggering and nearly falling.

We can't get everybody. But we have to open that gate.

We reach it and there's a man in front of it, but he's slumped over against the fence, and when Harmony shoves him, he falls limply. Dead.

The gate's got two sliding metal bars across it. Both are secured with combination locks, like I have on my locker at school.

Like the one I'd planned to cut off my dad's cell.

It doesn't make sense, but I feel like I'm making a choice here. Like if I cut these locks, I can't cut Dad's. I have to choose him, or the people who are helpless here at the gate.

And I know what he'd want me to do.

I use all my strength to cut through the first lock, then the second, and Remy slams the metal bars back, and he starts to charge through the open gate.

"No!" Harmony shouts, and takes his gun. She throws it away. "No weapons! No weapons!"

She's right. The FBI's out there. If we come out with guns and knives, they're going to think we're the problem.

I put the bolt cutters down. Harmony puts her knife down. She grabs Rose, disarms her, and puts the woman's hand in that of a little, crying boy. Then she shoves them out the open gate. Then Remy. Then one by one the other women and children.

She turns to me and Vee, and coughs out, "Go!"

"You first," Vee says.

Harmony vanishes through the gate. I can't breathe, I have snot running down my face, and tears, and I want to throw up. I turn and pick up the bolt cutters again. Vee stiff-arms me back. "The fuck are you goin', boy?"

"Dad," I croak.

She takes the bolt cutters away and tosses them into the mist. I yell and swing at her; she ducks. She's coughing and gagging, too, but she manages to say, "Your dad's okay. We have to *go*." Then she's dragging me through the gate and into clearer air, and FBI agents are shouting at us to keep moving, keep moving, hands up, keep moving, and I'm stumbling and falling to one knee. I look back at the big steel fence, the closed gates, and I hear something weird.

They're singing in there.

Father Tom's people have stopped shooting. They're singing some kind of hymn. Mostly men's voices, but I can hear some pure, high notes. Some of the women too. The ones who wouldn't leave. The true believers.

The FBI has us sit down on the side of the road, and they wash our faces and give us oxygen masks, and I start feeling better after a few minutes. It's dark out here, cold, and the singing hangs in the air like the tear gas clouds. A few more people come out of the side gate. None of them are my dad, and I tell the man rinsing my face a second time that I need to go back in, that my dad is Sam Cade and he's in there and they have to *find him*.

"Connor?" A big man in a dark windbreaker kneels down next to me. "Connor Proctor?" I nod. I don't know him. "I'm Agent Torres.

Special Agent Lustig asked me to find you and stay with you. You all right?"

I have no idea. I don't know what *all right* means anymore. The burning in my eyes is gone, but I keep crying. Is that all right? Is this *feeling* all right? I don't even know what it is. Only that I'm so tired I want to sleep, and at the same time I have to go back. "My dad's still in there," I say. "He's still in there." I start to get up.

Agent Torres puts his hand on my shoulder and pushes me down. "Agent Lustig and several teams are already over the wall, and they'll bring him out. You stay here." He stands up and looks toward the fence. He seems tense and worried, and I realize it's probably because of the singing. They shouldn't be doing that. They ought to be surrendering.

His radio crackles, and he answers it. "Status?" he asks. I'm close enough to hear the reply from the other end.

"They've retreated into the church building. It's rigged to blow. We're working on it now."

"How many in the church?"

"Maybe twenty-five men and women, no children we can see. We've disarmed two devices. Just one to go. Advise Agent Lustig that the leader is not, repeat, *is not* in the church."

"Wait one." The agent pushes buttons on his radio and says, "Special Agent Lustig, please be advised that explosive devices are in place at the church and are currently being defused, but the cult leader is still at large, do you copy that?"

"Copy," the radio says. "Did you locate Connor Proctor? Sam Cade?"

Agent Torres cuts a look toward me, and I feel sick all over again when I realize what he's about to say. "We have Connor Proctor safe, sir. No trace yet of Sam Cade."

"Acknowledged, Lustig out."

I lick my dry, still-tingling lips and say, "Check the shed, the one at the end of the concrete building. He's in there, I think. Or at the lake.

He could be at the lake." I hope he isn't. I don't even want to think why he would be, but I remember seeing him there, seeing that last look he gave me, and even though my eyes are burning and leaking, now I know I'm crying for real. *Dad, please. Please be okay. Please.*

Torres passes what I said along. Before we get an answer, the radio says, "All clear at the church. Located another device in another building, but it's empty and—"

In the next second, there's an explosion that tears the whole night to pieces, and it's big enough to send pieces of wood and concrete flying through the air up, out, every direction. We all duck and cover, and when I look, part of the fence is mangled and bent from the force of it. My ears are ringing, and I just stare numbly at the fire rising on the other side of the gate.

Nobody is singing anymore, not that I can hear.

"Jesus, tell me that wasn't the church," Agent Torres says into his radio.

But I already know the answer. It was too close. They've blown up the Garden. And if not for Sister Harmony, they'd have killed all the women and children inside it.

"Devices in the church confirmed rendered safe," the radio says. The agent on the other end sounds unsteady. "We pulled back before the building blew, no casualties. Those in the church being taken into custody now. Not putting up a fight."

They didn't manage to kill themselves. That's good.

But we haven't got my dad.

I stare off at the fire until Vee puts her arm around me. "It's okay, Connor," she says. Vee Crockett. Comforting *me*.

"Yeah," I agree. I don't mean it.

Because it isn't.

28

GWEN

I think nothing will stop me from getting to my son, but something does. I'm running up the path from the lake, exhausted, legs like jelly, my lungs aching from exertion; I've shed my tank and mask and regulator, but I'm cold. So cold. I'm forcing speed from my unsteady body and am halfway up the hill when there's an explosion that whites out the night and sends me staggering, and the sound claps my ears an instant after. Like lightning striking. It hits me like an ax to the chest and nearly sends me to my knees. *Connor. My son is there.* I can't believe that he was in that fireball. No. I can't. I need to *find him.*

I realize that there's someone walking toward me, coming down the path away from that hellish flame reddening the night. And he's singing. I recognize the hymn. *Yes we'll gather at the river, the beautiful, the beautiful river.*

He's got a beautiful voice, and it feels like the worst joke of all that this man can create something so lovely.

He sees me standing in his path, dripping wet. I'm aiming my gun at him, and he stops singing. "Who are you?" I ask him. He stops walking. I'm boiling with rage and terror, but outside I'm completely still. Completely steady.

He slowly raises his hands. "My name is Father Tom. I surrender." *Father Tom.* He looks almost angelic in the moonlight. But I know he isn't.

"Where's my son?" I ask him. My voice sounds almost quiet.

"Gina Royal. I knew you'd come. Well, if there's any God in heaven, your son is in hell," Father Tom says, and I hear the awful, smug delight in that. It shatters me like that explosion shattered the night, and for an incandescent moment I imagine emptying a clip into his face until I obliterate it, until there's nothing left of him but blood and shards, and then I will reload and keep shooting.

I break free of that with a gasp and realize my finger is a microt-witch from making it a reality. I can't, because he *did not* say my son was dead. He said, *If there's any God in heaven.* But he wouldn't hesitate to tell me directly that Connor was dead. I have to believe that. I have to, or I'll lose my mind completely.

He slowly lowers himself to his knees. He winces a little, and smiles. "Old bones. I'm not the man I was." If he's trying to convince me he's a human being, he fails. He's playing with me. "You brought evil into our garden, just as women always do. You're Lilith and Eve and the serpent all in one. You're the mother of all sins."

I walk right up to him, crouch down, and shove the gun under his chin. "Including murder," I say. "Did you kill my son?"

"He was in the Garden," he says, and I see hell in the smile that spreads across his lips. "The Garden and our meeting hall are ashes now. Go sift through them and find what you can."

I hate this man; I hate him more than I've ever hated anyone in my life. Even Melvin. I want to rip him to pieces, and I can do it with a touch of my finger. No effort at all.

"That isn't an answer," I tell him. "Did. You kill. My son."

He's gone pallid now. For all his grinning and pretense, he's afraid of something. Not the gun. Not that I'll kill him.

He's afraid that I *won't.*

317

"Yes," he says. "I did. He's with the saints." He looks toward the lake.

And I know he's lying.

"You've got a way out of here," I guess, and I know I'm right, because for the first time I see surprise flash in his eyes. "A secret only you keep. Where is it, near the lake? Behind the waterfall? Doesn't matter. You're not getting to it." I stand up and back away, still aiming. "Where's my son, you asshole?"

I hear footsteps on the path. See flashlights. "Gwen!" It's Mike Lustig's voice. The FBI's here. I don't relax, but I feel the warm curl of relief. I can get Connor now. I can get out of here. We've made it.

"I killed your son before I left," Father Tom says. "With my own hands. And he died crying."

The only thing that saves his life is Lustig shouting, at the same time, "We've got Connor, he's safe!" And I take my finger off the trigger because I might *still* shoot, and the second the FBI agents arrive, I crouch down and put the gun on the ground and cover my face with my hands and scream, scream out the fury and frustration and overwhelming relief.

I feel Lustig's hand heavy my shoulder. "Where's Sam?" he asks.

I take a deep breath and look up at him. "Safe. SUV on the south side of the compound, where you stationed us. We got to him before he drowned. He's safe."

My voice breaks on that last, and I feel the first stirrings of real hope.

"Come on," he says, and pats my back this time. "Let me take you to your son."

We pass Father Tom lying on the ground, face in the dirt, screaming as the FBI handcuffs him. I'm glad I didn't shoot him.

I want him to suffer.

29

GWEN

I never want to let my son out of the embrace I wrap around him. I hold him so close, for so long, that he finally squirms in discomfort, and I let go. "Dad—" he says. There are tears in his eyes. On his face. I gently wipe them away, even as I know he can see that I'm crying too.

"He's on the way to the hospital," I tell him. "He's going to be okay. He's cold, and he's got a wound they need to treat. But he's going to be all right." I don't know that, but I have to believe it. J. B.'s brought Lanny, Kez, and Javier, and I hug them all. I cling to Javier a little longer and say, "Without you, I'd have lost him."

"Make sure you tell him that," he says. "He was bitching about learning to scuba dive. Soon as he's better, he has to take the full course. You too. You fumble around like a puppy."

I laugh and hug him again. "I promise," I tell him. "As soon as I get a few other things straight."

He nods and takes Kezia back to the SUV. They want to take Connor in an ambulance, too; it's a close fit inside, with the paramedic, the two of us, two women from the compound, and an FBI agent. Connor tells me the blonde woman is Sister Harmony, and a woman with a gunshot wound is Sister Rose. They look exhausted and disoriented, but Harmony looks at my son and says, "We did it."

Connor nods. "Where are you going to go?"

Harmony blinks. "I—I don't know." She smiles, and I don't know that I've ever seen anything like it before. Wonder and fear and hope all at once. "Somewhere else. Isn't that amazing?"

Sam's being rushed to surgery as we arrive, but he's conscious enough to grab Connor's hand on the way, and he gives us both a weak, too-pale smile. We have to stop at the door. It's a long few hours in the waiting room with Kez, Javier, Lanny, and J. B., and I'm shocked to see Vee Crockett join us. "I was looking for you," Connor says, and hugs her. "Where'd you go?"

"I got the fuck out," she says, and slides a glance toward me. "Sorry. I had to ghost before they made me go back to foster care. They're probably pretty mad."

"Probably?" Connor snorts and shakes his head. "They're going to come and get you. They want to talk to everyone who was in there. Including you."

"Including you," I repeat, staring at Vee. "How the hell did you get there?"

"She stole a truck," Connor says. "She knows how to hot-wire cars. She did it to the RV and—"

I hold up a hand, still watching Vee Crockett. "I don't want to know. You're okay?"

She lifts one shoulder. "Sure."

She isn't, really. None of us are. But we're all pretending hard.

She's surprised when I hug her tight, and when she relaxes into it and hugs me back, I feel her shudder in relief. "I'm okay," she whispers. This time, I think she means it.

Sam comes out of surgery without complications.

Two days later, we want to take him home, but Kez tells us that home probably isn't where we need to go now. She shows us pictures. There's an army of reporters camped by the lake. There's graffiti on our garage door and the side of the house. Somebody's broken out the front window and tossed in paint. We're infamous. Again.

And I let it go. Finally, completely, I let it go. Norton. All the people wanting me to leave. My instinctive need for *control*, for defiance.

I don't need Stillhouse Lake anymore. I have what I need right here. All around me.

J. B. facilitates the return of Remy Landry to his parents at the hospital, and I don't think I've ever seen three people come alive like that. Remy is a shadow of the photos I've seen, down to skin and bones and raw will, but he's survived the impossible. And so have his parents. I can see the joy ignite in all of them, and it makes me feel all this has almost, almost been worth that.

There are seven bodies retrieved from the pond at the first Assembly of Saints compound. Another ten emerge from the lake at Bitter Falls, including the body of Vernon Carr, the leader of the Wolfhunter cult, who'd run to Father Tom for protection. He hadn't found the welcome he expected.

I get an anonymous postcard delivered to me via J. B. Hall's offices. It's handwritten in a childish scrawl, and it says, *Thank u for my life.* There's a big, flowing *D* at the end. *D* for Daria. I don't look at the postmark. I don't want to know. I shred it.

We go to therapy twice a week. All five of us, including Vee. It helps.

Sam and I put in adoption papers. He's adopting my kids, formally, as my partner. And we help Vee put in paperwork to become an emancipated minor. She'll be staying with us, at least until she can find her own way. Lanny and Vee seem to gravitate toward each other like magnets, and yes, I worry about that. Vee's got a long way to go to get to stable.

We definitely need to find a house big enough to contain the drama.

The last thing before we leave Stillhouse Lake, I handwrite a note and mail it to Lilah Belldene. It says, *I keep my word.*

I'm not surprised when I don't get anything in reply. Life goes on. We have Father Tom's trial to prep for. A new home to find.

And like Sister Harmony, I don't know what's coming next.

And that's amazing.

SOUNDTRACK

Music inspires me and carries me forward through the long and sometimes difficult process of writing a book like this, with so much intensity and emotion. So here are the songs I've chosen that help me stay in the world with these characters. If you like them, please support the artists and buy their music.

- "Monsters," Shinedown
- "Forever & Ever More," Nothing But Thieves
- "Split In Two," Broken Hands
- "What Happened to You," Black Honey
- "Get Up," Shinedown
- "Some Kind of Rage," MONA
- "Gods," Nothing But Thieves
- "Rolling with the Punches," The Blue Stones
- "Graveyard Whistling," Nothing But Thieves
- "Ghost," Badflower
- "Do Your Worst," Rival Sons
- "Live Like Animals," Nothing But Thieves
- "Holding Out for a Hero," Nothing But Thieves
- "Pressure," Muse
- "Propaganda," Muse
- "Sorry," Nothing But Thieves

- "Lowly Deserter," Glen Hansard
- "Philander," Glen Hansard
- "Take the Heartland," Glen Hansard
- "Who by Fire," Leonard Cohen
- "The Next Voice You Hear," Jackson Browne
- "Morning Mr. Magpie," Radiohead
- "Season of the Witch," Donovan
- "It's Not Too Late," T. Bone Burnett
- "Poison in the Water," Von Grey
- "Even the Devil Gets It Right Someday," Chris McDermott
- "Karma (Hardline)," Jamie N. Commons
- "Rumble and Sway," Jamie N. Commons
- "The Preacher," Jamie N. Commons
- "Last," Nine Inch Nails
- "Blood Like Lemonade," Morcheeba
- "Run Boy Run," Woodkid
- "I Love You," Woodkid
- "Ghost Lights," Woodkid
- "The Other Side," Woodkid
- "In the Air Tonight," Joseph William Morgan
- "Enjoy the Ride," Morcheeba
- "Change," The Revivalists

ABOUT THE AUTHOR

Photo © 2014 Robert Hart

Rachel Caine is the *New York Times, USA Today, Wall Street Journal,* and Amazon Charts bestselling author of more than fifty novels, including *Wolfhunter River, Killman Creek,* and *Stillhouse Lake* in the Stillhouse Lake series; the *New York Times* bestselling Morganville Vampires series; and the Great Library young adult series. She has written suspense, mystery, paranormal suspense, urban fantasy, science fiction, and paranormal young adult fiction. Rachel lives and works in Fort Worth, Texas, with her husband, artist/actor/comic historian R. Cat Conrad, in a gently creepy house full of books. For more information, visit www.rachelcaine.com.